Andalon Awakens

Dreamers of Andalon - Book 1

T. B. Phillips

Deckplate Publishing LLC

Andalon Awakens
Dreamers of Andalon, Book One

Published by Deckplate Publishing LLC
Copyright © 2019 by T.B. Phillips.

Cover design by Lynnette Bonner of Indie Cover Design
Front cover art by Jenny Kuehner Bechtold
Book interior design by Stewart Design, https://StewartDesign.studio

ISBN 978-1-73318-050-4

This is a work of fiction. Names, characters, places, and incidents are a product of the author's imagination. Locales and public names are sometimes used for atmospheric purposes. Any resemblance to actual people, living or dead, or to businesses, companies, events, institutions, or locales is completely coincidental.

To my children, Breana, Jennie, and Cooper
I wrote this story with hope that you will someday unlock all of the potential that awaits inside of you and reshape this cruel world into yours

To my wife, Jaana
No one has loved me or shown the support that you have. You are my Sippen Yurik, faithful and supportive while unwavering and innovative

To my mother, Jennie
Thank you for letting me use your typewriter when I was a child, always urging me to create, and always my biggest fan

To my friend and artist, Jenny
You see beauty in the world differently than most. Thank you for reading and painting my words so that She Wolf may finally set sail

Part 1
Kraken Rises

From the corners of Andalon children awaken,
Remembering not their past nor the powers that slumber.
The pain of their suffering increases with numbers,
Come, witness the birth of their salvation!
Rise the Kraken from the depths,
Dealing destruction and slaughter.
Watch him destroy our legacy.

- The Oracle of Astian, 134th year of order

PROLOGUE

A small, bespectacled man stood on the deck of a creaking battle frigate. Unable to sleep, the little man kept first watch, eyes on the desultory nighttime waves lapping at the hull of *Wench's Daughter*. The ships stood stranded on the open sea, thirsty for the air that had been strangely still for an entire day and night. He watched as the lack of wind seemingly laughed at the impotent sails hanging on their masts.

Complete lack of movement is rare at sea and the eerie calm had already worked on the imaginations of the crew. Fear had slowly built within each man during the night, and the abrupt appearance of eighteen sails sent panic through every topside sailor. The little man pushed back his spectacles and sounded the alarm before dropping down a hatch to wake the captain.

Inside the main quarters, a large man opened his eyes and groaned. The noise grew louder at his door, a rhythmic thumping that wrenched him from the dream. He fought back a euphoric shudder as the memory of his lover's embrace faded with the pounding of reality. He had only briefly held her in life. But in this recurring fantasy, she met him with the same tender they shared as innocent youth.

Her warm scent of spring lilac lingered momentarily, as did the soft caress of her lips. Braen Braston groaned as he awakened, fighting against the urge to draw his knife against the neck of whoever pounded on his door. Tears squeezed from his eyelids as he tightly closed them against the waking world.

If only he could return to the world where sweet Hester had

briefly met him. He yearned to rejoin her warm bed and to feel her silky skin against his rough hands. Having once been a nightly occurrence, Braen had languished without the dream for more than a span, each evening wishing that slumber would transport him to her realm. Now that she had again visited, he worried that he would not remember her facial features after he fully awakened. Faded love and death are the only promises that time gives to mortal men, and Braen secretly hoped for the second. *Does death include dreams?* He was almost willing to find out when awareness of the waking world shook him violently.

The heavy door to his cabin nearly splintered, keeping time with the pain between his temples. Panicked fists beat upon its planks as he briefly considered death once more. His eyes shot open with alarm. Somewhere nearby men shouted, and a feeling of urgency rocked the ship. The pounding that drew him back to reality had nearly broken the oak from its iron hinges. The shouting that accompanied the beating came from topside as his men ran to their battle stations.

He furiously threw the wool blanket from his body, sweating from the adrenaline of either passion or terror, whichever his faded dream had held. Wincing, he realized that her face had completely gone from his mind. Awakening had also robbed him of her scent. *Wasn't it lilac?* He could not remember. Reality and rational thought drew him out of bed to face the unknown foe who had attacked his ship while he dreamed of impossible fancies.

His boots slipped on easily enough and Braen did not bother replacing his shirt. Running bare-chested he emerged from his cabin and collided with Sippen Yurik, his engineer and first mate, lifelong friend, and make-shift cabin steward. The small man stopped beating down Braen's door when it suddenly opened inward.

"What is it?" Braen shouted over the sounds from above.

"Lady E-e-e-sterling's main fleet has found us." Sippen stuttered as he spat out the words.

The captain ran past the impish smithy and raced topside. As he emerged from the hatch the icy northern wind met his muscled chest. The blast nearly took away his voice. His long blonde beard kept most of the gust from off his face and he turned to see that Sippen had followed. The small man reached out a hand holding a thick coat. *Thoughtful Sippen*, he thought and surveyed the scene.

Across the choppy, greyish water he saw the faint white of sails against the dawn. He quickly counted the masts while Gunnery Sergeant Krill relayed a signal to ready the guns. While the cannons were loaded and range was elevated, Braen looked for a target. Four large galleons loomed between him and a large fleet of eight cargo ships that were accompanied by six smaller escorts. Both fleets closed on his with vengeance. He stroked his chest-long beard. *How do they have wind and we don't?* He glanced at his now raised battle sails, dangling limp and useless.

Braen had expected to cross the trade convoy in the night before. When he had lost the wind, he assumed that they would suffer the same hinderance as *Wench's Daughter*. He had not expected the main fleet to be so close. But it had appeared, oddly timing the arrival with the cargo ships. How had they coordinated pursuit in open waters?

"Get us some wind!" He shouted at the helmsman. "Hard to port! Drop those battle sails and put up the mains! We need speed!" Braen had not yet fought atop *Wench's Daughter* and cursed as he thought about the speed of his own *Ice Prince*. Suddenly, Braen remembered that *Wench's Daughter* promised bigger fire power. "Belay my last! Keep the battle sails," he ordered, "hard to starboard and all guns to port!"

With or without wind, his heavy ship would not outrun the swift imperial galleons. The large captain cursed again as he remembered how he had been talked into leaving his own sleek-lined vessel at Pirate's Cove. Worse, the belly of *Wench's Daughter* brimmed with heavy stores stolen from Esterling's winter warehouses.

Wench's Daughter drifted where the larger warships preferred.

He would have to fight on their waters with reef shoals directly south. He carefully chose and called out his first target, hoping that a hit below waterline would drag the lead galleon in front of the other vessels. However, such a first volley would be a marvel of the gods if it actually found wood to splinter. For that task, Braen Braston trusted his loyal friend Sippen.

The little weapon smith was not much to look at. Small framed, he was slightly larger than a ten-year-old boy. His head was too large for his body and his arms were twigs. Sippen Yurik was useless in a fist fight, and deathly afraid of sharp blades. He preferred mathematical equations over human interaction. Other than remembering small things like coats during a cold morning battle, the man appeared worthless on a war-going vessel. That is, until you witnessed him sighting weapons.

He had been the royal engineer at Fjorik and designed and oversaw the building of *Ice Prince*. Even earlier than that, a close friendship bonded the two men from boyhood. When Braen fled the city two years earlier, Sippen had been waiting on the docks with his tools and the ship, refusing to allow his friend to flee into exile without him. For all of this, Braen was eternally grateful.

From the corner of his eye Braen saw the unassuming man help the gunners make final adjustments for windage, furiously scribbling with chalk on a slate. Sergeant Krill called out distances, bearings and speed while Sippen calculated. "Guns readied," bellowed Krill, after Sippen had nodded to the one-eyed man. Braen briefly considered how a one-eyed gunner judged distance with such accuracy, but, as always, he did not openly question Krill's knack for timing and range.

"Stand by to fire!" The large, bearded captain gave the preparatory, "Make your mark. Now, batteries release!" On Braen's command the cannons exploded toward the largest of the galleons. Perhaps a lucky shot, Braen halfway smiled as most of the projectiles struck below the waterline. The large foe listed as a sudden rush of seawater entered its hold. It semi-capsized as he had hoped, and it listed before drifting with the current toward the trailing fleet. As he had hoped, the sinking vessel briefly blocked the passage of the other warships. Braen finally enjoyed time to think the battle over.

Oddly, he noticed a sudden coldness pass through his body. Most likely the retreat of adrenaline after the initial chaos, he tried to dismiss the chill until it had grown into a storm on a mountain summit. Braen felt his skin raise into bumps such as you would find on a freshly plucked fowl. Chicken-skin, his mother had called the sensation when he was young. It radiated from within, almost as if his blood had cooled several degrees during the time to aim the guns and fire at the other vessel. Braen pulled the collar of the heavy coat up against his neck.

While he pondered his next movement three massive dark shapes rushed beneath his keel toward the wounded galley. At precisely the same moment that the shapes passed underneath, Braen saw sails flutter. *Gods be praised*, the pirate captain thought as the wind caught. "Full to port. Ready the guns at starboard and prepare to take wind!" The dark shapes continued to speed toward the other vessels, and he briefly glimpsed long, trailing tentacles on the water.

Braen blinked as his eyes played tricks. *They're only mythological creatures*, he assured himself, but Artema Horn's prophetic words resounded through his memory. He was growing colder. Everything was colder. Even the wood of the railing had grown icy.

He signaled for Krill to prepare to lob the next volley over the wounded ship. Just as he prepared to call for the second attack, three large monsters emerged from the water.

"Kraken!"

Braen did not know who screamed the word. His only assurance was that it might not have been him. He watched helplessly as large tentacles reached out of the water and grabbed all three of the enemy galleons. Huge suction cups curled around the warships as desperate cries for mercy reached his ears. Then, the hardwood splintered as all three ships shattered like glass ornaments against stone. Stunned, the pirate captain prayed to the gods for the first time in two years.

Through the smoke and early morning haze Braen spotted more sails on the horizon. Hurried calculations revealed at least twenty more of Esterling's fleet, at least five of them flagships. Those, along with the six escorts, would make for overwhelming odds. As if timed with the sinking of the third galleon, the sails on *Wench's Daughter's* again fluttered, then fully caught the wind.

The ship lurched with a sudden jolt as the wind favored their escape. The captain smiled and gave the command to turn hard into the blessed current. Braen barked at his crew, "Square away these sails and get us away from this cinder cursed place!" Using the creatures and the wrecked galleons as cover, he silently hoped that the pursuers would remain distracted. He smiled and his crew let out a whoop as the now westerly blowing wind carried all of his vessels out to the safety of open sea.

Ashima Nakala, the lead sister of the winter oracle in Astian, broke from her dream with a scream. Initiates clustered around her and helped to ease her onto the dais. She was still writhing in pain from the bead, feeling it loosen the grip on her muscles as it left her blood.

The worse part of the Da'ash'mael was the intensity of the release. In fact, most dreamers feared the deadly rush of endorphins that ended the dream state, brought on by large quantities of the oracle bead as the muscles absorbed its potency. Dreaming was a dangerous art that promised no result but always offered pain and the risk of death.

She arched her back, writhing as her white robe slipped back to expose her dark brown breast. The curve of the ribs beneath her bosom drew in an exaggerated collapse as she gasped for oxygen against a sea of air. Her muscles instantly knotted along her spine and she finally caught the breath. Her next came rapid and beat out a tempo with her racing heart.

Ashima was the most accurate oracle produced by the coven in generations. She had predicted twenty years of changing weather patterns, including two significant blizzards and three gripping winters that lasted into the late moon of planting. But aside from weather phenomena, she had never dreamed anything that compared to the vivid cold that she felt inside the large bearded captain.

Although the oracles were called dreamers, the Ash'mael was more than a sequence of patterns from the subconscious. The Da'ash'mael provided omniscience that delved into the very existence of the dream state, often seeing current or future events from the perspective of another.

Indeed, Ashima had shared the pain of the huge sea captain as he had lain in his bed, smelling lilac, wishing for death, and remembering his lost love. Likewise, she had empathically enjoyed his surge of adrenaline as he raced topside to fight the imperial fleet. But the terror of watching the sea monsters rise from the depths had made her cry out in agony as a resurgence of the bead coursed through her blood. She convulsed as she watched the creatures tear apart the ships. Tears made pink trails as they streamed and mixed with the blood that trickled from her cheek, bitten through by her contracting mouth.

The initiates fought to hold her on the raised platform as she entered the Ka'ash'mael, the dreaded second phase in the telling of Ash'mael. This stage rarely occurred, but when it did the oracle prophesized the connection of the Da'ash'mael and how the viewed events affected the future of her Astian people. The accuracy of the dream depended on the true strength of the oracle, and only occurred after the drug had finally released its hold on their body. Since this particular Ash'mael was so strongly woven into the future of mankind, the transition from Da' to Ka' was amplified beyond any she had ever known.

The change gripped her body and she shuddered in orgasm as the bead released her muscles. She drew in a deep breath as the pain turned into a physical pleasure that simultaneously stimulated every nerve stem. Ashima knew, as did all dreamers, that the euphoria was a chemical response to the drug. But she welcomed the change as an awakening of her mind as it freed itself from her body.

Her eyes flitted in euphoric rushes as the sensation grew inside her body. Slowly, almost rhythmically, the knowing occurred. Feeling as if she were floating above her body, she began to recite her experience in the language of the oracle. The initiates relaxed and loosened their grips on her body. Each leaned in to listen and record her revelations as Ashima began to speak with slow and deliberate speech.

Fatwana Nakala watched quietly as her sister breathed her final words. The tall raven- haired woman did not give away any expression as the initiates carefully transcribed the Ash'mael. In stunned silence she took every word to heart and was not surprised when she saw the attending priest draw the shroud over Ashima's head. Her body surged up from the table and convulsed before settling onto the stone altar with a shudder, her final words spoken.

Ashima Nakala spoke truth in her Ka'Ash'mael, prophecy that transcended the physical plane and reflected changes threatening the existence of the Astian lifestyle. This particular Ash'mael held importance to all of the oracles and would no doubt shake the very core of their existence. After she had collected the transcriptions, Fatwana walked to the altar and placed her hand on the husk that had once held her sister's soul, speaking softly. "Rest sister and join our brother. I shall carry this warning to all, so that they must heed." Turning, she strode from the temple, ignoring the warm tears that slowly fell from her eyes.

Chapter One

The sun rose over a green valley in Loganshire, casting shadows on the rich farmland as it peeked around the clouds. Rivers and streams rabid with white froth raced between the hills, anxious to be free of the mountains to the north. Winter was arriving late, explaining why the grasses clung to their green hue. Despite the unseasonable warmth, the trees had completely let go of their leaves. Their shed foliage danced in the brisk wind that rolled down the mountain into the valley.

Loganshire was a quant farming region nestled between the kingdoms of Fjorik in the north, and Eston which lay to the south and west. Once, long enough in the memory of the old-timers, the valley was the focus of countless raids from the northern men. Those fierce raids signified the end of fall and the start of winter to the anxious people of the valley. For the past ten years, under the stability of the Esterling Empire, the raids had stopped completely, and the people enjoyed peace and prosperity.

One farmhouse had enjoyed a tremendous comfort, and Mauri hummed and danced as she washed the family laundry, hanging it on lines to dry in the breeze. That same wind tossed her red hair gently, nipping at her rosy cheeks as she spun and hummed. Her husband, Thom, baled hay with his brothers Franque and Jean on this day, and she had a stew warming on the hearth for their return from the labor.

Mauri and Thom had two children. Anne was three years old, and she resembled her mother with red hair and freckles from a life spent mostly outdoors. Ann played in the grass with a doll that her father had fashioned out of straw and burlap. Occasionally she would lean over and talk to her baby brother, Clauvis, as he cooed in his basket. He was a perfect baby, hardly cried, never fussed, and brought so much hope to the family for the future of the farm. Boy babies were lucky, at least that's what Mauri's grandmother had told her.

A hawk flew overhead, circling the field. Mauri took a moment to watch as it glided against the clouds and then as it dove. With grace it swooped toward a group of men riding horseback up the lane. It rested on the gloved hand of a tall man riding in the middle of the formation and Mauri froze. Wearing a hood with a feathered collar he sat high in the saddle, glancing sideways around him and darting glances like the oversized falcon perched on his arm. Abruptly, the hawk squawked a shrill, high piercing sound and the man focused his eyes directly at the farmwife. Her load of laundry fell onto the grass and she screamed a blood curdling sound that brought Thom running from the field.

He reached his wife just as the riders halted their beasts in front of Mauri and the children. His brothers, still wielding scythes from the harvest, dropped the blades in the grass as Constable Wimbley, local magistrate and leader of the group, spoke, "Thom and Mauri Thorinson. The Falconer claims that you delivered a living child sometime after the fifth day of the month of fall planting."

Wimbley should have been a military man. He was prim and proper, and, unlike other constables and their deputies, he wore his uniform clean and pressed, with his black beard and hair closely cropped. His harsh eyes narrowed on the family, as he asked, "Why did you fail to report the birth to a midwife or a constable?"

"We … We were afraid, Shon. You know we lost our second child after the beast examined her."

"Nonsense and superstition!" The Falconer behind the constable bellowed. The man was a hideous specter, one whose eyes seem to pierce through the hood and into another's soul. "The examination is a blessing, and infant mortality is a natural occurrence, not to be blamed on our ministrations."

The constable tried to keep everyone calm, "Thom, all you have to do is allow him to look your child over. Don't make this harder than it needs to be."

Thom's face was scarlet with anger. "Shon, you of all people should understand!"

"Let him work, Thom. Otherwise I'll have to hang the both of you." Wimbley rode his horse between Mauri and the baby, forcing her and her husband to step backward. "I'm sorry about this. Really, I am. Just do as he says, and all will be fine."

Dismounting, the Falconer approached Clauvis in the basket laying on the grass. Anne scurried away from her brother's side and hid behind the legs of her father, still clutching her little doll. The Falconer paid her no mind and knelt beside the younger child. The bird of prey on his shoulder stared intently at the baby, switching his head back and forth to view him with each eye. Mauri watched as her child stared intently at both the man and the bird, making no sound.

With a squawk, the bird spread its' wings and flew up into the air to resume circling. The hooded man pulled out a small jar of oil and removed the blue lid. He rubbed two fingers into the mixture, and placed it under the tongue of the child before standing to address the family, "I find your baby healthy and free of defect. Enjoy a long life with the child." Turning, he added an admonishment. "In the future report your offspring to the authorities." The man strode back to his mount and swung into the saddle.

The constable looked intently at Thom, who was grinding his teeth and seething with anger. "Your penalty will be an extra percentage of taxed goods when payment is due." To Mauri he added, "Be happy your child's healthy. Some of your neighbors weren't so lucky." He tipped his hat to the couple, and the group rode back down the lane the way that they had come.

As soon as the riders had turned their horses, Mauri rushed to the basket and swept her child into her arms. Holding him tightly, she ran back into the house with Anne chasing behind, her doll swinging wildly in her hand as she sprinted up the walk. Thom turned to his brothers, who picked up their scythes. He shook his head and cursed the hooded man, rejoining his brothers as they walked slowly back to the field to finish their duties. The laundry lay in a heap upon the grass where his wife had dropped it, but that task was long forgotten after the tense meeting.

After Thom and his brothers had finished in the field, they washed in the stream before making their way back to the cottage. Dodging chickens on the ground, they walked and talked about the earlier event. Thom, although relieved that his baby was healthy, still worried over the incident. Their other child, Grace, had been two weeks old when the other Falconer had come. Like today, he had blessed their child and proclaimed her healthy and whole. The young parents had considered themselves luckier than most, as other families had had their sickly or mal-formed babies taken from them.

They both felt that she was a special infant. Like Clauvis, she never cried nor fussed. They felt generally happier and more connected around their little Gracie and also thought of her as a lucky child. Thom remembered vividly awakening to the sobs of Mauri on the night of the last visit. Grace had died in her sleep. Crib death, the old-timers had called it, but he and his wife had distrusted their visitor and attributed the sudden death to his blessing.

A scream from within the cottage sent Thom and his siblings running the final steps toward the door. Thrusting it open, they halted at the display within. Mauri knelt over the crib, clutching the infant close to her breast. She wailed in grief as little Anne stood in the corner, also crying and squeezing her little doll in fright as she watched her inconsolable mother.

Thom broke free from the invisible grip that had held him, and stepped forward, placing a hand on his wife's shoulder. As Mauri turned to look up at her husband, he saw that Clauvis was lifeless and completely blue. The farmer's brothers took in the scene, then headed back outside to work. But this time the job was to dig a deep little hole.

A few days later, in city of Logan, Constable Wimbley sat in the corner of the *Mangy Dog* tavern. The tavern was noticeably empty on this day, despite that the city bustled with activity. The constable was not alone. Across from him sat the reason that the tavern was empty, in the form of the cursed Falconer.

Shon Wimbley loved his job as constable, and it had been his desired career since childhood. As a young man he served as a deputy to his brother in Brentway where they had fought against northern marauders during the most recent raids. He loved his duties and served them well, but his two least favorite tasks included tax collection and overseeing the child blessings. Those blessings were the reason that he had been stuck escorting this Falconer for an entire week.

Shon frowned at his mug of ale, unusually bitter for the season. "Are you sure that you don't want a mug?" When the beastlike man did not respond, he answered himself, "No, of course not." Then, under his breath he muttered, "You never do. You don't drink spirits; you don't eat rich foods or sweets and you don't look at the tavern wenches." After he had said his piece, the two men again sat in silence, the Falconer staring straight ahead, the constable's hard green eyes focused on his mug.

Shon found solace in the thought that he was nearly finished with his current duties. They had three more children to inspect in the city and had planned to begin at first light. So far, the blessings had gone smoothly. Only two farmhouses had produced children with defects, and those had been removed to the Rookery with little resistance and with only the expected grief by the parents. Since the Empire had gained a foothold in Loganshire, the tradition of culling the lame had become more widely accepted, possibly since more families were having healthy children with their newfound prosperity.

Only a few had tried to hide births, one of those being the Thorinson farm. How the Falconer had discovered the child was strange. It was almost as if he could communicate with his bird, or worse, see through its eyes. The thought unnerved Shon, almost as if the creatures shared foresight. But that theory was impossible, since all religions, regardless of belief, strictly prohibited telling the future or working magic. Both crimes were rewarded with the penalty of death in the Esterling Empire. Of course, magic did not exist, so that part of the edict never made sense to Constable Wimbley. He chalked it up to superstitious nonsense.

Still, something about the Thorinson exchange did not sit well with the constable. So far, fifty children were inspected during the week, but Shon had noticed that the blessings had included two jars of oil. Every other child had been anointed with the jar with the red lid, but that baby had received the substance from a jar with a blue lid. When he had asked the administrator why he had used a different jar, the beast-like man had lied and stated that he only has one jar.

Abruptly, the Falconer cocked his head to one side, suddenly alert. "Post men by the door. Trouble is coming."

Shon looked up from his ale, incredulous and feeling somewhat suspicious given his recent thoughts. He motioned his deputies, who stood from the table and moved into position like bookends on the inside of the oak frame. After posting the guards, the constable asked, "Did you hear something?"

Just then, the door burst open from the force of a large man kicking it in. Thom Thorinson charged through, wielding an axe and rushing directly for the Falconer. When he reached the chair, the hooded figure, who had never turned around, leaped from his seat and sidestepped a blow from the hatchet. The head of the tool sank deep into the table, spilling the plate of food and mug of ale that Shon had been working on.

Suddenly, with a screech a dark winged blur swept through the opening, sinking its talons in the back of the raging farmer. With its strong beak it tore at the man's flesh, ripping out chunks as it tried to peck out his eyes. Thom screamed and the bird squawked until the constable intervened. "For Cinder's sake restrain the man!" Only once they controlled his arms and pinned him face down on the floor did the raptor release its grip and return to perch on the arm of its' master.

Thom Thorinson bled onto the floorboards, weeping and sobbing in pain of both body and spirit. The deputies stood him up and fastened manacles on his wrists. Shon approached and demanded explanation. "What the hell are you about, Thorinson? Explain yourself!"

Thom sputtered, "That abomination killed my wife and child!"

"Nonsense! Both of them were very much alive when we left your spread, and he's been with me the entire time! You know DAMNED well that he had no hand in their death!

"Clauvis died mere hours after his blessing and Mauri slit her wrists in grief that very night!"

"A coincidence, I assure you!" Shon was very disturbed by this exchange. *The blue jar*, he thought and silently wondered if Thom was correct in his accusation. He stared up at the ghoul with an expecting glance, watching for any change in demeanor but none came.

The Falconer spoke up from where he now stood in the corner of the tavern, bird roosting on his arm. "Attacking an agent of the Queen Regent is a hanging offense. This was attempted murder."

Shon shook his head. Turning to look at the hooded man, he said, "Thom is grieving. I've known him and his entire family since their births. He's no murderer." He leaned in close to the farmer, and grimaced, "Smell him, he's drunk and acting out of grief."

"Death by hanging." Turning to look at the constable, the

beast-like man added, "Certainly you will not disobey an administrator in his duties? Men have hanged for that, as well."

Shon muttered under his breath, "Well, shit." After pondering for a moment, he shook his head and faced the others. "Take Thorinson to the jail. I'll speak to the magistrate and turn him over to the city officials for a trial." He placed emphasis on the final word as if willing it would ensure justice.

The next day, Shon wrapped up his duties, finally able to part ways with the eerie hooded beast. None too soon, he packed his saddle bags, mounted his mare, and spurred her flanks to a fast trot. As he rode out of the city, he tipped his hat to the swinging corpse of Thom Thorinson, the ripped-out portions of his face hidden within a hood of his own. The once stalwart lawman unpinned his badge and tossed it in the river as he crossed the bridge out of town.

Chapter Two

Mattie rose early before Alec and the children. Quietly tiptoeing across the room, she stepped over Liza and Alexa asleep on their pallets. Liza's sixteenth birthday celebration was a few days away, when they would hopefully announce her marriage to the son of Captain Dominique. That is, if Alec could arrange the match with a suitable dowry.

She took no time at all crossing their tiny apartment, stopping to tidy up a few items her husband had dropped when he returned home. Among these she found a letter from Artema horn, thanking the Captain for his faithful years of service to The Cove and the entire Pirate's Guild. *So that's where he'd been out so late,* she thought. Mattie Pogue loved Alec but wished that he wasn't so dedicated to his career.

Looking around the hovel she smiled. Although small, it was more than most of the palace officers could afford. As the captain of the guard, he provided well for his family. She only wished that he could spend more time at home with her and the girls. She loved him all the same, and that was the reason she had risen so early.

Moving into the cramped kitchen she examined the hearth. The embers had burned down in the night, so she added a few more logs and brought them to life by blowing into the coals. Within moments a fire burned warm and she started on his breakfast. Hazel had dropped another egg during the early hours, so this went straight into a pan of water set to boil. They had saved some fatback from dinner, and she cut this into strips like bacon. It wasn't the same, but he wouldn't complain. He never did.

His uniform lay spread with care atop a chair in the sitting room. Frowning, she eyed a spot of grease on the sleeve and carried the coat into the kitchen. As breakfast cooked, she dabbed at the stain with a cloth and white vinegar. She eventually felt satisfied that no one would notice and set the iron atop the stove to warm. Then she spread the jacket across the table so that she could flatten the wrinkles. She wanted everyone to respect him in his flawless uniform.

By then the water boiled and the fatback sizzled. She flipped it with a fork. While it cooked, she set a waterskin beside his boots and hung his sword belt on a peg above where it had fallen. *Really, why is he always so careless when he returns?* Of course, she knew the answer to her question. He worked tirelessly to protect the Pirate King.

Movement caught her eye as she pulled the boiling water off the fire to cool. "You're up early."

"Aye. Three of my men are ill and landed in the infirmary, yesterday. I need to cover their shifts."

"Why does that always fall on you?" She tried but failed to keep the resentment out of her voice as she spoke. "You're Captain of the Guard! Doesn't rank have privileges that allow you to spend time with family, once in a while?" Mattie didn't mean to sound like an angry wife, but the words had slipped out.

Alec wrapped his arms around her and brushed her long auburn hair from her shoulder. He examined her pale skin for a moment and then kissed her gently. All at once her anger left and she wrapped her hands around his arms. "That's exactly why I can't take time off, my love. Duty demands extra hours."

She both loved and hated when he kissed her like that. She wanted so badly to be angry, but he loved her like no man ever could, and so she always let it go. "How late will you be, tonight?" She turned to face him, wrapping her arms around his waist as she smiled up at his beautiful green eyes.

"I think I'll make dinner."

"Well, you'd better. I have an extra ration of loin that I'm cutting up in the stew. I want it tender so that you enjoy it."

"Mm. I always enjoy your food, Mattie."

"Oh? Well my husband deserves to eat as well as the king he serves." She pushed him back and grabbed the iron from the heat, carrying it to the jacket that dried on the table. "Have you talked to Dominique?" She tried to sound casual as she ironed out the jacket with crisp military creases.

"I think that an arrangement has been made. He offered twenty talents."

"Twenty?" She never looked up from the steaming iron as she moved it across the sleeve. "She's worth fifty or more."

"She's worth what he'll pay, Mattie, and I'm not noble. We're lucky that his whelp is interested in her at all, given that his family is of merchant birth."

She continued to iron, not wanting to answer. Finally, she sighed and responded. "You're right. I just hope he's a good man. I want her happy."

"As happy as us?"

"Come home on time and see how happy we are, Captain Pogue." She hid a devilish smile from him.

"I'll be home for dinner."

"That better be a promise." Finished, she pulled the jacket off the table and held it out while he slipped it on. "There, you look like a general."

Alec laughed. "Even generals don't look this good, Mattie. You spoil me."

"Yes, I do. Don't forget that."

He leaned in and kissed her passionately on the mouth. Pulling back, he added, "I never will."

Mattie forked the fatback onto a wooden plate and set the egg next to the meat. "Do you think we'll ever leave, here, Alec? I want so badly for you to retire."

"I... I don't know. Artema asked me to stay on a while longer. He wouldn't say why, but he was insistent."

"I want us to buy a farm in Loganshire. You'd make a fine farmer, Alec."

"I don't know. I'd miss the fighting, and you make my uniform look so good." He playfully winked as he spoke.

She smiled. "Fine! Be a constable, then. Just get us out of here."

"Soon."

He spoke the word, but she knew that he would never leave the service to his king. His duty was always to The Cove. "We have enough saved, Alec. Take me away from here."

He kissed her sweetly, dismissing her protests. "Soon. I promise." He pulled on his boots and strapped on the sword belt, dangling two cutlasses at his sides.

Mattie wrapped the breakfast in a sack and handed it to her husband. "I might not wait for you."

He smiled and kissed her. "I think you will." Then he turned and left their tiny apartment, walking the long road up the hill to the palace.

Mattie watched her husband walk away with silent tears in her eyes. After a while she returned to her chores. The girls would awaken, soon, and she wanted to prepare the house. She set some porridge on the stove so that they wouldn't be hungry and went outside to sweep the porch. The morning sun was just breaking the horizon and the salt smell in the air calmed her as she worked.

A strong hand grabbed her from behind and she dropped the broom. Before she could scream a knife flashed to her neck and a low voice whispered, "If you make a sound you'll die, Missy."

She nodded, careful not to cut herself on the blade. In a soft whisper she answered, "What do you want? My husband will return, soon."

"No." The man behind her laughed. "No, he won't. The Captain's working three shifts, today, because his men are ill."

"How? How do you know that unless you...?"

"Quiet, Missy. You'll do exactly what we say, and you'll live. Don't and you'll watch your two daughters die."

Two more men walked up the steps onto the porch. One of them, the smaller of the two, licked his lips as he looked Mattie up and down. "Time for some fun, then?"

"No." The other cautioned him with a look of disgust. "Boss said that they'll leave untouched. Unless they resist, of course."

The man holding Mattie guided her inside and rough hands forced her into a chair. Panic rose inside and she begged, "We have nothing. Please, leave us and don't harm my girls." Her eyes betrayed her, shooting a glance at a large sugar bin on the top shelf.

The first man smiled devilishly and stood on a chair to reach the container. Opening it he found a large cache of gold and silver. "Seems the Captain likes to live a quiet life, while saving his coin for a rainy day."

"Take it!" Mattie hoped that they would leave now that they had Alec's life's savings.

"It's not that simple, Missy." The first man bit one of the coins, testing it's worth. Satisfied with the soft give of the gold, he turned to the second man. "Boss doesn't know about this. We should keep it for ourselves." Both of the other men nodded in agreement.

"Please!" Mattie pleaded. "Take it and go!"

"I think not, Missy." The man laid out a piece of parchment. "Write out this letter exactly as I say, and your girls won't be hurt."

Her hopes lifted at the offer. "I promise! Anything! What do you want me to write?"

The large man whispered the words into Mattie's ears, sinking her hopes and heart. She took the quill and tears welled in her eyes as she wrote to her husband.

Alec returned home late, breaking his promise to arrive in time for dinner. His feet ached as he climbed the steps to the porch, and the muscles of his back knotted from the stress of the day. Yawning, he closed his eyes and wished that he was already inside and asleep beside Mattie. Long days like these made him consider giving in and taking her and the girls away to a quieter life.

The key turned easily in the lock and he stepped inside to an impeccably clean home. *She is so orderly, always taking care of everything.* He unhooked his sword belt and set it on the floor, relieved at the freedom from the added weight. Kicking off his boots he looked longingly into the small kitchen, hoping to spy the stewpot his wife had promised. *Strange, usually the kitchen smells wonderful.*

Something felt out of place. He made his way into the kitchen and saw an empty pot with dried porridge stuck to the sides. Beside it were three bowls and spoons coated with the same residue. Alec raised an eyebrow. In twenty years, his wife had never left a dirty dish on the counter. The table caught his eye and he turned to find an empty sugar container holding down the edge of a note. He swept the parchment off the table, holding it up to read in the soft glow of moonlight.

Alec, I'm tired of living in The Cove. This kind of life is not what I had wanted for our daughters and so I've taken them away. You are married to your career and I refuse to be second behind that kind of mistress. Don't try to find us. Mattie.

The Captain of the Guard felt his knees buckle and he sunk into a chair, reading the words over and over. Tears formed in his eyes and fell down his face, smearing the ink as they landed on the parchment. He had loved Mattie his entire life. They had played together as children and had married as soon as they were old enough. *How did I not see how badly she hated this life? Hated me, even?* Another thought crossed his mind and he looked again at the handwriting, more tears falling after confirming that it was hers.

Panic and doubt consumed him as he stood and rushed into the tiny bedroom. Both her and the girls' trunks were gone, not a stitch of their belongings left behind. On the bed lay a small box. He bent to open it, finding her wedding band laid gently atop every letter from his times at sea. Misery rushed in as Alec Pogue realized that he had lost everything important in his life. He lay down on the bed and wept, clutching the little box to his chest.

CHAPTER THREE

The hot, west wind burned at the face of the brown Pescari youth. He raced atop a sleek mare who frothed with sweat. The beast breathed heavy beneath the light frame of Taros and seemingly flew. He scarcely felt the light stamp of her hooves across the thick grass, pushing her toward home. He knew that she could stand only a few more miles before needing to slow once more. As the sun raised over the boy's left shoulder the smoke before him grew black against the red glow of morning.

Whispering promises of rest, he coaxed her ever faster as they raced southward. "Get me home, Falia. Get me to Mother."

Taros had been well north of the village snaring small game during the night. He had already checked most of his traps when he noticed the glow in the direction of home. Leaving the others unchecked he mounted Falia and pointed her nose directly toward the disaster. For the better part of an hour he had raced across the fields while his mind produced visions of his mother burning in agony.

Taros reached his village just as the sun had fully emerged. The smoking pyre wells that gave the Steppes of Cinder their name darkened the western horizon, with the fumaroles emitting a strange orange glow. Fiery plumes were a daily occurrence on the steppes, but seldom had this much of the plain fallen away into the erupting caldera. His village, once bordered on three sides by a raging white river, now stood on the edge of a burning chasm. The elders had not foreseen this disaster, and little could have been done to prevent the fire that rained down from the massive field of hell.

Looking around he tearfully saw that very little remained. Fewer than fifty survivors had gathered on the edge of the southern marshes a few hundred yards away. Taros dismounted Falia and ran to them, searching for his mother. Not finding her he rushed west toward the inferno. By now the village was fully engulfed in red flames and black smoke that filled with such heat and ash that it burned both his eyes and his lungs. Ignoring the pain in his chest he ran onward to his mother's hut.

Cornin, the village chieftain, shouted. "Leave her, boy! Leave her with the others!" Several of the firesiders lay on the blackened ground, overcome by the smoke and heat and unmoving. "Their fate is the will of the goddess!" His voice rang in competition against the roar of the inferno. Pushing forward, Taros flinched as the flames were made fierce by the westerly winds. "I said leave them!" The voice commanded, but he paid no heed and sprinted toward his mother's hut.

Large arms grabbed hold of Taros and he screamed against their grip. "Let me go! I must go to her! Let me save Mother!"

"Listen to Cornin," a faceless warrior whispered in the boy's ear. "You can't save Lynette. She died on the day of her shunning, boy! Let her be the sacrifice that the goddess demands!" But Taros could not believe that the voice, who he now recognized as his mother's brother Teot, could merely watch his own sister burn. The defiance in the boy's eyes turned to rage as he looked into those of his uncle. The rage grew into fury as he stared deeper into the man's face.

Screams rang out from Teot, hands burning with sudden pain. His grip on the boy failed and he dropped to the ground, writhing in agony and holding his forearms to his chest.

Ripping free Taros ran headlong into the smoke. As he did, he heard a woman whimpering from the direction of Lynette's crude shelter. Her cries confirmed his fears that she faced certain doom. Somewhere in the madness of his charge, the boy considered that she had not shed tears since they had buried his father two winters before. Even during the shunning ceremony, she had defied the elders by shamelessly holding up her head. The event was meant to appease their angry goddess by displaying only the weakness of her followers. But on that distant day his mother had looked each man in the eye as she led Taros to the far eastern side of the village toward the eye of Felicima.

In Taros' culture the eastern side was the fireside, or the part of the community given up to their goddess. She rose daily as a fresh fireball, surveying her people as the winds blew her across the sky, finally cooling in the western smoke of the fumaroles. She would return the next morning and do the same, seeing first the outcasts who lived under her gaze.

While the fireside contained the lame, the sick, and the widows, the last visage Felicima viewed was of the strongest warriors and most honored elders. They remained out of sight until her anger had cooled. Pescari valued tribal humility foremost among all virtues, and as long as they hid their strength from their deity, they could avoid her outburst and eruption. The western section of the village held the wealth and food of the people, and the furthest that tribal members resided from the goddess' eye was determined by their status.

Taros followed Lynette's cries into the wretched outlying in which she lived. Ignoring the putrid aroma of burnt hair and flesh that filled the smoke, he stepped through the flames toward her hut. Searing heat roared at the entrance as he peered in, hoping to Felicima that she lived. Something inside caught his eye, and he strained through the smoke at a dark pile of furs in the corner. *Is that her?* He closed his eyes and began to move forward when a sound caught his attention.

Lynette cried out from behind. "Taros! I'm here!"

He turned and saw the large clay oven where she normally spent her day baking bread. Luckily the eruption occurred early enough that she had not lit the space beneath. Lynette lay huddled within as fire raged outside, the bricks keeping out the worst of the heat.

Tears of joy streamed down his face as Taros ran to her, flames licked at his legs as he pulled her free.

He had turned to carry Lynette toward the other survivors when a backdraft exploded around him. In an instant he felt all of the hair on his body singe and curl in the heat, but his skin did not burn. The heat should have been unbearable, but, oddly enough, he only felt a warm sensation throughout his body.

Flame danced around him as he first walked, then trotted. Reaching the wall of inferno, he sprinted through toward the watching villagers, emerging with only wisps buckskins remaining on his brown body, every strip of clothing having burned off both mother and son. Relief flooded his heart that her naked body did not reveal any serious wounds that he could see. Amazingly, he still did not feel any pain as he jogged across the small stream.

The elders stared in awe as he trotted past. He turned his singed head and drove an icy stare through the old men as he laid her down beside the wounded.

"Place the bitch away from the others!" The angry voice of the chieftain caused him to turn. "Now, boy, or we'll cast you both into the fumaroles!"

Taros could see his uncle beside Cornin, his arms somehow burned from his elbow to his hands. Looking closely, he could see that his chest was also blistered.

He no longer cared if he offended the others with his mother's presence. He hugged her with tears in his eyes until she patted his arm and whispered his name. "Taros," she said, "your name means brave, my son, and you are the truest named boy in the village. Your father would be proud." She smiled up at him with eyes full of love and adoration.

He said nothing in return but kissed her gently on her forehead. It was cooler to the touch than he would have thought after walking through the flames. In contrast, his skin seemed to burn from the core of his heart, radiating outward like a fever. Taros gently let go of his mother and looked her over for any burns that she may have received. Both mother and son would live with nothing more than singed baldness all over their bodies. He smiled at her and hugged her once more before rising.

Finally standing he turned to face down an angry Cornin. The chieftain had grabbed his spear and was walking toward them with murder in his eyes.

"Shapalote," Taros spoke quietly. The athletic man, muscles hard from years of hunting and horsemanship, strode toward the pair as if he had not heard. Tears fell from Taros' eyes. Instead of cooling his burning skin they turned to steam as they dribbled down his cheeks. Louder he said again, "Shapalote!" Fury now burning within, he turned his full attention on the chieftain. "I demand the right of shapalote!"

Cornin stopped in his tracks. Realizing that the small boy had meant the words, he spat toward Lynette on the ground. Standing over Taros with spear point at the boy's throat, he warned, "You are too young for shapalote, boy." The older man looked amused. "Move the shunned one to the fireside and I will forgive your insolence."

"I had my ritual last spring," the boy shouted at the shappan. "I am a full member of the tribe and I demand the right to challenge your leadership." Gesturing toward Lynette, he added, "And I will restore my mother to the village." The audience stared in silence as Cornin's lips curled up slightly at the edges. Seeing the humor on the man's face enraged the boy, "I invoke shapalote, now!" He stared into the eyes of his chieftain with defiance. He had planned for this moment each day over the two years since his father had died. He knew that he would someday challenge Cornin to single combat, but never believed that he would do so this soon.

Teot, still hugging his burned arms to the blistered flesh of his huge chest, stepped between the boy and the chieftain. "He had his ritual on his fifteenth naming day. No one can deny the boy the right of Shapalote. That is, not unless you defy the goddess herself." Shaking his head at his nephew, he added, "One of you must die for the right of leadership." The uncle could no longer protect the boy from the world.

Cornin growled, "Fine. Throw the child a spear so that we can get on with our business." His neck made a cruel cracking sound as he tilted his head back and forth. "You are a fool, boy."

"I need no spear, Cornin." Taros walked two steps toward the warrior and stood defiantly.

"Stupid child." Cornin set his feet in the attack posture, ready to thrust or throw as an expert could easily execute either move from the stance. With a grunt the spear hurled through the air.

A new sensation filled Taros. Sudden knowing rushed in, and he instinctively raised his right arm and planted his feet stubbornly. Refusing to step aside he stared down the charging spear which abruptly exploded in flames, instantly turning to ash before hitting his chest and harmlessly falling to the ground. The bystanders gasped at the intervention by their goddess, and chants of "Felicima" erupted.

Taros stepped forward hand still pointed toward the chieftain. Cornin laughed, standing with his back straight and ready for any pathetic blow that may come from the man-child. Taros stopped one pace from his leader, the source of his hatred. "Felicima damn you, Cornin." As he spoke, the flames that he had absorbed while rescuing his mother exploded from his palm. Struck in the chest, Cornin fell to the ground and screamed and writhed in pain. Taros stood over him with his hand outstretched while his dark eyes reflected the flaming man at his feet. In mere seconds the former chief fell quiet, his body blackened into charcoal and molded in the exact shape of the former shappan.

Taros dropped his arm and the inferno stopped. The tribe watched in shocked silence, stepping back as women hid their children behind their skirts. Lynette lay on the ground smiling at her son with a knowing look in her eyes. She knew. Somehow his mother had known that her son possessed a gift from the goddess.

Teot turned to the frightened villagers and quietly answered their unspoken question. "The right of shapalote has been decided and Felicima has chosen our new spiritual leader. She has witnessed our strength and our corruption and is not pleased. Today was a warning that we must leave the Steppes of Cinder." The least terrified of those looking on nodded in agreement. The others stared blank faced at the boy who had wielded the forbidden power of legends.

Taros heard the words that his uncle had spoken. Looking up from Cornin's corpse and into the terrified eyes of his people he measured their fear and awe of him. At barely more than a whisper he spoke, "We will first cross the steppes and then the Forbidden Waste. Once past, we will seek refuge with the people of Andolan." He turned and walked to where Falia calmly drank from the stream. He retrieved the field hares that he had trapped during the night's hunt, taking them from the saddle and giving the string to a nearby woman. "Skin these," he commanded, "feed the weak, the old, and the children so that they will have the strength to walk."

Turning slowly to face Teot with confidence, his voice did not waver as he spoke in a tone unusual for a boy of fifteen summers, "Tell the men to gather up whatever salvage can be found. Search the huts." Then Taros quietly strode toward the smoldering remains to see what he could find as well.

The boy later returned with a bit of rope and three long tent poles that were seared on each end. He used these to lash together the litter that would drag his mother and their meager belongings behind Falia. He glanced only once at what remained of Cornin but stared often to the west as he worked. Westward he looked, toward the angry caldera that was the bed to the sleeping Felicima, goddess of the Pescari. *Are my people damned or blessed?* He did not know.

Chapter Four

The swift black ship bounced across the choppy seas. Each time that *She Wolf* crashed onto the waves she groaned as if it would be her last. The air around her grew noticeably colder and the crew turned up their collars to defend against the spray. Atop the deck a small figure draped in leathers as black as the sails above. First glance always missed the tiny woman in the fur cloak. On land she was a mere shadow, but aboard her ship Eusari ruled as a goddess.

She had spent fourteen of her twenty-seven years at sea. Originally from the farmlands of Loganshire, northern raiders stole her at a time when she should have been flirting with the boys of her town. Instead of making happy memories, the fur-clad Northern demons sold her to a merchant captain with an appetite for young girls. Years of abuse robbed her of innocence, and where she had forgotten how to love, she learned instead to hate. Her childhood innocence had long been replaced with cunning, and what of hers that had been designed to create life was used instead to destroy men.

She avoided thinking about the life that she had lived before the ocean claimed her, keeping the pain at bay through sheer avoidance. She knew that she had family in the world. Perhaps her brothers lived, but her parents were long gone. Her previous world was dead to Eusari, and she accepted that her family were pirates. In spite of their constant company, she lived a lonely existence. She hardly spoke to her few friends, and, when she spoke to her enemies, she preferred to let her blades do the talking.

Unimposing, the small and quiet woman captained *She Wolf*

while demanding absolute discipline. This allegiance was ensured by Sa'mond, her hulking first mate and extremely capable sailing master. His instinctual mastery rivaled any man of seasoned practice or schooling, and his crew worked with perfect timing and quiet precision. But most of all, and despite her stature, Eusari of Loganshire commanded the loyalty of her crew without the utterance of complaint or questioned order. Fear ruled *She Wolf.*

Eusari knew the clouds by their color and shuddered at the pea soup sky. She glanced at the northern horizon and it reflected against her own green eyes. As a child working the western fields of Loganshire, she learned early on when to seek cover from a storm. These clouds had grown black with fury, deepening the dark gray of the cold water. They raced toward her ship with a quiet calm that was broken only by the increasingly colder air. Her suspicious eyes darted once more to the horizon and her instincts screamed to steer a wide berth.

On this day she chose to ignore her gut. Her mission was urgent enough to push *She Wolf* to splinters. Her crew seemed to share her anxiety and busied themselves by clearing the decks and tying down loose objects under the watchful gaze of Sa'Mond. The dark skinned giant also took notice of the pending storm and nodded a reassuring smiled as if he understood her worry. She turned one more glance at the clouds then headed below to check the hold and her cargo.

The dark ladder did not bother Eusari. She knew every rung, every board, and every ounce of pitch that held *She Wolf* together. The vessel had taken her in and out of harm's way for ten years and the fact that she only needed a small crew to sail the ship worked in her favor. The petite woman exercised a pervasive lack of trust in men and large crews were difficult to control. Her cautious nature obviously dashed out any hope to take an enemy ship by force, instead taking on smuggling jobs that required stealth, speed and silence.

Artema Horn had personally chosen Eusari for the current job, telling her that it required her "feminine talents." She had nearly run him through with one of her many hidden blades, staving off for the fact that Artema was one of the three men whom she trusted. Of all the men that she had run across or through during her life, he was the first whom she thought of as she once did her father.

"You are the best wolf that I know, Sari," he had said to her. "Now, I need you to sneak into the flock and steal the shepherd's prize."

"Artema," she had protested, "I'm better in the shadows. I'm a smuggler and assassin, not a spy. Don't make me do this. Don't force me to be seen in daylight."

"I've never forced you to do anything for The Cove."

"Fair enough, and that's the only reason that I've stayed. I go where I choose, take the jobs I want, and kill anyone who tries to force me to their will. I tie up *She Wolf* without any expectation of fealty."

"Eusari, take this job because I ask it of you, and not because you'll profit from it. Which you will, I assure you."

She had scoffed at the mention of profit. "I have plenty of gold, Artema." She had turned to walk away from him, intent on turning down the job.

Artema cleared his throat, then added, "Sari, I found him."

Her eyes had grown wide in disbelief and turned around to face her friend. "Don't tease me, Art. You know what this means to me."

"This is the last time that I'll ever ask you to do something for The Cove. But if I'm right, this job will reward you greater than any of us. This is what you've been waiting for. I found him, Eusari. I'm certain."

Regardless of the promised reward, she had accepted his job out of loyalty though not out-right submission. Her body was hers to use as she wished and Artema was correct in assuming that daggers were not her only weapons. The job took her into the imperial city of Eskera, a small port on the tip of the Southern Marshes. Venturing north of Eskera and west of the marshes would subject a traveler to the hot winds of the Steppes of Cinder with its dangerous fumaroles, steamy caldera and savage Pescari people.

She had spent a full month in the port town watching her prey, learning his habits, and easing her way into his confidence. In the end she had worked over the mark like a professional. Under the guise of a wealthy Westonese merchant's daughter, and after only six months, she had gathered enough intelligence to bring down half of the empirical noble class. Then, the perfect opportunity finally presented itself to Eusauri and she seized it. She had quickly made her final arrangements, called in her crew and loaded her newly won cargo aboard *She Wolf*. The first part of her mission completed; she had left Eskera on the same winds of the night that she had ridden in on.

Now, as a result of her promise, the tiny girl from the Loganshire would be forever branded an enemy to the crown. Her face had been drawn from the shadows, would be remembered by those on whom she had played her game of confidence, and worst of all she had made an enemy of the most powerful family in the realm. She risked everything for a promise to Artema Horn.

Eusauri descended the final rungs of the ladder that led below decks. Here, the sound of the sea was louder, beating against the hull like a battering ram on a castle gate. The first time that her younger version had heard that sound she cowered in the corner and wept like a lamb that had seen the knife before slaughter. This time the sound reminded her that she was at home, and that no man would take from her anything that she would not willingly give. She blinked her eyes, adjusting to the faint light and then opened the door to the hold. The cargo that she had seduced sat upon a wooden chair in the corner of the room. A chain ran from his neck to the wall and another connected his wrists to his ankles.

"Go to hell, Bitch." Marcus Esterling spat in her direction. Eusauri watched the spittle fall to the wooden floor.

"I most likely will." Nodding her agreement to the young lord, she again closed the door and made a careful effort to lock it behind her as she did.

"What have you done, stupid girl?" she muttered to no one as she slowly climbed up the ladder, worrying once more at the storm on the horizon.

Sa'Mond approached her and trained his eyes in the same direction. "It be a bad one, mistress, a bad one indeed. I presume that the mission be worth our while?" He patted his large black belly with a hand as dark as the clouds that she watched. "May we be seeing some gold or rum in Sa'Mond's future?"

"No, we will see none of that Sa'Mond, my old friend." She turned and reached up on her toes until she could place her gloved hands on his cheeks. She was always gloved. "This mission will bring death and destruction to the life that we know."

"Ah, me be seeing the truth. We be doing the same job as that we always be doin', then." Pausing, he turned to look at his mistress with a look of amusement. "We be about to kill a man?" Smiling, he bowed deeply before his friend, grasping the haft of his cutlass.

"No, my gentle and loyal friend, we are about to topple an empire and betray everyone who trusts us." Closing her eyes, she kissed the forehead of her first mate. She kissed him gently, as a mother would kiss her simple-minded child. Leaning in, she whispered into the big man's ear, "Then we get to destroy a man."

Sa'Mond's eyes grew large and alert but his face showed neither pleasure nor thrill. "Which man, Sa'Mond be wanting to know?"

"A dangerous man, Sa'Mond," her voice barely reached his ear, but it held his face with intensity. "A man who has grown too big must be taught to stay small, brother of fate. Artema has promised him to me."

"Then we best be gettin' back to The Cove, then, mistress." The dark eunuch turned and glided across the deck toward the crew. Eusauri accepted the storm.

Chapter Five

Braen felt his warship jerk as if she were desperate to escape the mooring lines keeping her prisoner against the pier. He watched the handlers tie off the chocks and wrap the bits, although he admittedly watched out of a sense of duty that only feigned interest. The raid had yielded scores of foods which was a commodity worth more than gold to The Cove. Although his haul may save the smuggler town from winter starvation the stolen cargo did little to improve his anticipation of walking on dry land.

He was certainly not happy to return home despite that his master had prepared a hero's welcome in the castle. Or, perhaps that was the source of his anxiety. His ship had barely moored when his insides wrenched at the thought of celebration waiting in the keep. Artema Horn had asked him to do the impossible and he succeeded. An ambitious man would eagerly rush toward the wine, women and roasted meat that conspired to defile both mind and body.

But no one had accused Braen of ambition in two years. Perhaps once, in a previous place and life, Braen Braston had held the desires that drove mortal men. That version was a different, younger, man who viewed the world with optimism. Older and much wiser, he now avoided any responsibility that exceeded that of his ship and crew.

Braen served the outlaw, Artema Horn, who governed Pirates Cove. As the name implied, pirates had built the simple town inside a reef laden cove. At the center of the town a strong keep stood long abandoned by its founders and had been reclaimed by several recent pirate kings. Artema was only the most recent of these self-crowned noblemen of common birth.

Dark hearted residents called the town, "The Cove," and it was positioned in the most defensible harbor within the Islands of Deception. The nearly impenetrable waters attracted the worst of the damned and had always been a known den for smugglers, pirates, and mercenaries. Treacherous currents kept it safe from invaders, and only the trusted few members of the war council knew the secrets to navigating the numerous reefs that protected the rear access to the island. Ship captains who were privileged to visit The Cove were forced to pass between two large batteries of sixteen-pound cannon. Those who crossed the entrance of the main inlet did so under the watchful eyes of town militia perched atop rounded stone parapets.

Horn had handpicked Braen for the mission from which he had just returned. Those two months at sea found the captain anxiously thinking of ways to turn down his pending reward if he returned successful. Horn had promised him a spot on his private council upon mission completion. "Braen, you've served The Cove for a year without asking for anything that benefited you." The self-made king had stared the northerner down with dark pools that swam with a deadly current, "What is it that you came here for if it wasn't for glory or gold?"

"There is more to life than gold, Art, and keep your damn glory. I'm a simple sailor, now."

"You're a nobleman. Your family is one of the most powerful in Andalon."

"Despite my breeding I only want to be a humble servant to The Cove. I follow your orders, captain my ship, and just want to keep a low profile."

"Spoken like a piss-poor nobleman," Horn spat on the ground. "You were half-starved when I found you, fledgling as a rogue pirate and begging me to give you a letter of marque despite being a wanted criminal in your kingdom."

"I didn't kill my father, Art."

"I believe you. But I honestly didn't believe you, then. I disbelieved even though I saw something in you. I saw a piece of me, Braen. But surely you have ambitions beyond captaining that leaky piece of driftwood?" Artema had a way of searing your soul with a stare and his gaze often exposed a lie before it could even be uttered. The way that he looked at Braen at that moment had caused the larger man to shudder as if standing in an icy wind, albeit ninety degrees on the pier.

"I'm no longer a nobleman, Art. I told you that I shed that skin when I fled the northern peninsula." Braen wished that Horn had never learned of his birthright.

When he and Sippen had escaped Fjorik, they had ridden *Ice Prince* to the Southern Continent. There, they had waited an entire year in exile while Braen appealed to the Fjorik nobles and proclaimed himself innocent to his brother's false charges. But no answer came. He was forced to seek out Artema Horn and Pirate's Cove, if only to escape the assassination attempts and legitimize himself as a licensed pirate of marque in the guild.

"Old habits die hard, Northerner, but sworn oaths find ways to topple the strongest men to their knees. I trust that you're loyal to The Cove and I accept your story that you fled here to escape that tyrant of a brother." Artema's eyes narrowed. "But you have a duty to serve and help lead the people of this island. You're drawn to that duty by your nature, and you've been trained to lead men since you slithered out from between your mother's slit."

Braen towered over his master by a measure of six inches, a feat given that Horn stood over eighteen hands. When he drew himself to his full height, the broadness of his massive shoulders could not be missed. Sir Braen Braston, as he was called in the northern kingdom of Fjorik, was a giant among giant men. Standing within the piercing eyes of Artema Horn, however, the colossus wavered. "What is it that you'll have me do?"

"That's much better," Artema smiled. "Take *Wench's Daughter* and raid Lady Esterling's eastern cache in Noston. They are holding winter stores that her barges will soon transport to her main palace in Eston. You will have to move in quickly and leave before the bulk of her fleet arrives. My frigate has more firepower than your pathetic *Ice Prince* and will hold more of the food in her hold."

"How many ships do you think I'll face?" Braen had not expected to captain *Wench's Daughter*. Horn's private ship was not the fastest in The Cove, but she truly packed the strongest punch and he would only lend her to him if he expected resistance.

"About three times as many as you will be commanding, and I am giving you ten." Artema loved to joke, and he let out a chuckle as he added, "Be careful. Some say the Kraken himself resides in the waters off Estowen's Landing, and you'll be sailing straight through his territory."

"I will use that to my advantage." Braen laughed as he turned and strode toward the docks. He smiled despite the weight of the duty. Horn was likable, and Braen viewed him more of a brother than his own blood.

"Bring back that bitch's stores and I will make you lieutenant next to Kernigan." There was the catch. There was always a catch with Artema Horn.

Braen turned back from the brow of *Wench's Daughter* and looked down at Horn. "What about Nevra? Doesn't blood course his veins? Or do you have plans for him?" Lord Stefan Nevra was a southern continent nobleman who had served Artema for ten years as his right-hand man. He and the mysterious Samani Kernigan were the most trusted in Horn's council, and the bravest of dissenters gossiped that they were the true rulers of The Cove while Artema focused on the spoils.

"People come. People go. Some stay longer than others." Narrowing his eyes, he had added, "Others overstay their welcome."

The red hair on the pirate king's head shone with a brighter fire when the sun caught it fully, glistening with radiance as he whirled on his heel and marched up to the keep. Braen knew that Horn's image more closely resembled a god than a man when he chose. Good thing for Braen that he did not believe in gods in heaven nor on earth.

The men had finished tying off *Wench's Daughter* and Braen turned command over to Krill. Turning to Sippen, he smiled. The nervous little man outwardly looked like a librarian more than he did a weapon smith and first mate. His glasses were too big for his small face and he stuttered whenever his nerves overtook his confidence. The Captain gently slapped the little man on the back, and asked, "Are you ready to get this party over with?"

"I cuh... cuh... could use a dri... drink." Smiling up at his friend he added, "Or tuh... two."

A simple cart waited for them at the foot of the ship's brow. They strode toward the driver, giving orders to drive to the keep. The ride across loose cobblestones nearly jarred the teeth from Braen's head. The sun warmed his face as he tried to clear his mind of the things that he had seen during the battle against the Esterling queen's fleet. Knowing that the creatures existed did not bother him, but he wished that his men had not seen the Kraken as it appeared to come to his aid.

The entire week's return to The Cove earned him even the most loyal crewman's amazement. Surely, they knew that Braen had no effect on the sea creatures, but the prophetic words he had told Artema Horn were overheard and rumors spread faster than lice in a whorehouse. "I'll use that to my advantage," he had told the pirate king at the time. Obviously, word had reached The Cove and Braen noticed that even the carriage driver could not help glancing back in awe. He would celebrate the night as the man who had driven the man who called forth the Kraken.

The carriage finally rolled to a stop before the massive doors of the keep and Braen and Sippen strode up the stairway then made their way to the grand hall. The cut stone of the walls were remarkably well crafted. Not as well built as Fjorik Castle by a stretch, but Braen never failed to muse that surely the long-lost builders of the city employed guild artisans. As he opened the iron doors his ears welcomed the sounds of feasting and merriment that rushed out. His stomach betrayed his irritation by growling at the smells of roasting meat and spilled mead.

As he crossed into the room a cheer went up from the pirate rabble. Someone in the room shouted, "The man of the hour has finally arrived! Three cheers!" The revelers clapped, laughed, and then turned up their mugs to the large Northman.

Artema Horn sat on a simple wooden chair so that no one would confuse him for a nobleman. Despite his best efforts his regal stature betrayed him, and he prominently stood out at the head of the feast. His people revered him as the king, and he did nothing to dissuade their allegiance. He looked up from the busty blonde sprawled across his lap and locked eyes with Braen. "I hope you don't mind that we already started?"

"By all means, Artema, don't let me hold you up." The blue eyes of the large Norseman settled on the flag opposite the hall. It was a blue square adorned with a black squid. Braen frowned when he realized that the squid was crushing several small ships in its tentacles. The king watched Braen's eyes wander.

"I commissioned your new sigil, Sir Braston!" Artema stood quickly, tossing the blonde to the floor as he rose. "Ladies and gentlemen! I present to you Braen Braston, prince of the northern waters, king of ice and snow, exile to The Cove, and now lord of the KRAKEN!" The hall erupted in laughter as a topless woman dressed as a mermaid presented Braen with a scepter made of driftwood. Another adorned him with a crown made of seaweed. The two women then draped a wool blanket with a painted squid across his shoulders.

Braen caught the smile in Horn's eyes and breathed a deep draw of smoke-filled air before shooting his master a cool look. "Lord Horn, I graciously accept my new title!" Braen bellowed out his acceptance amid the good-natured laughter. "Whatever new duties that it may entail, I swear my protection to my watery realm and will ravage all of the mermaids that I encounter!"

"You DAMN WELL BETTER!" Horn thrust a frothy mug into Braston's huge hands and gestured toward an empty chair at his side. "Now DRINK!"

Braen seated himself and leaned in towards his liege. "Word travels fast, I reckon?" He whispered into the smaller man's ear.

"Aye, it does indeed." Artema agreed.

Smiling, he lightheartedly whispered, "Fuck you. You know I can't control those beasts."

"Fuck you, MY LIEGE, Braen." Artema corrected with an even bigger smile, emphasizing the words with a slight wink.

"Ok. Fuck you, MY LIEGE. You KNOW that I can't control those beasts."

"I do. But do you see the effect that rumor has on the entire cove?" He gestured at the revelers. "They love their new nobleman. The fact that you arbitrarily may or may not have influenced a pod of Kraken during battle is something that even a pirate king is smart enough not to question." Artema spoke the last statement with a finality that stung Braen.

"Art, I told you that I've no interest in leadership. Those days have passed, and several ships have sailed off with any aspirations I may've once had."

"Then you're more suited for the job than you even realize. Anyways, what is done is done and there is no changing my mind. If you don't want it then don't let the reef sink your ass on the way out." Artema turned from his chalice and his eyes met Braen's with that look of leadership that could force the most rebellious of men into kneeling. "We have a meeting of the sanctum in an hour. Don't be late."

Looking more like a regent by birth rather than happenstance, Artema Horn rose from his chair. He paused to tear a turkey leg off the roasted carcass on the table then strode toward the door. As he rose to leave the entire room leapt to their feet and emitted a cheer of praise. In his other hand he grabbed the busty blonde by her arm and turned to escort her from the hall. Pausing first to kiss his companion, then to rip off her corset, he turned his head and hollered back to Braen, "Better make it TWO hours!" The men cheered even louder.

Braen scanned the merriment. Across the table Captain Pogue nursed his drink. The man, usually lighthearted, wore a heavy burden on his face. "You aren't enjoying the feast, Alec?"

The man looked up with eyes red from grief. "Mattie and the girls left, Braston."

"What? When? I thought she was happy in The Cove."

"Apparently not. I came home from a late watch and they'd left. She packed all their belongings and slipped out while I was on duty." Tears misted his eyes, "She always hated it here. She felt isolated on the island and always talked about returning to Eston."

"I'm sorry, Alec."

Lord Nevra had been listening intently to the conversation and interrupted, "That kind of thing happens all the time in The Cove. Wives leave their husbands because they can't handle the pirate life."

Braen had never heard Stefan Nevra speak. The chief advisor to Artema Horn avoided conversation with anyone not in the inner circle, and his interest unnerved him. He looked the small, aged man over and the effort made his stomach queasy. Pox had pitted the man's face at an early age and the scars forced the Northman's eyes to look elsewhere. His head was mangy and patched without any pattern to the hair loss. Worst of all, was the way that his voice made the listener's skin crawl as if infested with insects. Braen swallowed hard and addressed him. "Yeah. I've seen it, before. I just never thought that Mattie would leave Alec."

Pogue downed his mug and tried to refill it, finding the pitcher dry. "Braen, you've never been married, have you?"

"No. I came close, once, but fate steered me south." The bearded man's thoughts flashed to Hester, and how she had once promised to share the world with him. She now lay with his brother Skander, the northern king.

Braen liked Pogue but let out a sigh of relief when the surly man rose to move to another table, carrying his nearly empty mug to find more ale.

"Thank the gods that depressing man left." Samani Kernigan had spoken, also a member of Artema's Inner Sanctum.

He started to defend his friend, but movement in the hall caught Braen's eye. Peering into the shadows he caught a glimpse of a small woman adorned with a black fur cloak with a hood raised on her head. Closer inspection revealed that the hood was the head of a wolf. "Sam," he said over the merriment. "SAM," he nearly shouted. Lord Samani Kernigan glanced up from anther busty mermaid astride his lap.

"What?" He asked with half interest.

"Who is that woman?" Braen gestured toward the shadows but the fur cloaked woman had disappeared.

"I see many women, Norseman. Just grab whichever one catches your eye." He answered with disinterest. The brunette was doing a fabulous job of keeping his eyes on her. With a dismissive gesture around the room he added, "According to Artema you're the man of the hour, and I doubt that he'd mind if you claimed any that aren't lying with him at the moment."

"That is not what I mean," Braen persisted. The woman intrigued him even though he had spent the past several years avoiding women. True, he had quenched his physical thirsts from time to time, but he steered clear of the treacherous reefs of long-term involvement. The large, quiet man had loved only one woman. Hester had been his friend since youth, and it was never a secret that the pair had been betrothed as soon as they could walk. No matter how many women he had taken to bed, Braen had loved only his lady of the north.

Thinking of Hester made him think of Skander and he boiled with rage. He was about to push Lord Kernigan about the cloaked woman when Lord Nevra spoke again. "You mean the maiden dressed in black? She who danced through the shadows with grace and intrigue? Was she the one, Lord Braen?"

He jumped when the small man spoke, having nearly forgotten that he was there. "Yes. You saw her, too?"

"Stefan. Please call me Stefan."

"Do you know her, Stefan?" Braen's eyes still scanned the room but she had long disappeared into either the shadows or the crowd.

"Her name is death, Lord Kraken. You'd do well to remember." The rat faced man laughed until he began to choke on his wine. Braen looked away with disgust and again checked the crowd for the mysterious woman.

"Oh, you meant the Lady Eusari," Lord Kernigan said with disinterest. "I know of none other who bears the name of death as well as she." Although he spoke, he did so without diverting his gaze from his mermaid. "She's part of our Inner Sanctum."

"I've never met her. I've never even seen her, before now." Braen scanned the room as he spoke.

Nevra commented, "She handles the 'darker' business of the guild. Like Samani and myself, she reports directly to Artema, but even we don't know about all of her secret missions." Stefan seemed put out at that fact.

Kernigan finally looked away from his whore to flash a sly smile toward Nevra. Then, he turned seriously toward Braen and warned, "She truly is named death, Braston. If she was here, and you actually saw her, then you missed seeing her eunuch. Sa'Mond never trails far from his mistress. The story is that she gelded him with her teeth."

"No, Samani," Stefan interrupted, "her gelding was already cut as I heard it. He fed his previous captain's stones to her during a mutiny."

"Either way, Norseman, she'll cut the balls from a man and devour them while he watches in fright." Lord Kernigan finally looked away from his mermaid and added with a stern narrowing of his eyes, "Steer a wide berth unless you relish losing your entire rudder as well."

Braen finished his meal in silence. After a time, he stood from the table and strode toward the door through which Artema Horn had exited. No guards barred the way, but he knew that two were posted within. He pulled on the heavy oaken handle and slipped inside the narrow passageway. Blinking in the torchlight, he focused on two brutes lurking in the shadows.

"Tired of being king for the day, Braston?" The larger, more muscular of the two men spoke with a western accent.

"Greetings, Amash. Yes, Artema needs the attention returned to him. Do you reckon he's finished with his blonde?" Braen liked this man. Of all the pirates in The Cove, very few sought out books for study with as much zeal as the large man from Weston.

"With as much beer as he's consumed, most certainly."

The smaller brute quipped. "I hope he's left her with an appetite. I wouldn't mind a go at her, myself." This man was one who Braen disliked. He watched as the guard licked his lips lecherously, most likely thinking of her ample bosom.

Amash slapped the man in the small of his back, "She likes sausage, Turat, not that pathetic green string bean that you are always pulling on."

"You two are missing out on the party," Braen observed, "I hope that your watch ends soon and without incident."

"Well met, Northman," Amash offered.

"Well met." Turat grumbled while glaring at his larger companion."

Braen followed the winding corridor past several turns. Although the torches lit the way, he knew that murder holes lay in the darker shadows, with men silently watching his passage. Braen felt an unnerving claustrophobia as the hidden eyes followed his movements. He was a great fighter in single combat, but assassins poised a different kind of threat. He forced down the panic and kept his pace slow and confident. Finally, after only several minutes that felt an eternity, the sea captain emerged into another antechamber of light. Another pair of guards cleared the path, opening the door to allow him into the private quarters of the pirate king.

Artema sat at a table that could easily accommodate six persons. He was not alone. To his left sat the small woman dressed entirely in the black leather armor of a night thief. On her back was a furred cloak that terminated into a hood made from a wolf's head, and her hands were clothed in thin black gloves. Directly behind her, about two paces back from the table, stood an extremely large man with skin as black and tough as leather dried and aged in the sun.

The woman and the king sat with their heads hunched closely together in private congress, obviously disputing a matter with passionately quiet words. The small woman was outwardly agitated and flashed a look up toward Braen. Her eyes conveyed both anger and disgust. Artema regarded the northern captain with a bemused smile, nodded, then whispered a few words that succeeded in clamping the woman's mouth shut. She sat steaming with anger with her arms crossed against her chest, most likely with dagger hilts close to her gloved fingers.

"Braen!" Artema gestured toward the other two people in the room with beckoning arms. "Meet Eusari, lady captain of *She Wolf*," He inclined his head and gestured with his eyebrows to the eunuch. "And this huge hunk of meat is her bondsman, Sa'Mond. Please join us!"

Braen nodded to the lady and her man, "It's my pleasure to meet you both, My Lady. Sir Sa'Mond." He drew a chair from the table and sat across from the small woman. She did not answer his greeting, and instead shot him an icy glare that caused him to shiver slightly. He glanced up at Sa'Mond, who still had one hand on the hilt of his curved blade.

Artema quickly got down to business. "Eusari has a special cargo in the hold of *She Wolf*. Your raid on the Esterling stores was a distraction to draw their fleet away from the real operation, the kidnapping of a high-profile Imperial agent."

"I was a distraction, Artema? That would've been nice to know at the time." Braen felt the anger rising inside. He had fully trusted Horn's earlier motives for the raid, which had nearly cost him valuable men and ships. Only his respect and admiration for the man held his temper in check.

"Yes. I couldn't let you know at the time, since your capture and questioning were a possibility." Something else hinted with Horn's words.

"What if we had failed? Would our deaths and the loss of the ships have been worth the extraction of this agent? Who is that important that they are worth losing ten ships, including your own flagship? Much less the loss of the highly skilled and irreplaceable crews?" Braen had stood up from the table, unable to further hide his anger as it grew.

A soft voiced purred out of the mouth of the woman in black, "Marcus Esterling. Youngest son of Lady Crestal Esterling. The second heir to the Esterling fortune and potential ruler of the Empire." Eusari never looked at Braen as she spoke, looking down at the table. The words seemed to growl as they left her mouth, heightening her feral persona.

Slowly, her eyes rose to meet his. *Gods! Was she smiling?* Beneath her beauty was a dangerous, if not rabid woman waiting to attack her prey. Braen could not help but wonder if madness loomed behind those eyes. "You. You kidnapped the second heir of Andalon?" Braen felt a surge of panic rise at the implications of their bold move. Lady Esterling would surely be launching the largest fleet ever amassed. "Gods, Artema! That boy is a whelp of only, what? Fifteen?"

"Sit down, Braen." Artema Horn rarely lost his smile when he spoke, but he cast the Northman an icy glare when he again spoke. "She thinks that someone else has her son. One of her vassals has been plotting against her and has donated much to our cause. The disappearance of Marcus Esterling won't be traced to us in any way. Also, I assure you that he has been treated well."

Braen quickly sat down. He respected Artema and admired him, greatly. In truth, he owed his life to him. After he had fled Fjorik, Horn had been his only option to which he could run.

Artema kept his eyes trained on Braen, voice flat and calm, "You and Eusari are to work together on a top-secret mission. I want you to sail with her in three days, when she takes the Esterling pup for the exchange. Tell no one of your destination. This is clandestine shit that I normally give only to Eusari."

"Then why am I going?"

"Because I need you to do that 'Kraken Trick' that you did, last time, off Estowen's Landing." Artema laughed as if he had been saving the joke up all evening.

Braen hated thinking about those monsters being real. Even worse was the thought that he had felt something from them when they swam under his ship. It was almost as if he could sense them. Not their presence, but their sentience, as well.

"But seriously, tonight, you are elevated into my 'Inner Sanctum' and become one of my most trusted advisors. If you are to know my secrets, then you will need to trust those whom I have believed in for years. Foremost of them being Eusari. She has been like a daughter to me and handles my 'darkest' business. I want you to see how she operates firsthand. Tell NOONE, not even that weird little Sippen, where you're going."

"And where is that, precisely, Artema?" Braen was still stewing with anger on the inside, but the prospect of a secret mission was indeed alluring.

Artema smiled as Braen took the bait. "Back to your favorite place!" He winked and added, "Estowen's Landing." Eyes serious he added, "Again, tell no one."

"I promise. And... I'm sorry that I got angry, Artema." Braen looked again toward Eusari as he apologized, nodding again to her. As he did, a second glance revealed that beneath her anger, something was deeply troubling the woman. He looked back at his mentor, "Regarding this promotion. I'm not worthy of being your advisor. I've told you many times that I..."

His words were cut off by the pirate king, who once again had return to more customary jovial demeanor. "Enough of that whale piss of an excuse. You're a nobleman and were trained since birth to rule over a kingdom. You lead like other men drink ale. Leadership is in your birth and your station, Braston."

Eusari's face softened at Artema's words and looked up at Braen with a surprisingly adoring look. "So, you're the oldest son of Lord Braston?"

"Not anymore." Braen averted his eyes from hers. At that moment, the door opened and Stefan Nevra and Samani Kernigan joined them at their table. The hulking Sa'mond turned quietly and left without an order from anyone. The eunuch knew his place. Braen lifted his gaze back to his mentor.

"Let's get down to business," a very serious and now dangerous Artema Horn proclaimed.

"Let's not," Samani Kernigan protested, "there are tavern wenches dressed like mermaids in the banquet hall, and better food." Something about Kernigan chaffed Braen's sense of duty and propriety, but Artema smiled and winked. Of course, his mermaid was waiting for him in his chambers, just down the hallway.

Eusari was obviously irritated at their lack of respect for women and shifted in her seat. Stefan Nevra starkly contrasted the other two men with his pox-scarred rat face. He stoically narrowed his eyes at them and opened a fat ledger. His fingers glided across pages until he stopped at a line, moving his fingertip under each work like a child learning to read. "Our business is more important than your cock or what you put into your mouth, Kernigan. We must discuss the defensive fortifications of The Cove. Especially after our newly crowned 'Lord Kraken' has pissed off the entire Imperial Fleet."

"Isn't cock the ONLY thing that you put into your mouth,

Stefan?" Kernigan quipped from behind his mug of ale. He downed it, refilled it and quickly winked at Braen as if he had just won a debate. Nevra scowled while Artema and Samani chuckled.

Braen watched as Horn and Kernigan shared the joke, still smiling like teenage boys in a brothel. In the years that he had spent running missions out of The Cove, he had never had much dealing with any of the counsel of Artema's 'inner sanctum.' He silently wished that he had taken more interest in their politics over the years, instead of acting as a private mercenary for Horn.

The rat-faced man ignored the joke and continued. "We need to move some of the batteries off the walls and place them closer to the entrance of the harbor. That would require placing more men on the walls to increase our ability to repel an amphibious assault."

"Since when are you a general, Nevra?" Samani asked, "You seem to have gone beyond counting sacks of flour." Shrugging, he added, "I guess that I can go back to my mermaids." Kernigan poured another mug of ale as he looked at Nevra. There was obviously some division to the counsel that he could not pinpoint. Kernigan finally looked away from Horn and added, "Artema, we'll need to dispatch our flagships to rejoin their battlegroups, so as not to get trapped in the harbor. I recommend that we do so quickly. We should keep them close by, but out of the eye of the Imperial scouts."

"Agreed." Artema drank from his mug and then continued, "In case Esterling does see through my ruse, we'll need to scatter to the seas. *Wench's Daughter* included. *Ice Prince* will remain behind, since Braen and Eusari will be on *She Wolf*. The others will be given a rotation to return after four weeks at sea. That should allow us plenty of time. Nevra, you and Kernigan will run things in The Cove while I'm away on *Wench's Daughter*. It's been a while since I've raided. After having some fun, I may head down to the Southern Continent for a break."

Braen rose from the table after all the business concluded. He

watched Artema leave the room toward his private chamber. Lord
Nevra brushed passed Braen like a slimy eel, twisting his head to
whisper as he passed, "We need to speak in private, soon. There's
much that we have to discuss." Braen shuddered slightly at the
strange encounter, as brief as it had been. He could not fathom
how such an odd man had wormed his way into Artema's private
counsel. He stared after him as he left, much as sailors watch
sharks that swim off the stern.

Braen watched as Lord Nevra also pushed past Eusari, knocking
her slightly off path. A look of disgust flashed briefly across her
face as she watched the eel swim into the passage before her.
"Goodnight, Eusari," Braen offered. She returned his greeting with
a flat stare, nodded, and then she turned to follow Nevra into the
silent dark. She intrigued him. Although attractive, Braen knew
that his interest was not sexual. He was intrigued by her mystique
and composure, and the prospect of learning her story bolstered
the excitement of their mission.

After Eusari exited Braen realized that he was left with
Kernigan. The man appeared to want to talk with him further
and alone.

"He's a true lord, you know," Kernigan indicating that he was
speaking of Nevra with a brief nod toward the door.

"I'd heard." Braen looked from the door at Kernigan, then
turned to follow and try to catch up with Eusari.

Kernigan must have had business to discuss on some private
agenda, and spoke flatly as if Braen had no pressing matters, "Do
you trust him, Lord Braston?"

Braen paused with irritation. "Not a lord, and barely a Braston.
Why wouldn't I trust Nevra? Artema seems to trust him fully."
Again, he tried to make for the door, but the persistent man's next
words froze him in the doorway.

"I wasn't speaking about Nevra, I was speaking about Artema."
Kernigan held out a hand toward the chair nearest Braen.
"Nobody trusts Nevra. Well, nobody except you, apparently." His

face scrunched as if eating a sour pickle and then took on a more serious, thoughtful look. Artema keeps him around for his logistics expertise. He's no tactician, a piss-poor sailing master and a slimy weasel with a knife in someone's back at all times. However, he keeps our mercenaries and taxes paid and ensures that the Empire is always looking the other direction. No, Lord Kraken, I want to know if you trust Artema."

"Of course, I do. He allowed me into The Cove when I had nothing." His blue eyes burned with distrust at the politician gesturing to the chair. "He's trusted me, mentored me and today raised me to his private counsel. Yes, he has my unwavering loyalty." Braen refused the chair that Kernigan offered. He narrowed his eyes further and looked closely at the shorter, seated man. He was more muscled than most men of luxury and held a posture of confidence that was often masked by his aloof personality. Braen realized that he had never really looked at Samani Kernigan, before, and realized that this man was more dangerous than he had thought.

"Where is he sending you and Eusari?"

"I can't tell you, that."

"Of course, you can't. He has your 'unwavering loyalty,' doesn't he?" Rising, Samani offered his hand to Braen. The larger man ignored it, causing him to smile and walk out of the room. Pausing as he opened the door to leave, he spoke without turning his head. "Be careful, Northman. Squid is a delicacy, and pirates are no different than nobles when it comes to politics."

Braen waited a few minutes, then followed hoping that Kernigan had exited the hallway. Passing Turat and Amash, he shook hands with his large friend. "Come by the apartment, tomorrow night, for cards. We need to catch up."

"That we do. I heard rumors about the voyage."

Turat's ears perked up at the mention of cards. "I just came into some coin. May I join the game?"

Braen flashed a smile, "Only if you want to risk losing it to Sippen."

Amash nodded. "You'd better have a plan to get the little fella drunk, this time. Did you pick up any of Esterling's private stock during your raid?"

Braen feigned a hurt look, "Do you not know me at all, Amash?" Smiling, he added, "Of course, I did. I stole ten cases and held back six for myself and Sippen. Why should the Esterling family be the only people in Andalon to enjoy a fine vintage?"

"Which year did you take?"

"Why, only the 754, my friend."

Turat, who was listening, turned with eyes round with shock. "754 is their prized year! One bottle is worth a fortune!"

Braen beamed a smile, "It WAS their prized year. I took ALL ten cases and smashed the rest of their collection."

Amash laughed hysterically while Turat stared dumbfounded. "You smashed their ENTIRE collection?"

"Well, not entirely. I left years 772, 773 and 781. I didn't want to be a COMPLETE asshole."

Amash looked thoughtful, "Wait a minute, weren't those all extremely hot summers?"

"Your memory astounds me. Yes, in those years the grapes were drying on the vines and ripened unevenly. Right about now, Lady Esterling is drinking what amounts to piss and vinegar."

Both large men laughed while Turat stood with mouth agape. "You really ARE an asshole, Braston."

Braen smiled and nodded agreement as he opened the door. He quickly dropped his smile when he realized that his party was still going strong. Pausing only to help a drunken Sippen up from the floor, he left the merriment behind and guided his little friend back home.

CHAPTER SIX

Taros sat tall astride Falia and stared intently at his small band. A hot breeze warmed his cheeks reminding that they neared the Forbidden Waste. The eruption of an angry goddess had reduced his people to a pathetic pilgrimage of tattered desolation, and less than fifty villagers remained. Before him stretched a small assembly, a wretched lot that had traveled for several days. He was beginning to grow accustomed to their looks of despair.

The difficult trek across the steppes provided little in the way of forage. His people had salvaged anything useful from the village and packed their meager supplies onto sleds of animal skins stretched over three lashed poles. These dragged behind horses and dogs, but desperation demanded that some follow behind men. Taros' people carried both their past and their future on the sleds, but they carried their present on their faces.

Taros thought about the day of the fire. His power had rivaled Felicima's, but he sensed that was his problem. *Am I her equal? Or had she "blessed" me with her power?* By now, killing Cornin was only a distant memory in his mind, but the tremendous power troubled him as he ruminated. *I held the flames in my body. Absorbed it, somehow.* He thought about how the inferno had boiled up to match his rage. *I was angry. Anger belongs to Felicima. Am I like her?* Every Pescari knew that fire belonged to the goddess, and to hold wrath is to challenge their matriarch.

Others doubted that Felicima's had blessed him. He had heard the elders' whispers behind his back, especially those of Daska, the most powerful. He openly speculated that their shappan had erupted with the power of the goddess, a power that he had stolen with his hatred for Cornin. Indeed, he had harbored years of animosity toward the chieftain, and that horrible emotion must have fueled the flames. But hatred was the way of the goddess and not the way of men, so the elders feared their young chieftain. Ultimately, they had agreed to watch and wait.

Pescari legend warned against a fabled ability to control the power of Felicima. The elders taught that those who wielded the power in these legends were not heroes to the Pescari, but rather abominations to be feared. As a rule, Pescari children learned early in life to put aside their hot emotions and taught instead to embrace the cooling of humility. That was the reason for the tradition of the fireside. Only by keeping from her gaze could they avoid her fiery eruptions.

Taros did not know what to believe. Though it was true that he was angry when his blood had boiled, part of him believed that the fire came purely from within and not from Felicima's wrath. He had felt in complete control of the fire, as if it had danced to the rhythm of his heartbeat. Indeed, while walking through the fire he had been focused on keeping it away from his mother. At first the heat had been searing. After a few moments, he felt as if followed his will and avoided them both. *The flame obeyed me as it's master. It lived and I controlled it.* The last thought brought a smile to his face.

Most strange was the sensation as the fire grew within his blood. Although the flames had licked at his skin, the searing merely warmed him while his insides felt as if his soul was boiling. A torrent stormed as his anger had raged, and his mind was consumed by the anger. He had seen Cornin burning in his mind before the flames had even exited his body. *But how? How had my body produced the flames?* Regardless, he was happy that the man had burned.

"We should stop for the night, nephew." Teot's voice shook Taros from his thoughts. "Your people tire, and Felcima will sleep soon." He pointed to their god as she dipped toward the horizon. "See? We have wandered far, and she is soon to slumber before us."

"You speak true, Teot. I will tend to mother." Taros nodded and Teot rode off to check in with his scouts.

The elders had gathered nearby. When he approached, he spun from the saddle and dismounted in one graceful motion. After his feet had landed on the sand, Falia nudged him with her long nose and whinnied. "Easy, my friend. I will find you water, but first I must tend to mother." Falia protested by showing teeth, spitting and snorting her disdain. Soon, she busied herself with some blades of tall grass. The shappan ignored the men looking on.

Kneeling beside the litter he examined her, motionless on the ground. He felt the heat in his body rise momentarily as he felt a surge of panic, but then she coughed and wheezed before finally catching breath in a smooth rhythm. He placed a waterskin to his mother's lips. She was so weak that she could barely lick at the moisture. Once, he would pray to his goddess to heal her, but he could not bring himself to do so on this evening.

Rising from his mother he turned back toward Falia. She had turned up some roots and was grazing lazily. He unhooked the litter and laid it on the ground. Then, he hobbled the mare's left leg. She bit at him and neighed in disgust. "Easy, girl." Falia would never hurt him. Their friendship was too strong, but she always showed teeth when he took away her freedom. "I know, girl. But we're near the waste. If you wander, you'll not easily return to me, and that would make me sad."

Taros heard someone clear a throat behind him where the elders milled around nervously, awaiting his attention. He smiled to himself as he finished wrapping the restraint. *Let them wait*, he thought. *They have been the center of the tribe's strength for too long, but no longer.* He was the strength, now, and they needed to know that a dying woman and a horse took precedence over their audience.

"Taros," a voice stammered and cracked out his name, "we need to discuss some matters of importance to the tribe." Taros slowly turned and recognized Daska. The man was the oldest and known for his legendary bravery as a youth. He had apparently retained that trait, as he demonstrated by stepping forward from the others who huddled in a group looking aghast. Despite their protests, he continued. "Even the moon knows a destination when it travels, Taros. Why are we wandering like the bison with no clear certainty that the next valley is greener?"

"Daska, all valleys are turning brown by Felicima's wrath," Taros responded, turning and respecting his boldness. "Her fire spreads and pushes us to Andalon. He glanced at the horizon and watched as the last of the goddess dipped into the western inferno. Disgust rose up in his belly, as he realized that Daska had only displayed bravery after she had shown her people her back. "The people of Andalon have food and we do not. They will share with us."

Daska stole a look at the others who were notably silent. Their eyes gestured for him to continue. Shaking his head, he turned back to Taros. "You are young, but you know the story of our people. I taught you, myself. You know about our treaty with the Andalonians."

Taros nodded. "Yes. But you are old, Daska. Your time is over, and I lead with the authority of Shapalote."

Daska bowed his head in respect. "You speak true. Cornin lost favor with Felicima and you lead us. You have our support."

"Fear. I have your fear. Not one of you want to follow me. I am a youth, and you think that I lack wisdom." Taros took a step toward the elders. All but Daska stepped backward in response. "See? You all cower like old men."

"Not a lack of wisdom, my shapan, merely experience." Daska had used the word "shapan" to stress his support for Taros, and the boy recognized the strength of the word.

"You call me father?"

"Yes. You are shapan to our tribe. You will protect our wisdom as duty to all of your people."

Taros let the power of the old man's words sink in. "You are trying to caution me to listen to your counsel. You think that, despite my intentions, I will lead you to death or starvation, instead."

"Yes. We are not like the bison. We lack the fat and fur to protect us if the next valley is as brown and burned as the last."

Taros placed his hand gently on the shoulder of Daska, who somehow managed to only flinch a little at his touch. The boy narrowed his brow and looked through the cloudy grey eyes of the sage. "That is the problem. We see ourselves as bison, a mere herd upon the plains. We must learn to become wolves. We should take down the bison of the world with our numbers."

A tear formed in the old man's eye as he realized Taros' intention. "We are smaller in numbers than we were, Shapan. Even if Felicima allowed us to attack them, we are few."

A smile formed on the face of Taros. "She does not decide for us in this matter. I do. I will that we seek shelter in Weston city. If they do not offer it freely, then we will take it. We are few, but the Pescari are many and we will gather-in the scattered." Taros removed his hand from the elder's shoulder and turned his back to finish tending to Falia.

A shout brought him to his feet, and he look up to see Teot riding fast and hard toward him. His uncle wore a look of concern on his face and his mount screeched to a halt in front of his nephew.

"What is it, uncle?" Taros felt alarm rising in his gut.

"A war party is approaching!"

Taros jumped into action, quickly removing the hobble from the leg of Falia while Teot rounded up the warriors. In a moment, nineteen men were mounted next to him, riding to meet the attackers.

The raiders were from a tribe as desperate as his, having fled and left their belongings behind. Mostly opportunists, they were more dangerous than a hungry wolf. Squinting to see farther, Taros scanned and saw dust kicking up from the plain. Approximately fifty riders were pursuing two of Teot's scouts, each pushing their horses to near-death sped. The attackers were close and were closing.

Felicima had not yet set beneath the horizon, and an orange glow lit the plain. Turning to his uncle, Taros ordered, "Nock arrows, but do not release unless I cannot hold them back." Teot looked concerned but relayed the order with quick hand motions. Meanwhile, the scouts were gaining ground and nearly joined with Taros' meager group. The pursuers pulled back on the reigns and nocked arrows of their own. One of the raiders, a large man on a blazing black steed raised his hand and the boy chieftain marked him as the leader.

When the opposing shapan dropped his arm, arrows darkened the sky and begin falling as a cloud toward the small group of men. Each of the warriors felt afraid, but the man-child stood tall in the saddle before them. Anger filled Taros as the arrows flew, and he thought about Lynette laying in her litter where he had left her, rambling on about some distant memory with his father. With one motion of his hand, the arrows burst into flame. Simultaneously, every campfire in the campsite blinked dark without even a wisp of smoke as Taros took the heat from the burning logs and dung.

The raiders nocked again and fired, but these arrows met the same fate. Frustrated, the other shapan ordered a charge, and the men began to close the gap of fifty yards at a sprint. Taros rode out a few more steps, then focused his energy. All of the enemy's wooden weapons burst into flame. Each man screamed and cast their arms to the ground. The horses bucked in fear at the flames on their backs, flinging men through the air and onto the ground.

Slowly, Taros rode toward the other chieftain. The man lay on his back and looked up with dark eyes full of fear. "I am Taros, shapan through the right of shapalote. Tomorrow I lead my family across the forbidden waste to demand succor from the people of Andalon. I order you to bring your people to join with us, or to curse them to stand alone and face the wrath of Felicima. But if you try and molest my people then you shall face my wrath."

He motioned for the man to rise. Terror filled the warriors and they huddled in front of the boy. Their former chieftain knelt before their new Shapan and the others followed suit. Taros dismounted and walked toward the man with his hand outstretched, placed five fingertips on the man's face and branding him with his inner flame. He then walked among the warriors, and did the same to each, making them his own. After he had finished and remounted, he led his men back to camp after dispatching the branded to recruit. "Bring every Pescari to me, so that I may lead them to Weston."

The next morning, Taros and his uncle looked out with shock at the new faces that had joined them in the night. Fifteen tribes had joined in all, swelling their numbers to more than two thousand, of which more than nine hundred were mounted warriors. Teot had agreed to take a team of scouts back toward the steppes to gather and spread the word to others about the Shapan's power, and to bring them across the desert. They were free from Felicima's wrath and would create a new life on the Andalonian side of the waste.

The Pescari slowly began their trek each daybreak amid a parade of misery and hard-faced determination. The slowly moved away from the rising eye of their goddess, and, when she settled her gaze ahead of them, they were forced to make camp and wait for her to again sleep. Thus, they rested every night until she awakened behind them, allowing them once again travel across the hot and barren desert that lay between their steppes and the Imperial city.

Taros rode, flanked by his branded followers, reflecting on the surrealism of his position. Outwardly, the youth displayed strength and stalwart confidence. Inside he boiled and steamed with such ferocity that even the goddess of the caldera should tremble at his wrath. He felt as if he were in a dream, wandering through the waste with his people. Occasionally he would return with brief clarity and speak with an odd confidence when his people asked him for guidance. They were his people. *By the fire of Felicima, they had become my people!* He felt driven to protect them with as much determination as he had when he pulled his mother from the burning village.

Thinking of Lynette, he glanced behind Falia at the sled that she dragged. His mother rested on the skid, looking up with a serene smile as she watched the goddess' eye. Taros worried about his mother. She was not physically harmed in the fire, but she had not yet recovered enough of her wits to walk on her own. The elders feared that, although she had been shielded from the flames by her son's grace, her mind may have been boiled by the heat. She stared up at the goddess with an odd smile that troubled the boy.

Taros hated that his mother looked so reverently upon her goddess. To him, Felicima was a jealous woman. She cast judgment on those who walked openly with strength. She was no better than Cornin had been, using her strength to oppress the weak who cowered beneath her. Tradition demanded that the Pescari people hide their strength from Felicima in humility and reverence, but Taros had begun to think differently.

Daska rode along with the elders, away from Felicima's eye. Occasionally he raised his hand to his shoulder and felt where the boy had touched him, feeling the hot and flushed skin. His deepest fear had been confirmed, that the blaspheming child intended to challenge the wrath of their goddess as well as that of Andolan. The old man felt tired and weaker than he had since the eruption had begun. Taros would have to be stopped and order must be restored.

After the procession had camped for the night, he dismounted and walked slowly to his sled, old bones aching as the temperature continued to drop with the onset of night. Stooping over his belongings, he flipped over furs until he found a wooden chest. The vessel was very old. Older, Daska believed, than his own people.

His bent fingers tripped the latch and drew out a hide, rolled and tied with a leather strap. With the dying light of Felicima, his weak eyes focused on the drawings. Each depiction was of a boy standing in fire, the eye of the goddess burning overhead. The angry deity grinded her teeth in dismay as the boy stole her power and destroyed her people.

Daska focused on one drawing which showed the boy standing elevated above the walls of an Andalon city. Fire welled around and swirled in cyclones, anger pouring out of his eyes in the form of flames. Before him lay an army, burned and black with steel weapons laying useless in the ash. Off in the distance, a much larger army marched with drums and banners bearing a sea creature rising from the water. Wolves and birds alike fled before the army as it marched. With trembling hands, the feeble fingers of the old man rerolled the skin and returned it to the box. Tears rolled down the old man's face as he realized that he was fighting against a god.

Chapter Seven

Robert Esterling stepped into the fighting pit. His shield was heavy in his left hand and the leather armor restricted his movement. He could barely breathe against the straps around his sides, and felt claustrophobic from the pressure on his chest. The sound of the sand crunching beneath his boots pounded in his ears under the padded leather helmet as he tentatively walked toward the hulking man facing him.

"Lift the shield and keep your sword elbow up." boomed General Reeves on the sideline. Robert complied, but the sword felt so heavy that the tip dragged atop the shield. "Not so low on the tip, Princeling! That's it. Small steps. More of a shuffle. Now halt!" The men on Robert's left and right halted alongside of him, feet stomping and setting in the sand. His own left leg braced against the shield. "Now, SHIELD … WALL." The two words gave both a preparatory and a command and all three shields set into the sand with a clap as Robert and his companions squatted into a ready position against them. Two more shields slammed overhead, and Robert could barely see the opposing man. He ran directly toward him, shield up as if he held a battering ram.

The impact of the collision shook Robert and he fell hard against the man behind him. He lost the hold on his shield, and he collapsed on the ground, causing the men on his sides to fall atop him with the full weight of the opposing soldier. He felt his sword tip fall into the sand, sparks of pain flashing through his right hand as his wrist bent in an awkward manner.

"STOP!" The general's voice bellowed. "Dammit Robert! You

must brace against the shield on the left, NOT the right! Strength
to the left! Reset and begin, again!" The older man ran into the pit
as he shouted, lifting the armored men off the boy as if they were
sacks of flour. Reaching his hand toward the prince, he grasped his
jerkin and pulled him up with one arm, bringing him to his feet.

"I... I'm sorry. I always confuse that."

"Then pay closer attention! You can't allow a single man to
break the wall. What would happen if an entire line of men had hit
you, instead? That was one man!" Robert again lined up, and the
men shuffled in the sand as before. "Shield ... Wall!" This time, he
braced to the left, wedging his shield properly against that of the
man on his right. When the man behind him set his, he felt more
stability in the line. With a roar, the opposing man again threw
himself into Robert's shield, which thankfully held. "Much better,
Robert! Thank you, men!" The general beamed. "The princeling
has learned enough for one day. You may return the practice gear
to the armory and head to dinner."

Robert fumbled against the straps of his jacket and tossed it
atop his shield laying in the sand. He turned and looked toward
the general, flinching under his gaze. "I'm sorry, Maximus. I am
trying my best."

With a grunt, the older man walked over and slapped him on
the back. "It could've been worse."

"How do you suppose?"

"You could have had a breathing attack, again."

"Yeah. That is true." His private lessons with the general were
mostly due to his breathing disease. He trained with a special
cadre of his private guard, handpicked for their loyalty and, most
importantly, their discretion. "I know what to do."

"I know. But it isn't about knowledge, my lord. You know
everything about warfare. Your problem is strength and execution.
You lack both." Maximus Reeves was like a father to Robert, and
their relationship centered on honesty.

Robert shook out his black hair with his hands, airing the sand back into the pit. After he was certain that most of it was gone, he turned his dark eyes back to the general. "I'll never be strong like the others, will I, Max?"

"Perhaps not, but strength also lies in wisdom."

"If you ask my family then you'll know that I am lacking in that area, as well." Robert looked down as he said this, kicking at the shield with his foot. "They judge me because I struggle to learn."

The older man sighed and put his arm on his shoulder. "Yes. You read slowly and remember little."

"The words get all mixed up on the page, and the letters play tricks on my eyes."

"That doesn't mean that you lack wisdom."

"That's why she hasn't agreed to relinquish the regency, isn't it? She thinks that I am a simpleton."

"Robert, you're seventeen years alive. The law of succession clearly states that you'll have a regent until you are eighteen if you pass the trials. Twenty-one if you cannot."

"No. If I can't pass the trials, then a witan may or may not choose me at twenty-one. It's not guaranteed. They may even choose HER over me. Worse. They could choose my brother." Tears welled in his eyes as he thought about his family. It had been two years since his mother had sent him to the frontier. She had wanted to 'toughen him up enough to be worthy of his father's crown.'

The general squeezed his shoulder in a fatherly way and then slapped his back with pride, "See? Wise. Who needs to read when you have a full grasp of the law of succession?"

"I would rather have strength of body and mind." Robert could not help but smile up at his friend when he spoke. But the smile faded quickly as some dark thought formed.

"What is it, son?"

"She isn't going to abdicate to me, is she? She is going to keep it for herself. I know it."

Maximus Reaves lost his own smile as he met the boy's eyes.

"No. She probably won't, not if you can't pass the trials and prove your worth to her."

Robert contemplated his friend's words as he rolled up his sword in the jerkin. "Would you fight alongside a weak simpleton, General Reeves? Would you support my claim to the title if it came to civil war?"

"My lord. You're like a son to me, but I look up to you as my liege. You have my loyalty now and will have it forever."

"Then I'll see you back in this same pit in the morning. I have to practice my footing if I am to pass the trials. And, I WILL have to pass them if I want to keep you from dying for a weak half-wit." He picked up his shield, sword, and jerkin and walked to the armory with a smile flickering on his face.

A few hours later Robert had bathed and put on a simple linen blouse and pants. He always wore silk or linen, since the breathing sickness attacked him when he wore wool. Under his left arm he tucked a large volume of *Common Law and Trial* and left his chamber to walk toward the kitchen. As he passed the dining hall, he heard the commotion and revelry. As appealing and fun as the laughter sounded, he fought against the urge to join in. He had a lot to think about, and the crowded hall of the Weston governor was the worst possible place for reflection and study.

Life in the governor's palace was not too bad, even if you considered that it was on the western border of the Steppes of Cinder. The grassland prairie that rolled westward was dry and windy, preventing many trees from growing. The rivers were mostly alkaline, meaning that they were not fit to drink and could cause a man to shit out his guts. Robert privately thought that the steppes were beautiful and spent most of his time outdoors, looking west toward the glow of the distant caldera. It had been eight hundred years since the last eruption, but it had been glowing hotter and redder in the past month.

Not all his days on the frontier were good days, though. Sometimes the wind chased him indoors when it blew from the west. On those days, the hot westerlies breathed smoke and dust, choking out his lungs and causing him to wheeze. When he had first travelled to Weston, he had hoped that the prairie air would help his breathing. But more frequently he dreamt of returning east to the cleaner water and air free from ash.

Robert rounded the corner to the kitchen and froze in his tracks at the door. Sarai Horslei sat at the breakfast nook with two plates of food and two glasses of milled wine in front of her. She met his shocked look with a warm smile and motioned to the empty seat across from her.

"It's about time that you made it down here. When I heard that you were drilling late, I assumed that you would not want to eat with the others."

Robert warmed and forgot about his melancholy when she spoke. He always forgot to fret when she spoke to him. Just being around her caused him to forget even to breathe, sometimes. "You brought me a plate from the feast?"

Her smile turned shy and her cheeks reddened when he sat down at the vacant seat across from her, setting the large tome on the table. "I figured that you'd be hungry." Before he could respond, she snatched up the book and feigned interest in the words on the pages. "You pick the strangest bedtime stories, Prince Robert."

"I need something way more interesting than fairy tales if I want to distract my mind from your beautiful yellow hair and gorgeous blue eyes, lady Sarai." A thought flashed in his head, "Sarai even rhymes with eye. Sarai's gorgeous eyes!"

"Oooooo! Scandalous flirtation!" Her smile deepened, and her eyes shone with laughter as she chastised him. "How DARE you try to woo me without a proper chaperone, sir!"

"The scandal would be to let you fall for another suitor, my lady."

Abruptly, Sarai stood and leaned across the table, kissing Robert on the lips. "Flattery will get you everywhere, Prince Robert." She sat down and looked at his expression. "Don't look so shocked. You've been wanting me to do that for two years."

"I... er..."

"Oh stop." She said as she picked up her wine glass. "We both know that we'll be betrothed, soon." Pausing mid drink, she eyed him coolly as she looked over her glass, "unless you don't WANT to admit that you are madly in love with me and choose instead a pretentious upstart from Eston over the royal belle of Weston."

"Royal belle? Don't you mean 'royal pain in the ass?" He laughed and ducked as Sarai threw a bread roll at his head.

Their laughter abruptly stopped when a figure barged into the kitchen. Looking up, Robert and Sarai saw the strained expression on the face of the page boy.

"Prince Robert, come quick! Something terrible has happened!"

"What is it?"

"The caldera! It erupted! The steppes are on fire!"

At his words, Robert and Sarai ran from the kitchen, down the corridor and out into the night. They raced across the courtyard and up the nearest ladder to the parapet. Sarai slipped and nearly lost her footing on the top landing, crying out as she fell backward toward certain pain. Robert reached out his arm, catching her hand in his, pulling her toward him in an embrace.

Sarai grinned at him through her curls, eyes flickering devilishly, and whispered, "My hero."

Robert was too out of breath from the run, and felt his lungs burning from the exertion. He couldn't answer through his wheezing but managed a quick kiss to her still grinning mouth. By the time they reached the western facing wall, a large group had already congregated. The two teens pushed their way to the front of the line, still holding hands. A large man wearing a white tunic glared down at them with disapproval. On his tunic he wore a crest of a horse rearing against the sun. Sarai dropped Robert's hand like she had been stung at the sight of her father's gaze.

Robert did not notice the slight. His eyes were fixed on the western sky, which glowed with the brightest orange and red that he had ever seen. The spectacle nearly caused him to forget his breathing exercises, and he fought against the excitement to slowly breath in from his nose, and then out slowly from his mouth as if he were tickling the flame of a candle. Careful not to extinguish.

He felt another large man approach and heard the voice of his mentor address the small grouping. "This will certainly drive the Pescari people to your walls, governor. They will be a wretched mass of sick, lame, hungry and poor. You should prepare to receive them as refugees," was the advice given by General Reeves.

"More wretched than the savages already are, Maximus? I assure you that the rabble will not receive succor within these walls." The governor set his mouth in a line, clenching his teeth and wrinkling his nose against some horrible smell that only he could sense.

"Abe, you should at least send scouts to determine how many days until they arrive, and to estimate their numbers," the general pressed.

"What? And risk losing valuable men, REAL men to the devils? No, Max. I will send a Falconer."

Aghast, the general stepped back with real fear flashing in his eyes. "A Falconer is here? When did he arrive?"

"Two of them, actually. They arrived this morning. Both have been touring the city, blessing the new births."

Maximus Reaves shook his head and then spat over the wall. "Blessing, indeed."

Robert realized that he had stopped watching the horizon and instead stared at the men after mention of the specters. He started to speak, but the general quickly motioned for him to stop and cocked his head toward the stairs. After a quick glance at Sarai, Robert turned to follow the man the way that he had indicated.

Once they were out of earshot, Maximus warned, "We need to leave. NOW."

"No, Max. I want to see how this plays out. I may be of use."

"You don't understand, Robert. This is bad. REAL bad. We need to get you back to Eston. It will not be safe for you once several hundred thousand Pescari arrive, hoping for food and shelter, only to be turned away by the governor."

Robert blanched at the number. "Really? THAT many? How dangerous can they be with their sticks and clubs? We have steel."

"Gather enough insects into a swarm, and bones can be cleaned in minutes, Princeling. Trust me. No good can come from a flood of Pescari. And the presence of Falconers? That can only mean one thing... The people of Weston will be unsettled and looking for a scapegoat VERY soon."

"What are you talking about, Max? The Falconers do Mother's bidding."

The general's serious expression unsettled the teen and his words sent a shiver. "Quite the contrary, boy. Your mother is a slave to THEM. It's time that you learn the truth about your family."

Robert watched as his mentor strode away to confer with the captains of the city guard. As he did, Sarai approached and touched him on his arm. "You don't believe them, do you?"

He turned toward her, raising his eyebrow slightly and chuckling. "That the caldera is erupting? I can see that it is."

She wrinkled up her nose and hit him playfully on his arm. "No, silly. That one hundred thousand Pescari are marching toward us."

"Honestly, I think that number is high. It is probably less than ten thousand, but I suppose that if the eruptions continue then more will make their way into this territory. Are you afraid?"

"No. They are poor people. Refugees who have lost their homes and we need to help them." Sarai looked thoughtful as she spoke. "I know that my father and your general feel differently, but I think that we should help them." When she mentioned General Reeves her face momentarily took on a sour expression. "Do you think like they do, Robert? Or do you want to help them?"

"I don't know, Sarai. This isn't my city and I'm not supposed to interfere. I'm here as an ambassador and to study, that's all." He watched her face turn thoughtful as he spoke. She was so beautiful to him. Inside he kicked himself for making her more worrisome. He could tell that the fate of these people was important to her.

"Robert!" Maximus called to him, beckoning him over.

"I need to go, Sarai."

She smiled up at him, eyes again playful. "Better go, Prince Robert. Your general is calling you." She kissed him before he left. As he strode away, he briefly saw her throw Reeves a look of disdain. He was beginning to understand that she despised warriors, especially the men who led them.

As he walked over to the group of men discussing city defenses, he watched as Sarai was approached by one of the city councilmen. Cassus Eachann, he thought was the man's name. He watched them for a while, jealous of the time that the older man was spending with his love. Sarai smiled as she spoke with the man, intently listening.

"PRINCELING!" The word from Maximus snapped Robert from his jealous trance. "Did you just hear a damned word that we were saying?" The city commanders had finished conversing with the general and had already departed.

"I'm sorry, Max. My mind wandered."

Reeves shot a look toward the blonde girl with blue eyes. "Looks like you are thinking with the wrong head. That can get a man killed, you know."

Robert nodded at the general's words, again drifting off to watch Sarai and Eachann. They had been joined by Abraham Horslei, and the two older men were in a heated exchange, although he couldn't hear their conversation. Sarai stood off to the side, watching her father with anger and resentment in her eyes.

"Those two hate each other." Max gestured toward the two men.

"Yeah. Eachann is Horslei's arch political rival. He works to oppose him on every topic.

"Abe could say that the sky is blue and Cassus would argue that it was sapphire. Two sides of a coin, those two men. Never seeing eye to eye and equally as powerful as the other, depending on which side landed by chance." Max spit on the ground and turned to leave. "We should go and prepare our men. If there's going to be a shit show, we must decide how to best proceed. This is one fight that we cannot participate in."

Robert watched as the two men argued. "Can we trust Eachann, Max?"

"I don't trust either of them. Watch your step when around snakes, boy."

Sarai looked up and saw Robert watching. When their eyes met, she managed a weak smile which he returned before turning to follow the general.

CHAPTER EIGHT

Lady Crestal Esterling captivated every room she had ever entered. It had always been that way. Her status as Lady Regent of the Realm increased the number of eyes that followed her movements, and she bore that burden with grace and charm. A flawless woman in both appearance and politics, she exuded grace and steadfast leadership. On this day, however, the lady trembled with fear beneath her political mask.

Half an hour before, Crestal had presided over winter solstice celebrations atop the Eston Span. The sprawling capital comprised two high-walled cities that overlooked the traffic on the Logan River. The span connected the cities and loomed over the vital trade route, demonstrating the ruling family's power and dominance over both the farms of Loganshire and the resources of Weston. The Square of Unification sat atop the middle of the high bridge, recognized as the heart of civic events.

All activities in Eston were celebrated in the square. A normal day would witness thousands of vendors crying their wares while thousands more travelers passed by, intrigued by the lure of exotic fruits, spices and cloth from the Southern Continent. A festival would add to the excitement, filling the square with mobs of menageries, circus performers and bards. The annual blessing that the Esterling matron gave on this day drew the entire city. Hundreds of thousands of Estonians crowded the massive span in hopes of catching a glimpse of the Lady Regent while her personal guard stood vigil over the proceedings.

Crestal kept her attention on the city dwellers presenting

offerings. She made a brief gesture of acceptance to each tribute, all the while taking in the peripheral activities. An Imperial messenger had interrupted the ceremony with a whisper in the ear of Matteas Brohn, Captain General of Lady Esterling's guard. She curiously watched as the little courier reached up on tiptoes to relay his message. The massive man gave away no indication whether the news wrought tragedy or triumph. He merely nodded and casually walked toward two of his men, quietly giving them orders.

A farmer approached and placed a basket of gourds at her feet. "May the three bless you and the Esterling Empire, My Lady." He looked older than he probably was, the result of spending his life under the sun. Beside him was a woman with long hair grayed before her time. Crestal thought that it may have been blonde in the recent past. She looked down at the woman's hands, calloused and strong from working alongside her husband. One of them held the hand of a fiery haired girl with a burlap doll gripped tight against her chest. An eye was missing from the pitiful toy and an arm dangled loose.

"Your daughter has the most beautiful freckles."

"She is our niece, My lady." The farmer's wife nudged him with her elbow, correcting his slight. It was improper to correct the Lady Regent.

Crestal ignored the impropriety and smiled down at the little girl. "May the three bless you through the winter with a warm hearth." Something about the child unnerved the monarch as she stared sightlessly ahead, seemingly oblivious that she stood before a queen. She looked up at the farmer's wife. "What is the child's name, dear?"

Shocked that the regent had addressed her directly, the woman dropped into a panicked and pitiful curtsey. "Anne, My Lady."

"Anne, would you like a new doll for the festival?" She gestured to her attendant who produced another in an exquisitely made princess gown. The girl's eyes grew wide in amazement and nodded, still clutching the tattered toy to her chest. "I pray that she keeps you company through the winters to come. May she remind you of this day, when your family were blessed for their sacrifice." Anne nodded and let go of the woman's hand, reaching out to take the doll.

After the family had moved along, the regent stole a glance at movement to her left. Her carriage had been brought early and stood ready for a swift departure. The captain of her guard had his head down, near the ear of the driver. *Something is wrong.* With a smile painted on her face, she accepted the next offering. A brewer presented a keg of ale. *Ugh. Wretched stuff for the lower classes.* She preferred fine wines and would send the swill down to her guards. Nonetheless, she accepted the gift graciously.

Finally, after what had felt more like hours than mere heartbeats, Matteas calmly strode toward his lady. He confidently bent down as if he were about to discuss the price of grain or the weather. After whispering briefly, she felt her soul rip out. The news hit her heart like a scythe on wheat during reaping. Maintaining her ever-existent composure, she nodded to confirm her understanding. To onlookers, Lady Esterling had received the news with as much disinterest as her captain had displayed to the courier, but internally she screamed and cried with indignity.

She continued to welcome each offer with a warm smile. After she had listened to every petitioner, she completed the ceremony with a prayer for fertility and bountiful spring planting. Then, she listened patiently while the priests blessed the crowd. Exhausted, yet fueled with a flame of intensity, she walked with purpose toward the awaiting carriage, telling the coachman to ride with haste.

They careened through the wide streets as the people of the city parted before her. The wooden vessel was flanked on both sides by an honor guard of the fleetest horses and bravest men that her empire could offer. The hard men and their queen blurred through the sprawling city until they finally reached the Rose Palace. The massive structure was beautifully adorned in the spring with massive blossoming foliage, but that beauty had retreated in advance of the winter months. Crestal always preferred the spring version of her city when the blooming vines reflected the vibrancy of her thriving empire.

As the coach lurched to a stop at the base of a broad staircase, she winced at the news she had received. She swallowed back both tears and anger before stepping down from her carriage onto a velvet stool. Briefly accepting the hand of Captain-General Brohn, she seemed to float from the coach to the wide carpet bearing her family crest. She glanced at the sigil, noting the rose in the mouth of the eagle. *Which one am I,* she pondered privately, *am I the eagle or the rose?*

Without losing her step she glided across the stairs and into the palace. She paused only once, turning to blow a kiss to her adoring crowd that had gathered with hopes of sighting their beloved Lady. They roared with delight. *To them I am the rose,* she muttered through clenched, yet smiling, teeth. She could barely hold back tears and she seethed with anger as she walked with majestic grace through the double doors.

Quickening her pace, she entered the palace. Walking with regal determination she made for the Room of Light on the far side of the great hall. The Room, as it was called among her advisors, remained closed to all but her most trusted and loyal administrators. It was here that she truly dominated and only those few advisors ever witnessed her lioness ferocity. This room of decision making, politics and intrigue is where she set aside false niceties and ruled her empire with true despotism. She walked with haste toward this room, hoping to reach it before both her smile and her patience had faded.

The air within grew thin and cold when she strode inside. "In here, I am the eagle," she muttered and dropped her mask. The gilded iron door to the council chamber slammed shut behind the trailing Matteas Brohn. The fury that she had suppressed through the city erupted as soon as the doors shut. She looked around at the assembled faces. "How in the name of the gods did you imbecilic bastards allow my son to be kidnapped?" She hissed these words more than shouted them at her gathered assembly.

The men seated around the table gaped with their mouths open and their eyes on the stone floor, appearing even more idiotic. They had not had time to rise when she entered and sat, staring at the floor. *Is Matteas the only man in the room who possesses a backbone?* "I will repeat my question for your simple minds," she went on, separating each word, "How...did...pirates...kidnap...my youngest SON, the second heir to this FUCKING KINGDOM?"

She emphasized the word "son" by slapping the aged chancellor across the face. The gray-haired man fell from his seat and lay in a heap on the stone. He was so feeble that he struggled to right himself. Instead, he pulled his feet to his chest and placed his hands to his face. None of the other men moved to help him. They stared silently at the floor, looking pointedly away from the chancellor and Lady Crestal.

After what felt an eternity, Crestal heard a throat clear from behind her. "Your majesty, uh, Lady Regent," a voice stammered. She whirled around to see that a familiar looking man kneeling behind her. He forced the words out of his mouth and continued, "Lord Esterling, um, your son, was in the company of a whore when he was taken." As he spoke his eyes darted at Matteas as if he were about to take off his head at any moment.

Heavens! He looks like he does want to remove a head. She raised a finger to stay her guard. "Go on."

"He had left his personal guard outside of the room with instructions not to be disturbed. I believe that his orders were, 'Interrupt me during the next three hours and you will find yourself six inches shorter,' or something to that effect."

Matteas had grabbed his sword, intending to draw it. She shot him a look and a large hand released the hilt.

She looked closer at the man. *His name is Shol... something,* she recalled. She had seen him attending the feeble old chancellor throughout the palace. *He's the chancellor's assistant,* she thought.

"The men stationed outside the room heard nothing, suspected nothing, and even had to beat down the door when the three hours were up. Upon entering there was no trace that the prince had been inside the room at all. Quite perplexing, actually."

Damn Marcus' whores! She had made a mistake of allowing him his fancies, hoping to distract him from finding a suitable wife. No doubt every woman in the realm would saddle him at the prospect of ruling the empire beside one of her sons. But she would not allow a fluffed up noble hussy pry her own hands from the reigns. The realm was hers until her oldest son, Robert, came of age in the next year. *Only if the pathetic and sickly weakling actually passes the trials.* Even then she planned to rule it through him.

"You are Lord Shol, are you not?"

"I am Lord Campton Shol, your majesty."

"That is right. The council appointed you Deputy of Information. But that doesn't explain why you are here in the Room with my advisors."

"I am assistant to Chancellor Gedon." He gestured at the old man lying on the floor. "In his current state of mind and body, the council has asked me to attend him more closely."

She started to protest, intending to remove him from the hall. *Fires of Cinder! Is he just going to lie there, crying like a baby?* She motioned for Brohn to restore the old man to his chair.

Shol quickly added, "We know where your son is, your majesty. We received a ransom demand for his release. Our sources tell us that he was kidnapped by a known outlaw to the empire, one Braen Braston, the oldest son of the late Lord Krist Braston of Fjorik."

The queen met his eyes as she absorbed his words. She could feel herself calming down, yet the anger was still seething beneath the surface. "Didn't he flee to exile a year ago?" She looked at the old man, now seated. *Blast it but he's still crying. I didn't hit him that hard.*

"Two years, my Lady Regent. His brother revealed his murder

and attempted usurpation of Lord Krist after he had fled on his father's flagship. I believe that it was called the *Ice Prince*, my Lady."

"I don't give a demon's ass what the name of the ship was!" *This man could be useful. He may be the only man besides Matteas worth his salt in this palace.*

Campton Schol continued, "My apologies, my Lady. The ransom demand marked Estowen's landing, a week's sail up the coast to the northeast, for the exchange." He rose from kneeling on the floor as he spoke and drew a folded parchment out of his coat. "The details of the exchange are included." Shol said, as he held the document out to Matteas. The large man said nothing and turned to study it against the maps on the chart table near the windows.

Crestal assumed that Shol had reached the end of his information and turned to deal with the imbeciles seated at the table. "Does anyone else have anything to add?" She emphasized her words as if she had dared them to volunteer for the gallows.

"My Lady Regent," the minister pressed, "there is one more issue." She turned back to meet his eyes. They were narrowed, and his face bore an intelligent and perhaps ambitious expression. "Our sources suggest that Braston was the same pirate who plundered our winter stores on the week before last."

She met his intent look with one of her own. "Is that the same raid that resulted in the loss of six of my war galleons?" She felt the room spin slightly as she remembered the details of how they had been lost.

"Yes, Lady Esterling. He led the vessel that escaped upon the arrival of the...the beasts."

"So that really happened as it was reported." she whispered. She chuckled slightly despite herself. "Braston really escaped while our fleet was attacked by the mythological kraken of the deep?"

"Yes, my liege. Several of them, actually."

"OUT!" She commanded. "All but the captain general." As

the men scrambled to leave the room, she briefly glanced at the chancellor. He was still crying and held his hands to his face. "Lord Campton Shol?"

"Yes, my lady?" He bowed deeply again, this time with his eyes to the floor.

"You are to report directly to me and General Brohn." She gestured at the Lord Chancellor Gedon as she spoke." Show us your reports BEFORE you show them to this sniveling bag of bones." Picking up a glass of wine from the table, she took a drink to calm her frazzled nerves. She immediately turned her head and spat the entire mouthful on the chancellor. "This wine tastes like piss."

Matteas Brohn took the glass, sniffed it and made a disgusted face. Shrugging, he downed the remains. Shol helped up and half carried the old man out of the room, the heavy door slamming behind him as he did.

After everyone had departed, a door on the opposite wall slowly opened. A tall man with foreign features entered the room wearing a simple robe and a feathered stole around his shoulders. His head was completely bald, and a large hooded hawk perched on his arm.

Looking up at his yellowish face and slanted almond shaped eyes, Lady Esterling softened her tone. "Weren't the other Falconers with the fleet?"

"Yes, Madam. We lost a total of four."

"But you had the wind. You had used your magic and stolen his wind, right?"

"Yes. We had the wind and had stolen his. There is no way he should have survived our arrival."

"Then how? I thought that only Falconers had the power?"

"The other powers have been latent for 800 years, My Lady. Despite our efforts, they may be finally awakening. We have already culled fifteen gifted infants this year."

"Then we need to destroy them. Crush them."

"We are working on that, My Lady."

"Giant squid? Really? Of all latents to awaken, it had to be water?"

Matteas Brohn spoke up and answered for the Falconer, "We will make a plan to capture and kill him, Your Highness. It'll be during the exchange for your son, if you allow us to proceed with it."

"He really took him. That ABOMINATION has my son?"

The Falconer nodded, "That is confirmed. We received a ransom request for one hundred thousand gold tenets. He wishes to trade at Estowen's landing in a week's time."

"Braston wants gold. Why does an exiled prince want gold?"

"We think he is building an army to challenge his brother."

Brohn interjected, "This act should revoke his letter of marque. Unless of course that sleazy Artema Horn sanctioned this kidnapping."

"No. Horn isn't stupid." Crestal walked to the window and looked out at the city, deep in thought. "No, Matteas. Horn wouldn't stand for this. I placed him in charge of Pirate's Cove, and he pays his taxes on time, every time. No. Braen Braston is rogue, most likely hell bent on retaking his kingdom from his brother."

"Why not just ask us to back him, instead?"

The Falconer broke his silence, "If he has awakened, then he likely sees himself as a god. If he is making a move to avenge his brother, then he will also raise an army against you."

"He will be powerless on land, will he not?"

The eerie man nodded, "That is our understanding of the winter art. He needs access to water in order to work his power. There are no forecasted rainstorms for that night, and the trade will be made far enough from the pier that a tidal wave will not be too damaging."

"Then I will be with you when the exchange is made. Gather the gold. I will take the most elite of my guard, Matteas. We need to restore order to the Empire." Both Brohn and the Falconer nodded, then the tall, robed specter turned and glided toward the door from which he entered. After it had shut behind him, Crestal turned to Brohn, "They creep me out, Matteas. I'll never grow accustomed to them. Make the arrangements and let's go get my shit pot for a son."

"Aren't they both shit pots, Your Majesty?"

"They take after their father." Crestal spun on her heel and made her way to the main door. "I'm retiring to my chambers." As she opened the door, she spoke without turning to look at her captain general. "I'm done dealing with this shitty day. Have someone send up a decent bottle of wine."

"All that we have left is the piss, My Lady." This stopped the Queen Regent in her tracks.

"Then I really am going to kill that abomination. I'm going to kill him and pour a bottle of 781 down his fucking throat." The door slammed shut behind her.

Matteas picked up a glass of wine from the table, sipped it, and muttered, "At least the bastard left the 772."

Chapter Nine

Amash laid three cards face up on the table. "Three fools and a knight. Read 'em and weep." He started to reach out for the pile of coins in the middle, until Braen raised one hand to stop him.

The big northerner took his time, then said, "Three queens and a fool are a better hand. I win this one, Amash."

"Ahem…" Sippen cleared his throat then spread out three kings and a queen. Without saying another word, he used his hands to pull all of the coins to his side of the table.

"Gods be damned, Sippen! Were you dealt those kings?" Braen picked up the discards and began searching the deck for another king. He could have sworn there had already been two turned over.

"Yuh… yes. Puh… pay better attention." Smiling, the engineer began stacking his new coins in orderly rows next to his towers of gold and silver.

Turat rose from his seat in a huff. Most of the coins lost that night were his. "I'm out. Besides, Lord Nevra asked me to do some extra work, tonight."

"You're working for Nevra?" Braen shot a confused glance at Amash.

"You think that guarding Artema brings in enough coin for cards? Nevra always has extra work to do around town." He grabbed his coat and downed his mug. "See you tomorrow, Amash."

"He's right, Braen. We don't get paid very well for guard duty. All of us take other jobs around town from time to time." Amash took another sip from his glass and Braen topped it off from the bottle.

Sippen waited for the door to shut behind Turat. "I don't trust him."

"Turat? He's not a bad guy. We stand a lot of shifts together and I trust him to have my back. Also, he's decent with a blade." Changing the subject, he pointed at his glass. "Well, at least this wine is as good as its' price tag."

"Better, it would seem, except for the fact that there will only be nine cases left in existence, after we are finished with this one." Looking at the bottle, the big man contemplated, "I could literally sell a single bottle and retire to a nice chateau. I could sell an entire case and buy back my kingdom from my brother. Sippen, the other cases are safely snug on *Ice Prince,* right?"

"Yuh... yes. In the suh... secret hold."

"Good man." He took a sip from his own glass and smiled, "Damn if this isn't perfectly aged! Such aroma! Such bouquet!"

"Such a waste of the rest of the collection!" The three men laughed until Amash cleared his throat and asked the question that Braen had hoped to avoid. "Is it true, Braen? Did Krakens really come and attack the ships?"

"Yes."

"Demon's Ass! What did they look like?"

"Just like the storybooks. Giant squids with tentacles and suction cups. Huge eyes that were the size of an amidships." Braen tried to pour wine from an empty bottle, looked down its neck at the dry bottom, then set it down. Reaching for another, he added, "And before you ask, no. I didn't call them."

"Have you been able to do other things? Like stir tea without a spoon?" Amash was not poking fun. He was a true friend and seemed honestly interested and eager for fables to be true.

"No. Well, I've never tried." He poured his wine and then stared at it, squinting his eyes and scrunching his face. "Nope." He drank a swig from the glass. "I'm as normal as you, Amash."

"Wuh... well. The air has been getting ruh... real cold around him when he is scared or excited." Sippen was looking at Braen when he answered Amash.

"Gods damn it, Sippen!" Braen drank another long draw from his glass. "You, too?"

"I... It's true, Braen. Weird things have buh... been happening, uh... a lot." Sippen looked toward Amash, "Eh... especially when he's sleeping. He starts dreaming and the ship is fruh... freezing cold beneath decks!"

"Braen, that's how the legends work."

"What do you mean?"

"Have you heard about latency?"

"I'm not superstitious nor religious." Braen set down his glass and looked at Amash with a serious expression. "But tell me about it. I know that you read books. Get it off your chest so that we can get back to cards."

Amash cleared his throat and began as if he were a professor teaching a class. "Legend has it that before the Esterling Empire was formed eight hundred years ago, mankind was engineered by a master race of beings."

"Engineered? What is that load of nonsense? Made, like constructed by gods?" Braen chuckled and shook his head with doubt.

"Sort of, I'm afraid. They bred us like cattle, according to the legend."

"What were these people called?"

"No one knows their real names. The legends call them overseers."

Braen shook his head, again. "If a master race of people bred us like one of Sippen's science experiments a mere eight hundred years ago, then why isn't there a record of it in historical accounts? I mean, seriously, I've read historic records dating back eight hundred years regarding crops and weather, and something THIS extreme would have been mentioned."

Amash began, again. "The legends. Some believe that they are more of an oral history than a fable. After we were scattered, stories were handed down and still remain."

"Scattered?" Braen realized that he had not had a sip from his cup in a long while and forced himself to take a drink.

"Scattered. They culled out anybody who showed signs of the power, and then divided up the people based on whatever latent power they possess. Earth in Loganshire, Fire in the Steppes of Cinder, Air in the East..."

"And Water in the North," Braen whispered.

"Yes, Braen, Water in the North."

Sippen, who had been listening intently, asked the scientific question, "Huh... how does it wuh... work?"

Amash shrugged his shoulders. "I have no idea." He stood up and walked to the fireplace, picking up a poker as he did. Stoking the wood, he watched as sparks rose into the air, disappearing into ashes. The fire strengthened when he leaned the poker against the wall and blew at the base of the logs. "But I think it works like this." He pointed at the flame. "When the fire grows, the heat is dissipated throughout the room. Someone with latent powers can take the heat from the air and store it their body like a waterskin."

"Now you lost me." Braen laughed at the thought of storing fire in a waterskin.

Sippen nodded. "Nuh... not a waterskin. Like uh... a rock."

Braen looked at Sippen, "Rocks don't burn."

Amash nodded and smiled his agreement. "No, but they hold heat! A person with a fire latency can absorb heat in their bodies and seemingly be unaffected. Then, they can disperse it at will."

"That actually sounds dangerous. Why in heavens would someone breed THAT ability into mankind?"

"Exactly. That's why they dispersed us. Gave us rules and religion and set up the Esterling dynasty to rule over us."

"Why them?" Braen was growing interested in the logic.

Sippen answered before Amash could open his mouth. "Buh... balance. If they ruh... rule the air, then thuh... they can maintain buh... balance by keeping us suh... separated."

"Yes. Except for the fact that we're not as separated as we once were. The Cove is an example of a heterogenous society."

Braen choked on his wine. "A what? Really, Amash, where did you learn to speak with such an advanced vocabulary. And, why aren't you a scholar?"

Amash looked down at the ground. "I was. I was training to be a scholar in the University of Eston, but I wanted adventure. Also, I couldn't stand those damned Falconers walking around everywhere." He shuddered at some distant memory. "So, I left. I came to The Cove because I couldn't return home."

"Yeah, those bastards creep me out, too." Braen refilled the glass in front of Amash. "How do they fit into your legend?"

"They're what's left of the overseers. Everyone knows that they are the special police of the empire, but they also control the air." Amash paused to take a sip, and then sat back down at the table. "Did you notice any weird weather phenomena when the fleet caught up with you?"

Sippen answered before Braen could open his mouth. "YES! The wuh... winds were still for a duh... day and a half. Also, they cuh... caught up to us with two suh... separate fleets sailing from two suh... separate directions."

Braen nodded his agreement. "That's right. They met up on the same morning and seemed to have five times the wind than should be had for the season. That was the creepiest part of the entire day. Well, except for the Kraken showing up at just the right time."

Amash stared at Braen with a most serious expression. "My friend, if you, or someone on your ship has a latency for water, then you or they can also control creatures of the sea."

Braen drank straight from the bottle.

Lord Campton Shol sat at a writing desk in his office. Since Chancellor Gedon had lost his wits, the council had maneuvered to place him as his assistant and as Deputy of Information. As such, he enjoyed certain luxuries and wielded authority beyond that of the Queen Regent. Although, that authority was kept secret even from her. A knock at the door signaled that his visitor had arrived, and he rose to open the latched door. A robed Falconer with a feathered stole and a bald head followed him into the office.

"Greetings Kestrel. I assume that you reinforced my information to Lady Esterling?"

The Falconer nodded, "I did. She is convinced that the Braston pirate is the kidnapper, and intends on paying the ransom, herself."

"She's an idiot. She's so damned emotional and has no concept about the truth." Shol picked up a communique from the Oracle of Astian. "There have been another six martyred Dreamers in the past week, each having entered the Ka'ash'mael and failed to return. The entire Astian council is concerned that we're losing control in Andalon."

Kestrel snarled at the implication that his Falconers had been failing the council. "My men and their casts are working daily to suppress the abominations as we find them. Too many have been born and many have slipped past our identification. After six months we cannot detect latency, and more and more families have been hiding away their infants."

Campton nodded. "I empathize, my friend, but the council has demanded our discretion."

"That discretion has allowed many to slip past."

"Times are changing in Astian and the council is filled with a new kind of politician. Too many progressives have risen to power and they fail to see that the situation is dire. Especially now that the caldera is erupting. As it ionizes the atmosphere, more and more latent abilities will awaken."

"What about 'Society' agents? If the council would allow us to, we should be arresting them and returning them to Astian."

"True, Kestrel, but our focus remains on Braston, since he was prophesized. Go with the Esterling bitch and ensure that he doesn't survive the exchange." Kestrel nodded his compliance and turned to leave the study. "And Kestrel," the Falconer turned to meet Shol's hardened gaze, "ensure that the bitch stays alive. She's easier to control than either of her sons will be."

After a curt nod, the specter exited the room and Campton chose a dispatch from his agent in Logan. *Outlaws attacked a food caravan headed from Diaph to Logan. Sixteen carts of grain and five carts of salted pork were stolen along with 50 horses.* Slamming the paper back onto the desk, he walked to a large perch in the corner of the room. Atop the roost sat a regal falcon adorned with red feathers around its' head with white along the edges of his wings and tail.

"Reaver, my sweet, I need you to pass on a message." Leaning in, Shol closed his eyes and spoke with his mind directly to the bird, *Fly straight away to the rookery. I authorize a full caste to aid a cavalry regiment out of Diaph. Find the outlaws operating in the forests north of there.* When he had finished, the great bird flapped its wings and flew out of the widow to relay his command. Lord Shol returned to his desk to muse over the remaining dispatches.

CHAPTER TEN

Robert Esterling had risen early for sword practice and beamed as he made his way from the fighting pits to the palace. Even Maximus had been proud of the prince's progress in the single combat, praising him in front of the armorer. "Like an eel in the sea," he had described the fluidity of his footwork and agility. Most importantly, Robert had endured the entire session without a single onset of his breathing sickness.

As he walked, he pulled a blanket tighter around him. Winter was trying to grip Weston City. He looked out over the wall. Cold rain had fallen during the night, flooding the fields west of the Misty River. Robert had never seen anything more beautiful, but he worried that the cold and humidity would hurt his lungs in the night. Looking out over the great expanse of water, he could still see the red and orange glow and worried also over the distant fire.

Robert had performed so well in the morning exercises, that Max had wrapped them up earlier than usual. The prince had extra time to study for the intellectual portion of the trials. Studying had become more fun, as of late, but not because he had experienced anything near the success that he had with swords. No, he smiled outwardly at the thought of spending more time with Sarai. Since their kiss a week ago, she had grown from being his best friend into his heart's desire. And, more recently, had become his tutor.

She was not only beautiful with her yellow hair and frost blue eyes, but she was intelligent and such a strong reader that Robert admired her ability. She could read things once and then know it by heart. Most importantly, she was patient with him and did not ridicule his slow reading or scold him when he mixed up the order of the letters. Thinking about his love, he hurried to their usual meeting place, the breakfast nook off the kitchen. The place of their first kiss had everything that they needed, a warm hearth, access to food, and it was the last place that her father would interrupt them.

Abraham Horslei was a proud nobleman with old-fashion views. He was also an elitist who looked down on anyone who was not high-born, so he would never be found near the cooking or waitstaff. According to Sarai, he was a bigot and biased against anyone who was not born a man of wealth or perfect health. He loathed the dark-skinned people of the Southern Continent and abhorred the Pescari people of the plains. A hardened chauvinist, Sarai had told Robert that her father had wanted another boy so badly that he had beaten the doctor senseless when her mother delivered her, instead.

Robert arrived at the nook and found his love sitting at the table, a plate of food covered and awaiting his arrival. She had cut pieces of paper into rectangles that were spread out on the table. Sarai jumped up when he arrived, genuinely excited to see him. She threw her arms around his neck and kissed him long and passionately before pulling back with a smile on her face, obviously eager with some news.

"I made something for you!" She grabbed his hand and led him to the table, pointing at the rectangular cards.

"What are they?"

"Pick one up." Her smile radiated and was so infectious that he could not help but smile back.

"You wrote on them." He focused on the letters, sound them out in his head. "Wait, this is about taxation rates." Smiling, she held up a large blue book. He looked closer and remembered it as the one that he had left in the nook on the night of the eruption. "You wrote down the taxation rates of villages and towns throughout the empire?"

"Yes!" She laughed with joy that he had figured out her cleverness. "I realized that the tables were just too much and too confusing for you to learn at once. So, I broke it down. See? This side of the card has the city of Logan written on it. And if you flip it over you will see the rates in order of livestock, goods and foods."

"You are a genius, Sarai." Robert marveled at how clever she truly was. In the months they had spent time together, she constantly astounded him with her ability to teach him. Everyone else who had tried had failed. He kissed her then pulled back and looked into her icy blue eyes which were beaming with joy. "I love you. I truly do, so much, Sarai."

Her smile turned devilish, "Of course you do, Prince Robert! I cast a love spell on you. A spell to trick you into marriage and making me your queen."

After a few more flirtations, they finally settled down to study. After only a few hours, Robert felt confident about the tax rates for the various counties and was ready to move on to the more difficult task of studying global economics. "What is heg...uh... moan...ic the...or...eee?"

"Hegemonic theory. I'm really not sure." Taking the book, *Political Theory and Practice,* she found the reference and read aloud, "Hegemonic theory is the principal that, in an international economic system, stability depends on a single nation-state rising as the world power. Thus, is the premise for the formation of the current Esterling Empire."

"Way to go, great-great-great Grandpa." Robert chuckled.

Sarai kept reading, "The strength of the unification between Eston, Weston and Loganshire established a military force that can withstand attacks from Fjorik or the Southern Continent with little consequence. International order breaks down in the absence of a single powerful nation-state, resulting in higher impacts from famine, crime, terrorism and warfare. The Empire, or a semblance of such, must be maintained at all cost."

Robert nodded. "That's true. There hasn't been a real attack from outsiders since my father drove back the Braston family. Now, Mother talks about them as if they're her puppets. The same can be said for the Pirate's Guild. Did you know that they pay taxes on their spoils from attacks on all trade ships? That includes attacks on our own. That has minimized their impact on the economy and was easier and cheaper than destroying them completely."

Sarai stared at him in disbelief. "You aren't serious! Your family taxes their raids?"

Robert laughed, "We also collect the insurance money paid out after their attacks, and, now that I think about it, we own the insurance companies. So, we receive a portion of the premiums on every shipment. We allow them to take a few each year to appease their animalistic need to pillage, and we're paid either way."

"Wow," Sarai feigned shock, "You are wealthier than I thought." After a pause she added, "And you had BETTER make me a queen." They laughed and kissed and then both paused when their thoughts drifted to the current situation in Weston. Sarai broke the silence. "I wonder what impact the arrival of the Pescari will bring."

"There'll be a humanitarian split in the minds of every person in the Empire. Some will view them as people in need, refugees in need of a hand up. The social aspect of their welfare will be a concern of those in Eston or Loganshire, those furthest from the actual migrants."

"But people in Weston will fear their coming, won't they? They'll fear their competition for jobs or worse, the crime that they may bring as a desperate culture with a different view on social norms." A tear streamed Sarai's face as she thought about the next option, "And then there are the bigots like my father. They will want to cut them out like a disease or send them back to face the erupting caldera. Either way, they'll refuse to accept responsibility for their welfare."

"Exactly, Sarai."

"Then what do we do? Do we let them in the gates, or feed them outside of the wall? We can't send them back."

"But we can't let them in. This is the need for a hegemon, to provide the welfare where they live, in their home nation-state. We must create an arrangement that is like our relationship with Fjorik or even the Pirate Guild. Only then will they be able to self-govern themselves within the construct of their own culture, while we minimize the impact of disaster."

Sarai let Robert's wisdom sink in, before adding, "That's considering that they'll even want us to affect their culture. They've been wronged by the people of Weston for years. We've exploited them for their furs, made treaties that they kept but we've broken. And we forced them to stay on their side of the forbidden waste with the threat of war. Now that they're crossing, we have no choice but to modify or keep the terms of the treaty. I fear what my father will do."

"I fear what my mother won't."

Sarai sat up with a new thought. "What about Cassus Eachann?"

"Isn't he your father's political rival?"

"He is." Sarai was aglow with excitement at the prospect of reaching out, even if it went against her father. "But he's the wealthiest man in the city, next to my father, of course. He leads most of the programs within the city to help curb vagrancy and to help create and find jobs for the beggars. He's a humanitarian. He'll have ideas."

Robert shook his head. "That's dangerous, Sarai. Your father rules Weston under the favor of my family. If you were to go against him, then he'll resent you."

She smiled. "Then he'd have to marry me to you, to curry back more."

Robert laughed. "Just be careful what you set up with him.

Politicians are snakes, and only act when something benefits them, even when they appear to be helping the unfortunate. There is always a motive, whether it's to gain bigger popularity or political base."

It rained during the night, but Taros did not feel the cold. Rather, his body burned with internal heat, most likely from excitement and anticipation. During the past week across the desert his group had grown to ten thousand Pescari. All viewed him as a savior or a god who held the power of Felicima. When they camped, strangers would stroll by where he and Lynette bedded down, just to get a glimpse of him. When they trekked during the day, he rode at the front of the procession, leading them further into the desert and closer to aid.

Surprisingly, not a single member of his troupe had died during the march. Unfortunately, Lynette had never regained her lucidity, and had begun talking to Felicima as she stared up at her all day long. After a few days in the desert, she had lost her sight completely. An image of Felicima burned across both eyes from exposure. At first, Taros had tried blindfolding her, but to no avail. She always managed to wiggle the cloth from her face. As a result, her mind was as burned as her eyes.

When they had camped during the previous evening, scouts reported that the Andalonian city of Weston lay a mere thirty miles ahead, one more day's trek if they did not experience any setbacks or obstacles. As a precaution, he ordered his warriors, now a force of three thousand, to march in the front of the formation, range weapons at the ready, just in case. All spare mounts were saddled with the best warriors, and each sled was fitted with a knot that could be released very quickly if they ran into trouble that required fighting.

Overhead Taros noticed another hawk. He squinted and knew that if he looked hard enough, he would see the second falcon keeping pace with his group from the air. They had strange behavior for birds of prey. At first, he thought them to be buzzards, circling and waiting for scraps or for a weak member of the party to fall out. Something did not bode well with the presence of these birds.

Ahead he could see the walls of the city appearing on the horizon and sat a little taller in the saddle. Glancing back at the hawks, he called a woman over. Flaya was older than he, and he should consider her pretty like the other men did. But he could not see her in that fashion. Lynette had long urged him to find a woman who was pure, and to be wary of women who lied or had many partners. He was discouraged that Flaya was very popular among the warriors, many of whom had known her.

He whispered in her ear, in case the hawks could hear, and she walked quickly away to a skid to retrieve a torch. This done, she lit the end and walked alongside Taros. He smiled as he thought about what he was about to do and wondered why he had not done this sooner. As the torch suddenly snuffed out, Taros tested his range and looked at the closest of the hawks. They circled just a little bit higher than the arrows had been when he burned them in the air. Abruptly the bird squawked, and his tail feathers smoked and singed, sending both birds flying very quickly toward the city walls. This made Taros smile.

CHAPTER ELEVEN

Skander Braston wrapped his fur cloak around his burly frame as he walked toward his father's former chambers. The chill had finally cooled the thick walls of the keep so he assumed that winter was close to gripping the kingdom. Huddled so against the cold, the large prince thought about his father.

Skander had hated the man. Truth be told, he had hated his father more than he hated his own mother and brother. The Braston family crest proudly displayed a winter cat with saber teeth tearing apart a lifeless wolf on a blue background. Skander frowned at the thought that his father had resembled a craven more than a saber cat, with palace doors open to allow the lowly wolves entrance for an easy handout.

Krist Braston had ruled the northern city of Fjorik more than thirty years and his people had loved him. Skander felt that the elder lord had lived more to pander to their open jowls and had fed them better than he had his own family. True nobleman enjoyed feasts such as those thrown by the Esterling Queen Regent. During her coronation tournament ten years ago, however, the "Lord Craven" had refused to allow his sons to compete because he had felt that the northern people faced a longer winter than they had in past years. Lord Krist had instead forced his sons, both eligible princes, to remain at the hearth to oversee "building strategies" for the grain silos and salt cellars.

But now Skander Braston ruled the entire northern peninsula and mined its wealth and splendor from its snow-capped mountains. His mountains contained resources that could fuel an empire.

Fjorik could potentially surpass the Southern realms in both power and might, perhaps even rising as a rival to the Esterling Empire. Skander knew his duty and would correct the order of the kingdom. He would return Fjorik to its ancient glory and break apart the southern empire.

Alas, this year an early winter had set in, much as it had ten years earlier. His people faced another harsh famine, and Skander was not prepared. He frivolously spent too many resources from the mines in his attempt to industrialize, ignoring his father's warnings to horde grain. Feeling like the failure that his father had predicted, he had been forced to broker a trade deal with the Esterling family. In return for allowing the Falconers unfettered access to conduct a census of the Northern people, he would receive grain and meat. Of course, they sweetened the deal by promising weapons if he sent them extra iron. He had accepted out of desperation.

He felt the walls of what had once been his father's room, absorbing the winter spirit of the stones. Dark and icy rage had pierced them, and he heard his father's words belittle him in his head. *Why can't you be as levelheaded as Braen, Skander? Think before you act, Skander.* He felt cold fury enter his skin. Once inside, it cooled his heart and lungs. He then breathed out an icy mist that coalesced around the stone in front of him, then froze as a thick sheet of ice on rock. *You will never be the ruler that you brother will, Skander.* He hated his father, but his father was dead. He also hated his brother, and Braen was alive.

"You should light a fire in here." Hester spoke from the doorway.

Without turning, Skander responded, "I won't be here long."

"It should be yours. You're the king, and these should be our chambers." Hester knew that he would refuse to make this room his own. Skander ordered sealed like a tomb after they had removed the body of his father.

"Not as long as his spirit walks."

"You need to get over that superstitious nonsense. His ghost doesn't haunt these walls. And if it does, it's because it fears your strength."

"If it does, it's because it couldn't get into the Heavenly Hall." *And who's fault was that, Skander? You didn't even place my axe in my hand when you killed me.*

"That's his problem. He was a cowardly king." Hester entered the room, wrapping her fox fur against the chill. "He didn't deserve to rule, and you were the one who told me that he must be removed." Grabbing his forearm, she turned him to face her. "Be the king that I married."

"I killed him in his sleep and now the warriors won't welcome him. He at least deserved to hold an axe when he died. I didn't even give him that courtesy." *No, you didn't, did you? After all that I taught you about respect for tradition, and you slit my throat and ran.* Skander raised his free hand to his head, closing his eyes against the voice of the spirit.

"Your BROTHER killed him." Hester dug her nails into his arm and screamed, "Don't you ever say otherwise, or you'll lose your kingdom while he still lives!"

Skander pulled away from her touch, blood oozing from several places on his arm. "Your nagging killed him, you witch!" Seeing the blood, he raised his arm to strike her with the backside of his hand. Before he could level the blow, she slid swiftly closer and he felt cold steel touch his belly through his furs. He pulled back his hand and looked down at the drawn dagger pressed against him.

"Hit me. Hit me and I'll tell the kingdom the truth of your father's untimely passing. I'm pretty sure that Braen would drop everything to come out of hiding and take your place by my side."

Skander growled as he stepped back from her blade. He calmed himself, drew a breath, and changed the subject. "Speaking of my dear estranged brother. I received word from Marcus Esterling that he's been found. He's been living as a sanctioned pirate for the better part of a year."

"And?"

"He has a plan to capture him and bring him to me." Skander walked to the window and looked out at the snow.

"When did an imperial messenger arrive?"

"That's the oddity. It arrived this morning. That little shit of a prince was kidnapped by pirates in Eskera, three weeks ago."

"A message from Eskera takes four weeks to reach Fjorik by Imperial ship."

"Exactly." He held up another message. "A message from Eskera takes three weeks to reach Fjorik by one of OUR ships. This is the message informing me of his kidnaping. Also delivered this morning, by one of our information gatherers." He again held up the first message, "He sent this to us exactly one week to the day before he was taken." Skander turned to look at his wife and handed her a letter that he had produced from his belt.

"He knew that he'd be kidnapped?" Hester snatched the parchment from her husband's hands.

Skander nodded. "Or he orchestrated it."

She read the note quickly, then asked, "Do you think we can trust him? What does that whelp of a spoiled brat really want?"

"He wants a kingdom, most likely. But he's only asking for gold, for now. Lots and lots of gold."

"If he was kidnapped a week after he sent this, then he may have arranged for his own capture. He has a plan."

"Exactly. I'll meet with him where he wants. I think he's a spoiled brat, but we need an ally in the Empire. His bitch of a mother and idiot for a brother are out of our reach."

CHAPTER TWELVE

Braen stood on deck watching Sa'mond order the crewmembers atop *She Wolf*. They tossed lines and made preparations to sail with unmatched precision. He marveled that the crew worked with the same eerie quiet as their mistress. Whereas his crew would have been singing chanties or laughing as they worked, Eusari's crew responded to the eunuch's orders with rhythmic strokes as if a silent bass drum were beating in their hearts. The spectacle ran chills up the Northman's arms.

He continued to watch as Eusari walked across the brow. *She is so beautiful and so dangerous,* he thought. She walked by two crewmen without saying a word, seemingly ignoring them. They reacted with quiet fear, both backing up to give her room. *Or was that disdain?* He kept watching and realized that all orders continued to come from Sa'Mond, despite that their captain walked the deck. His eyes followed Eusari, marking that she hadn't even spoken to Sa'Mond, before retiring below decks.

Sippen stood beside Braen, arguing against his orders to stay behind. The impish man begged to get underway, "I pruh...promise that I would sur...serve you better underway!"

"Not this time, Sippen. I need you to stay here and keep watch. I don't trust Kernigan and I feel that a mutiny is stirring up. Be my eyes and ears in Pirate's Cove. We only have a ten-day sail via *She Wolf,* so I will be back in three weeks, depending on weather."

"*Ice Prince* could make it all in a week," the small man reminded.

"Yes. But this is Eusari's mission, and stealth is her cover whereas speed is mine." Both men stood in silence for a moment as three deckhands removed the doubled line from the bits. After the sailors moved on to a different line station, Braen added, "Keep to the shadows in The Cove. Find out just what the hell is going on." Turning, he added, "And Sippen, watch Kernigan. If something goes wrong, it will be because of him."

"What if Kuh...Kernigan is right, and we cannot trust Nevra? Wuh...what if we can't trust Artema?"

"If we can't trust Artema Horn then we have bigger problems, my friend."

Sippen and Braen embraced in a brotherly hug, then the little man scurried off the deck. A few minutes later the brow was hoisted, and the crew heaved in the lines. An hour later *She Wolf* was clearing the channel toward open sea. Several men climbed the main sail when Sa'Mond yelled, "Make READY!" The sails unfurled on his next command. Not long after, they squared away for full speed. Only then, as The Cove disappeared behind the stern, did Braen lay below decks.

His small stateroom lay directly aft of Eusari's. He went inside and readied his gear for the transaction. If there were trouble during the exchange, he wanted to stand ready. A standard and boring looking cutlass hung from his left hip, readied for a cross draw. Braen had adopted the shorter, slightly curved blade not long after leaving his home in the north. Liking its' feel, it quickly became his daily carry and most trusted fighting tool. As a youth he was trained in the traditional way with a broadsword, but shipboard fighting differed greatly than open battlefield. Tight spaces, overhead rigging, and cramped quarters rendered a long blade useless.

In the small of his back he wore a short blade sheathed horizontally on a riser from his belt. The long knife was more of backup weapon, but could be drawn by his left hand, giving him a quick thrust following a parry with the cutlass. Like the cutlass, the knife was basic in appearance. Leather wrapped the handle which swelled to steady his grip when fighting while coated in blood, sweat, rain, and sea water. The blade itself was cast in folded steel with dark swirling patterns. He trusted the knife for its strength and had often wielded it to deflect against full swings from larger swords.

On his right hip hung a small axe. The blade was of the same steel as the knife, and held a dangerously sharp edge, even after battering doors and cutting down riggings during ship to ship battles. Although Braen could throw an axe with accuracy in a contest, he had only thrown in a battle one single time. That decision had ruined his life and was a moment that he regretted every night since, when he had lain awake staring at oak ceiling boards. Suffice to know, that Braen Braston had once carried a matching set of axes.

He knelt before his footlocker and pulled out a long sword wrapped in rolled leather with rawhide ties. He laid it on the stretched canvas of his hammock and untied the straps. He drew a deep breath and held it in briefly while unrolling his father's broadsword. The "Guardian of Fjorik" was majestically folded steel with a deep blue sapphire on the pommel. The hilt was intricately carved with the crest of his family, a winter cat tearing apart a wolf with long sabre teeth. Braen remembered to exhale and let out long cold mist from his lungs. The sword frosted slightly as his breath brushed the steel.

A soft knock on the stateroom door jarred him from his trance. He quickly rolled the blade back into leather, then replaced it to the footlocker without bothering with the ties.

"Enter!" He called toward the door, shutting the lid with a sweeping motion.

Eusari glided in with confidence, then drew her furs closer around her shoulders. "Why are your quarters so cold? These rooms are usually the warmest." Braen had not noticed and shrugged. *She Wolf's* captain glanced at the footlocker and then back up at him.

"Thank you for the quarters. They're fine." Braen was not usually this uncomfortable around women, but the captain of *She*

Wolf unnerved him. He found her stunningly beautiful with her pale complexion, dark hair and green eyes, but he could not help but notice the anger that she carried in those orbs.

"Captain Braston, I..."

"Braen, please. And may call you, Eusari?"

"You may. Braen. I want to apologize for being so rude on our first meeting." Her words seemed forced, as if she were not accustomed to exchanges of pleasantries.

Braen watched her soften. *Maybe the rumors are wrong and she's only an introvert,* he thought. *She doesn't act like a maneater.* "It isn't a problem, really."

"I resented Artema forcing me to bring you along."

"I took no offense, Eusari. I understood."

"Regardless, I would like to start over. I want your journey to be pleasant aboard my ship. But I warn you that crew is wary of outsiders. We rarely take any on. Our visitors are usually kept in the hold and wear shackles instead of steel blades. Please understand that they don't mean offense if they're not friendly."

"I understand, completely. They're highly efficient and quite remarkable, by the way." Braen had been watching her closely as she spoke. She stood in complete control of her body language, small and contained within her furs. Eusari appeared to have no movement at all, gloved hands near her knives and legs positioned as a dancer ready to leap into movement. She could best be described as a cat wound tightly before pouncing.

"I'll pass along your compliments to Sa'Mond." She shifted her weight before adding, "Captain Braston...er, Braen, I'd like it if you'd dine with me in my quarters."

"Of course. I look forward to that."

Eusari nodded, and then turned to leave. She opened the door and paused, looking back over her shoulder. "Are you really the son of Krist Braston?"

"Yes. Will that be a problem in the way of our friendship?"

"Perhaps. I'm originally from Loganshire." Eusari stepped out of the room and the door slammed into place. The chill in the room returned immediately as Braen drew in a sharp breath. When he finally let it out, another chilling cloud of frost formed.

Loganshire was the historic enemy of his family until they fell under the protection of the Empire. He and his family had raided their fertile farms on occasion as marked on their crest. The wolf in the teeth of the snow cat depicted the dominance of his people over hers. For the first time in his lifetime, Braen Braston felt queasy at sea.

Sippen watched from the pier as the *She Wolf* dropped her sails and caught the wind. Samani Kernigan strode slowly up to the small man, much as a predator would stalk its' prey except that his hands were harmlessly clasped behind his back, masking his danger. "He's your friend, is he not?"

"He is muh... my best friend in thuh... the world." Sippen was not sure if he fully trusted the lord, but he could not ignore some underlying respect for the man. He did disagree with Braen, who categorically distrusted anyone in The Cove except for Artema Horn. Interestingly, Sippen hated the king.

"I've noticed that you don't always stutter. Does it come and go?"

"It is anz... anxiety. I literally choke on the words."

"I see. I hope that you can relax around me. I wanted to ask about your projects, Sippen. I was told that you are more than his friend and steward, and that you're a keen engineer with a knack for invention."

"I dabble."

"That. Is total Bullshit, and you know it."

"How duh... do you know?"

"You did not stutter, my good man." Samani slapped him on the shoulder like he had told a joke, and Sippen was forced to smile. "I would like to play you in poker, some day. I think that I may have finally found someone whom I can out bluff."

"Thu... That sounds like fu... fun. Yuh... you shuh... should teach me to play." Sippen smiled, remembering the game the night before and his piles of gold.

"I'd love to. Now, please show me what you've created. I want to see your genius."

Sippen nodded, and the two men turned to make the walk through the town. As they talked, four soldiers passed in formation. The men looked like the typical brutish city guards who watched over The Cove.

Kernigan watched the men cross the street, then remarked, "You can take the pirate off of the ship, but you can't take the pirate out of the pirate. Each of them looks like trouble."

"There have been muh... more guards, of late. What is Ah... Artema planning?"

"The tensions with the Empire have been wound up tight since Artema thought it would be a good idea to kidnap Marcus Esterling. Nevra placed some extra guns and soldiers on the walls in case they try to enter the harbor."

"Thuh... they never have buh... before. Why would they truh... try, now?"

"Exactly. They have the numbers, but they would lose an entire armada if they raided the Cove. I think that it's a show of power by Artema. He's the Pirate King and likes to remind us. It's almost like Artema has his own agenda, other than officiating the guild." He glanced over his shoulder as *Wench's Daughter* shoved off the pier adjacent to the one from which *She Wolf* had recently departed. "Like that, for instance. Why the hell is he leaving on his flagship? We'll need him, here."

Sippen frowned, "Aren't you loyal to Horn?"

Kernigan stopped walking and his smile disappeared. "Sippen, I'm loyal to The Cove and to the Guild. Artema's the elected king, but I believe in Social Contract theory. He commissions our letters of marque to raid as pirates, and we in turn prey upon the Empire, the Southern Continent, and the Northmen of Fjorik. He taxes our acquisitions and commerce of the town, and provides the army that you see, here. He also provides for infrastructure so that the town can thrive. When a contract is violated, either side may demand recourse. He presides over our judicial system and can punish the citizenry and any rogue pirates acting without a marque. But it's a two-way street, and we should be able to remove him if he fails to uphold his side of the contract."

"Then why haven't we been ruh... raided by the thuh... kingdoms? Together, they have greater numbers."

"Two reasons. First, we're surrounded by a system of reefs, and only one ship can enter or exit at a time. It's folly to send an amphibious assault, and a blockade is impossible, due to the spacing that they would have to maintain. Also, they don't have access to the secrets of the reef. Only the Inner Sanctum are entrusted with that passage. They can't keep us in or fight us as we come and go as we please. The unified Empire is our only threat. The Cove pays a 'tax' each year to the Esterling family to keep the heat off. They know that if we wanted, we could completely disrupt their entire global enterprise and could tear apart their tenuous hold on the empire itself. So, they usually turn a blind eye to our malfeasance and take our bribes."

"Won't that change, now that one of their sons has been kidnapped?"

"I honestly do not know, Sippen. That move was unexpected and may signify lack of prudence on the part of Artema."

"Thuh... this is our apartment." The men had arrived at a small two-story building in the merchant quarter. Sippen unlocked the door, and they entered. The downstairs was outfitted as a smith shop with small kilns and furnaces but were unlike any that Kernigan had ever seen.

"Why are they shaped like that?"

Without stuttering, the little man proudly explained, "I can get the impurities out of the iron, better than traditional methods. My steel is stronger and cleaner than most."

"I see. Can you make these bigger? Can you mass produce?"

"That was the plan when I designed them, but then we fled Fjorik and I have been using them simply to resource my puh... pet projects."

"What's this?" Kernigan picked up what appeared to be a small cannon with a wooden grip fashioned to hold the barrel away from the person wielding it.

"I call it a huh... hand cuh... cannon. But I cannot get the ruh... right steel hardness to contain a buh... big enough explosion. I keep cuh... cracking the barrels. I think that I also need hotter buh... burning powder. Right now, the projectile is only effective at tuh... ten paces. I would like to make it more accurate and uh... able to enter a pig cuh... carcass at twenty paces, before I trust it with my luh...life. I hate swords and I luh... love cannons."

Samani stared blankly at Sippen. Finally, he spoke, "You're a genius. If you can get this worked out, then you'll have single handedly changed warfare. How fast do you think these will take to load?"

The impish man smiled at the flattery. "Fuh... faster than a real cuh... cannon, but sluh... slower than a sword. I need to fuh... find a way to defend against muh... more than two ah... attackers during a minute's luh... loading. That depends, of course, on how I will carry the puh... powder to keep it dry."

"Can you make it into a longer-range weapon? Something that could pick off lines of men from range on the battlefield?"

Sippen looked thoughtful and then nodded. "If I can get the steel right, then yes. The luh... longer barrel would be more accurate, but more likely to spuh... split due to how thin it would have to be. If it isn't thin enough, then not muh... many men could carry it into battle.

"Amazing..." Kernigan's next words were cut off by cannons exploding in report.

Both men ran upstairs and Sippen threw open the door to the master balcony. From their vantage point on the harbor, they could see that *Wench's Daughter* had been fired upon by both Northern batteries. The ship's main mast ripped free and fell with a crash into the deck. The batteries fired another salvo, directly impacting the main body of the wounded ship and crew. Artema Horn's flagship imploded from both sides, splintering into pieces. A third salvo fired, and the magazine exploded in the entrance to the harbor.

Chapter Thirteen

Braen left his stateroom and approached the oak door leading to Eusari's cabin. He knocked and she swung it open, motioning for him to enter. She wore a flowing robe of black silk, with very little underneath. He could make out the small shape of her nipples as they lightly pressed against the cloth, reaching up to touch the cold night. On her hands she wore black silk gloves. *Always gloved,* he thought to himself, painfully keeping his eyes on hers. Although she was pleasing and he was a man, this woman was not his Hester. He finally averted his eyes from her to take in the room.

A table had been set with rich foods from her homeland. Loganshire was filled with fertile farmland, and hogs and beef cattle augmented diets of corn, wheat, and barley. The nearby forests provided her people with venison, truffles and root vegetables, all of which were represented in the feast. The table was set with fare that would be found in a farmland banquet or celebration.

"That's quite a spread, Captain Eusari." Braen tried to focus on the food, and not what else might be offered on the menu.

"Your family has raided my people for generations. Always taking what's not yours." She smiled. "I thought that I'd offer on my own what your family has always taken from mine." She ran her hands down the sides of her breasts as she said this, insinuating much more than the meal.

"That isn't what I came here, for, tonight. I'm sorry, I need to go."

Eusari moved to block the door, grabbed his hand and tried to lead him back to the table. "Have a seat, Braston. I was only teasing."

Braen sat in the chair, but his mind was swimming. This woman, who had been so cold in their first meeting and so nonchalant in their last was acting so brazen. She was an enigma. "I... I'm not comfortable with this. If it's some kind of a joke, or if you're trying to make me feel bad for some reason, then it's working. I've never taken from Loganshire."

Eusari's eyes narrowed. "Oh really? The son of Krist Braston has never raided Loganshire?"

"No. Well, not really."

"Which is it, Prince of the North? Did you, or didn't you?" Eusari's eyes changed during the exchange. Braen recognized a deep hatred within the dark green ring against the white.

"I... I'm sorry. Tradition has guided my people for centuries. When I was eighteen, my father brought my brother Skander and me on a raid."

"And?"

"Is this why you have scorned me since we met? Because I tagged along when my family raided yours? Eusari, I've left my clan forever, and I reject their tradition. I hope that you can forgive me. I feel nothing but remorse for my past life and for the sins of my father."

"Relax. I didn't bring you here to dig up the past." Eusari replaced her vixen charm with a disarming smile. Pausing to pick up a robe from her bed, she draped her shoulders. Much to his relief, the robe also covered her breasts. "We're partners on this venture and Artema has entrusted you to my care. I just want to make up for the rocky start to our friendship." She picked up two cups and held one out to him. "Can't we let bygones be bygones?" She toasted her goblet against his and each of them sipped.

Eusari sat down across from Braen and cut a beef rib from the rack. Gone was the sensual nymph that had opened the door, replaced with a girl in a robe wearing black gloves with her elbows on the table and gnawing at the meat on the rib.

"Seriously. What's all of this about?" Braen's shock was gone, replaced by a little anger at the insults. He took a long draw from his goblet which Eusari re-filled immediately.

"I hate your people."

"I see."

"Well, not all of them, really. Mostly just your family."

"I need to go." Braen tried to push back from the table, but she held up a hand.

"Hear me out, Braston son of Braston." Braen downed his cup which she quickly refilled. "I was thirteen years old when your family raided my town. Your father was battling my father and the other men of my village on the edge of the square. Most of us women and children were huddled in our homes, but I watched from my door with my mother."

"A teen wearing your family crest, pushed into our home and struck my mother in the head with the hilt of his axe, knocking her to the ground. Two other men followed him in, and they grabbed my arms. They leaned me over a table while the boy brutalized my mother. He raped her with his axe until she died, Braston."

"I... I'm sorry. I had nothing to do with this." Braen tried to stand, but he felt the wine spin in his head and fell back into the seat.

Eusari stoop, picking up the rib bone off her plate and waving it in the air as she talked. "He screamed at her while he raped her, calling himself the 'heir to the north.' When he finished, and after he had brought the axe down, burying it in her skull, he turned on me with the weapon between his legs."

"Wh... What is this?" Braen could not focus. "What does this have to do with me?" His senses spun within the room and he picked up his goblet. A sticky residue clung to the sides. "Did you drug me?" Everything in his sight was blurred, except for the gloved hand holding the rib bone like a scepter.

"When you were finished with my mother, you ruined me, Braen. An innocent girl, years younger than you. After you stole my mother from this earth, you stole my innocence and pride. You called yourself the heir to the North. That was you. The oldest son of Krist Braston. The heir to the Northern Kingdom."

Braen's vision swam. He looked at the wine in his goblet and then up at Eusari. He tried to reach for the knife on his back, but felt his weight shift in the chair, suddenly losing balance and falling to the deck. Light flashed in his head as he struck hard.

"Careful, Lord Braston. I'd hate for you to be unconscious, too soon." Eusari strode to where he lay, reached down, and gently pulled the cutlass and axe from his side. These, she nonchalantly tossed on the bed before returning to retrieve his knife. "You know, the best way to disarm a heavily armed man is to charm him into submission."

"B...But..." Braen stammered as he sluggishly tried to reach out toward her, grasping only the air where her arm had once been. A soft rapping came from the door, and Braen watched as several Eusaris made their way to answer the knock.

"I hope that you haven't killed him, we need him for a higher purpose, Eusari." A low rumble of a male voice reached the prince as he lay on the floor, helpless.

"Not at all. I just started to have my real fun." Her voice purred with glee.

"Do you mind if I watch?"

"You're a sick bastard."

"I'm the sick bastard?" The male's voice rang out in laughter.

Her footfalls were always soft, but this time they thumped in Braen's ears like large drums in a tiny room. "Braen. Listen to me, Braen. A wolf doesn't always kill its prey outright. Sometimes... Sometimes she will toy with her food before devouring it with a beating heart. The meat tastes sweeter from the fear."

Braen tried to answer. He tried desperately to speak through the sludge of his mind but could only manage a low groan.

"Don't speak, Lord Braston. You're drugged with a special concoction. You're not paralyzed, only nearly so and your senses are heightened so that you'll feel all the pain of my family. All the violence that I've endured, you'll experience." From out of nowhere, something hard struck his left ribcage. A cracking sound rang from his side. "But it'll not be enough because I hate you. I hate your entire family. In fact, hate does not even come close to the pain that you're about to receive." Another blow struck him between the legs, sending a rumbling sensation through his stomach. Braen wretched.

His heightened senses revealed that another person had entered the cabin, and the male's voice boomed in his ears like an unholy choir, "Marcus! I see that you are up and about. You couldn't stay away from this fun, either?"

"Just ensuring that she keeps him alive, Artema. His brother will pay me handsomely for his living body, and nothing for a corpse. Another blow struck Braen in the crotch. Unable to fight back and now fully paralyzed from all bodily function except thought, he felt Eusari removing his breeches. When he realized why she was still holding the rib bone, he wept.

The explosion in the harbor blasted warm air through the open window, knocking both Sippen Yurik and Samani Kernigan onto the floor. Both men briefly lost their breath as a deafening explosion rocked the entire building and plaster and dust fell around them. Samani quickly scrambled to his feet and gave a hand to Sippen.

The little man felt around on the floor and retrieved his glasses. "Suh... someone assassinated Horn!"

"Nevra."

"Thuh... that must be why he posted the extra puh... patrols!"

"Aye. He owns the city guard and apparently the guns on the walls. *Why didn't I see this coming?* I've been watching him all this time and knew that he was up to something.

"Whuh... we need to fluh... flee. Geh... get out on *Ice Prince.*"

Samani looked at the little man standing in the center of the room covered with ash and wiping his lenses on his dirty shirt. "Can we get past the batteries?"

Sippen returned the glasses to his face and and focused his eyes on Kernigan. With a mischievous grin that gave him a childlike appearance he said, "Yes. Yes, we can." He did not stutter, and so Kernigan believed him.

Samani chased the little man down the workshop. Sippen stopped to load objects into a canvas bag and thrust a second into his arms, directing which of his many inventions were the most important to save. Loaded down, both men ran out of the building and into the streets. As they emerged outside, they collided with a warzone.

Troops loyal to Artema Horn fought desperately against their mercenary counterparts but were rapidly losing ground. The keep must have fallen quickly, possibly even before the batteries turned on the ship, as infantry in tight and organized formations filed out. Troops loyal to Nevra had been pre-positioned in key areas around the city and quickly captured men, killing those foolish enough to fight back.

Samani pointed to the merchant square. "A six-man squad is headed this way. Do you think that they're looking for us?"

Nodding agreement, Sippen handed his new friend one of his hand cannons and pulled him down an alleyway. The squad started running and were quickly closing the gap.

Looking at the cannon, Samani asked, "Has this one been tested?"

"No. Luh... let me know if it works."

"Great. I will write a full report after I field test it. Where're we going?"

"Wuh... we picked this apartment for a reh... reason. Quick eh... escape to the puh... pier." At the end of the alley was a bluff overlooking an embankment. Hidden behind a planter box was a rope with a grappling hook. Sippen attached this to the wall, and then pointed to another string attached to the hook. "Ruh... rappel

down the rope, buh... but duh... don't touch this struh... string."
He disappeared over the side and skillfully rappelled twenty feet
to the ground. Tucking his cannon into his waistband, Samani
followed him over the side with much less grace.

The squad reached the top of the embankment at the exact
moment that the fugitives' feet hit ground. The lead pursuer
grabbed the rope and started climbing over the edge. Sippen
reached up and tugged the string, slipping the rope free of the
grappling hook. The guardsmen plummeted twenty feet to the
ground with a thud that sounded like glass shattering. Turning,
the two men ran raced full speed toward the pier. Shouts of pursuit
from above warned that their lead was short lived.

They reached the pier after *Ice Prince* had tossed lines but
pulled the gangplank. Guardsmen fought on deck with Krill and
the rest of the crew, the men of *Ice Prince* gaining and pushing
them back. Five guardsmen with swords drawn stood between
Samani and Sippen's freedom, five more quickly closing from
behind.

Sippen recognized Amash leading the group with his partner
Turat. Turning to Samani, he said, "Ih... It's ok. That is our fuh...
friend, Amash. "Wh... what is guh... going on?"

Amash stared beyond Sippen toward the five assailants. "Get
us the hell out of here, Sip. With Artema gone, we'd rather take
our chances and meet up with Braston."

Turat, his smaller partner, nodded in agreement. "Yeah! Nevra
is leading a mutiny, and we want off this island!"

Amash pleaded, "We know that you can get out of here, Sip.
Take us with you."

Kernigan pointed behind him. "Get them off our tail, and you
have a deal!"

Amash and his squad formed a line in front of the two men, out
of breath and panting. Turat, as usual, stood next to his partner
as they stood their ground. When the squad was nearly in sword
range, Turat pivoted and stabbed his sword into the side of Amash,

finding the exposed ribcage between the plates of his light armor and driving the point into his vital organs. The big friendly guard spit out red blood and fell into a heap on the pier.

Turat then wheeled and faced the two very startled men. Samani, without thinking, drew the borrowed hand cannon, pointed it at Turat's head and pulled the little lever on the handle. Half of Turat's face exploded in blood, brains and shards of skull that shattered onto his advancing friends. The sound was deafening and everyone on the pier shared the same ringing of the ears. Kernigan and the eight remaining guards stared at the cannon while Sippen beamed like a proud father. Knowing that it was empty, and knowing that they did not, he raised it toward the advancing five. They fled the way that they had come.

Handing the cannon back to Sippen, he said, "It works."

"Kuh… keep it. And thuh… thanks for the report." The little inventor smiled as they turned and raced down the pier. The ship's crew had fought off the wave and yelled for them to hurry aboard.

Gunnery Sargent Krill met them as they stumbled across the brow. "Your orders, First Mate?" Sippen, still smiling, pulled the one-eyed man to the side for a brief conversation. When they finished, Krill loudly yelled to the crew, "Avast! Lower the yardarm and full sails! We be about to slide outta this harbor like cum down your mudder's leg! Gunners! Load the cannon with carcass!"

Samani, ears still ringing from the hand cannon, asked Sippen, "Did he say carcass?"

The little man, smiling even broader and said, "Wait until you see THIS shit!" After the way that his morning had gone so far, and, since the strange little man did not stutter, Samani Kernigan knew that it would be the truth, he would not believe ANY of the shit that this little genius pulled off.

Lord Stefan Nevra sat on the throne in Pirate's Cove. The entire Coup lasted only a half hour, and most loyalists had quickly surrendered once it was obvious that Horn had "died" in the explosion. Of course, he hadn't really died. He had slipped onto *She Wolf* and was currently sailing off to trade that idiot Northman to his tyrant brother. Artema had promised Stefan that he would take the reins when he retired, and he had gone out in style. Nevra knew that pirates didn't care who issued their marques or levied their taxes, quickly forgetting their past loyalty to Artema Horn.

One problem nagged Stefan incessantly and it stood in the way of a perfect transition of power. Samani Kernigan had somehow disappeared during the brief fighting and had most likely hidden on the island. He would send his city guard door to door until he turned up. Of course, this was a pirate town. Pirates were consummate smugglers who shared an obsession with hiding people and goods. If he didn't find him soon, Kernigan would turn into a ghost whispering, "rebellion" into the ears of the sheep.

"Lord Nevra!" Captain Pogue entered the hall.

"What? Tell me you have him."

"We almost did, sir. He ran onto *Ice Prince* and they're trying to get underway from the harbor. We'll have him soon, since he can't get past the batteries."

Smiling, Nevra stood and walked to the balcony overlooking the harbor. There, on the water, he could see the northern lord's ship pulling away from the pier. Grapeshot was firing out of the starboard guns, keeping the city guard at bay and out of reach. The ship was racing down the length of the pier and starting to catch wind. "Those idiots have their full sails open in the harbor. They're trying to sprint by the guns."

Pogue nodded. "All batteries have orders to sink any ship that tried to follow *Wench's Daughter*. They won't succeed. Today is your day, Sir. Congratulations."

Nevra nodded absently and continued to watch as the ship tore down the pier, noting its' shallow hull and sleek design. *Those north men really know how to make a boat.* Clear of the pier, the ship raced headlong toward the opening. The northern battery reported the first cannon salvo and *Ice Prince* snaked hard to port, underneath the shot and carful to stay out of range of the southern battery. It turned again to starboard and exposed itself. Shrewd move, but when they come around again to port, they will be in range of both batteries.

A salvo exploded from the portside guns. This was not a problem to Nevra, since the reinforced bunkers fully protected the batteries. The only vulnerability was from above, and cannon balls and grape shot were not effective in a lob. Nevra leaned over the rail of the balcony. "What the hell kind of ordinance is THAT?" His pox covered face scrunched up into a sneer, as he watched twenty-five canvas wrapped projectiles burn in the air as they lobbed over the rampart. As soon as they landed on stone, each exploded into a puff of smoke. Combined, the smoke cloud of fog clung to the parapet.

Nevra recoiled in horror as his gunners chocked and gagged in the cloud, some leaping off the battery and into the water. *Ice Prince,* instead of racing toward the open sea, turned in the harbor and moved out of range of the southern guns and toward the pier. The cloud lingered on the parapet and Nevra stood aghast, staring at his unmanned arsenal. Turning hard to port, *Ice Prince* again turned away from the pier, this time making a beeline to the southern battery. A gust of wind caught the open sails, propelling it at breakneck speeds. The lone battery fired.

Nevra held his breath. The ship was moving so fast that the salvo sailed over the mast and harmlessly into the water. Turning to port, the starboard guns fired and lobbed those funny canisters up and onto the parapet. The result was identical to the previous attack. The fog quickly enveloped the entire area, forcing the men to retreat from the smoke.

Ice Prince sped off between the batteries and cleared the entrance of the harbor. Forty men could be seen bending over on the fantail of the ship, exposing their buttocks to the harbor and sticking their middle fingers up, into the air. Although he could not distinguish between asses, Lord Stefan Nevra knew that Samani Kernigan was among them.

Chapter Fourteen

Robert Esterling observed the arrival of the refugees from atop the westernmost city gate. The young prince pulled anxiously at his white military jacket, straightening it and tucking the shirt underneath.

"Stop fidgeting, your excellency. The men are watching."

Looking up at his mentor, Robert apologized, "I can't help it. It's itchy and keeps sliding around. It's also too stiff and I can barely breath."

The general let out a chuckle. "That symbolizes how uncomfortable leadership is at the top."

Eyes growing wide, the prince remarked, "Seriously? Why would they do that..." He cut off when his mentor began laughing. Some of the gathered politicians shot the general admonishing glares in response to his inappropriate humor at such a serious event. He just waved and smiled back at them. When one of the officials continued to stare, Max blew him a kiss. The man turned around in a huff, face red.

"Sarai says that it doesn't look right on me. That I am a statesman, not a warrior. She said that I look like a child wearing his father's clothing when I put it on."

"Wise girl. She has you pegged, princeling." Looking back over his shoulder he frowned at the sad state of the city defenses. He scanned the full squad of city guard, a force of one thousand, spread thin along the wall and also in reserve inside the city square. "This lot is pathetic. I wish that I could commit our own troops to help.

Unfortunately, we're merely observers until the walls are actually breeched."

"Rules of engagement…"

Maximus nodded. "Rules of engagement," he agreed. The general commanded the Imperial army in Weston, but his detachment sat in reserves further within the city for the reason that Robert had stated. It pained him to stay out of the potential conflict, but he had no choice. Without orders from the Queen Regent and the Chancellor, his troops, a contingent of two thousand, could only engage if the Pescari actually invaded the city and broke through the walls. Politics, the prince thought.

Changing the subject, Robert pointed over the side of the wall. "That's a lot of Pescari, Max."

Reeves estimated that the strength was fifteen thousand men, women, and children as they assembled before the gates. So far, they had not displayed hostility, perhaps realizing that they lacked the siege equipment necessary to fell or get over the wall. "It's the biggest assemblage that I've ever seen. Usually they stay in groups of no more than one hundred, with mounted squads of fifty warriors, at most." He looked through the spy glass. "I estimate nearly eight thousand warriors. This is insane."

"Why are they lining up with the warriors away from the walls? They're putting women and children between us."

"Religion, Boy. Their god rises in the East and sets in the West. The ever-watchful eye of Felicima, they call it. They hide their strength from her so that when she rises, tomorrow, she will see the women and children instead of the warriors."

Robert nodded, "So we are only threatened if they move the warriors to the walls, and the women to the rear?"

"Exactly. But an attack like that will only happen after sunset, when their god isn't looking."

"Does Horslei know that?" Robert and Max looked toward the city official, nervously talking with the officers of his guard.

"I sure as hell hope so."

"I keep hoping for a peaceful solution, Max." Robert thought again about Sarai, considering their earlier conversation about the humanitarian faction within the city. "Would it be so bad if they helped teach the Pescari how to farm and live as neighbors?"

"Why the fuck would you think that's even possible? You're a smart kid, princeling. You can train a dog but not these savages."

Robert cringed at the harsh words. "Please don't call them savages, Max. They're refugees." Movement in the camp caught his eye and he pointed, "Look! Two of them are approaching the gate on horseback."

Max raised his eyeglass, aiming it at the duo. "That's just a man and a boy. A teen, by the looks of him." He continued to watch carefully. "That can't be right. Even if the man is one of the Shappans, he would not be speaking without the authority of the elder council. This must be a messenger."

As they neared, the man began to address the gate, shouting his words loudly in broken Andalonian. "Your Shapan is invited to feast with us. Bring your council and meet with our elders in peace, and you will not be destroyed. You have the promise of Taros." After speaking, the man and the boy turned their horses and made their way back to the westernmost extent of the camp.

Robert looked to Horslei, watching to see his reaction. As he feared, the city official had taken offense to the invitation to parlay. Max grabbed his shoulder, "Come along boy. We need to fix this before it gets out of hand." The general collapsed his spyglass and returned it to a pouch on his belt before hurrying Robert into the palace.

Abraham Horslei, after hearing the challenge from the savage, called an emergency meeting in his war room. The room was filling up fast, as most of his advisors had been on the gate and heard the challenge. Abe was seated at the head of the table, with the captain of the city guard, Sam Troly, on his immediate right.

General Reeves and the Esterling child were seated together on his left, and the rest of the city leaders were scattered around the table. One of the Falconers stood in the corner, looking menacing in his hood and feathered collar.

The governor watched as Cassus Eachann slid into the room and stood near the wall, shadowed by some of his political patsies. They would no doubt push for a humanitarian solution, rather than the military option that he was about to propose.

Abe ordered a guardsman standing nearby. "We have everyone that we need, seated here." He gestured to the host of people, mostly noblemen and heads of the most influential houses. "Get the rest of these onlookers out into the hall."

Eachann protested, "Abraham! We are invested in this city and have a right to hear what is decided!"

"Only in a democratic meeting of the council, and this most certainly is not. This is different. We are defending the city, Cassus."

"But the charter states that defense of the city is decided by council!"

"The charter also states, that in times of imminent danger, the governor has the right to order martial law!" Abe's face was red with anger and did not have time for politics.

"By a vote of the council!" The noble had pushed past the guard and was challenging Abe, standing directly over him in his chair.

"Except when a foreign army stands on the doorstep to the city!" Abe stood up and screamed into the challenger's face.

"That is NOT an army! Those are refugees demanding food and shelter!" A host of cheers erupted from the multitude of politicians standing around the room as Eachann made his push.

Abe went quiet. Perhaps he had underestimated the sympathy that the city leaders would have for the host of hungry animals at the gates. When he finally spoke, it was with determination. "Captain, remove the civilians from this chamber." As an afterthought, he added, "Also, take Mr. Eachann into custody and confine him to a cell."

Cries of protest erupted, as Captain Troly and his men ushered them out.

Casus Eachann shouted, "This is against the charter, Horslei! The people of Weston will not stand for this!" Two guards grabbed him and dragged him from the room.

After the room had cleared Abe looked toward the men still seated at the table. "What is our food situation?"

The minister of agriculture cleared his throat, "We have an abundance in the silos. We could easily feed the refugees and our city patrons for the entire year, at least long enough for aid to arrive from the Imperial stores."

Abe looked at the old man with a scathing frown, "Not the rabble. I do not give two shits about the savages. Do we have enough food to survive a siege?"

"Yes, your excellency, we can easily survive two years." The man squirmed, and looked at General Reeves, who stared straight ahead.

"General, what are your thoughts on mustering an attack on their camp?"

The general turned and looked at the governor, a look of shock and disbelief on his face. "Say that, again, Abe. But slower and in your own head, before you make a total fool out of yourself."

Feeling his face again turn scarlet, Horslei asked again, "I'm attacking their camp. Do you stand with me, or not, General Reeves?"

"I'm not authorized by the Queen Regent or the Chancellor to dispatch my troops in an offensive campaign. If you were to do so with your company of guard, devoid of cavalry, you would lose your city in a matter of minutes." The general spoke slowly and deliberately, but the undertones were there.

Abe did not like Maximus Reeves, and barely tolerated his presence in his city. *But he's right.* Without him committing his troops, an attack would be impossible. "Perhaps, but I certainly cannot meet with their elders."

The general looked back at him. "That is actually very true, Abraham. You are prevented from doing so by decree of the Empire. Only an ambassador named by the Esterling family has that authority to negotiate with foreign nations outside of your walls. That includes the "rabble" as you called them, that grossly outnumber your pathetic little force and stand outside of your gate."

All eyes in the room looked at Robert Esterling, whose official title was Imperial Ambassador to the City of Weston. He sat up straighter, trying not to fidget, as they focused on him.

Abe Horslei slammed his fist down on the table in anger as Maximus and Robert rose together and left the room.

Sarai rushed up to Robert as he and General Reeves left the war room, letting the door slam behind them. Robert turned to his mentor, and said,

"I'll meet you in the stable, Max. I need to talk to Sarai for a moment." The general nodded and strode off down the hallway.

"What happened in there? Why did they arrest Eachann?"

Robert smiled, "There is a definite split in city leadership, Sarai. Eachann and his faction dissented and want to feed the refugees."

"Then my urgings to him worked. I didn't think that he was actually listening to me, when I met with him." She beamed with pride that she had planted the seed in the politician's head.

Robert frowned, "Sarai, your father wants to attack the Pescari, but Max will not commit my mother's troops."

Her smile dropped abruptly, and a tear flowed down her face, "What are you two going to do?"

Robert smiled, "We're going to meet with them and figure out a compromise. As the official ambassador, I'm the only person in Weston who is authorized to meet with the Shapan."

Sarai reached up and kissed him. After she pulled away, she smiled said, "Do the right thing, Robert. Be the humanitarian."

A few moments later, Robert and Maximus sat atop their horses at the city gate. The guard refused to let them leave the city and had quoted some directive from the governor. The general raised up his hand, and six of his elite force moved out of the shadows to stand next to the city soldiers. They quickly acquiesced and opened the gates, allowing the two men to ride out into the night. Robert turned, and saw that the gate closed behind them.

"Don't worry, they'll also ensure that they let us back in when we return."

Nodding, Robert swallowed, and followed Max through the Pescari camp. The people had erected tents constructed from poles that they had dragged behind them when they arrived. By lashing them at the top, they stretched furs and skins around them, forming a cone-like structure in which they could sleep away from the elements. Although he had read about and studied the Pescari, seeing them up close gave him an entirely different respect.

They were a wretched people. Even in the dark of night, he could see that. They looked half-starved as well as leathery and sad. He noticed that even the children wore the same hard expression on their faces as the adults. Sarai had warned him of this. She had taught him that they had originally controlled the plains east of the Misting River, where Weston currently stood. But when the Westonese people had arrived with their superior weapons, they had driven the Pescari deeper into the steppes and across the Forbidden Waste. The treaty was the beginning of their misery, he surmised. Hopefully, he and Sarai would be able to reverse their fate by securing some semblance of humanitarian aid.

They finally approached the large tent at the westernmost edge of the camp. They dismounted and made their way to the opening. Two warriors met them at the entrance and held back the flap to grant them entrance. Robert turned to the general and whispered, "They didn't even take our weapons!"

"Shh, Boy! Quiet!"

Inside sat a circle of elders, just as Max had told him that they would find. What he did not expect was to see the same young teen that had ridden with the man to the city gates. The boy sat in the circle of the elders as if he were equal among them. The man who had spoken, presumably the Shappan, sat on the right hand of the teen. A man with a brand in the shape of a handprint sat on the teen's left. Robert and his mentor took their place in the circle and watched as one of the men sprinkled a bowl of herbs on the fire in the middle. The flame turned blue and roared to life.

After a few moments, the boy spoke in Pescari, and the man on his right translated. "Taros, Shapan of the Pescari welcomes you to his council. I am Teot, uncle to the Shapan, and I will mediate."

Max sat up at the words, and asked, "Which tribe?"

The man spoke to the boy, apparently called Taros, who answered in his language. With a smile, he addressed the general. "All of them."

Robert had known Maximus Reeves his entire life but had never seen him stiffen in shock as he did at that moment. The general swallowed and tried to appear as calm as possible when he answered. "That isn't the Pescari way. On what authority does he claim the right of Shapan?"

The man answered, "By right of Shapalote, Taros speaks for all clans."

"No. Felicima would not allow this. Felicima demands homage and acquiescence, not strength. Not a unified Pescari."

This time, the teen spoke without using his translator. "Felicima has given her power to me and I rule the Pescari while she spends all of her time riding the sky. I am the god, here."

Max looked at the boy's translator, who simply nodded. Turning back to look at the boy, he asked, "What do you demand, from my people, Taros of the Pescari?"

"I think that you mean, HIS people." Taros pointed at Robert, who blanched at being singled out.

Breaking his silence, Robert asked, "Yes. What do you want from MY people, Taros of the Pescari?"

"I want food. And I want you to share your city with my people. It is large and we are desperate for protection from the caldera. The eruptions have been more frequent, and we are no longer safe on the Steppes of Cinder."

General Reeves spoke up, cutting off Robert before he could answer. "We can't agree to that. That's a decision for the council and must be put to a vote."

"I will bring it to the council." The words had left Robert's mouth before he knew that he was going to answer.

Maximus shot Robert a glance that chilled his blood. "What my esteemed comrade means, is that we will discuss the matter and let those with the power decide.

At that moment, a Pescari woman entered the tent, earning protests from the elders within. She pushed past the warriors and spoke in rapid Pescari to Taros. He abruptly jumped to his feet and ran into the night. Many of the elders gave chase, and Robert looked to Max with shock.

"Stay close," Max warned, "we're winging this, and something is wrong. Be ready to flee."

The two men left the tent, and saw a group gathered at a smaller tent just a few mounds over. They pushed their way through the crowd and gained a front row perspective. Taros screamed and wailed inside the tent, and the Pescari became extremely agitated at his outburst. Robert leaned and peaked through the flap, gaining a glimpse of Taros. He appeared to be kneeling beside a woman, lying in blankets.

The man who had been translating, approached the two men. Robert recognized that his name was Teot, as he said, "My sister lies dying in that tent, and my nephew will not take this, well. Please leave, and we will meet again, soon."

Max nodded and tried to steer Robert toward the horses.

"No." The prince pulled back his arm. "I have a duty to protect these people, Maximus." Robert pointed at Taros in the tent and began walking backward toward him, his eyes on the general's. "The nobles of Weston agree, Max! We MUST help these people!"

The camp abruptly went dark. Max and Robert looked around. Thousands of fires had suddenly and simultaneously winked out. Everything was suddenly thrust into blackness. Robert, who was looking toward the city wall, watched as every torch on the wall followed suit, one by one until they entire city was extinguished. And then the boy roared.

Robert turned as Taros screamed from within the tent and a sudden ball of light emanated from within, exploding in a brilliant fireball.

The Pescari man who had been urging them to flee, began to cry. "Run. Please go. This is our burden. GO!"

Robert felt himself lurch into the air as Max threw him over his shoulder, running toward the horses. Looking back, bouncing as the general ran, Robert's eyes reflected the bright light that burst from the boy's body, scorching the still body of his mother. In Robert's eyes the fireball grew, and then exploded into thousands of smaller fires that shot out from his fingertips as he pointed toward the city. The Prince could hear screams of terror as men burned alive atop the wall.

The elder Esterling son felt his air leave his body in a single blow, as Maximus threw him across the back of his steed. Sitting and trying to right himself in the saddle, his head turned to face the city wall and gate. The wooden door was aflame as men ran and threw themselves from the rampart, screaming in terror as their clothes and bodies burned. General Maximus Reeves grabbed the reigns of Robert Esterling's horse and led them full gallop into the forest and away from the city.

CHAPTER FIFTEEN

Braen lay on the soft grass, eyes closed with a gentle spring wind brushing against his face. He breathed in deeply, smiling wide as the breeze brought the soft scent of lilac to his nose. He held that breath in, praying to the gods that he would never forget both this moment and her scent.

Her body was pressed against his, her firm breasts exposed against his bare chest as they slipped from her half-unbuttoned blouse. His arms held her warm body and his mouth searched for hers, joy rising within him as her soft supple lips danced and teased with his own. His own body pulsed with blood as he felt her hips press into his, rubbing slightly with pressure.

After they had pulled away, she whispered, "I wish that you were not leaving me, Braen."

"I have to go, Hester. Father is taking us raiding in Loganshire at a place called Brentway. He said that we're to become men."

Smiling, she reached her hand down and grabbed ahold of his pulsing manhood through his breeches. "You are more than a man enough, now, Braen."

He laughed and kissed her again, rolling her over on her back as he did. She squeezed tighter and tighter, the pain radiating through his crotch and into his stomach as she bore down with all of her strength. He opened his mouth to breath, feeling several of his ribs crack against the knife that she had plunged into his back.

Opening his eyes, he saw the stale floorboards of a ship's hold, soaked and stinking metallic with his blood. Tears rolled down his face as he realized that he had again held and lost his love.

The door opened and footsteps approached. Braen resigned to lay on the floor, all his strength drained over several days of beatings. Although he knew that he was to be sold to his brother, he silently wished that he would die along the way to the exchange. He growled as rough hands grabbed his bound arms and heaved him from the floor.

Eusari's voice could be heard directing her thugs. How could so much hate exist within one person? Why couldn't she believe that he had nothing to do with the death of her family? Two of her brutes dragged him from the room, pausing briefly to allow someone to punch him in the nose.

He awoke a few moments later to muffled voices. Someone mentioned payment and he recognized Skander's voice among the rest. Braen felt a small chuckle leave his mouth. He opened his left eye as much as he could, unable to open his right one at all. As he peered through the blood, Skander's face came into focus and Braen struggled to lift his head. Any fury that he had previously held toward his brother momentarily faded as he glimpsed the face of his childhood playmate, confidant, friend and brother.

"Skander," the name crawled as a whisper from his lips.

"The younger Braston brother stepped up to lean his ear closer to hear his plea, "Yes, Brother?"

"I..." Braen struggled to speak through the copper taste of blood in his mouth. "I love you, little brother."

"Of course, you do, Brother. You always were the sentimental type." Skander laughed, and the other attendees joined in. Still leaning in, he said, "you never would've hurt a soul if you didn't have to. Always the thinker, never mean enough." He then brought up his steel gauntleted hand into Braen's ribs, cracking some more. Braen again passed out.

Estowen's landing was an abandoned port town with a functional pier that could accommodate smaller ships such as *She*

Wolf. The empire had long abandoned the town and its small port when it adopted larger vessels. Its' Navy preferred the larger, more secure ports down the coast, farther from the Northern Kingdom. Although the town was devoid of human life, climbing vines had overtaken the crumbling buildings had no doubt become home to lesser, four, six or eight legged lifeforms.

Standing at the hatch that led below deck, Eusari motioned for two men to retrieve the Northman. At some point Braen had passed out from the pain, and they had little difficulty picking him up from the floor after unlocking his chains. As they dragged him toward the hatch, she watched him with satisfaction, knowing that he would soon fully pay for the crimes against her and her family. She had wanted to kill him, but she had been made to promise an intact, live delivery. Instead, she motioned for the men to pause at the doorway. In a quick motion, she punched his nose, breaking it cleanly. His body went limp as blood stained his blonde beard orange. Eusari smiled and motioned for them to move him along.

She followed behind as her men dragged Braen's limp body across the brow of *She Wolf* and down the gangplank. Marcus Esterling and Artema Horn emerged from the quarterdeck a few minutes later. Eusari could not help but notice that the Esterling whelp bore a smug and knowing expression. The look bothered Eusari. Everything about that man disgusted her. From the moment that Artema had made her release him, she had regretted allowing him to survive the kidnapping.

The two crewmen dragged the northern prince onto the pier and down a muddy path that led to what had once been the town square. The crewmen tossed Braen in a heap on the ground before three hooded figures. One, she knew would be Skander Braston, younger brother of Braen and the current ruler of Fjorik. The others would be his guard. Behind him was a large wooden chest. Eusari scowled at the thought of trading this rapist and murderer for gold. Sa'Mond took his place beside Eusari and placed a calming hand on her shoulder. She reached up and touched his hand, ever thankful for her eunuch friend.

"Skander!" Marcus pushed by Eusari, shoving her into Sa'Mond. His big hand tightened on her shoulder, as if to warn her not to act rashly. She regained her footing and settled back to watch the exchange. The two men grasped forearms in the northern custom. Obviously, they had met in the past. Also, it was equally obvious to Eusari that the Esterling pup was currying the northern king's favor. "Did you bring my payment?"

The younger Braston pointed to the chest, "Count it, if you like, but it's all there. Let me see what you brought for me."

"Skander." Braen's voice barely squeezed past his lips.

The northern king walked toward his older brother, and leaned in with a smile, "Yes, Brother?"

Eusari strained to listen to their exchange.

"I... I love you, little brother." Blood spilled from his lips as he sputtered out the words.

"Of course, you do, Brother. You always were the sentimental type." Skander laughed and the other attendees joined in. Except for Eusari. If she could, she would feel sorry for the big man about to be sold and slaughtered. But then again, justice is justice. Still leaning in, Skander said, "you never would have hurt a soul if you didn't have to. Always the thinker, never mean enough." Eusari watched as he cracked Braen's ribs with a steel gauntleted hand. He again passed out.

Skander laughed, his hood falling back from his face as he did. Eusari stared at his features, aghast. "This is the Braen who I remember. Weak and defeated, crying and preaching love and forgiveness. Did you know," he said to Esterling, "that this great big 'warrior' never took part in the raping and pillaging during raids? No. He was so self-righteous that he would slink back to the ship after the fighting and pray for their souls. He always hated the spoils part of war." The two men exchanged a laugh before switching to talk business. Eusari could not divert her eyes from Skander Braston.

Eusari felt a pit of despair hit her stomach. Although the men looked so much alike, the crumpled heap of a man on the ground was not the rapist and sodomizer who had killed her mother and sold her into slavery. No, Skander Braston's face was unmistakably memorable and opened an uncontrollable flood of both memories and emotions. She absently stepped forward and started to draw a knife, when four more cloaked figures approached the pier. Two of whom carried another large chest. Three of the figures were clad in Imperial armor and trailed by a woman in flowing white robes emblazoned with an eagle holding a rose in its talons.

"What kind of unholy alliance is this?" Crestal Esterling, Lady Regent of the Empire, stepped out from behind her guards and addressed the men standing over Braen's lifeless body. She looked down at the unconscious prince and then at her son and the ruler of Fjorik. "You've been busy, son."

"What is in the box, Mommy?" Marcus laughed hysterically at his own joke.

"I think you know. Apparently, you manipulated this ransom. What did you do, bribe Artema horn to sell your captor to his brother for an extra bonus? That is Braen Braston, is it not?"

"What's left of him." Marcus laughed, barely containing his merriment at the joke he had played on the most powerful people in the world.

Eusari's head spun. She felt Sa'Mond's hand on her shoulder, but she was quickly losing feeling in her entire body. She looked at Artema, who laughed along with Marcus.

She shrugged off the hand and moved up to the younger Braston. Her knife flashed from her furs and sliced at the man who destroyed her family. Unfortunately, his guard saw the movement, and shoved him just enough that she missed. Her weak attack barley sliced his fur cape. Reacting, Braston's gauntleted fist came up into her face, and she fell to the ground beside Braen.

Marcus laughed harder, and his maniacal tone convulsed above her as a leather boot connected with her ribcage. She rolled and tried to stand but pain stopped her. From her hands and knees Eusari looked up at the Esterling prince. Through her thin gloves she felt the ground, wet and sticky from the blood of Braen. Her anger raged and Eusari yearned to lunge and rip out the throats of the men looming above. Her eyes met those of the prince, and she growled low and menacing.

The surrounding air fell as cold as a frozen winter night and the ground shook. Eusari could sense everything around her, the earth, the vines and even the insects crawling in the undergrowth. The earth shook more violently, and the men staggered, several leaning on a nearby wall for support. From the edge of the forest a wolf howled into the night.

The vines closest to Skander and his guards began to twist and seemingly come to life. They coiled around the Northmen like pythons, constricting and squeezing out their breath. Hundreds of spiders crawled from their cover, and up the legs of the men, biting the most tender parts of their exposed skin. The younger Braston screamed alongside his men, trapped in the vines as if they were a web.

A large hawk dove from the sky with a loud screech as it opened strong talons to grasp at the flesh of Eusari's back. Sa'Mond grabbed the falcon under its wings and ripped it from her skin, taking a chunk of leather that had once been her armor. Blood poured from her wound and she screamed. All at once, the earth stopped shaking. The vines fell limp and lost all animation as the men brushed the spiders from their faces, coughing and sputtering little black objects from their mouths.

Regaining his balance, Marcus turned to the soldier behind Lady Esterling and ordered, "Matteas, Kill the bitch." The soldier took a step forward, drew back his hood and drew his sword.

Of course, Eusari thought, this was the famed Captain-General Matteas Brohn, chief lackey of the Esterling empire. *At least I'll die at the hands of a legend.* Grasping another knife in her left hand, she rose to meet her attacker with her right arm limp at her side.

Brohn turned and swung his sword at Lady Esterling. Marcus laughed at the shocked expression on her face as her head rolled between him and Artema. Skander Braston, free from the spiders and vines, laughed nearly as maniacally as the boy. Eusari stood dumbfounded and frozen in her stance. Sa'mond and the others formed up around her. Moving together, they started shuffling her toward *She Wolf.*

She screamed, "Wait!" The man she had broken during the voyage lay on the ground and Skander's men moved toward him. "Get Braen, too!"

Sa'Mond bent to grab Braston, but the Esterling guards also advanced. The two small forces clashed before him. He shouted to the crew on the ship to make ready, then tried again to grab the unconscious man. Finally finding an opportunity to step in, he grabbed him by the tunic and began to run toward Eusari.

She felt drunk. Her shoulder ached, and warm blood oozed underneath her leathers. Staggering, she turned and tried to run toward the gangplank. She looked over her shoulder to see Sa'Mond dragging the fallen prince behind him. Safely aboard *She Wolf,* she scanned the pier and spotted a grinning Artema Horn waving farewell. He blew her a kiss and laughed.

A loud thud tore her eyes from her former friend and leader, and the lifeless body of Braen Braston fell in a heap beside her. She looked first at him, then up at Sa'Mond. Her two other guards had fallen in battle on the pier, and Sa'Mond fought two men at once on the other side of the gangplank. She started to run toward him, but he shook his head at her, and with a single kick he shoved the plank into the water, cutting off both his and the attacker's path to the ship. He shouted to the crew to shove off and they did, wind catching the sails as they pulled away. He killed both of his attackers, then turned toward his mistress with a sweeping bow.

As he raised up, the falcon returned with a screech, diving and ripping its talons into the back of his neck. He screamed as the giant bird ripped out his right eye with its sharp beak. Eusari screamed and then fell to the deck in tears, wailing as she watched Skander Braston drive his sword into the back of her comrade, the only man whom she could trust after Artema's betrayal. No, not a man. Sa'Mond was a eunuch, a former man, she realized, as the loving and tender giant died on the pier. *Will I ever trust a man, again?*

Stricken with grief she stared at her friend, bloodied and being ripped to pieces on the pier that grew smaller as *She Wolf* departed. A groan finally pulled her eyes away and she watched Braen Braston's tattered body convulse at he tried to lift himself from the planks. Kneeling, she reached out a hand and placed it on his shoulder. "I'm sorry." Tears of remorse overcame her. "I am so, so sorry, Braen."

He turned his face, blackened from the week-long beatings that he had received, and smiled softly with his magnificent icy blue eyes. "I... I forgive you."

Eusari wept.

Fatwana Nakala walked with long strides into the council chamber. Her black hair was neatly pulled back and wound into a tight bun that revealed her almond shaped eyes. Her fair skin sharply contrasted her hair, and her silk robes clung to her form as she walked with confidence and authority. Her held her stern mouth in a tight line that narrowed the look in her eyes.

As usual, the chamber was full of chatter and debate when she arrived, as the ruling body of Astian argued the catastrophe that unfolded in Andalon. The panic had grown, and Fatwana was the bearer of their anxiety. She strode directly to her chair beside the other oracles and sat down with an air of authority. The room immediately noticed her arrival, and the chatter died down as a wave of silence followed her entrance. She knew that their eyes were on her and she waited.

Chancellor Jakata slowly stood and gestured toward the oracles. "Does the Winter Oracle have information for the council?"

Fatwana stood and addressed the entire room, "It has been confirmed that the recent volcanic eruption has affected the ionic atmosphere, thereby intensifying the emotional latency of powers in certain Andalonians." She did not flinch as she spoke and paused to allow the eruption of dissent and discontent to fill the room. The chancellor tried for several minutes to calm them down until she could finally continue. "This is not a worst-case scenario, rather, we have agents in the field working to minimize the impact."

A voice shouted from the gallery, "What powers have awakened?"

Fatwana answered honestly, "So far, we have witnessed two of the four powers with Da'ash'mael." The anger in the room exploded with greater force than before. The chancellor banged his gavel repeatedly to regain order from the delegates and she continued, "The culling process has been largely successful, and the emergence seems isolated, at least for now. Unfortunately, we have an outlier. Although we earlier witnessed one of the Latents control sea creatures, we have not been able to view him or his abilities since. Our endeavors have resulted in the death of some of our coven members."

This time the chancellor spoke. "How many is some?"

Fatwana finally blanched at the question that she had hoped would not come. "Nine, your excellency."

"Nine? Did I hear you clearly? Or did you hopefully say, 'none?'"

Fatwana's calm composure broke, and she finally started to sweat under the pressure of the day, "Nine."

The room exploded in shouts of condemnation. Chancellor Jakata had no choice but to recess the council session.

PART II
WOLF OF NIGHT

On land the monster roars and walks,
Death surrounds in light and shadow.
Destroy the seed before it roots.

- The Oracle of Astian, 805th year of order

Chapter Sixteen

Chancellor Jakata wasted no time summoning Fatwana Nakala to his chambers after her report. She rapped three times on the door and was surprised when he immediately opened it, himself. Soft orchestral music played in the background.

"Light level six." At his voice, the lights in the room brightened, revealing an old-fashioned study with surrounding bookcases and antique leather furniture. "Music, stop." On his command, the music halted. "Ok. You have my attention. I hope that your plan to solve this mess is better than the speech you prepared this afternoon." He sat down in a large, brown overstuffed chair and waited patiently for her to speak.

"The experiment has not failed."

"Doesn't sound like it. Try again."

"We are not talking about a widespread awakening. So far, it has only been two Latents, and their powers are still weak."

The older man shook his grey head with disagreement, "That's not what I'm hearing. The summer oracle is talking about a very strong awakening. Full channeling of fire and his emotancy is off the charts hot. Their coven has been in a nearly constant state of Da'ash'mael since his powers awakened."

"Yes. I 've read their reports." Fatwana walked around the room as they talked, pacing with anxiety, but playing it off as if she were calmly admiring the decorations in the room. She paused in front of an Andalonian vase, Eskeran artwork, by the looks of it. "Have there been any Ka episodes?"

Jakata sat silent, watching her survey his office.

"Then our Latent is the one." She turned from the vase and looked intently at the politician. "And as soon as we find him, we can deal with him."

"I wish that it were that easy, my dear. The spring oracle also reported a Ka prophecy." Jakata smiled at the reaction on Fatwana's face when he revealed his news. He enjoyed knowing key information before the oracles.

"That. That isn't possible." She shook her head in disbelief, stunned and waiting for the joke to be revealed.

"I am afraid that it is. Apparently, a female reached full emotancy in a single instance, albeit brief. The revelation of the Ka was incomplete, and we are unaware of the significance. That's the only reason that I've not ended this experiment entirely and signaled the kill order."

"You cannot end the experiment, Jakata."

"And why is that, Fatwana?"

"I believe that there has been interference."

"Interference, how?"

"I am not positive, but I think that The Society is involved."

The chancellor shook his head in denial. "No, The Society ended with his death, Fatwana. Your brother and his followers were killed in the explosion, before they could go public."

"Perhaps so." The leader of the winter oracle left the vase and walked to the bar cart in the corner. On it was a bottle of Estonian wine, label embossed with the numbers 7, 5 and 4. She picked it up, pulled the cork and smelled it before replacing it in the bottle. It smelled like a nice vintage. "I think that members of the Humanitarian Freedom Society survived the assassination. I have reason to suspect that they are operating on Andalon and are meddling with the political framework that we instituted."

"I haven't heard of any evidence, but I have an agent placed high in the ministry of information. I will have him fan out with the Falconers to sweep and verify what you say. If any Astian is living among them, then he'll find out. I'll bring in technology, if I need to."

"That is dangerous, Jakata. You remember how much things changed when we gave them cannon to fight the Pescari?"

"More dangerous than allowing emotionally charged Latents to discover and hone their elemental powers? I'll do everything that it takes to protect the Astian way of life, Miss Nakala."

"Even genocide?"

"Yes."

"Careful, Chancellor. Talk like that could cost your re-election, and next year is an election year. The humanitarian faction has a very strong impact on your constituency."

"Get out, Fatwana. I need to think."

She bowed respectfully and then left the room. The sound of an orchestra returned, and the closing door muffled the tones of a mournful cello.

CHAPTER SEVENTEEN

The Black Forest of Diaph served as a border between Loganshire and Fjorik. Tall spruce and fir trees reached into the heavens, dropping their needles onto a carpet thickened by moss and ferns. Rainfall was abundant, and the growth tremendous and thick. Had the forest not been such a dangerous place, men from both sides would exploit it for the large game and ship-perfect lumber.

Like most borderlands, this forest was home to outlaws. They hid their camps well under the pine canopy, keeping most of their activities from even the sharpest of eyes. Travelers who dared to pass through this territory paid with either their lives or their gold, occasionally parting with both. It was for this reason that most of the shipments into and out of Diaph came strictly by sea. This prime location made the city a burgeoning trade spot, as barges and transports stopped along their way to Logan and eventually Norton.

Recently, Imperial caravans transported high-risk goods through the forest into Fjorik. These shipments were prohibited by the council, but kept certain promises made by the Esterling family in their arrangement with Skander Braston. The northern king had ample supplies of resources but no means to mass produce useful products, so the family exchanged food, plows and goods for rich iron and lumber. In return he kept his armies to the north and allowed the Falconers to freely move in and out of his kingdom.

Shon Wimbley crouched low along the roadside as one very special caravan approached. He, like his men, was camouflaged and blended into the forest. He identified the wagons using a hooded eyeglass. He quickly confirmed that they had recently left Diaph and would contain special cargo. Smiling inwardly, he thanked the reliability of his spies.

He counted twenty mounted escorts with two Falconers. He strained his eyes skyward spotting two large hawks circling the forest. Staying low to the ground, he hoped that it was not too late, and that his cover was not already blown. They possessed remarkable vision and very little escaped their gaze. As a constable he had worked closely with these monsters, strongly suspecting that they shared one mind.

Regardless of the risks involved, he and his men were searching for a special item worth the risk of death. He signaled Marque, who hid deeper in the forest away from the road. The camouflaged man crouched over several boxes with holes drilled in each. He squatted, ready to release the weapons. Waiting till the large birds were nearly directly overhead, Shon gave the second signal and Marque opened lids. He muttered a prayer for luck as dozens of black ravens flew up into the sky, directly for the hawks. Instantly, the sky filled with a cacophony of cawing and screeching as the crows harassed the larger raptors.

Wimbley stroked his black beard and signaled again. Ranged archers took advantage of the distracted birds and dropped both Falconers instantly. After they had released and nocked again, they disappeared deep into the forest to cover a possible retreat. Camouflaged crossbowmen rose from their concealment and fired bolt after bolt into the armored cavalry, catching them unaware and clearing the mounts within seconds. Overhead, the blackbirds continued to harangue the larger raptors, distracting and forcing them from the area.

The battle ended swiftly, and Shon and his men emerged from the woods. Men leapt atop the wagons, throwing back the blankets and revealing several caches of crates and boxes. These were quickly unloaded, and his small army moved like ants clearing a carcass. They removed every bit of useful material. Shon slapped Marque on the back victoriously. It had been his idea to use the ravens. "Great job, my friend. Today is yours."

Marque beamed with pride for the recognition from his leader. "Thanks, Boss."

A shout came from one of the men searching the fourth wagon. Hurrying to see what the excitement was about, Shon climbed atop the buckboard. The man held a blanket, pointing down at his find. Like the other carts, inauspicious pine boxes contained food and weapons of fine steel. But this wagon also held the treasure that he and his men sought. An intricately carved chest lay among the rest, secured by an iron lock and embossed with a falcon.

"Good find!" He waved another man over, and each of them grabbed an end of the chest. He directed the others to quickly unhitch the horses and to strap the cargo atop the animals. He wanted to make a clean getaway without blazing a road directly to the boats. Hopping down from the cart, he moved to search the Falconers.

Both specters lay on the ground, felled like common men. Marque joined Shon and stared down, sharing hesitation at touching their bodies. "This feels like the first time I gutted a deer. I knew that I had no choice, but I still felt weird about cutting open the animal."

Shon nodded his agreement. "And just like in the deer, there's shit inside and we have to grab it with our hands." He knelt next to the first corpse and ran his fingers through the pockets of the robe, turning up only a few items of necessity like flint and steel. Placing his hand under the feathered neckline, he felt and came away with nothing.

Enough of the cloth moved away to reveal skin. *Why not? We may as well see how ugly they are.* With a tug Shon removed the hood. A man's face stared up at him with open eyes as dark as coal. His black skin appeared darker than any shade he had seen, even from the Southern Continent. He was bald, without wisp of hair on head or face.

"He's definitely not from around here, Shon." Marque knelt

down beside the other and ripped the hood with more force than the bandit leader had. His Falconer stared back with large eyes of light brown, accented with thick dark eyebrows. His face was tanned olive with sharp features. He, like the other, was completely bald.

"No, Marque. They most certainly are not." Wimbley spotted what he was looking for dangling from a string around the man's neck. A key as intricate as the lock it opened shone in the light of the afternoon. He pulled it over the head of the dead administrator and shoved it down deep into the pocket of his buckskins. A thorough search revealed a small pouch hanging from the belt of the second Falconer. He cut it free. A peek inside revealed several black beads. Smiling, he turned to his partner. "Let's go." Both men hurried off to rejoin the others.

Chapter Eighteen

General Maximus Reeves held the reins of Robert's horse. They were galloping south toward the forest and away from the cacophony of fire that pummeled the city wall of Weston. The Prince looked over his shoulder at the spectacle, dazed and possibly even in shock from what he had witnessed. "Wait!" The youth shouted over the sound of the hooves on dirt. "Wait! Stop!"

Maximus pulled back on both mounts, slowing them. The seasoned soldier looked past the boy toward the refugee camp. "What is it?"

"Why are we fleeing? We have to go back!" Robert wasn't sure if he was thinking about Sarai's safety or the people of Weston, but he felt obligated to act.

"Absolutely not, I have to get you to safety." Max started to spur the horse forward.

Robert snatched his reins from his mentor. "No," he shouted, pulling his mount to a defiant stop.

"What is this? After all my tutelage, all the training that I have given you, how dare you defy me!"

Max is right, Robert thought. He had been his mentor and teacher for his entire life and deserved more respect than he was currently receiving.

"And one more thing!" The imposing general spun his horse around and stared Robert down with a mixed look of disappointment and anger. "How dare you make those promises, back there!"

In a commanding voice, Robert defiantly stood up to the ranking officer. "I am the heir to the throne, General Reeves! I have the full authority of the Imperial family and a sworn duty to act as ambassador as I see fit, and I command you to take me back into the city."

"Listen here, you little whelp of a boy! I have a sworn duty to your 'Mommy' to keep you out of harm's way. That's why she sent us to this backwoods hellhole in the first place! I'll take you and hide you in the forest, then go back and get my army out of the city."

"You'll abandon the city?" Robert's eyes looked on the general with a steady gaze, silently accusing him of cowardice. "I thought you never fled from the enemy."

"Gods be damned." Max shook his head. He spat on the ground and then smiled, proudly. "Looks like you finally found your father's blood, you little shit. Fine. Let's go see how bad this really is." He wheeled the horse around and led Robert to the north, this time toward the fire.

As they topped a hill overlooking both the gate and refugee camp, Max again pulled back on the reins. "Whoa..."

"What is it?" Robert strained his eyes to see. "Why are we stopping?"

"They've formed up. The women and children are at the rear and moving toward us."

"So, the warriors are lined up at the walls? They're attacking the city?"

"Yes. This isn't good, Robert. After that fire attack, my troops will have to engage. But with that fire flinging, tantrum throwing child leading the attack, they'll be destroyed. Gods! They'll be cooked in their armor like lobsters."

"What about the archer corps? Won't they be effective?"

"Given what we saw earlier? He'll most likely burn their arrows in the air. If we're to get in, then we need to push through, past the archers and rush the gate in the confusion." Max shook his head, "That is assuming that we don't get our backs filled full of arrows. Looking back at his protégé, he said, "Robert, we can't win this without some serious firepower."

"Max. We must try. Earlier tonight I thought of them as refugees. I wanted to be the superior but benevolent leader. You know, as my duty as a prince of the free and master world. I felt that I owed it to them as lessors and as those in need."

Reeves chuckled, "Someone's been reading too many books."

"Yes." Robert blushed a little at how naïve he and Sarai had been, thinking that they could reason with the Pescari. "Max, I thought that I owed it to them. By overruling Horslei I thought that I could secure the support of Weston's progressive nobles and legitimize myself as the future ruler of the Empire."

"And now?"

The prince let out a brief uncontrolled chuckle and answered honestly. "He's a fire flinging, tantrum throwing child who must be put down before he burns down the free world."

Max nodded. "And how will your lovey-dovey pro-humanitarian nobles feel if you ride up and stab the little shit in the back? For that matter, how will your precious Sarai feel about you?"

Robert sat up taller and his eyes narrowed, "Leave her out of this."

Max's eyes gleamed and he drew out his sword, "Just ensuring that you've covered all contingencies before we die, your excellency." With that said, General Maximus Reeves spurred his horse into a gallop and raced down the hill, breaking through the ranks of the Pescari horse archers.

Robert let out a war whoop and followed. Together they rushed the rear of the Pescari line, wind blowing past as they rode. Women and children parted like a sea before their horses and Robert made the mistake of looking into several of their faces. Once again, as before, his heart began to hurt for the struggle of these people, but he pushed this feeling down deep with the thought of Sarai still inside the besieged city.

Soon they reached the flanking horse archers. None of them were firing, rather were milling about and staring at their boy leader. *That's good,* Robert thought. *If they're not attacking, then there's a chance to get through.* His heartbeat throbbed in his ears as they sped past the bewildered Pescari.

By the time they reached the front line, arrows whizzed by him and Max. Crouching close to their horses, he marveled that none found their mark. *Aren't Pescari expert marksmen?* They had passed the line and the gate lay one hundred feet ahead. That distance displayed a horrifying sight. The boy Taros was fully engulfed in flames. The flames were emanating from his body as blue, orange, and yellow danced around him like an aura of searing light. The boy himself was untouched and unharmed.

As they rushed by Robert met the red-hot embers that had replaced the eyes of Taros. They burned fiery like a demon's as he flung death toward the city, hell bent on destruction of the gate. When those eyes locked onto his, the prince felt a surge of fear rise and he continued to stare as they raced toward the now burned-out gate. He watched in terror as a firebolt flew directly at him and Max, screaming as the ball of flame struck them.

Only it missed. Somehow, the fire curved around the two riders and their horses without singeing a hair on man or beast. Turning his head, Robert spurred his animal forward and arrows flew past on both sides. Ahead, the general leaned against the mane of his own horse, clinging and giving him his head with the loose reigns. At his side his right boot kicked spurs against ribs. Like the flames, the arrows glanced around the two men as if they had bounced off some unseen force. Despite the heat in the air, the prince felt icy cold and the breath of both horse and man turned to mist in the night.

Sarai Horslei stood in her chambers, looking out from her western facing window and thinking about Robert. *Will he be successful? Will his negotiations force father to grant entrance to the Pescari, allowing the humanitarians to aid and feed the homeless?* This thought troubled her the most as she thought about the long walk that the Pescari people had made, how they had been forced from their homes by the erupting caldera. *Why can't he understand that they didn't choose to come to Weston?* She wished that he would listen to the nobles, men like Cassus Eachann.

Cassus was a good man. He cared about the poor in the city as well as the less fortunate throughout Andalon. When she had discussed the Pescari with him, he had lit up immediately and beamed with excitement at the idea. He proposed building a new ward in the city, temporary, of course, until the Pescari could be taught farming and granted plots of land on the steppes across the river. That land was ideal and largely unfarmed. *Why can't father be as open minded as Cassus?*

Suddenly a flash of light exploded over the wall. It startled her so much that her heart raced. She breathed slowly in and out to let her mind catch up to her eyes as she reasoned with a suddenly horrifying display. She watched as guardsmen exploded into human fireballs, screaming and leaping from the parapets and from the wall itself. In seconds, the heavy wooden gate erupted with red and orange flame that lapped and scorched the brick of the defensive armaments. In no time, the flames reached the black powder stores and sections of the wall exploded in quick succession, tossing men like ragdolls into the black of the moonless night.

She raced downstairs but was stopped by palace guards. "Sorry Lady Horslei, but your father gave strict orders that you're to stay in your chambers."

"What's going on?"

The men refused to answer. They looked anxious at the palace door with nervous apprehension, as if it would explode inward, at any moment.

"Where is my father?" Sarai pressed, stalling with hopes that she could either learn more or have an opportunity to run out the door and lend aid as needed.

"I'm here." Abraham was hurrying down the stairwell in his military uniform and light armor. Sarai was shocked to see that a sword was strapped on his side. In all of her life, she could not remember having seen him wear one. "Go back to your rooms and bar the door. Don't come out until I release you." When she hesitated, he shouted, "Go!" Immediately she raced up the steps.

Once safely in her rooms, she moved a couch in front of the door. Frustrated, she rushed to her window to watch and learn what she could. The searing flames burned her face as the wind blew into her window, but she stood defiantly and watched as tears poured down, vaporizing from the heat.

Below, her father had mounted his horse and formed up the city guard's reserves. He had moved archers away from the walls, and they lobbed arrows over the stone ramparts into the night. These burst into flames as they flew, disintegrating into ash. Her eyes grew wide in amazement. What kind of weapon were the Pescari using?

There had been at least five hundred men on the wall when the attack began. By now the wall was devoid of life and those who survived ran into the square behind the reserves. Her father's fighting force had been reduced by nearly half. She knew that he was nervously waiting for the gate to fall, and his little army made a pathetic sight.

Suddenly, the gates crumbled from the heat, revealing a Pescari teen on the other side. The debris exploded inward with so much force that it panicked the destrier beneath Sarai's father. The beast, normally calm and controlled in battle, reared in fright, throwing Abraham to the dirt and hard against the city fountain. In panicked fear he stomped and kicked, massive hooves striking the motionless man on the ground. Tears again flowed down Saria's cheeks vaporizing immediately into puffs of steam as she willed Abraham to stand up.

Two dark figures approached the gate. Sarai watched with hope as they walked toward the boy with confidence, hooded heads held high as if they would end the entire affair on their own. Above, a screech broke above the roar of flames and Sarai saw two large birds of prey circling overhead. Silently she prayed that they wouldn't harm the boy, and that there was still a chance for a peaceful settlement. Another tear rolled down her cheek as she glanced toward her father's lifeless form.

The Pescari boy raised his hands up into the air toward the great birds above. In a flash two streams of fire shot out from his outstretched form, briefly turning the circling shapes into legendary phoenixes. For several seconds the fiery falcons flew, screaming painfully into the night.

On the ground, the Falconers fell to their knees, paralyzed from the pain that their vestiges endured. In a flash, one of the men erupted into flames and took off running toward the horse stables. He threw himself down and rolled in the hay hoping to put out the flames, instead spreading the inferno to the neighboring buildings and trapping him with the beasts that remained in their stalls. The second specter grabbed the reigns of the governor's horse and swung atop the beast. Turning its' head, he raced eastward toward the far gate and freedom.

The rhythmic stomping of armored boots on cobblestone turned her attention. The Imperial troops marched into position behind the city guard, despite that their commander was beyond the wall. Halting, they too waited for the Pescari to enter the gate, not wanting to rush into the chokepoint and certain death. Sarai peered through the firelight and saw that the buckskin clad warriors had lined up, most atop horseback with arrows nocked. At their head stood the boy, fully engulfed in flame and not appearing to feel the heat.

Having seen enough, she raced back down the stairs and halted. The guards from earlier stared through the open door into the square. Taking advantage of their turned backs, she crept silently across the main hall toward their quarters. The room was empty, all occupants having been called to action, and she broke into a heedless run as she crossed through the bunk room. On the other side was a sentry office, and she screeched to a halt as she entered.

This room was smaller, adorned with a single desk, a chair and several locked trunks. Weapons of differing varieties hung on the wall, but she ignored them and ran to the desk. One by one she pulled open the drawers until she found the item she was looking for. A ring of five keys, one of which must open the cell that held Cassus Eachann. Keys gripped tightly in her hand, she ran from the room and back into the main hall.

The guards still stood at the door, hands on their sword hilts nervously shifting their weight from one foot to another. They appeared terrified and Sarai frowned as urine flowed from the pantleg of the smaller man, forming a puddle around their boots. Beyond them the motionless form of her father lay at the base of the fountain.

Their lack of action enraged the Lady Horslei. Pushing past the cowards, she rushed to her father's side. Blood trickled down from his temple and his eyes were closed as he breathed slow and shallow. He was unconscious and showed no signs of awakening any time soon. Tears again filled her eyes and hoofbeats drew them away from her father and toward the charred remains of the gate.

Two figures on horseback raced through the opening, a firebolt exploding behind them. She blinked away tears and realized that she was watching Robert and General Reeves return to the city. She hugged her father's lifeless body and cried for their help. In a moment, her love had dismounted and knelt by her side. He wrapped his arms around her while the general took charge of the city defenses.

Robert pointed at the two guards standing in the palace doorway. "You two! Come here!" The men hesitated, looking at each other and then at the gate. Robert screamed forcibly, "COME HERE NOW!" They broke free of their fear and ran into the courtyard, kneeling beside their fallen governor. "Let's carry him inside! You grab him under his armpits, and you support that leg. They lifted him on the count of three and scurried toward the palace.

Firebolts and arrows flew as the battle reached the courtyard.

Sarai stood and hurried after the men as they carried Abraham's lifeless body toward the doors. She screamed out when an arrow flew directly at her betrothed's back. "ROBERT!" He spun around, still holding her father's leg and frowned at the projectile. It narrowly missed his chest as he flinched at the last minute and it grazed his triceps, the red streak marring the white jacket. In that moment she realized that he finally fit into the once silly costume, or rather, it finally fit him.

The small group carried the governor into the bunkroom. They laid him on a cot and Robert sent one of the men to retrieve the surgeon. Sarai watched with love as her betrothed took control of the situation, leading the men into action to save her father.

"Sarai." Robert looked exhausted as he talked. "The Pescari. They're not what we thought. They. They're dangerous, Sarai. We must help keep them out of our city."

Shocked, she glared with mouth agape. "Who. Who ARE you, Robert?" Anger rose within as she processed his words. "And what do you mean by 'our' city? This is MY city, Robert! After you Imperials leave and return to Eston, we're the people forced to live with regret if we don't help them."

"That boy." He pointed to the window. "That boy is shooting fire from his hands and eyes, Sarai! He killed a Falconer! He's dangerous and will hurt you. We must fight and drive them back across the river. I'm going to rejoin Max and lead this fight!"

Sarai could not believe her ears. "No." She shook her head. "I think that you and your nursemaid started this fight during your 'parlay.' Is this what you wanted all along? Were you just giving me the same diplomatic lip service? All our previous talks about humanitarianism and rights for all Andalonians were... were what? To woo and build my trust? Well, I've never felt so betrayed. I'll let those people in and treat them as guests!" Pointing down at the lifeless form of her father she added, "You're no better than my father, Robert Esterling!"

Robert approached her slowly, arms out and trying to hold her hands. Voice soft he said, "Sarai, please open your eyes and see that these people are not what we believed. I love you, Sarai. I wanted to help them, but they're evil. They're destroying the city and killing innocent men."

Aghast, she pulled back from his touch and ran from the room. Crossing the great hall, she did not stop until she rounded the corner to the kitchens, where she and Robert had spent so much time together talking and dreaming about a peaceful and inclusive empire. She had thought that her Robert would be a different kind of ruler, and she had truly believed that she would stand at his side and rescue all poor and wretched people from poverty. She looked at the breakfast nook where their books and study cards lay in stacks and she cried.

CHAPTER NINETEEN

Eusari sat in a sobbing heap on the deck of *She Wolf* as the ship pulled further from the harbor. Shock consumed her as her eyes fixated on the lifeless body of Sa'Mond on the distant pier. Beside her, Braen lay in a heap, bloody and beaten by her hand. She trembled and wished that it had been her, instead, on the pier. She watched as one soldier used his foot to push her friend's corpse off and into the water, causing her to cry out into the night.

Transfixed, she hardly noticed as Skander Braston fled with his guard as soon as Imperial soldiers secured the scene. The Queen's head lay discarded in the square, and Marcus had no doubt accused her or Braen when the soldiers arrived. She and her crew would be hunted down and killed for transgressions against the crown, and so many lives had been ruined by her hatred and arrogance.

The rest of the world blurred, and she could only make out muffled sounds aboard the ship. Her crew, if it was still her crew after Sa'Mond death, made preparations to turn out to open sea without interrupting her mourning. No one tried to comfort their captain. Eventually someone, she did not know who, helped her up and escorted her into her cabin where she eventually fell asleep.

She awoke the next morning and found a tray of food on the table in her cabin. She glanced at it and felt her stomach knot. She had no appetite for anything at all, much less food. Looking back at her bed, she considered returning to it and staying below decks forever, but she knew that she could not. Instead, she made her way to the room where she had previously kept Braen. She tried the handle and the door opened easily. Inside, she found

Braen sitting up with his wounds tended, eating his breakfast. He seemed to have regained much of his strength despite the broken ribs and nose.

"I owe you an apology, Braen."

Smiling back at her, he pointed at his meal, "Don't worry about it. These runny eggs more than make up for the past couple of weeks."

"Seriously, Braston, how can you be so lighthearted about everything after what I did to you?" There had been quite a lot of trespasses against him, during the voyage to Estowen's Landing, and she owed this man more than she could ever repay. "I almost sold you off to that monster." She thought again about Sa'Mond and tears choked off anything else that she could have thought to add.

"Really. I understand. You thought I was my brother, or that he was me."

"Why didn't you correct me?"

"I was embarrassed." He shrugged. "Eusari, I was also guilty of crimes on that day. I fought in the streets and killed innocent men who were protecting their families. They protected you, even. Besides, I didn't stop Skander from having his fun. I knew that he was looking to rape villagers, and all that I did was return to the ship to pray. I'm truly sorry and I hope that you forgive me."

"You're a strange man, Braen Braston, and I don't know what to make of you. You want no glory for yourself and refuse to take up arms to take back the kingdom that's rightfully yours." She shook her head. "You even rejected my sexual advances when I was practically throwing myself at you."

"To be accurate, you advanced pretty far after you poisoned me." Braen managed a shy smile, despite her violations of him.

Eusari winced at the memory. "I... I'm sorry. I guess that I'm no better than those who hurt me. I should never have... Revenge overtook me... I'm sorry, Braen." She cried again, this time burying her face in his chest.

Braen, despite the intense pain in his ribs, lifted an arm and placed it around her. He let her sob until there were no tears left. After she pulled back and wiped her face and nose on Braen's table napkin, he addressed her. "Eusari, you don't have control over this crew, do you?" He made a statement and not really a question when he spoke.

Eusari shook her head, "no."

"I feared that was so. Sa'Mond led them, and you were a figurehead."

"Yes. How? How did you know?"

"When we first got underway, I saw how the men looked at you, and how they worked with precision for him. They work out of pure fear, and now that he is gone..."

"Yes. Now that he is gone, I'm afraid that they will turn on me. Women are unlucky on a ship, and I am the worst kind of woman. I killed their previous captain."

"Yes, I heard that story. I also heard that you ate a part of him."

Hearing her own legend made her smile, just a little bit. "You heard about that, did you?"

"I did. Was there any truth to that story, or was it just a legend? Please, I am dying to know." His smile was disarming, and a little bit charming despite his battered face.

"The captain had raped me for too many years. After a while, I just stopped fighting. Stopped struggling. But when you stop struggling against a monster, they find new ways to make you."

Braen had lost his smile as Eusari told her story. "I'm sorry for asking, you don't have to continue."

"It's ok. I've never spoken any of this aloud and I think that it may be time. Sa'Mond knew. Well, most of it, anyway, but he's gone." Tears returned but there were fewer than before. "One night was particularly bad. That butcher was carving on me and I just couldn't take it." She lifted her shirt and showed him her back. She was covered with thick deep scars that ran all the way down to her buttocks. "Sa'Mond heard my cries and couldn't stand by any longer. But by the time that he kicked the door in, I had already taken the knife and had the captain pinned on the bed. I held him with my legs while I reached down and castrated him. When I saw Sa'Mond, I thought that he would kill me. I wanted him to. He was a eunuch, and, because of that, I feared that he would take greater offense to what I had done."

"He understood, though?"

"He did. He helped me tie him, and then escorted him to the main mast. He lashed him, weeping and wailing to the post. He was naked and the men stared in awe at the gaping hole below his limp dick. It was the quickest mutiny in history, I think. I sat at a table, calmly smiling at the former man. Sa'Mond went below decks and brought me out a plate of two ordinary meatballs. I ate every bite while staring and smiling, and the entire crew and captain believed that I had eaten his manhood. Eventually, he bled out on the deck."

"Sa'Mond ran things after that?"

"He did. He supported me and that added to my mystique. I think they believe me to be a witch, or something worse."

"Do you know any of them? Do you know any of the crew by name? Their stories?"

Eusari did not hesitate to answer, "No. I left that all up to Sa'Mond. I never even spoke to them. I did my jobs and to me they were nothing more than my crew. They're certainly not my friends."

"How many crewmen are onboard *She Wolf*?"

"Thirty-two. Wait, twenty-nine after Sa'Mond and the others fell, last night." She choked up when she said had to form her friend's name in her mouth.

"Then we have a hell of a lot of work to do, or we're going to die."

Over the next few days, Eusari followed Braen's advise to the letter. She got out and met the crew, worked alongside them and ate with them in the crew mess. At first, they were leery and standoffish. Some even avoided her altogether. He assured her that was normal, and that she would never be able to win them all over. Eventually Braen built up enough strength to go topside, and he worked with them, as well. She watched how he interacted, treating them like individual people who were special. He listened to their complaints and talked them through their fears.

At first, she had thought Braston was insane. Her experience was that pirates were rough men that needed to fear their leadership if they were to be kept in line. But he eventually proved to her that all people are the same, even the roughest of characters. People crave to be treated with respect and listened to, and the northern captain was a good listener. She learned a lot from Braen, most importantly, she learned the importance of building trust. She had lived her entire life avoiding relationships and the change proved hard for Eusari.

Quick enough, she learned that Devil Jacque was the Quartermaster who had picked her up off the deck and placed her in her room. He had also brought her the meal that she had never touched. Peter Longshank had lost his leg to a cannonball while serving as a gunner in the Imperial navy. He hated when the others called him "Peg leg Pete," so she agreed to call him Peter. Gorgeous George was the hideous pox-scarred cooper who had lost an ear and half of his nose fighting against a merchant from the southern continent. The rest of the crew each had a story, a life before crewing *She Wolf.*

A week into the voyage, Braen pulled Eusari aside. His body had mostly healed, except for the ribs, and he had color back. She couldn't help but notice that his face was a handsome one, beneath the long, blonde beard. Guiding her by the arm, he pulled her into her stateroom. He shoved a knife into her hand and shushed her when she had begun to protest. "Have this ready at all times." He warned. Something had changed in his tone, and this version of Braen was on high alert.

"What's going on?"

"I think it's what we feared. I heard some of the men talking, and they plan to take over the ship." Looking around, he asked, "Where did you stash my blades?"

Eusari led him to a chest beside her bed, opened it, and took out his items. Laying them out, she noted, "You know, I just realized that I've always seen you armed but I've never actually seen you fight."

"Let's just hope that I don't have to." He strapped on the longsword first, then placed the cutlass and axe in the hoops on his belt. Finally, he placed the large knife in the horizontal sheath in the small of his back.

She pointed at the longsword, noting, "That is a little overkill on a ship, isn't it? How can you swing it in such a tight space?"

"I don't. It belonged to my father, so I carry it for sentimental reasons." The sword indeed had sentimental meaning to Braen. Highly effective in open combat, the blade had cut down many a Loganshire defender that went against his father and grandfather before him. Braen had learned sword stances and strokes from Krist Braston as soon as he could walk and hold a wooden version. Of course, he would share none of this with Eusari. Looking up at her, he asked, "Are you ready?"

Her green eyes lit aglow as she threw off her fur cloak to reveal at least twelve knives sheathed in strategic places along her leather breeches and tunic. The pathetic kitchen blade that he had handed her appeared comical in her gloved hand, and she winked at him as she tossed it aside. Pushing past him, she opened the hatch from her room, letting in screams and the sounds of struggle, above. The mutiny had begun.

The duo raced up the ladder and emerged in a nighttime cacophony of fighting. Braen pulled his cutlass and knife from his belt and looked every bit as menacing as the man she had heard rumors about. Up until this moment she had doubted the stories, and fully believed that his prowess had been greatly exaggerated.

But when Gorgeous George swung at him with a club, Braen moved like a boxer, dodging the blow and returning with a jab of his knife hand. The blade plunged in and out of the neck of the hideous creature, blood spraying as the northern captain spun, slicing his hamstrings with his cutlass and dropping him to his knees to bleed out.

"Braston, look there!" Eusari pointed at the forecastle, where six crewmen were pinned down by ten mutineers. The men loyal to Eusari were armed with whatever they could grab. One man, Giovani, was fresh from scullery duty and was armed with a meat cleaver. He swung violently and screamed obscenities while the more confident mutineers watched and laughed at his foolishness.

Braen seized the opportunity and ran behind the group. He flung his knife, burying it deep in the back of Theo the linesman. Flowing inside of them with his cutlass, he sliced the Achilles tendon of another man. Spinning low he pulled his knife from Theo and braced for a blow. Two men lunged from both sides and he parried a cudgel with the curved blade, ramming his knife into the attacker's groin. He turned the man like a shield so that the other's blade sank deep into his back. Stepping aside and swinging his cutlass, he left the second attacker's hand still gripping the knife stuck in the back of the first.

Braston was an artist with his blades and painted the deck of the ship red with stroke after stroke against the mutineers. Eusari, not wanting to let him have all the fun, became a flurry of steel, herself. She quickly dispatched Raulphe, the navigator, by flinging a knife into his neck below the base of his skull. As soon as she released the blade, she had produced another from her collection, embedding it in the chest of Simone. She could not remember the role he served on her ship, only that he was a total asshole when they had played cards.

Inspired, several of her crew members joined the fight and she saw that Peter had turned a small two-pound cannon. He laughed as he fired it into the face of a man she didn't recognize. Turning to her right, she saw that Devil Jacque had moved into a defensive position beside her. The remaining two mutineers threw down their arms and surrendered, but she dispatched them quickly with a flung knife to each of their throats.

"Why the FUCK did you do that?" Braen screamed across the deck.

Eusari tilted her head to indicate the hatch leading below. "We have bigger problems. There're fifteen more in the hold, and only eight of us."

Smiling and holding up his cutlass, he asked, "Why is that a problem?"

"Because they've probably broken into my armory, by now."

Braen dropped his smile and shrugged. "Well then, that's a problem, isn't it?"

Peter spoke up, "Can't we just chain them in, Captain?"

"Not if we want to share their food and water. Jacque, gather up weapons from the dead and redistribute. Pete, roll that cannon over the hatch so we can rest while recovering our wits."

Braen sheathed his weapons and pulled the captain of *She Wolf* aside, whispering in her ear. "Turn back to Estowen's landing, Eusari. With this wind, we can be there in two days, less if lucky. We have enough dried foods and water above decks to make it if we conserve. We can trawl fishing nets, to help."

She nodded and gave the first real order as a legitimate captain on her own vessel. They brought the ship about and stood watch over the captives below, ensuring that the hatch remained secured. *She Wolf* had a captain, a cook, a master gunner and a quartermaster. She would need a navigator, a first mate and new cooper. Her green eyes met the icy blue of Braen's, and she mouthed a silent, "thank you."

CHAPTER TWENTY

Lord Nevra sat in the great hall relishing his new title. Artema's plan executed perfectly and handed over power just as promised. His mercenaries had quickly dispatched the loyalists, and everyone in the town had witnessed the fake death of the former king. Stefan should have been happy with his new title and power, but instead worried over the little things. Those being the many loose ends that had failed to tie.

The first of these was Samani Kernigan. That man posed danger while loose and would no doubt raise support to challenge his rule. *If only I had access to his network of spies*, he stewed. He had lost many nights of sleep over this problem, and ultimately decided to send his own agents to ports throughout the empire. Their primary mission was defaming his opponent's name and blaming him for the death of Horn. A bounty of ten thousand Imperial marks was placed on the capture or death of the man wanted for regicide.

He concocted the story as plausible as possible and word spread quickly that Kernigan had bribed Horn's guard to fire upon his ship as it left the harbor. His plan had failed after destroying *Wench's Daughter,* when a battle broke out between Stefan's guard and Samani's loyalists who conspired against the beloved Artema. After the assassination, Lord Nevra was the hero who dispatched his own men to put down the revolution in the streets. Facing certain death and humiliation, Kernigan fled on *Ice Prince* with the crew of his co-conspirator.

Braston made an easy patsy, and it was believable that he was power drunk on his newfound success as the "Kraken." Stefan had spread word that Braston wanted to ride that glory and rule alongside Samani. He also placed a bounty on his head, five thousand marks to the man who captured the Kraken and brought him to kneel before the King of The Cove.

Nevra laughed at how easily the guild accepted the story, and how Horn's own "Inner Sanctum" had been his downfall. He convinced them that he should rule as a singular despot over the guild. He did not need advisors, only followers. He owned the army, the financial system and was the wealthiest man in The Cove.

He heard footsteps approaching and then a clearing throat broke his concentration, snapping him from his thoughts. "What is it?" He growled.

Alec Pogue stood in his perfectly arranged uniform. "My Lord. One hundred fifty men have refused to surrender. Should I dispatch them or exile them?"

"Exile?" Nevra sneered. "If you capture a rat and set it free outside of your house, it will gnaw its' way back in. If you kill it, then you starve its' children."

"So, I should kill them, Your Excellency?"

"I haven't decided, yet. Put them in the lower prisons until I do." Nevra picked up his ledger book and opened it to review his inventories. "Yes. We have enough rations to support them, I think a month in the cells may turn a few more. How many of Horn's former supporters have already surrendered?"

"Two hundred, Sir."

Nevra chewed on his quill while he thought aloud, "So that brings the wall strength up to seven hundred men with another five hundred in reserve." Flipping pages, he opened the book to update those numbers, as well. "That includes another two hundred housed in the barracks and supplementing the city patrols." He slammed the book shut with a satisfied smile. "Have any of the evacuated ships returned?"

"No sir. We only have the twelve moored during the turnover."

"Who is due in, first?"

"Captains Dominique, Gordman, and Creech were out raiding the Southern Continent, and are unaware of the change in power. They're due back any day."

"As soon as they arrive, dispatch Harper, Lindeman and Schott to patrol the northern coastline. I think Kernigan will head to either Eston or Diaph."

"Their orders, Sir?"

"Here is a list of names who I trust. I want them delivered to ports all along that region and set up as legitimate business owners. They'll be my eyes and ears."

"And the funds for that, Sire?"

Nevra's brow furrowed, questioningly. *The nerve of Pogue. Is he implying that I should pay for it from my own funds?* "Take it out of the treasury. Here's a writ for the withdrawal."

"Aye, Sir."

Stefan picked up a general news dispatch that had arrived that morning. Reading it, he motioned Pogue over and handed it to him. "It seems that the western empire is having some difficulties. The caldera has had some minor eruptions that have driven the Pescari to the walls of Weston. Is that special prisoner still alive?"

"He is, My Lord."

"Good. When he reaches full health, I want to ransom him. He'll bring in a good sum if his father becomes desperate or sentimental enough."

Pogue nodded. "Will that be all, Sire?"

"No. Did the engineers figure out what those projectiles were?"

"Yes, my lord. Apparently Braston's assistant had a laboratory in their apartments. We brought everything to the keep and set it up here to research."

"What did they find?"

"The rounds were filled with several chemicals, mostly pitch, Sulphur, and turpentine. As they burned, the released gas drove off our crews."

The new king nodded thoughtfully. "Is there any way to counter the effects?"

"The engineers are working on a device that our men can put over their faces if the same rounds are used. They think that they can be effective against all types of smoke and gas. Well, for a short amount of time, at least."

Clever, he thought. *Braston and his team are always clever, but not cleverer than me.*

"You did well, Pogue. Now go deliver that writ." Nevra waved his fingers dismissably and the Captain of the Guard again left him alone to his musings.

After a few moments he decided that his concentration had been broken for good and went for a walk to get it back. Three of his personal guards flanked him, and he was thankful for their presence. Unlike Horn, Nevra was not a fighter and depended on the loyalty of his personal cadre of thugs. He paid well for their loyalty and slept well knowing that they were outside of his door.

As he walked, he passed a detail of soldiers carrying his trunks and books to Horn's former chambers. If he were the new Pirate King, then he wanted the most secure quarters in the keep. One of the men stumbled on a loose brick in the floor and tumbled backward, spilling a chest open. Dozens of Stefan's precious and personal ledgers fell out, dumping pages out like loose leaflets into the hall.

Rage burned inside of the little pox-faced man as he screamed, "Be CAREFUL with those!" He quickly scrambled to his knees, scooping up page after page of several decades of his life's work. After he had finished, he rose to his feet and turned on the man. A knife flashed from the soldier's belt aiming for the King's neck. Nevra stepped back with a scream and two of his guards moved in to grab the arms of the soldier. Once they immobilized him, another drove his sword into the gut of the would-be assassin.

Once the soldier was on the ground and the knife removed from his hand, Stefan began kicking and wailing on the corpse with his fists. Stooping down, he picked up the knife and stabbed it into the corpse, over and over. His guards watched with smiles on their faces as he cut off ears and disfigured the man's face.

Alec Pogue raced up the hall, having heard the commotion. He was halted ten feet away by one of the private guards. Just beyond, Nevra sat on the belly of a bleeding corpse, plunging his knife into the chest with his face distorted in an angry sneer.

"Let me through." He tried to push his way past the guard.

"Sorry Captain. We're gonna let the king have his fun." The man was a brute, one that Pogue didn't know. *He must be one of the hired mercenaries.*

Finally, the king was out of breath, energy spent on his tantrum. "I already dismissed you, Captain. Go about your tasks."

Pogue stepped into attention, saluted, then turned an about face and headed down the hall. Looking down he still had the writ and the instructions with agent's names in his hand. It was crumpled into a ball within his fist.

Chapter Twenty-One

Marcus Esterling walked with confidence, smiling as he took each step leading to the Rose Palace. Matteas Brohn and twenty sworn soldiers flanked the prince, six of whom carried a simple pine box. The parade made quite an intimidating sight as they approached the stairs, and the palace guards saluted his return.

The squad slowed as they approached the doors to the Room of Light. Marcus had never been allowed in during council, but he had snuck in on many occasions when it was not in use. He smiled and waved for two sentries to open the doors before him.

One of the men cleared his throat and addressed the prince. "I'm sorry, Prince Marcus. Only the Queen Regent and her cabinet are allowed beyond this door."

"Well, that won't be a problem. You see, the Queen Regent is dead and in that box." He turned to indicate the coffin. "Open the door."

The sentries looked at each other with shocked expressions, then looked to their captain general. "Um... Sir?"

"For fuck's sake." Brohn strode forward and kicked the doors open, startling the cabinet members inside. The sentries jumped out of the way and stood useless, watching the prince and his entourage march by.

Marcus entered the room with his smile plastered on. He waved his fingers at the old men sitting around the table playing their political games. "Hello, useless sacks of wind. Kindly go with my soldiers and no one will die."

The chancellor sat in his usual seat. He wore an irritated and angry expression, but Marcus noted that he was far too old to stand and argue. "What is the meaning of this?"

"I am dreadfully sorry to interrupt your geezer party. Well, not really. Actually, I was looking quite forward to this." Still smiling, he added, "While my Mommy and Captain General Brohn were 'rescuing me,' the outlaw Braen Braston killed my mother, lopping off her noggin." He snapped his fingers and one of his soldiers handed him a velvet sack. Marcus reached in with his hand and pulled out Lady Crestal's head by the hair. He looked at it adoringly for a moment, then kissed the severed head on the lips and left it as centerpiece on the table. Frowning, he turned it so that the open eyes stared vacant, directly at the chancellor.

While the men gasped in horror and moved their chairs backward, Marcus pointed at the head and said, "Look Brohn. She's still seated at the head of the table."

The chancellor finally found his voice and courage as he stammered, "You can't do this! This is disrespectful and a desecration of her body."

"No. The disrespect was when you paid off the Braston pirate to kidnap me. She was forced to ransom me back, and your thug killed her in the process." He slowly walked around the table as he talked, until he stood directly behind the older statesman. Leaning in close to his ear, he whispered loudly for all to hear. "Unfortunately, he told us of your involvement. Also, that it was your plan to have him kill my dear mother so that my brother would take the throne."

"That's preposterous!" The man's face turned scarlet at the accusations.

Brohn spoke up next. "Actually chancellor, you have the most motive to overthrow the Regent and place Prince Robert on the throne. Everyone in this room knows how she despised and often humiliated you behind these doors. In fact, the last time we met you were crying and pissing yourself."

The other men around the table nodded their agreements,

murmuring as they remembered the events of him lying on the floor of this very chamber. The man began stammering, tears flowing down his eyes as he looked at each face around the table, recognizing the guilt that they attributed to him.

"No! I'm loyal to the people of the Empire!"

Marcus shook his head. "Tsk. Tsk. You're loyal to the people, but not to my mother. Those are the kind of words that incite revolutions."

Brohn continued, "You conspired with a northern aggressor and promised that you would help overthrow his brother in Fjorik."

Marcus acted shocked at the accusation and feigned surprise. "Why! That's TREASON, chancellor!"

Brohn motioned for two soldiers to take the man into custody. "Chancellor Gedon, you're under arrest for soliciting the murder of the Queen Regent and for attempting a coupe."

"Show of hands. Anyone against placing emergency powers of succession in my hands while we investigate the involvement of my brother with the chancellor?" Marcus looked around the room at the shocked faces. "None opposed? Good. Then it's settled. Now everyone, get the fuck out while I start my investigation." He held his fingers up as quotation marks when he said, 'investigation,' laughing as he did at his private joke. The cabinet scrambled away as quickly as they could, not staying to watch the soldiers chain the chancellor.

After the room had cleared, Marcus watched Matteas Brohn casually stride to the doors, closing and barring them from the inside. "What is this, Matteas?" He asked as he poured himself a glass of wine. "Why are you locking us in?"

"Because, your excellency. We're in need of a conversation." A deep voice from behind drew his attention. The prince looked up to see a Falconer, having entered from some secret entrance.

"Oh, we are, are we? Wait. Aren't you the Falconer from the exchange?" Marcus looked thoughtful for a moment and then added, "You witnessed how my mother really died." Taking a long drink, the prince gestured toward the intruder. "Matteas, Tie up this loose end."

The specter walked toward the table, dragging a fingertip along the cheek of Lady Crestal's remains. "I am your overseer, Prince Marcus."

"Listen to the man, Marcus." Brohn poured himself a glass, sniffing it before downing in a gulp and pouring some more.

"Don't you and the other freaks work for my family?"

"No. Actually, your family works for us."

"Matteas, run this idiot through."

"Can't do it, My Lord." Matteas held up a finger, wagging it back and forth as he talked. "I said to listen to the man."

"My name is Arch-Falcon Kestrel and I represent another party. One highly interested in the success of your family in the domination of this continent."

"We already rule the world."

"If you say so." The large bird man chuckled breathlessly, letting out a little squawk as he did. "As I was saying, I represent a party that placed your family on the throne eight hundred years ago and has an interest in your success. Your mother cooperated and was allowed to rule after the death of your father." The Falconer mimicked the same finger quotations as he said, "father."

Marcus looked at Brohn, and the Captain General smiled back, lifting his glass into the air in a silent toast.

"This is preposterous." Marcus spoke to Brohn. "If you don't shut him up, then I will."

"Listen to him speak, Boy."

"No!" Marcus drew his knife and charged at Kestrel, but the creature-like man stepped aside at the last moment and the blade slashed only the air. Turning, the specter raised his hand and a gust of wind blasted Marcus backward, hard against the wall. The Falconer strode calmly toward him, smiling. All of a sudden, wisps of air began wrapping themselves around Marcus' wrists, legs and ankles. It felt as if he wore invisible shackles and the prince could no longer move. "What... is this..." Before he could finish his sentence, another band of air wrapped around his mouth, gagging his speech and cutting off his breath.

"Listen to me speak, Boy. You have interrupted far too often in this little exchange." The young prince's eyes grew wide and tears slowly trickled from their corners. "Your weapons are useless, as I can see your every move before you even think about making it." Bending down, he picked up the fallen blade and then strode back toward the boy on the ground. He stooped low beside him, blade out reflecting the light from the window.

Marcus felt terror within his gut. Even when the pirate bitch had kidnapped him, he wasn't afraid. But this large man dressed in feathers and holding his own knife induced panic like the prince had never known. He fought to breathe against the invisible gag but failed. Warm urine flowed down the front of his trousers, spilling out onto the marbled stone floor.

Kestrel looked down at the mess and smiled. "Thank you for your undivided attention." He leisurely returned the boy's knife to the sheath on his belt, then rose and stood over him. With the wave of his hand a gust of air rushed in and Marcus could breathe. He gasped and cried as the panic subsided.

"As I was saying. I represent another party. No, before you ask, the party is not a single nobleman in your kingdom. I represent a people who you've never heard of. Their technology far surpasses your own, and they are in fact the benefactors who gave your family the advantages that you currently possess."

Marcus looked toward Brohn who nodded at the truth in the words. "That's how we got the cannons and black powder, boy. The Pescari used to be more numerous than they are, now, and even occupied the eastern side of the Misting River. The Falconers brought us the technology that drove them back, forcing them to live across The Forbidden Waste."

"Cannons. How quaint." Kestrel had returned to the conference table and absently twirled Crestal's hair with his talon-like finger.

"You'll rule this land, Marcus Esterling, and the Falconers will assist you in your civil war against your brother. We'll even grant you technologies to tip the odds in your favor, if need be. But make no mistake in believing that you are in control. You will rule within the boundaries that we set, or we will replace you. Other than that, the Empire is yours."

Marcus coughed and asked, "What is it that you want me to do?"

"Much better. You will do three things. First, you will allow the Ministry of Information to operate as a sovereign entity and you will never meddle or allow meddling in their work. Secondly, my Falconers will continue their work uninterrupted. You will never allow anyone to question their valuable mission on this continent. And finally, you will keep a chancellor of our choosing as the head of the council for perpetuity." The Falconer turned the head so that the vacant eyes of Crestal Esterling stared back at her son, bound and laying in a puddle of urine. "Any questions or complaints?"

The prince shook his head.

"Good." With the wave of a hand the restraints disappeared, and Marcus sprawled on the floor. "You may start by elevating Lord Campton Shol to chancellor as soon as you wrap up Gedon's trial. Oh, and go clean up. The future king of the Esterling Dynasty should not be lying in his own piss."

Chapter Twenty-Two

Robert watched Sarai run from the room and shook his head in wonder at the angry display. The still form of Governor Horslei lay on the cot, and he watched the man's chest slowly rise and lower with shallow, rhythmic breaths. *How can she fail to see that her father might have died at the hands of those savages? Is she so blinded that she can't see the danger that they pose to lawful citizens?*

His thoughts were interrupted by the return of the palace guard with an older man, slightly bent and carrying a medicine bag. The surgeon pulled up a chair and began examining the governor, carefully looking over his body for unseen and internal injuries. After a few moments, he opened the man's eyelids and checked his pupils for reaction.

Nodding, he looked to Robert and gave a positive prognosis. "He has a head injury and may regain consciousness at any time. We will have to wait. In the meantime, I am going to have to reset this leg of his that was broken in the fall." Robert nodded and then left Abraham Horslei in the capable hands of his guards and his surgeon.

He walked outside of the palace and immediately saw that General Reeves had organized the line of troops. A command was given, and shields moved on the line to reveal the aging mentor. A squire ran up and handed Robert both shield and sword, then they both hurried to rejoin the formation. As he ran, he glanced over his shoulder at the gate and line of Pescari. Where a ten-foot-solid wall had once held the gatehouse, a gaping hole smoldered from the explosion of powder stores.

"Well boy, it looks like our friends are afraid to come in." The general pointed toward the Pescari boy, Taros. He still stood before the entrance, but he no longer burned with flames. Not an inch of his body appeared to be harmed by the fire that had raged. "He's been standing like that for about ten minutes. His flames puffed out and he quit burning when you and your girlfriend ran into the palace."

Robert nodded, staring wide-eyed at the remains of the gatehouse. "Are we going to advance the shield wall? If we move the line to where the gate stood, then we can hit him with crossbows from behind the shields. Those bolts move faster than arrows and can probably get through without him burning them."

Max smiled in approval. "You're getting better at this soldiering thing, your highness. I was thinking the exact same tactic and was waiting for you to arrive. Are you ready to die for your crown, Prince Esterling?"

A small laugh escaped Robert as he nodded his agreement. "I'm ready to kill him for it, like you taught me, General."

"Then give the command, boy. The army is yours."

"SHIELD. WALL." Robert's voice boomed and two thousand soldiers snapped to attention, banging shields against one another in a chorus of metal. "FORWARD, MARCH!" Boots hit the ground in unison, stomping and advancing toward the hole where the wall had once stood. Step. As they marched Robert watched Taros. *He's just standing there, looking exhausted and worn out.* Step. *Something's wrong,* he thought. Step. *Is this a trap?* Step. The Pescari warriors raised their bows from atop their horses. Step. The boy wasn't even flinching. Step.

"STOP!!!!!" A female voice came from the palace doors.

Robert turned his head and saw that Sarai had emerged with a man. Step. *Is her father awake?* Step. Looking closer he realized that the man was Cassus Eachann, leader of the Humanitarian faction. Step. *Wasn't he imprisoned by her father just yesterday?* Step. *Surely Sarai did not release her father's political rival.* Step.

That would be a foolish move on her part, one that would have lasting effects after her father awakens. Step.

"HALT YOUR FORMATION!" Eachann's voice rang out from beside Sarai.

Robert looked at Max. Neither had any desire to halt, and instead wanted to end this battle and kill the menace that had caused so much bedlam the night before. Step. He watched as Sarai ran out in front of the advancing army toward the Pescari boy. Step. Cassus followed her and they raced across the courtyard toward the gap in the wall. Step. *No, she wouldn't be this foolish.* Step. *Yes. Yes, she would.* Step. From nearby buildings several other people emerged. Step. These, like Sarai and Cassus, also ran toward the boy. Step. Soon, a group of about twenty citizens, including Robert's love, stood before the boy unarmed.

"COMPANY, HALT!" The order came from General Reeves and the entire column of soldiers stopped marching with a resounding stomp of boot on dirt.

Robert watched dumbfounded as Sarai embraced the Pescari boy, hugging him while Eachann spoke with the man Robert knew as Taros' uncle Teot. After a moment, he turned to face the column of Imperial soldiers. In a loud and commanding voice, he addressed both the soldiers and the citizens, who were emerging from their homes to watch the spectacle. "The Weston governor is incapacitated and unable to rule. As lead councilman, I take control of the city. These refugees are under my protection and will be granted safe harbor within the walls until suitable resettlement can be arranged."

Looking toward General Reeves, Robert could see silent fury in his mentor's eyes. "Can he do that, Max?" He asked, softly.

"I'm afraid he can, boy. We have to stand down, unless Horslei wakes up and miraculously intervenes."

And then Eachann addressed the general directly. "General Reeves. Your army is no longer needed within the incorporated city walls of Weston. Per Article Five, Section Three of the Weston

Imperial Constitution, I invoke the right of the city to refuse martial law." The general's cheeks danced as he listened to the politician, teeth grinding against his anger. "I demand that you immediately turn your force around and march to a new position no less than ten miles from the border of our sovereignty."

"You are a fool, Cassus! You're putting all of these citizens in danger!" Robert could not hold back the words that flew from his mouth. He knew that he should remain silent, but added, "These Pescari are not refugees! They're invaders and possess dark and dangerous magic! You'll be begging the general to retake this city before long!" After he spoke, he cringed at the furious and hateful expression on the face of Sarai. Inside, he knew without doubt that he had lost her forever.

"Ambassador Esterling," Eachann addressed him directly, "you are an emissary of the Imperial crown and have a right to observe our self-governance without interference. On behalf of the ruling council I extend you further invitation to remain a silent witness to our generosity as we welcome our allies from across the Forbidden Waste. Any future meddles into our sovereign affairs will not be tolerated."

Mouth agape, Robert stared back at the council leader. "Future meddles? Are you implying that I had a hand in the breakdown of last night's talks?"

Nodding, Eachann continued. "Although you are young and most likely meant well, we cannot forgive the fact that your lack of diplomatic experience led directly to a breakdown of negotiations."

"Break down? Of negotiations?" Scoffing, the prince pushed aside the shield to his left, emerging from the formation and throwing his shield down on the ground. "What you are implying, Councilman Eachann, is treason! I am the crown prince and heir of the Esterling dynasty!"

"I see only a boy playing soldier and using real lives as his toys. You've not passed your trials, and the governors have not voted to pledge their allegiance. Your mother rules until you can gain their favor and claim the title of Emperor," louder and to the gathered audience he added, "if that ever truly happens."

This time it was Sarai's voice that addressed Robert. "Go with your soldiers, Robert. Leave the city because you're not welcome here." She then grabbed the hand of Taros and led him toward the palace. Cassus and Teot began waving in the warriors, women, and children who gingerly stepped through the burned out remains of the gatehouse. The wretched mass of people slowly streamed into the city, dragging their belongings behind them as they had done for so many days across the desert and plains.

Behind Robert, Maximus gave the order to turn, and the retreating boot stomps sounded the exit of the Imperial troops through the eastern gate. Standing alone in the courtyard, shield on the ground and sword tip angled uselessly in the dirt, the crown prince of the Esterling dynasty was bewildered, exhausted and beaten. He had finally found his strength as both a military leader and a statesman but lost all credibility as a ruler in one swift political move. His mouth gaped, devoid of words and as empty as his heart. Tears fell as he watched the love of his life take Taros by the arm, leading him toward the palace.

Sarai Horslei could not look at Robert as she passed by, leading the Pescari boy by the arm. She felt heartbroken by his betrayal. *He's no better than General Reeves or my father.* In her mind he was the same as them and she had no place in her life for warmongers.

She had believed that he was truly a humanitarian and would secure the refugees a place within the city walls. But he had lied and somehow tricked the Pescari into attacking. Where love had once filled her, resentment now boiled up instead. She refused to look at him standing in the courtyard, wanting instead for him to leave her city.

Yet, inside she felt conflicted. She had truly fallen in love. He was everything that she considered attractive and she also found him intelligent, vulnerable and honest with his emotions. She had longed for a marriage with him that would further strengthen the bonds of the eastern and western halves of the empire. Now, as she passed him by, her heart yearned for her eyes to meet his. Her lips longed to give his one last lingering goodbye. With Horslei stubbornness she willed her eyes and her body forward.

Her hands held the arm of the Pescari boy, leading him like a frightened toddler. She had expected his skin to be hot where the fire had engulfed him, but instead it was cold as ice. As they crossed the courtyard, she looked him over. His skin, browned by constantly living under the sun, did not show any signs of injury from the flames. Where he had been visibly angry when she and Eachann had first approached, his face now wore a confused expression that seemed to study Sarai. His eyes were fixed on her, two dark brown orbs that shown slightly with gold specks that danced in the torchlight of the courtyard.

Several warriors ran up alongside them as they walked. The boy waved them off, saying something in Pescari to make them return to their duty of ushering in their people. They cast several nervous glances over their shoulder, obviously worrying over his safety. She could sense that he was not afraid to leave his people as he walked with her to the palace.

Once they had passed out of earshot of Robert, she softly spoke to the boy. "My name is Sarai. I want to welcome you and your people to my city."

He opened and then closed his mouth, as if he were trying to form the words without actually producing the noise. After a moment, he replied in a deep accent, "I am Taros."

She smiled at Taros as warmly as she could, despite wanting to cry over Robert's lies and betrayal. "I'm pleased to meet you, Taros. I'm bringing you into the palace so that you can relax after your ordeal. You're very cold, so I'll have servants draw you a hot bath and bring you food before we meet with Cassus Eachann."

Taros froze at the doorway to the palace, muscles tensing beneath Sarai's hands on his arm. At first, she was confused, but then nodded and spoke to him soothingly. "Felicima sleeps and will not see you go into a building. Do not be afraid of her wrath. Come."

"I am not afraid of Felicima. I am a god like her. It... It is only that I have never been inside of a building of rock." She frowned at his words. *Surely, he struggles with the language*, she assured herself. She gently coaxed him inside, smiling at the wonderment that filled his eyes as they entered the grand hall. He looked around with amazement, taking in the banners and tapestries. Three attendants approached, and she motioned for him to follow them. After another brief hesitation, he stood a little taller and with more confidence. He turned his head with one last look before allowing them to guide him toward his quarters.

A few moments later a deep voice broke the silence in the hall. "Thank you for freeing me, Sarai."

She turned and saw Cassus in the doorway. She smiled. "You're the future of this city, Councilman. My father is not fit to rule in these changing times, and the Pescari people need your benevolence and compassion over his war hawking."

He nodded, striding up beside her. "You have a wisdom far beyond your years, Sarai Horslei, and you'll no doubt be a strong future leader of your house. I hope that your deeds here tonight do not earn you excommunication from your father."

Frowning, she pondered this possibility for the first time since she had stolen the key and freed Eachann. "Even if my father survives his injuries, he'll not be able to deny that is too late to turn them out of Weston."

"Plans are already underway to establish a temporary Pescari borough in the city. Taros' uncle Teot is moving them into the lower sector as we speak."

Sarai looked up with concern. "What about the citizens living in that sector?"

Cassus smiled disarmingly. "They will be… relocated. Trust me that their new accommodations will be a… a step up from their current situation. The removal is necessary in order to prevent those who resist their sanctuary from doing them harm."

She pondered his words and then nodded. "Yes. I see the wisdom of moving out the residents so that it will be easier to keep the peace." She stole a glance at the guard quarters where her father lay, still unconscious.

Following her gaze, Cassus nodded. "You should visit him. He's your father and it's normal to worry about his wellbeing, even if your allegiances differ."

"No. I no longer care if he awakens at all." A tear rolled down her face as she thought of all that she had helped to change in a single night. "I'd rather save several thousand lives by cutting out two that were dear to my heart. Especially when those would have contributed to the pain and suffering of the same several thousand."

"Your Robert?"

"Yes." *My Robert.* Sobs finally let loose from her gut as she thought about her former love.

Chapter Twenty-Three

Taros watched the attendants leave the bathing quarters. They had drawn a bath so hot that steam rose into the air above the pool. His joints had ached with dull pain while he watched the servants fill the tub and he longed to climb in. He felt cold. The feeling ran deep in his body as if it came from the inside out. He leaned in close to the water, hoping to absorb some of the heat but to no avail. He had never felt so cold in his life and had shivered since he and the girl entered the palace. As he stared at the water his muscles began to quake with spasms.

He stole a glance toward the door through which the attendants exited. Finally feeling confident that they would not return, he stripped out of his tattered and burned buckskins. With cautious steps he placed one foot into the tub and then the other. He stood like that, cold feet in the hot water with his naked body over the steam. He frowned down at his feet, realizing that he could not feel the warmth of the water. They were still cold. Slowly he sat down into the pool, picked up a bar of soap and washed himself between shivers.

He did not linger long in the tub. Feeling no comfort from the steaming water he rose and grabbed a towel from the edge. He dried himself and then wrapped the cloth around his shoulders as he surveyed the room. Before leaving the servants had taken care to lay out clean linens on a nearby bench, along with some clothes in the Andalonian fashion. He frowned at these, but his buckskins lay charred and unusable on the ground. Desiring to stop his shivering, Taros slipped into the clothing.

As soon as he finished dressing, he heard a soft knock at the door, and he watched a male attendant enter the room with a large, soft robe. The man tried to wrap it around his shoulders, but Taros stopped him, snatching it out of his hands and putting in on himself. Not appearing offended, the man stepped back and bowed deeply. "I am Philip, your excellency. I will be your steward during your stay in the palace. Is there anything else that I can bring before escorting you down to dinner?"

Taros paused, taking in the words. Although his mother and uncle had taught him the Andalonian language, he had only practiced its' use with the occasional fur trader. Once he was sure that he understood the man correctly, he responded. "Food is good. Take me to the food."

The man bowed and turned and left the room with Taros following closely behind, shivering from the cold.

Philip had a slight hunch to his posture that was more prevalent when he walked than when he stood. His hair was thinning more on the top than on the sides, giving it a horseshoe appearance. But the characteristic that stood out most to Taros was the man's smile. It was not bold, nor did it make him appear fake. Rather, his smile was as genuinely comforting as one a grandparent would give a child. Interestingly, he did not find it condescending.

When they passed through the great hall Taros immediately noticed that the girl, Sarai, was gone. He felt sad at her absence and hoped to see her again. He welcomed her friendly demeanor after the sudden loss of his mother and craved a friend with whom he could talk about things.

She was the most beautiful girl that he had ever seen. Pescari girls had dull eyes and everyone's hair was the same color amongst his people. But hers had been vibrant yellow and her eyes had shone with a brilliant sapphire blue. He was drawn to her stark difference.

Several city guards milled about in the great hall while some ran bandages and supplies outside to the injured soldiers in the courtyard. These men glared at him, contrasting the friendliness of Philip and Sarai with their resentful expressions. He knew that they had every right to distrust him after his display at the walls.

Unlike the other times that he had used Felicima's power, he felt remorse for what he had done to their comrades. Although they were warriors, they were defending their city and had not harmed him personally. In his moment of grief, he had lashed out and killed many of their comrades. They had every right to hate him.

He again shivered while entering the dining hall. The room was large enough to house hundreds of people, and rows of tables ran the length of the vast space. One large seating place was set apart from the others. A raised platform stood before a roaring fire in a grand hearth. He rightfully assumed that table was reserved for the most distinguished of chieftains, as he stared wide-eyed at the feast laid out before him. Roasted hams and entire chickens rested on platters, and fruits that he had never imagined were piled in bowls. His mouth salivated.

Philip indicated that he should have a seat at the banquet table. "The others will be joining you, momentarily, your excellency. Do you require anything else in the meantime?"

Taros shook his head and stared at the feast. Philip bowed and left the hall, doors closing behind him with a heavy echo. Flinching, the boy pulled his robe closer and shivered. Stomach growling, he realized that he was hungry. He didn't know where to start with so many options and tentatively took a step toward the platform.

He approached the table with eyes focused on the roaring fire, watching the flames and recalling the events from earlier. Tears rolled down his face at the image of men screaming and leaping from the parapet, desperate to escape his fiery outburst. He had not meant to kill them, but when Felicima's power flowed, he made no discernment for the lives of others. They were merely in the way when anger gripped him.

He thought about that anger. After learning about his mother's passing, he had been enraged that his people had not been granted access to the city and his singular thought was to open the walls and destroy the gate. Emotions flooded all at once and the grief gripped his heart and twisted his stomach. His chest heaved in heavy sobs as he lamented over Lynette. He curled up on the floor in front of the fire, shivering and shaking while he wept.

A soft and warm hand touched Taros on the shoulder, comforting and soothing him as he cried. He opened his eyes and looked up to see the face of Sarai, tenderly smiling down. "It's ok," she said, "cry it out. That's what often helps me."

"I... I didn't mean to hurt anyone. I only want my people safe."

"I know. Cassus and I believe you. That's why we intervened. I promise that your people will be fine, now." A single tear rolled down her own cheek as she spoke to him, and he believed her.

He thought again about Lynette, this time with sadness rather than grief. "My mother is dead. She died, tonight, and I need to bury her."

"That's awful, Taros. I am so sorry, and I'll make sure that you and your people can tend to her." She seemed genuinely concerned and he felt that he could trust her. He was about to thank her when she spoke, again. "I lost my own mother two years ago. When she passed, I felt like I had lost the only friend that I ever had beside my brother. It was made worse, because it was the year after he'd gone off to the university." Tears filled her eyes, thinking about her family.

"Is he there, now? Or did he return?"

"He died in an accident, there, and never came back."

"I am sorry, Sarai. Do you have a father?"

"I do." A look of concern crossed her face, and she added, "He's recovering from his injuries from tonight."

An anxious cramp gripped Taros. "Did I... Did I injure him?"

"Yes. You did, but it was an accident. He was also the reason that the gates were barred to your people, so it is a good thing that he is unconscious." Her face looked deeply troubled as she spoke, and Taros realized that she had risked much to help him and the Pescari.

"What happens, now? I only ever thought this far." The honesty of his words caused him to cringe, as he admitted for the first time since fighting Cornin that he lacked the confidence to lead.

"Don't worry about that." She patted his shoulder and he blushed at her touch. "Cassus Eachann and I will help. We're here for you, now." The sad look that she had been wearing instantly disappeared when she spoke. Her hand lingered on his arm and his pulse quickened as she said, "He is going to help you find permanent settlements."

A voice from the doorway broke Taros from his thoughts and Sarai pulled back her hand very quickly. "It seems that they could have at least lit a fire in the hearth."

The two teenagers stood, and Sarai greeted the newcomer. "Hello, Cassus!" Frowning at the simmering coals, she remarked, "That's strange, the fire was roaring a moment ago."

Taros turned and saw that the fire had completely extinguished. He realized instantly that he was no longer cold. He cleared his throat and addressed the man, "I am Taros, shapan of the Pescari and favored of Felicima. Thank you for allowing my people inside the gates."

The man bowed deeply before him and responded, "Greetings your eminence. I am Lord Cassus Eachann. Acting governor of Weston, city councilman and leader of the humanitarian party. You are most welcome in my city." Gesturing to the meal, he invited, "please join us in a meal so that you may regain your strength." Taros nodded and sat down in one of the high back chairs, noticing happily that Sarai had chosen the seat next to his. He hadn't realized how ravenous he was and feasted.

He ate so much that within minutes his stomach had begun to ache. Sitting back in the chair he felt tired. Feeling warm, he looked back at the fireplace. While they were eating, an attendant had scurried over to the fire, trying to relight it and struggling to do so. Taros noticed that the wood was half-burned and cool, making the man's chore difficult. Beside him, Sarai shivered and wrapped her arms around herself. Concerned about her comfort, he reached toward the hearth and with the flick of his wrist the fire roared to life. Both Sarai and Cassus jumped at the sudden combustion and the attendant fell back onto the floor in a terrified heap.

Cassus regained his composure quickly. "How do you do that, young Taros?"

"I do not know. I think that it is a blessing of Felicima, although many of our elders call it a curse. Sometimes I can control it." Frowning, he added, "Tonight I could not."

"Does the fire come from within you? Or elsewhere?" The man named Eachann seemed to be calm and comfortable talking about it, but Taros felt strange. He did not want to talk about this topic in front of Sarai.

"Both, I think. When I use my power all other fires go out."

Sarai asked the next question. "Where did the fire to light the hearth come from? There are no other fires around."

"I. I don't know. I do know that I no longer feel as cold as I did, earlier, but I am cooler after lighting it."

Eachann pressed. "Why did you light the fire, just now, Taros?"

He looked up into Sarai's beautiful blue eyes, blushing a little with embarrassment as he answered, "Because she was cold."

Sarai's cheeks went red at his answer, smiling shyly as she said, "Thank you, Taros. That was very sweet of you."

Raised voices were heard in foyer and the dining hall doors crashed open. Teot entered followed by two of his warriors. They were flanked by six palace guardsmen, all of whom had swords drawn.

"Shapan! These people could not keep us away! Are you well?" Teot narrowed his eyes at Sarai and Cassus, relaxing a little when he saw that Taros was unharmed.

Taros stood and greeted his uncle. "I am, Teot. Gather up the remains of this meal and distribute it to the people." Turning to Cassus, he added, "They will need more."

Nodding his agreement, the statesman responded, "Of course, your excellency." He motioned two of the guards and directed them to organize a detail to take more food to the Pescari. As they scurried off to take action, Phillip entered the room with a look of grave concern on his face. Leaning in, he whispered into the ear of Cassus who nodded a reply and then dismissed the steward with a flick of his hand.

"Lady Sarai. I am afraid that I have some dire news." Cassus did not blink as he relayed the information. "Your father has succumbed to his injuries and has died."

CHAPTER TWENTY-FOUR

The coastline north of Estowen's Landing curved slightly westward around rocky cliff outcroppings and the occasional tall mountain range. Evergreen spruce and pines reached upward toward the heavens, painting the landscape with dark color that contrasted the pink hues in the rocks. Winter had fully gripped the peninsula this far north, and the tree branches dipped with the heavy wet snow, letting the excess blow off with a wind so icy that it cut to the bone.

Skander Braston ignored this wind as his ship bounced on the choppy waves, having traveled far in a single night. He was already hundreds of miles north of the meeting place, but he could not shake the humiliation of the event. Thinking about the night before made his mind race. He had planned for the exchange perfectly, had the upper hand, even. But after Matteas Brohn had killed Crestal Esterling, chaos had ensued, forcing him to flee.

Flee. Such a simple word with intense connotation. The northern king grimaced at the thought that one simple word would brand him forever a coward in the eyes of his enemies. Outnumbered by the arrival of Lady Esterling's private guard, he had no choice but to run back to his ship empty handed when the fighting broke out. Hester had told him to keep the parlay a secret from even his own generals, so he had traveled with only a small cadre of soldiers and sailors.

The sudden arrival of the Falconer had also startled him, forcing him into panic. Their powers were unworldly, demonic even. Unnatural to the order of the gods. Skander felt another wave of rage rise from his belly, causing his chest to tighten. He was certain that in the bedlam the pirate wench had used similar magic on him and his men, wrapping them in vines and sending spiders to attack them.

He remembered her lunge at him with a knife. She had nearly killed him, and he was lucky that Artur interfered. Something had been oddly familiar about that witch, like he had run across her in his past. Perhaps she had some vendetta against him. He gritted his teeth as he thought about the feeble attempt on his life and her dark magic. The voice of his father returned. *Only a coward would fear a woman, Skander.*

Skander Braston was the most powerful man in the northern kingdom and he would never allow a woman to hold power over him. Flinching, he thought about Hester resting in luxury in his palace, ordering around his servants and conniving politics behind his back. She played the nobles against each other with her games and was a master in her craft. But, even with her manipulations, he refused to allow her an ounce of control over him.

He often regretted seducing her and taking her for his wife, but always understood that she was the only woman halfway deserving to stand by his side. Although it was true that he had originally only taken interest to slight his brother, she served more purposes to him than to warm his bed. Her family owned the iron mines and their wealth fed the empire. If she could produce a male heir, then he would dominate both houses.

Thinking about Braen enraged him. That sap had adored and worshipped Hester, mistakenly believing that she loved him back. While he wooed her with tokens and favors, Skander flexed his strength before the nobles and gained legitimate backing as the future leader. While Braen brought her poetry to win her affection, Skander had secured her future as a queen.

At least the Esterling bitch was dead. That thought consoled him a little, even though his brother had slipped out of his grasp because of her death. Worse, her son had taken his payment failed to deliver Braen. Fury rose as Skander thought about the humiliation of returning without either his brother's head or the bounty that he had taken to pay for it. Marcus had made off with a small fortune in coin, that night, and Skander wanted it back with interest.

A thought occurred to the northern king as his ship skimmed the coast for Fjorik. He would extract all that he was owed by renewing raids on the empire. Not just by raiding Loganshire as his father had done, the entire empire would pay the whelp's debt. A smile crept across Skander's face at the thought of war with the Esterling dynasty. With the mother out of the way the child had done the north a favor, giving him an opening to take what was rightfully his.

But the desire for war was something to satisfy in spring. Skander realized that he wanted a morsel of revenge, now, and so he scanned the coastline for any opportunity. Ahead, smoke billowed out of a few buildings in a small coastal village. The despair in his stomach eased at the sight, and he let out a slight chuckle of glee at the thought of a bloodying both his sword and dick. He called to a tall sailor on the port amidships, "Coxswain!"

The man hustled over. "Aye, sir?"

"Make for the smoke up ahead. Luff sails and lose this speed. We feast, tonight." The man ran off to make the adjustments. Braston looked up at the clear sky, nodding his pleasure that there would be no interruption by bad weather. He then turned to a large, bald man carving a piece of whalebone while lounging on a starboard crate. The sergeant at arms perked up at the sudden change of mood and the snap movement of the coxswain. Pausing in his ministrations he awaited orders. "Artur. Ready a landing party. The peace is over, and it's a beautiful night for raiding."

The man placed his scrimshaw into his pocket and answered the order with a wide toothless grin that formed a gap in his beard. Skander watched the man scurry below decks to gear up the soldiers, nodding along as he privately shared the excitement for bloodletting. As a king, this Braston loathed the duty of diplomacy. No, that was his brother's strength. Killing and violence was this brother's forte, and he was about to go to work.

About an hour later Skander led a force of twenty warriors through the forest. He smiled alongside his men, lustily daydreaming about the carnage they were about to wrought. As the sun dipped behind the mountains, the temperature dropped quickly but the men barely felt the chill for their excitement. It was approaching dinner time, so most of the occupants would be in from the field, boots off and drying by the hearth when the attackers arrived. After so many peaceful years, the raid would be a complete surprise.

He surveyed the buildings. There were very few, as this was a poor and simple village. It was so simple that there would be more bread than mutton in the crew's diet that night. That mattered not to Skander, as he scanned the hovels for movement. The sun had nearly set, and the small windows emitted faint and flickering candlelight.

Doors opened and women called to their children washing at the well. Laughter carried the children up the steps to their homes, oblivious to their fate. After they had all gone in for their supper, the northern king signaled for his men to split up and flank the buildings from two sides. The night fell suddenly silent as the insects and wildlife watched the men take up their positions.

Braston crept silently to the first home, looking across the square at Artur who had done the same across the way. Likewise, his men fanned out and took their positions in small teams at each of the other buildings. He shivered both in anticipation and against the air, now quite a bit colder than it had been moments ago. He let out an icy breath that turned into frost as soon as it left his mouth. Breathing in the cold, he filled his lungs for a loud and blaring war cry, "ATTACK!"

His crew answered his call by screaming and kicking down doors. Soon cries of a different sort rang out as the occupants responded. Skander swung his axe against the weak and pitiful door, and it splintered in two as it fell off its' hinges. Inside a man and a woman ate at their table, wooden spoons frozen at their mouths at the sudden arrival of a war-clad Northmen. With a backhand, he sent the man's head rolling off his shoulders and onto the floor. The woman screamed and Skander smiled. Somewhere a baby cried and sounds of battle raged in the night, entering through the open doorframe.

The woman tried to run to the baby, resting fitfully in a cradle beside a simple bed. It wailed in fear and the king roared with delight at the futile act of motherhood. She should have left the child, he thought, saving herself by running past him to escape into the night. By running toward the child, she had turned her back to him, making it easier to push her down onto the bed. She tried to get up. Again, the baby screamed.

He flipped his axe over and brought the blunt handle down across the woman's temple, dazing her and sending her crashing back down on the hard bed of straw and wood. The timbers cracked under the force and so did the bones of her cheek. The wailing of the child grated against the rage within him, covering the sounds of her dress ripping in his bare hands. This enraged his fury further, as the tearing of cloth was his favorite foreplay. The sight of her perfect ass infuriated him. He responded by laying his axe down next to her on the bed and drew out his dagger, cutting lines against her flawless skin like the scrimshaw Artur had cut into the pale whalebone.

Outside, pandemonium raged. Sounds of the raid intensified and Skander frowned at what appeared to be a change in momentum. Hearing shouts of resistance against his soldiers, he realized that a battle was taking place. He angrily put his knife away, smiling at his handiwork on the crying woman. Her once pretty ass was no longer perfect and bore instead his house sigil. Disappointed that he had not even unbuttoned his breeches, he grabbed his axe and strode into the night.

Outside there was no wind to carry the sounds of battle. The air was still except for large, wet snowflakes falling from the cloudless sky. Eerily, the snow had already begun piling despite the short time that he had spent inside with the woman. Skander smiled at the blood that poured over the white blanket, painting the snow pink. He quickly formed a frown when he realized the state of his attack.

He strode toward the center of the town and saw that several of his men had already fallen. Pushed back by villagers, Artur led a defensive shield wall against the organized line of ten men. Each one was dressed in tattered farm clothing but carried an exquisite quality of sword and shield. These weapons were made of top-grade imperial steel, far superior to the low grade that his men carried. Looking from corpse to corpse of his fallen comrades, he immediately saw that their weapons had been cleaved in half and lay broken in the dirt.

Furiously he ordered the charge. They may lack superior weapons, but sheer numbers should overwhelm the farmers and force them into submission. His men hesitated at his order, and Artur stared dumbly back at his king with defiant fear and trepidation on his toothless gape. Skander raged and threw his axe at the lead townsman, catching him in the center of his forehead and dropping him in the painted snow. He charged with a scream that shook his men into action as they chased after him toward the small line of men. Stooping low to retrieve his axe, he also drew the short sword from his hip. This he used to parry a blow from his left as he spun, swinging the axe down on the nape of the attacker's neck.

Bodies pressed in around him as a shield wall again formed on each side, this time making an offensive push toward the fighters. Discipline, inspired by his charge, won out that evening as his men restored the advance and dropped the last of the villagers in a pile on the square. Sounds of battle quieting, the wailing of children filled Skander's ears. He frowned as the cries of one single infant rose above the rest. Squeezing his eyes tight against the wails, he spoke loudly so that his men would hear, "Take what you want. Bring the women and the children to the well when you're finished." Smiling, his soldiers fanned out to enjoy their spoils.

Squatting down, he picked up one of the fallen swords laying in the snow. Smiling at its superiority to his short sword, he tossed his down and sheathed the finer on his belt. Turning, he slowly walked to the center of town, whistling a tune that his mother used to sing before bed. He continued to hum and whistle as he casually returned to his earlier business.

As he strode to the hovel where he had left the woman, he paused just outside the door. In the woman's arms was a crossbow. Somehow the bitch had managed to pull the instrument's heavy bolt back into place and held it pointing at his chest. "Don't you know that I like to play with my food, Dearie?" Casually he pushed the weapon aside, taking it from her limp arms and holding it downward in his left hand. With his right hand he reached up and grabbed her hair, dragging her exhausted frame to the well that stood in the center of the village. He tossed her against the bricks of the structure, laughing as her broken face hit against the stone.

Inside the hovel, the baby cried. The infuriating sound him irritated him to the point that he could no longer think rationally. All he could see was the snow falling around him, piling fast and burying the corpses. Above him shone stars against a cloudless sky. Crossbow in his hand, he held his arms against his ears, muffling the sounds of the infant.

Wails. Screams. Fury.

Artur stepped up beside him, corralling six or seven of the village's children toward the well as he was instructed. "These are all that we could find, Your Highness. We think that some escaped with some of the women during the fighting."

Lowering his arms, Skander's face contorted in rage against the sound of the crying baby. Letting out a scream, he reached out and shoved the first of the children over the ledge of the well, laughing maniacally as the body splashed into the water twenty feet below. One by one he threw them after the first, cackling and hooting as they fell. But still the infant cried. Even after the last child splashed into the well, the infant wailed.

He leaned over and looked down into the hole as his men watched on with credulous stares. From this angle he felt at one with the water below, warmed by the earth surrounding the pool. As his anger at the sound of the crying rose, so did the water in the well. Slowly at first, but then rapidly. The children below, some still conscious from the fall but suffering bruises and fractures, wailing along with the infant. All that Skander Braston could hear was the crying.

Slowly, the water churned and spun into a gentle whirlpool as he again raised his hands up to shield the sound. Around and around the children spun in the pool, water rising and frothing as it gained speed, sucking the children into the vortex and silencing them. But it wasn't enough. He could still hear that single infant. *Crying and useless. You cried all the time as a baby, Skander. Your mother and I couldn't stand the sounds that you made, so we left you with the nursemaid.*

With a final scream, Skander rushed into the hovel, still holding the crossbow in his left hand. When he emerged, the child dangled by its' foot in the right hand of the king. Still it cried. Still it wailed. Seeing her pride and joy swinging as he ran toward the well, the mother emitted a sound that was sweet to the ears of the northern king. Sweet because they momentarily muffled the sound of his torment.

When he approached the well, he swung both child and crossbow up at the same time, firing the bolt so that the shoulder of the infant was affixed firmly, nailed to the frame of the riser. He dropped the crossbow into the snow and instead drew his knife, still pink from the blood of the woman laying helpless at his feet. Her eyes were wide, but her mouth made no sound as she watched him draw a single line across the belly of the tiny, naked boy. In a final attempt to silence the cries, Skander Braston wrapped the neck of the child with its' own intestine. Even after it ceased to breath, he could still hear the cursed cries.

Chapter Twenty-Five

Ice Prince raced along the open seas, finding both wind and current. The sleek lines of the ship, low to the water, added to her speed. It had been nearly two weeks since the crew and passengers had escaped The Cove, and time was of the essence if they were to find Braen and Eusari. They had to warn them about the mutiny in Pirates Cove. Unfortunately, only they and Artema Horn had known the location of the transaction, so *Ice Prince* was winning a race with no destination.

"I'm telling you, Sippen! We need to head to Eston so that I can reach my contacts. I have eyes all over Andalon, and can get word to the rest of the fleet no matter what port they land in." Samani had been making the same argument for a week straight, but Sippen and the rest of the crew had insisted on systematically checking possible locales for *She Wolf.*

"We have one more spot to check, then we will heh... head to Eston." Estowen's Landing was high on their list but had been the furthest away. The first two places that they had checked were dead ends, and the men on *Ice Prince* were anxious and concerned about the whereabouts of their beloved captain. The Landing was an obvious spot, due to its' functional harbor and easy egress if something had gone awry with the trade.

Gunnery Sergeant Krill added his support for Sippen, much to the chagrin of Kernigan. "We be arriving at the landing, soon. Then, if the gods bless us with wind, we be arrivin' in Eston in three days. Five, if they piss on our sails, instead."

"Wonderful." Samani was visibly frustrated with the decision and seemed put out. "And very elegantly put, Mr. Krill." Not hiding his disappointment, he laid below decks to await their arrival at the Landing.

Sippen watched Kernigan leave. He had grown to like their passenger but was still leery. Although he was learned and charismatic, as well as a fun drinking companion, he had a lot of secrets and his "contacts" could spell trouble. Before leaving on *She Wolf*, Braen had warned of Samani's questioning loyalty to Artema Horn. *Why does he want so badly to get to Eston?* No, Yurik would not fully trust this man, no matter how much he liked him as a person.

They continued to hold the wind the entire day and reached the port just before sundown. As they rounded the jetty and turned west toward the inlet, their eyes beheld a magnificent sight. *She Wolf* stood boldly on the water, silhouetted against the orange and yellow blaze of the setting sun. She moored away from the pier with anchor in the water. There was no activity on deck, and the ship appeared more as an apparition than a corporeal object. Her beauty and presence instantly calmed the men of *Ice Prince*.

"All hands to deck!" Sippen shouted without a hint of a stutter. He stood smiling at the marvelous find, ready to embrace his friend and to open a bottle of 754 over a deck of cards and great conversation. Looking closer, he could make out Braen waving his arms frantically in excitement as they approached. "Puh... prepare to move alongside!"

As they made their approach, Krill took over the piloting and the little engineer went below decks to inform Kernigan that they had arrived. "Turn to starboard and head into the wind, you sorry sacks of blood!" Krill addressed the crew with a smile emblazoned on his face, the singular eye twinkling with excitement upon seeing his captain. "Prepare to slack sheet, you miserable sons of whores! Now luff sails and feather and drift!" When the ship had slowed to a crawl in the small harbor, the crew tied the main sail and made their preparations to moor alongside *She Wolf*.

After twenty yards, the big ship came about to port, intending to drift along-side the smaller vessel and tie off. Without warning, starboard cannons roared from *She Wolf,* placing a full broadside into the bow of *Ice Prince.* The ship rocked fore to aft from the blow, cracking the mast and sending it crashing across the stern. The crewmen tying off the mainsail flew into the dark water, screams abruptly stopping when they hit the surface. Several more of the crew slid across the deck into the rail, the impact knocking from them either wind or consciousness.

The concussion of the impact sent Sippen into the bulkhead. He scrambled to his feet and made his way topside to see what had happened. He emerged from the hatch just in time to witness the fall of the mainsail, as the tremendous post crashed into the helm where he had stood with Krill only moments before. Eyes wide in shock and disbelief, he took in the scene. The large helms wheel had been crushed. Beneath the large pole he could see the leg of his longtime friend, trapped beneath what was left of the steering mechanism. That was all that he could see of Sergeant Krill.

The lookout reported an incoming vessel and Eusari ran to the rail beside Braen, instantly recognizing *Ice Prince* rounding the jetty into the harbor. Eusari watched the burly captain smile at his friends' arrival with radiance that spread to his eyes. She silently wished she could experience his private joy, and, as he turned to look at her, she smiled back. A smile, something so foreign to Eusari that she could not remember the last time she had.

During the past week she had noticed things about Braen that she never looked for in other men. She admired the confidence with which he walked and spoke. She appreciated that, when they talked, he listened with intent and heartwarming honesty. His eyes always found hers, despite that she kept them hidden under her hood. Eusari was beginning to believe that she could someday trust or even have feelings for a man like him. *Maybe.*

"Help has arrived. See? The gods favor us, today." He shot and anxious look toward the hatch that locked their prisoners below. All night long the mutineers had banged their weapons against the door, causing the topside crew to fear that they would break free and overrun the ship. The banging had finally stopped a few hours ago but recommenced at the arrival of Braen's ship and crew. Frowning, he added, "They're banging with more fury, now."

"No matter. With the help of your crew we should be able to kill them all or convince them to surrender." Eusari glanced back at the cannon atop the hatch, as if willing it to stay in place.

Braen's attention returned to *Ice Prince* and Eusari could see that many of his crew were shouting and waving at him. A week ago, Eusari would not have understood the zealous loyalty they held for their captain, but after spending a week at sea, working alongside of him as he learned her own crew's names and stories, she could not help but admire and also want to follow him. He was a kind and loving man. The kind that she had not believed existed.

The ship turned its head into the wind and luffed sails to lose speed quickly. Braen smiled and let out a small laugh. "That is Krill's signature move. The crazy bastard must be at the helm."

As the ship slowed, the topside men furled the mainsail. Braen frowned and looked again at the hatch. The pounding had momentarily ceased. Eyes widening with concern, he suddenly addressed Eusari. "They have access to the armory."

It was more of a statement than a question, but Eusari answered as if he had asked. Realization crossed her countenance as she added, "they have access to the cannon powder..." Sudden awareness dropped her stomach with dread. The mutineers had control of her guns, powder, and shot. She screamed at her men to ready their arms and quickly led them to circle up around the hatch.

Braen waved his arms frantically at the crew of *Ice Prince*, yelling at them to move aft and away from the broadside. Too late, a thunderous boom exploded from below decks. A full salvo ripped through the bow of his ship, sending the forwardmost crewmen flying back with the hail of splinters. He watched in horror as the main mast ripped from the deck and fell with the lurching of the ship. The men who had been rigging the sail were tossed and Eusari saw them disappear into the dark water.

Her ears rang from the unexpected blast. She watched as the Northman drew his axe from this belt and ran to the hatch. With his broad shoulder he shoved off the gun, moving the heavy piece as easily as if it were a minor obstacle. The weight now removed, the hatch flew open from the banging below, revealing an unsuspecting mutineer holding an axe of his own.

With a downward motion, Braen swung his at the man's neck, severing his surprised expression. The rest of the men rushed up the ladder one by one, and he swung like he chopped wood. Violently lashing out and roaring like a snow cat, he severed piece after piece of the mutineers. His bloodlust changed him, and a primordial beast took his place.

Eusari had killed many men, several in cold blood and many out of vengeance. But she paled in horror at the wild turn in Braen. After watching the cold-blooded ambush of his ship and crew, he ceased to be the charming and attractive captain. He transformed into an animal dripping in the blood of his enemies, wildly killing and screaming inaudible curses and taunts. He was the most terrifying visage of fury she had ever seen.

Eusari and the rest of the topside crew stood around him, giving just enough room for his wild swinging, weapons drawn to assist. After a few minutes, the men below pulled back from the stairwell, realizing that to exit was certain death. A pile of body parts lay in a pool of blood beneath the ladder, and blood-soaked Braen bellowed rage. Gone was the easy-going sea captain, replaced by a berserker from the north.

When the mutineers had stopped climbing the stairs, Braen screamed at them in challenge. "Come out and face me, cowards!" Spit spewed from his mouth, mixing with the blood of the men he had hacked, causing a froth to form like a rabid animal. When no man would exit, Braen looked down into the hatch and saw nine men backed up against the door to the armory. With a final roar of anger, his wild face contorted behind his blood-soaked beard.

The air around the ship went ice cold. The night had already been cool, and the breeze had been the kind that you turn up your collar against. Abruptly the air around *She Wolf* became a winter storm. The change took away the breath of everyone witnessing the rage.

Suddenly, the ship lurched in the water. The pressure around the vessel increased, squeezing the hull from all sides at once. Braen breathed heavily, staring down into the hold as *She Wolf* slowly sank like a swamped canoe. The water seeped in from the spaces between the boards that strained against the pressure, flooding and filling the hold.

Below decks, the horrified mutineers cried and screamed for mercy as the entire cavity filled with water. One brave man tried to swim to the ladder, trying his luck against the devil above. Braen threw aside his axe and caught the man's face between his bare hands, pulling him close as one would a lover. Eusari recognized the man as Johon the Coxswain. She had liked the man, always whistling as he worked with a smile on his face. She tried to remember if he had a wife and kids.

Braen squeezed the sides of the man's face slowly. She did not recognize her friend in that moment, fully consumed by bloodlust and revenge. Tears flowed down her cheeks as Johon's skull imploded between those powerful northern hands. As if the action had been related to the pressure around the ship, *She Wolf* once again lurched.

Braen dropped the man's lifeless body into the water below and collapsed on the deck. Tears rolled down his face, streaking the blood. Instantly, the pressure around the swamped ship released, and *She Wolf* rocked precariously back and forth, ready to sink at any moment. Eusari ran up and closed the hatch, ensuring that the mutineers would drown in their tomb below her feet.

She carefully picked her way toward Braen as if he were a wounded animal that would lash out if she got too close. Pausing briefly, she motioned her men to help the crew aboard *Ice Prince* and looked down at the crippled Braston. He cried and coughed as the blood ran down off his body and onto the deck. His scarlet hand felt along his ribcage, tenderly remembering the pain from his beatings.

She could tell that he wanted to stand and run to his crew, but the captain from the north had no more energy. No more anger. He was spent. She knelt beside and hugged him close as he wept on her shoulder.

Chapter Twenty-Six

Eston City mourned her beloved Queen Regent. Citizens painted brightly colored roses on black backgrounds, lining the streets and bridges with the banners and pennants. The old and young alike wore black, and even the poorest found strips of black cloth to tie around their arms to display their loss. She belonged to the people, and they would forever miss their Lady.

Her funeral spanned six days of holiday, essentially cutting off the outside world. The closed gates and harbor operations halted commerce, and the markets and bazaars rolled up their tents. Locked in their homes, noblemen whispered stories of intrigue and deception within the Queen Regent's cabinet and the commoners retold grisly tales of the treasonous beheading. Each city dweller wished that the northern monster was in the ground instead of their beloved matriarch.

The story spread quickly of how the exiled prince, Braen Braston, had contacted Chancellor Gedon and struck a deal to restore him to his northern throne. He asked only for assistance in ousting his brother, the rightful heir chosen by the legendary Krist Braston. But the Chancellor had a more sinister and devious plan up his treasonous sleeve. He, after years of jealously, wished to remove the mother of the city, and the rapist and murderer from the north made his options viable.

The politician knew that he would never hold the throne, himself, but saw opportunity in Prince Robert. The boy suffered chronic illnesses, rendering him too feeble to wield either a sword or shield. Illiterate and dumb, the boy lacked the ability to read simple words much less lead the greatest nation in the world. Gedon had found the perfect puppet through which to rule over the masses while lining his pockets with the gold of the people.

The Queen had longed for retirement to their summer home but recognized that her oldest son was not fit to rule. Thus, she had expressed to the cabinet that she would hold onto leadership until her younger son, Marcus, could pass the trials and rule as well as she. The Chancellor had quickly ordered that the younger prince be kidnapped by Braston, taken across the sea and through the dangerous reefs of Pirate's Cove. There, he was beaten and tortured by the Northman until a ransom could be collected.

The leader of the Pirate's guild, the famed Artema Horn, became sympathetic to the plight of the prince, and even tried to rescue Marcus. He launched his ship to take after Braston for a daring high seas rescue, but the cowardly Northman had paid off Horn's personal guard to attack him. The cowards had fired upon and destroyed his vessel in the harbor of The Cove. The people spoke of the darkness in the heart of the prince of the north, and how he had brutally beaten Marcus Esterling each night at sea.

The Queen used her own wealth to ransom her son and met the pirates in a secret meeting place. There, Braston and his pirates had raped and beheaded the mother as she cried over her beaten and bloodied son. She was rescued by Captain-General Matteas Brohn who fought the blackhearts off and rescued the boy from certain death. His only regret, the story tells, is that the pirate had made off with the ransom money and escaped with his life.

Every citizen made their way to the square on the seventh day of mourning. They witnessed the most momentous day since the coronation of the first Esterling monarch, and no one missed the trial of the dastardly Chancellor Gedon. Marcus Esterling sat in his mother's grand chair in the center of the square, overlooking the assembled citizens, every eye watching him during the trial, pitying his plight at the hands of the pirate. They wanted to love him like they had adored his mother.

The young prince should have been happy with how the masses had played into his ploy, but he felt melancholy. He wanted better weather in which to hold the trial, the spectacle of a century. Winter had moved in quickly and cold wet rain chilled the morning. He wrapped a woolen blanket around his shoulders, shivering and fretting. He held up a mug and an attendant poured some hot spiced wine to help warm him.

An iron cage rested at the feet of the prince, too low for a man to stand to full height and built in a way that they could not sit, either. Movement caught everyone's attention as a prison wagon made its way toward the platform. Marcus smiled as the citizens threw rotten fruits and vegetables at the occupant. The guards led the old man from the wagon to the platform and someone found a rock to throw, striking him on the forehead and splitting his thin skin. A trail of blood ran down his face and the boy prince let out a little chuckle at the sight.

Ten Falconers emerged from their Rookery. The overseers would not participate in the trial, but their presence would legitimize the outcome. Chief Magistrate Frasier Boothe rose at the approach of the prisoner and beat his gavel violently to get the crowd's attention. "Order! Order!"

Several minutes of prodding from soldiers finally beat back the crowd, forcing them to quiet down. Prince Marcus Esterling stood from his throne, letting his blanket fall onto the platform as he raised his arms so that the crowd could see him. He was a splendid sight, dressed in a tunic adorned with the family crest. In his hands he held a single red rose like a scepter.

"I carry this rose for my mother. She was a child of spring and cared for her roses as she did her people, with love and patient compassion." The crowd erupted, this time full of cheers and adulation for the late Queen Regent. Marcus let them die down on their own, then continued. "But occasionally the gardener must weed out the undesirables that threaten to choke out the entire vine." Again, cheers erupted, and chants of, "Kill him!" echoed.

"My citizens! No man is innocent unless he can prove so in the eyes of the people. Today Lord Chancellor Gedon stands before you to answer allegations that he committed egregious crimes from his seat of power. A seat that he held in trust by the citizenry. By you!" Marcus fought to keep a smile off his face, enjoying the power of the frenzied mob as it grew beneath him. "I ask a personal favor of you, kind people. I ask that you judge him with compassion and patience just as my late mother, your adored matriarch, judged over you." The eruption lasted several more minutes before the soldiers could again quiet the near frenzied mob. Satisfied, the prince sat down to witness the show.

"Order! Order!" Magistrate Boothe banged his gavel with all of his strength, shouting over the mob. When it quieted down enough to speak, he asked the prisoner, "Lord Gedon." The old man straightened his back as much as the cage would let him at his addressal. "High Chancellor and representative of the people of the Esterling Empire, you are charged with crimes against the people and the crown." The magistrate read each charge aloud so that the crowd would have an opportunity to voice their dissatisfaction. "Kidnapping of a noble. Murder by contract. High treason! How do you plead to these accusations?"

The crowd hurtled more objects at the cage, several of which struck the chancellor directly. He would have brought his hands up over his face, except that they were shackled to a chain attached to his feet.

"Not guilty, Magistrate!" The elderly man fought to shout over the now murderous crowd. "I love the people of the Empire and it is my sworn duty to…"

"Order! Order!" The banging of the gavel drowned out the words following his plea. "The court calls Lord Cedrick Strader, Minister of Finance, to testify against the accused!" Strader strode forward with a somber expression on his face. He raised his hand to swear to the accuracy of his statement.

"Lord Strader. Did the Chancellor procure the sum of one

hundred thousand golden talents from the treasury, just a week before the death of the Queen Regent?"

"Aye, Magistrate. He did." The crowd roared again.

"And where are these funds, now?"

"I assume that the chest is in the hands of Lord Braen Braston."

"How can you make that assumption? Didn't the Queen pay him with her own funds?" Boothe spoke over the banging of his own gavel as he questioned the witness.

"The chest had gone with the Queen to ransom back her son, High Prince Marcus Esterling. She believed it to be from her own vault, but Chancellor tricked her into using the people's money. He provided an altered procurement form to the treasury, requesting public funds."

"Is it customary for the government to pay ransom to pirates, My Lord?"

"No, Your Honor. That's why I was shocked by the request."

"Who insisted that you deliver over the funds for the ransom?"

"Your Honor. That was due to the urgings of Chancellor Gedon. He signed the request along with a personal note demanding strict confidence and secrecy regarding the nature of the payment." The minister's face dropped, and his countenance was crestfallen, regretful, even. "I had to comply with the orders from the representative of the people, Your Honor. I had no choice." Again, objects began flying toward the caged man, accompanied by boos and more chants.

"Order! Order!" The magistrate addressed Booth, "You may step down, Minister. You were following orders and are not under trial, here." Reading from a paper, he called for the next witness. "The court calls Lord Campton Shol, Minister of Information and Assistant to the Chancellor."

Campton Shol wore a simple woolen tunic devoid of sigil and ornamentation. If he had been standing in the crowd it would have been difficult to distinguish him from the commoners. Marcus sat up taller, closely watching the man as he approached the witness platform. Like Boothe, the man swore his testimony and turned to face Chancellor Gedon.

"Lord Shol. Are you the personal assistant to the Chancellor?"

"I am."

"Have you heard him speak of intent to overthrow the Queen and to support the usurper against his brother?"

"Your Honor. Lord Gedon spoke often of the older brother, many times comparing the boy to his younger brother." At the mention of Marcus, he gestured toward the royal box. "He did not care much for the younger prince, and often expressed as much to me and whomever would pay attentions to his ramblings."

"Answer the question. Have you heard him speak of his intent to overthrow Lady Crestal Esterling?"

"I assure you. Had I overheard such treason I would have reported it immediately."

"I see. As Minister of Information, you have access to secrets that are little known to the rest of us for reasons of national security. Tell us. Who kidnapped Prince Marcus?"

"Why, Braen Braston, of course! I have the written request for ransom, right here." The crowd again exploded.

"Order! Order!" Once the crowd had settled, the magistrate pressed on. "What was the Chancellor's response when the Queen was informed of the kidnapping?"

"He was adamant that we pay the ransom. She was afraid to use public funds for such a folly, but he insisted. When she tried to argue against his insistence, he literally lunged out of his chair at her in anger." An inhalation of shock went through the crowd and the man in the cage began to cry.

"I see. Do you believe that the Chancellor intended to overthrow Lady Crestal in support of Prince Robert?"

"In my heart I believe that Lord Gedon would have rather placed a chimpanzee on the throne than any of the Esterling family. Prince Robert was just the easiest for him to manipulate, Your Honor." More rocks than fruits and vegetables began to fly at the cage, so much that Lord Shol had to hurry off of the platform. Marcus beamed as he watched the crowd intensify.

"ORDER!" The magistrate shouted to the chief of the guard, and soldiers fanned out. "This court calls Captain General Matteas Brohn to testify!"

Matteas approached the stand and swore in like the others. But when he turned to face the Chancellor he reared back and spit in the man's face. The crowd exploded in cheers. "Order! ORDER! I will remind the witness to refrain from making personal judgements while on the stand.

"I apologize, Your Honor. But I watched as Braen Braston struck the head from my Queen. Before he did so, he plainly stated that he was acting on behalf of Lord Gedon." For the first time that morning, the crowd had gone completely silent, tears filling the eyes of both the men and the women.

"Why did you let him live? Why did you let him escape?"

"Because he and his witch companion had worked dark magic, Your Honor." The crowd listened intently. "His witch called upon the roots and vines to tie my men and me up, while she sent spiders to crawl up and down our skin, biting us and trying to force their way into our mouths and noses. We were powerless against their magic, Your Honor. When he made his escape and we were free, he channeled water and waves to drive back my ship. We barely escaped before the Kraken himself could rise from the water." At this, the crowd wailed and screamed for the heads of both Braston and Gedon.

"NONSENSE! Those stories are superstition and nonsense!"

It was Marcus' turn to participate in the spectacle, and he rose from his chair. "Your Honor, if I may?" The magistrate nodded for him to go ahead and the prince began to speak. "More than a month ago, the same Braen Braston raided our winter stores. Just as our fleet had converged upon him, several of these Kraken rose from the water and secured his escape. We had multiple witnesses. CREDIBLE witnesses who will uphold the claims. Furthermore, I can personally attest to the use of magic by his witch accomplice." The crowd was in total shock and let out a collective gasp.

Two Falconers walked forward, followed closely by a young woman. She would have been beautiful had her nose not been recently broken and twisted out of shape so horribly. Both of her eyes were black from bruising, and she was almost two weak to climb onto the platform.

The magistrate asked the prince, "What is this about, then? Who is this woman?"

"This woman is the most recent victim of Braen Braston. After he had fled from the scene of the crime, and after killing my mother, he raced up the coastline to a small village." The people stared, dumbfounded at the presentation of the woman. "There, his troops attacked simple people without food or gold and ravaged them with his senseless violence."

"You, madame, what is your name, love?"

"I am Amira."

"Where are you from, Amira?"

"A small village in the north called Ataraxia."

"What did Braen Braston do to your village, my dear?"

Tears soaked the woman's eyes as she relayed all of the bloody and gory details of the raid on her village. She described northern monsters, tall and bearded who cut the men to pieces and brutally ravaged the women. She broke into tears several times in the telling of the story, especially when she described the fate of the children. She spun a tale of magic and demons, unbelievable, had they not been collaborated by the Prince's testimony. When she described the fate of her own child, she wept uncontrollably along with every mother in the audience.

"My dear, Amira," Marcus was on a roll, and ready to push the crowd one more time. "May we show everyone here the proof that Braen Braston was the perpetrator of these crimes?"

With a nod, she agreed and turned her back to the crowd. One of the Falconers let her wool dress drop to the ground, removing her clothing down to her undergarments. The other lifted her skirt, revealing several cuts and carvings in her white skin. The crowd gasped in recognition at the unmistakable Sabrecat devouring a wolf. After the crowd had seen her mutilated skin, she gathered up her dress and allowed the Falconers to lead her off.

Marcus cleared his throat and once more addressed the court. "Magistrate, I ask you to weigh the evidence that you have seen and tend to the issue at hand. Do it, quickly, so that I may ask the council, as representatives of you great citizens," he pointed to the crowd, "for emergency powers and recognition as the heir to my father's empire. I vow, that as your king, I will hunt down both the abomination Braen Braston as well as my treasonous brother." Bowing his head, he added, "I will kill them and all of their co-conspirators in the name of my mother, our beloved matriarch, Lady Crestal Esterling!"

The crowd tried to push past the soldiers. Some were chanting, "Guilty!" while others shouted, "King Marcus!"

The magistrate banged his gavel, finally screaming as loud as he could over the noise, "I FIND LORD CHANCELLOR GEDON GUILTY OF ALL CHARGES!" But, before he could pass a sentence and recommend that he be hanged by the neck in a public place, the crowd pushed forward, rocking the cage until it toppled over. Someone found a set of keys with which they opened the box, lifting out the old man. They raised him over their heads and delivered him to the center of the square.

The ravenous crowd tore off his clothing and began beating and kicking him. After his skull had been crushed and bones broken, his limbs were torn apart and tossed over the bridge into the river below. Matteas Brohn quickly escorted a smiling Marcus Esterling into a carriage, whisking him away to the Rose Palace.

CHAPTER TWENTY-SEVEN

It had been a week since the mutineers had fired upon *Ice Prince,* and Braen Braston had not fully recovered his strength. He had reinjured several ribs during his display on the deck of *She Wolf,* and Sippen and Eusari joined forces to keep him in bed until fully healed. They had taken charge of both crews, brought provisions ashore and essentially resurrected the ghost town. He proudly watched from his hospital bed as both of his friends worked side by side with the crewmen, strengthening bonds as he had shown them.

Braen turned to the bed next to him and smiled. "Looks like we own an entire town, my friend."

Gunnery Sergeant Krill spat over the side and remarked, "Wha' da devil do we be need'n with a fuck'n town, Cap'n?"

"I honestly have no idea," Braen tried not to laugh, but felt the pain in his ribs, nonetheless. "How's your leg feeling?"

"Fuck you, Cap'n." Krill was a comical sight, looking down with his one eye at his one leg, the other having been amputated several days before.

"Aww, don't be sore, Krill. I think it gives you character. Credibility as a pirate, even."

Krill smiled back, his one eye ablaze with sarcasm, "That's why I wear the eyepatch!" Gesturing at his stump, he added, "Now I be need'n a fuck'n peg leg."

Braen smiled. It was good to see his that friend had survived the blast, albeit narrowly. "All that you need is a hook hand."

"Gawds no, Cap'n! You kin put an eye out wit one of those!"

Both men laughed hysterically, resulting in a spasm that forced Braen to ease back down on the bed, wheezing from the pain in his ribs. A short time later, Eusari and Sippen walked into the room with plates of food for their recovering charges. Sippen took his plate to Krill, who instantly devoured the contents.

Eusari lifted the napkin over the plate, frowning down at the food. Blushing, she put the napkin over the food and stood to leave. "On second thought, I'll bring you some soup."

Braen raised an eyebrow incredulously, then looked over to see Krill gnawing on a spare rib. Looking back at Eusari, he nodded. "Yeah, that's a good idea. It might be too soon for ribs." He watched her scurry out of the room, red faced and embarrassed.

"Sippen, how bad off is *Ice Prince*?"

"Nuh... not bad. The tuh... top mast is gone. I need a new one."

"I was afraid of that. Take a team into the forest and find a good one. Take Eusari with you, when you do." He looked up to see her returning with a bowl of soup. Thankfully there were no bones in the bowl.

"Take me where?" She asked.

"Into the forest, we need a new topmast to get *Ice Prince* underway." He sat up and she wedged a pillow beneath his back so that he could eat.

"I kuh... cannot go. I nuh... need to finish pumping *She Wolf* and tuh... tar her seams."

Krill interrupted, "Tar... I love the sound of dat word, 'tarrr.' It rolls off de tongue, it do."

"Are you fucking serious, right now?" Eusari looked like she was about to shove her knife in Krill's one good eye. "People like you are the reason that Pirates have stereotypes, you know."

"Arrr, dat be true, but so do peg legs and eye patches, and I be the only one wearing those, arrrrrnt I?" He either winked or blinked, but his point was made.

"Your friends are fucking weird, Braston." Standing up, she started making her way to the door. Motioning for Sippen to follow, she added, "come tell me the dimensions that you need for your post, little man. I'll get it with my team."

Braen waited until she and Sippen were out of earshot before he turned to Krill and said, "Yes, I know that they arrrrrrrr." Both men laughed and Braen spilled his soup when he reached for his side against the pain.

Moments later a throat cleared in the doorway. Braen looked up to see Samani Kernigan standing in the doorway with a bundle.

"Come in." Braen still did not trust nor like this man, but they were stranded together, and he decided to make the best of it. "I've hardly seen you since you arrived. What have you been working on, Sam?"

"Sippen found blacksmith equipment in town and I've been trying to help him restore a laboratory."

"He's spread thin overseeing the repairs of two ships. His hobbies will have to wait."

Kernigan pulled the hand cannon from his waistband and held it up to the light, inspecting it. "This is a game changer, Braen. This and several other of his inventions could change this entire world, and I want to help him to do that. Please promise me that you'll focus on his development."

"They're novelties, Sam, novelties that lack accuracy and reliability."

"I disagree, but this is your command, Braston. I'll not interfere, but you're making a mistake if you don't let him focus on weapons development."

"Weapons? Weapons for what? Now that Nevra has The Cove, we're rogue outlaws and probably have prices on our heads as we speak. We need to leave for the Southern Continent and seek asylum."

"Braen, we have less than two more weeks until the flagships return to The Cove. The situation is getting dire, and I need to get to either Eston or Diaph. I have contacts in both ports." He pulled a chair beside Braen's bedside and sat. "If we move, soon, we can bring support over to our side and strike back at Nevra."

Looking thoughtful, Braen sat silent and rubbed his beard. Finally speaking he asked, "You know these men better than I do. What percentage will support you over Nevra?"

"That's hard to say. But the faster we move the weaker his position. Pirates follow power, Braen."

"Sam, I get that. But it'll be at least two days until *She Wolf* is seaworthy, and several more until *Ice Prince* is." Looking up at Kernigan, he noticed that something had changed in the man. For as long as he had known him, he was a wheeler dealer who constantly played with puppet strings. This new man looked humbled and concerned. Afraid, even. He reconsidered. "Help Sippen get a lab established so that he can build us some useful gadgets. Then, after we can get afloat, I'll drop you off with your contacts. I won't make any more promises beyond that."

Kernigan looked honestly appreciative when he looked up. "Thank you, Braen."

"You're welcome. We'll get you in charge of The Cove in no time, Sam. Then you can get back to your politics."

Samani looked aghast. "NO!"

"What's wrong?"

"I think that you misunderstand. I've no desire to lead The Cove." Samani's eyes pleaded with an honest disdain at the prospect, and, for once, Braen began to trust that he did not have an ulterior motive.

Pulling off the sheets, the bearded captain climbed out of bed and indicated for Samani to follow him to the kitchen. "I need ale for this conversation. Let's go drink." Once seated at the kitchen table, Braen posed the question that had been burning. "How did you know that I couldn't trust Artema Horn."

Sipping from his mug, Kernigan began, "I've been an officer and advisor to The Cove since before Artema took over fifteen years ago."

"Go on."

"I know everything that happens in Andalon. My spies are

networked in every city and major town throughout the empire, in Fjorik and even the Southern Continent."

Braen nodded, and commented, "That's quite a network. How do you finance that?"

"That's the easy part, and why I'm aligned with The Cove. I fund the web through a legitimate institution that is free from the oversight of the Ministry of Information."

"The guild, you mean."

"Yes," Sam nodded. "the Pirate's Guild. It's imperative that I keep my web out of the gaze of the ministry and their Falconers. You might consider me the counter organization to theirs."

"I see. So, get back to Artema. How did you know?"

"I didn't, exactly. That was a complete and unpredictable surprise. I knew that he was getting too close to the Esterling family, but that was it. I feared that he'd jeopardize The Cove and draw too much attention to the guild." Samani sipped from his mug. "I wanted someone more capable and less self-consumed to take over operations before that happened."

Braen nodded, "More capable than Nevra, and less self-consumed than Artema?"

"Exactly." Sam downed his entire mug and poured another.

"So, this was me taking over the guild before Nevra could, and before Artema destroyed us with his incompetence?"

"In a nutshell."

"Sam?"

"Yes?"

"I don't even want my own kingdom back, how can you think that I want The Cove?" Braen took a long sip from his mug.

"Because it was prophesized."

Braen spit the contents of his mug across the room.

Eusari went into the forest with six of her best fighting men, each armed with a crossbow and extra bolts. All week she had trained these men in stealth and knife throwing. She passed along every skill she knew, teaching them to fight up close like a thief with speed and agility as well as hiding in shadows. They brought the bows along with hopes they could train range weapons after completing their work.

She walked in complete silence through the woods, cringing when one of her men would misstep and make a sound. They were not perfect but improved daily.

Giovani, who had been elevated to cook in her crew, broke the quiet with a question. "Where did you learn how to walk like this? It's especially difficult in a forest."

"My father taught me. He was an excellent hunter and outdoorsman." Thinking about him brought back pain that had been absent for years. "He also taught me archery and how to hold a knife."

Jacques stepped on a branch, earning him looks of disdain from everyone in the party. "Sorry." He muttered.

They walked like this for about a mile, until they finally reached a grove of spruce. Eusari picked out a suitably sized tree that matched Sippen's requirements, and the men began to cut. She watched for a while, until the tree felled. She finally got bored watching them trim off the branches and walked away from the group to think and to focus on other thoughts.

Braen Braston was foremost in her mind. She had spent more and more time thinking about the Northman, and that worried her. She was not ready to trust another man, not so quickly after losing Sa'Mond and Artema in a single night. He troubled her.

She found a clearing and chose a felled log to sit on while getting lost in her thoughts. No matter how hard she tried, her mind kept returning to the bearded man. At first, she wondered about his swift forgiveness after what she had done. *How could he joke about the rib bone, the way that he did, earlier? Is he toying with me? Making me feel bad? Is he waiting for his chance to crush me after gaining my trust? And why did he help with my crew?*

The thoughts brought up anger, and she crossed her arms against a chill.

After a while, she thought instead about the way he had gone berserk on the mutineers with a bloodlust that nearly destroyed *She Wolf.* He had killed Johon mercilessly. *How had he done that?* If she hadn't of been there, to see the "power of the kraken" as the others had begun to call it, then she would not have believed that he controlled the waters.

What worried her the most, was recalling the night in Estowen's Landing when Sa'Mond had died. She remembered reaching out with her mind and hearing the answer of the vines and insects. *I did that. I called them. I felt them as if I were biting the soldiers and not the spiders.* Feeling the air turn even colder, she pulled her cloak closer around her body.

Trying to relax she stretched out and felt fur. Startled, she looked back and saw that a very large black wolf had sprawled out and lay beside her. She froze. The animal looked up at Eusari and yawned, exposing huge teeth and jaws that could rip her into shreds. It settled down and pressed against her. With her hand still on the animal, she began to pet. Slowly at first, then, when the animal did not protest, she began to stroke its' fur. When it allowed her to scratch behind its' ears, she laughed out loud. The wolf only glanced at her and then pressed into her hand.

"That is quite a pet, you have there."

Eusari was so focused on the animal, that she did not see the man walk up on her. She leaped to her feet, drawing a knife. The wolf stood and growled a low sound that made both her and the man uneasy. The newcomer placed his hands up, showing that he was not a threat. His only weapons were a bow on his back and an axe on his belt.

"I'm sorry," he said. "I didn't mean to startle you."

"Who are you?" She looked him over, measuring. He dressed in buckskins and a long black beard reached down his chest. His long black hair draped his shoulders.

"My name is Shon Wimbley." He reached out his hand, but she ignored it. After a moment, he put his back down. "I was hunting and heard the woodcutting. I'm sorry, I'll leave you, alone."

"Wait." Eusari detected something in his voice, something familiar. "Where are you from, Shon Wimbley?"

"I am from Loganshire."

"Where. Where in Loganshire?"

"My family is from Brentway, a tiny town about…"

"About six miles northeast of Logan." Eusari finished his thought.

"Yes. That's right. Do you know the area?" The man appeared noticeably shocked that she had.

The mention of her hometown took her back to her childhood. She remembered the dirt streets, the smell of the bakery and the sounds that came from the inn every evening. With her father being the constable, her family knew everyone in the town and surrounding villages. She even remembered a Wimbley, growing up. She narrowed her eyes and looked closely at the stranger.

"Ma'am," the man gestured toward the wolf at her side, "can you make your wolf stand down? He is quite unnerving, and I promise no harm."

Looking down, she realized that the huge animal was matching her own posture, defensive, unsure and wary. "um… Sit." The animal looked at her, and then sat like a trained domestic. Eusari shrugged.

"Thank you."

"You say that you're Shon Wimbley?"

"Yes ma'am. From Brentway."

"What was the name of the constable during the last Northern raid?" She narrowed her eyes at him, awaiting his response.

It was his turn to be taken aback. This was not a question that he had expected to ever answer, but he did. Without hesitation he responded, "Franque Thorinson was the constable during the raid." Standing a little taller, he proudly added, "I fought along-side him and watched as the northern devil killed him." She felt his words rip scabs over memories that had healed years before. "He was my mentor and my friend." Indicating he bow, he added, "He even taught me how to use this."

She fought back a tear, then asked her next question, "How many children did he have?"

"Four. Three sons, Franque, Thom and Jean and one daughter, Eusari."

"What happened to his children?"

He eyed her suspiciously, but continued, "Franque and Jean have nice little farms outside of town. Thom was taken by the gods, last year, along with his wife and youngest child. Franque is raising their oldest daughter, Anne."

"What about Franque's daughter? What about Eusari."

Realization spread across his face as he looked upon her differently. "You have my sister's eyes, dear. I don't know how I didn't recognize you at once. It is you, isn't it, Dearie?"

Tears flowing from her eyes, she nodded. "It's been a long time, Uncle Shon."

CHAPTER TWENTY-EIGHT

Maximus Reeves sat atop his destrier on a hill overlooking Weston. He winced at the memory of the last time he sat upon this rise, when Robert had pushed him to charge the city. That had been a foolish act, but the boy had finally shown his courageous spirit. *The boy no longer.* That was the day that Maximus forever considered Robert Esterling a man. He had shown more backbone and far stronger resolve than the most decorated general in the empire had shown on that day.

Thinking about Robert made him anxious. It had been more than a week since he had disappeared, and Max feared the worse. He wished that he had not turned the army around and marched away from Robert, leaving him standing alone shouting at the councilman. He had assumed that the prince would have followed the column, but he did not. Maximus felt personally responsible for leaving him behind.

A rider approached from camp and the general looked up to see Captain Titus approaching. "Sir." The man gave a crisp salute as he pulled back on his reigns.

"Well?"

"Still no sign of the prince, sir."

"What do our agents say?"

"We have twenty men within the walls, scouring the city. He's not imprisoned as far as we can tell, and he hasn't been staying in the palace."

Max let out a breath, relieved but feeling disheartened from the news. "Keep looking. Check everywhere, even the alleyways."

Grimacing, he added, "Every time that a body turns up, have one of our men check it. You know, just to be sure." Time was running out for the prince. Eventually, the army would have to break camp and move further away from the city, but he would drag his feet as long as he could. Robert was alive, or, at least he tried to convince himself that it was so.

Consumed in his thoughts, the general pictured the worse. If only he had more spies in the city. "Do we have any word on the Falconer who fled?"

"No, General. We assume he fled to Eston."

"Then that will be all, Captain. Let me know the moment any news arrives from Eston." He waited for the officer to leave him to his thoughts, irritated that he lingered. "Is there something else, Titus?"

"Sir…" The man shifted his weight in the saddle, then leaned forward to reassuringly pat the neck of his mount. Max frowned as he realized that the man needed more reassurance than the beast.

"Spit it out, man!"

"Sir, when you and Prince Robert charged through the gate…"

Reeves cut off the junior officer with irritation in his voice. "Yes. That was bold, brash and stupid. I know."

"Yes Sir." Max shot him a look of caution. "I mean no, Sir. I mean…"

"Well was it or wasn't it? Gods, man, how did you finish the academy?"

"General, what I mean is that… well… When you and the prince charged the gate the arrows were bending, Sir." Captain Titus stared at the ground as he spoke, ashamed, but evidently believing the words."

"For fuck's sake. What the devil are you talking about?" Max pierced the man with his eyes, clearly confused, irritated, and annoyed.

"The arrows. They flew directly at you both, but then bent around like you had a shield ten feet behind you."

"What?"

"They deflected. No. Diffracted around you with a curve. A parabolic curve, Sir."

"Captain, have you been drinking?" Max readied himself to dismount and strike the man from his horse and have him flogged.

"No Sir. I'm sober." He paused, then added, "General, the other men saw it, too. The entire camp is talking about it. They think that the Prince was divinely protected." The man lifted his gaze and looked directly into Max's eyes. Gods, he really believed what he was saying. "You too, Sir. The scuttlebutt is that you are both destined by the gods to lead the empire. They are happy to serve you both, Sir."

Max took this in. Although he did not believe in superstitious nonsense, this would be helpful. The Prince would eventually need an army of dedicated and zealous loyalists if he were to overthrow his mother. "Then pray, Captain. Pray that the gods are watching over him, now. That they're keeping him safe." He turned his head so that the man would not see the tears blurring his eyes for the boy. "Wherever the Prince may be."

He continued to look the other way as the captain gave another salute and then rode off to rejoin the main army. He immediately dismissed the officer's report as superstition. Useful superstition, but superstition all the same.

Maximus, again alone, felt the worry in his heart deepen at the lack of news. *Where could the prince be? He'd most likely stick close to the Horslei girl.* He shook his head at this, thinking about how she had manipulated and played Robert over the past months. He didn't doubt that her father had put her up to the relationship, to curry favor with the Esterling family. But the way that she had flipped on Robert in favor of the Pescari was a problem. His brow furrowed as he remembered. The heartbreak must have been devastating to the prince.

The general's eyes again rested on the city, pondering hiding places and wondering if Eachann would be bold enough to imprison the Imperial emissary. If he did, then Maximus Reeves would personally lead the charge to crush him.

A shout from the main camp snapped General Reeves to immediate attention. Another rider rode with haste to Captain Titus, who wheeled his steed and sprinted back up the hill to his commander. News of Robert at last? He offered a prayer to the gods above, that it was good news.

"General Reeves!" Both the man and beast were out of breath when they reached the hilltop. "The Queen Regent is dead. The younger Esterling brother has laid claim to the throne and declared Prince Robert an outlaw."

"Fuck." Max felt the bottom fall out of his heart and into his stomach. "Get your ass into that city and find the boy. NOW!"

Sarai walked beside Taros as they made their way to the newly designated Pescari district. Eachann had wasted no time clearing out the previous residents, relocating them to a more appropriate area on the far side of the city. The borough chosen for the Pescari had been run down and largely ignored in the past, but builders were hard at work making improvements.

Sarai briefly considered why this area had been neglected before the arrival of the Pescari but knew that it was part of Eachann's voting district. She speculated that her father and his cronies had blocked his efforts and prevented the vital monies necessary for improving the infrastructure.

The existing buildings had been emptied in advance of the new occupants, and Sarai noticed that the Pescari had settled in quite easily. "Have your people had any problem with the other citizens?"

"Just the expected. Westonians are afraid of us and think that we are savages. Every now and then, someone will throw rotten fruit or insults, but your city guards chase them away."

Sarai nodded. Cassus had given strict orders that no one would harm the newcomers, but he had doubled patrols just in case. "I'm so sorry, Taros." She placed her hand on his arm, letting it linger as they walked. She felt comfortable with the boy and wanted him to feel at ease.

As they strolled through the city Sarai thought about Robert and the similar walks that they used to take. She had not seen the prince since that horrible night and assumed that he had left with General Reeves. In a way, she was upset that he had not fought harder for her. She still loved him; despite that he had tried to march against the poor Pescari. In her heart she hoped that he would come back to her, realize his folly and apologize, then help her and Eachann to rebuild the city into a place where everyone would be welcome.

"Are you well, Sarai?"

"What? Oh, I'm sorry, Taros. My mind wandered."

"We are here. This is what I wanted to show you."

Sarai looked up and saw that they had reached the center of the district. Her eyes beamed when she looked at Taros' surprise, and she threw her arms around him in a big, friendly hug that nearly knocked him off his feet. The public display caught the attention of several nearby Pescari women who frowned their disapproval. Ignoring their stares, she grabbed him by the hand and dragged him inside the construction site, excited to see the layout of the new meeting lodge.

Flaya watched as the Shapan walked with the girl with the yellow hair. Her jealousy burned as the girl placed her hands on his arms in such an intimately familiar way, but she followed them through the streets just the same. He and Sarai had been venturing out publicly more often, and many of the Pescari had noticed that Taros spent more of his time with the Westonians than his own people. But Flaya had especially noticed that he spent more time with his yellow-haired princess then any of them.

She watched as the two stopped in front of the meeting lodge and felt anger well up when the girl wrapped her arms around Taros. Worse, the whore had grabbed the Shapan's hand and took him inside of the lodge, the most sacred of places in the Pescari culture. Squinting, she looked high up at the midday sky at Felicima, who had witnessed the brazen afront to propriety.

Flaya scurried to the elder's lodge, leaving her chores. Knocking, she waited until the door to the lodge opened and Daska stepped out.

"What is it, Granddaughter?"

"I watched the Shapan like you asked me, and I watched him take the girl into the new meeting lodge."

Daska bowed his head, shaking it with disgust. Squinting up, he remarked, "And in the eyes of Felicima, as well. Have you been able to speak to him or get him alone since we arrived at the city?"

"No, Grandfather. He is always with that girl."

Nodding, he reassured her. "Keep trying. Our people need to win him back from the temptations of this foreign culture, and you are key to that."

CHAPTER TWENTY-NINE

Shon Wimbley stared at his niece with shock and amazement. He had last seen her when Krist Braston of Fjorik raided Brentway fourteen years earlier. Looking at her, now, he had no doubt that she was truly his niece.

"Where have you been, Dearie? Where did they take you?"

Eusari wiped her eyes with the back of her hand. "That doesn't matter." Sniffling a little, she tried to regain her composure.

Shon showed concern when a thought crossed his mind, "Sari, are you still their captive? Do they still own you?"

Anger flashed across her face, "No man owns me, uncle!"

He flinched at her response and paused a moment before changing the subject. "I'm sorry that I wasn't fully honest when I didn't know who you were." Her head cocked at this. "I had been watching the boats in the landing and saw the black one fire upon the Northmen. I only know them to be raiders and opportunists. When I first saw you, I was trying to learn what side you were on. Sari, if you're in trouble, I can help you."

Nodding, she answered, "I understand, but it isn't what you think, Shon. I captain the smaller vessel."

"What? Truly?" This entire conversation baffled the former constable. "Why is the northern vessel, here? Are they raiding?"

"No. It isn't like that."

More concern crossed his face, "Eusari, are you with them?"

She shook her head. "Come back with me, and I'll explain everything. I need to help my men drag the new mast that they're cutting, and they should be finishing up."

They turned to leave and the large wolf stood and stretched. It followed, matching Eusari's stride. Shon marveled. "How long have you had this magnificent animal?"

His niece turned and looked at the beast. "I've never seen it before today." Shrugging, she added, "It just laid down by me."

The wolf unnerved Shon. Keeping his distance from the animal, he followed to where her men had cut the log. They had trimmed it and tied it with ropes to aid in dragging. At their approach, the men, who were resting on the ground, leaped to their feet, some drawing weapons. Shon watched as Eusari raised her hand.

"Stand down. He's with me." She nodded at the huge wolf and added, "So is the wolf."

One of the men asked, "What the fuck, Captain? Did you literally just walk into the forest, find a wolf and say, 'you're my puppy, follow me?' Because honestly, that's the sort of the shit that you'd do." The other men laughed and Wimbley watched as she smiled.

"Yes Jacques. I challenged the wolfpack and told the biggest, meanest beast that I'd castrate him if he didn't follow me."

The men laughed again, and the one called Jacques added, "Isn't that how you got us to follow, Captain?"

Shon could instantly tell that she captained these men. She had their total allegiance; despite that they were obvious cutthroats and pirates. Realization crossed his face, as he thought about her small black vessel and how it had fired upon the longboat in the harbor. "Eusari, do you captain the infamous *She Wolf?*"

She looked up and flashed a smile with a brief wink, taking away his breath. Tales of her smuggling exploits had reached as far as Logan. As a constable, he was well aware of the legal dispatches sent by the Empire, oftentimes describing daring and brutal actions by a 'lady pirate.' He stared in disbelief.

Pointing at the log, she asked, "Are you going to sit there and drool on yourself, or are you going to help us drag this back to town?"

An hour later the work detail returned to Estowen's Landing and a small man with a large head met them on the pier. Shon noted that both ships were tied, and both crews worked together.

The little man spoke with a stutter, "Wuh... what's with the wolf, Eusari?" It was sitting, yawning next to her. Even seated, the top of its' head reached her shoulder. Gesturing in Wimbley's direction, the man asked, "And huh... who is this?"

Eusari bravely wrapped her arm around her new wolf and answered, "This is my new first mate, Sippen." Indicating Shon, she added, "And this is Shon Wimbley from Loganshire. Shon, meet Sippen Yurik of Fjorik."

The former constable was reaching his hand in greeting but pulled back as if he had seen a snake. "Pardon me if I don't shake your hand, but I don't shake hands with murderers and rapists from Fjorik."

"Shon!" Eusari called out, shocked.

Sippen simply nodded and bowed gently. Without stuttering he stated, "If my people have wronged you then I'm truly sorry." Turning to Eusari he added, "I will fuh... fetch my captain." He made his way from the pier to the wharf and proceeded inside a building.

Shon turned to Eusari. "I can't forgive those vermin." Shaking his head, he said, "They destroyed our lives and took everything. How can you be walking among them, working with them after all that they took from you? My sister, your mother? I found her dead and raped in your home, Sari. Axe handle shoved up inside of her. And what about your father? I watched him die."

Eusari looked down at the ground, "I know very well what they took from us. But you've no idea how they impacted me." She looked up, anger smoldering in her eyes, "The fact that I trust this man and his captain should be enough for you."

"Don't betray your people, Eusari."

"My people?" Her eyes flared with venom and she took two steps toward her newly found uncle. "My PEOPLE?" The wolf emitted a low and rumbly growl, and Shon broke his eyes from Eusari's to check the animal. She took another step toward him. "I have no PEOPLE except them men who have sailed, stolen, and fought alongside of me. I have no family. No mother. No father."

Feeling something pressing in his groin, Shon looked down and saw that she had drawn a blade and touched it to his artery. He stammered, "Eusari... I... I'm sorry."

"My virginity was stolen from me before I'd even bled as a woman. I was taken only moments after I watched the same demon brutalize my mother, leaving her for dead. And you want to talk to me about the trauma from finding her DEAD? I WATCHED her die."

Shon's heart raced and he dared not move. The wolf had crept closer and lunged, standing with its' forepaws on his shoulder, snarling and panting a breath so hot that the foul smell turned to frozen mist in the cold air. "I'm sorry! You're right. I'll never know how that felt, will never know the damage that they did to you. But I'm here, now. Let me be your family, Sari. Let me protect you!"

"I know a hundred ways to kill a man, Shon Wimbley, and a thousand ways to make him suffer and beg for death. What could you possibly do to protect me?"

Shon was speechless. He couldn't truthfully answer and so he stood quietly, terrified, as his sister's daughter held a knife to his groin and her wolf stood snarling in his ear. He tore his eyes from her and looked up as the little man from the north walked with the devil who had killed Franque Thorinson.

Braen and Sippen emerged from the building. It was noticeably colder than it had been when they'd carried him into the house a few days before. Shivering, he pulled his furs closer. Far down the pier, he saw that Eusari talking to the man with whom she had returned. *Shon Wimbley*, Sippen had said that his name was. The name meant nothing to Braen, but he watched closely as Eusari pulled one of her knives and placed it against the man's groin.

Her anger did not surprise him, rather he smiled at the thought that the stranger had met his match. Braen knew firsthand that she was a dangerous woman to slight. She could also carry a grudge for decades. What surprised him was the huge black wolf that stood beside Eusari as if she had raised it as a pup. When the animal stood up to growl in Wimbley's face, Braston increased the speed at which he walked, suddenly worried that she or it would kill the man.

"Eusari," he called out in a cheery voice, as if he would invite the stranger to tea, "please introduce me to your new friend."

She withdrew the knife and stepped back. Her wolf did the same. The man, visibly shaken, just stood on the pier staring at Braen. He appeared too terrified to move a single step. Without looking away, Eusari said, "This is my Uncle Shon, Braen."

Now that is more surprising than the wolf, he thought. He smiled and reached out his hand in a greeting. It was ignored. "Well then, bring your uncle inside where it's warmer. I'm sure that we've a lot to talk about." He turned to return to the building, but paused then turned around with a smile, "Please leave the dog outside. We don't know if it's housebroken." Angling his head toward Sippen, he added in a whisper, "Hell, I don't think she's housebroken. The little man smiled as they returned inside to wait.

Samani Kernigan was already seated at the kitchen table when they walked in, and Braen chose a chair next to him. Sippen cleared the table of the old mugs and grabbed several new ones and a pitcher of ale, setting them on the table. A few moments later Eusari and Shon joined them, taking seats across from the two men. The wolf casually strolled in and took its place next to Eusari on the floor. Braen glanced at the animal and then raised an eyebrow toward its' master. She shrugged.

Braen looked at the newcomer, his eyes staring with obvious disdain. "Sippen tells me that you're not a fan of Northmen."

"You can say that, Braen Braston. That's your name, isn't it? The son of Krist Braston."

"You seem to have me at a disadvantage. And yes, it is I. We both know that you've several very good reasons to hate me, especially given that my family has not been kind to your people. Can we get this behind us and move on to business?"

Shon placed his hands up in a shrug. "What is it that you would like to know?"

"What I want to know is are you really her uncle? Also, how did you two meet up?"

Eusari answered for him. "He is my uncle. I was young, but I remember him. Also, he knows specifics about my family from Brentway."

Braen's perked at the sound of the town. "You're from Brentway?"

"Yes. My father was the constable, there. Shon was his deputy."

Shock flashed through Braen like a sudden kick to the stomach. He remembered the town very clearly, events about Eusari's past suddenly coming into focus. It must have shown on his face, because Wimbley smiled and sat up straighter.

"That's right, Prince Braston. Her father was the constable." Grinning as he spoke, he pressed, "Why don't you tell Eusari how her father died."

Kernigan set his drink on the table and watched Braen very closely. All eyes waited. The bearded man stared at the table, too embarrassed to look at Eusari. The details of that night were blurred, but certain details were still clear. Yes, he remembered the constable. He remembered him very well.

Eusari broke the silence with one word, "Braen?"

Staring at the table, Braen answered softly, "I'm sorry. I knew that my family had hurt yours, but I didn't realize how much until just now."

"Realized what, Braen?"

"Eusari. I killed your father."

She looked at Shon, eyes begging confirmation from her uncle. "Is this true? Are you sure?"

Her uncle nodded, "I'll never forget the face of the demon who diced up my mentor."

Eusari went silent. She swallowed and stared straight ahead, not looking at Braen. "Tell me the details."

Shon began, "He came at us..."

"Not from you." She silenced the man with a fierce look and turned toward Braen. "You. You will tell me everything."

"We attacked Brentway at dawn. The town slept and Skander took teams door to door, killing many of the men in their beds. I followed Father to the tavern. The constable, your father, had a contingent of ten or so men with him, many of whom were archers. My father asked them to lay down their weapons and come outside. He meant to spare them, thinking that they would just bribe us to leave like most other towns and villages."

Tears began slowly dripping down Braen's face. "One of them fired a crossbow at my father, striking him in the chest. He nearly died from that bolt." He looked directly at Eusari when he said the rest. "I lost my temper. Just like I did the other day. I went berserk and began killing."

Shon spoke up, "First you hurled your axe at the man who fired the bolt." He removed his from his belt and set it on the table. Braen stared for a moment, then reached down and removed his own. Two identical partners lay on the table. Eusari gasped at the sight.

Braen narrowed his eyes at Shon. "I killed that man. I know because that was my first kill."

"No Braston." He unbuttoned his shirt, revealing a large horizontal scar just right of center in his chest. "You missed the vital organs. Just barely."

"Then I guess we've no more quarrel, Wimbley." Braen retrieved his axe and returned it to his belt. He left the matching axe on the table. "You may keep that one. It seems to be a good luck charm for you."

"You were possessed, the way that you killed my friends." Shon pointed at Eusari and added, "The way that you killed her father."

"Yes. Yes, I was." Tears formed in Braen's eyes as he remembered charging the men, slashing and chopping them into pieces. "I was an animal."

"No. You were a demon. I wake at night, remembering the way you cut them apart like a butcher."

"I do, too, Wimbley. Not a night goes by that I don't remember the first night I killed." Looking at Eusari, he added, "I'm so sorry. If I'd known that I had killed your father, then I would've told you. Sincerely, I would have."

"The sad thing is that I believe you." She shook her head, turning hateful eyes downward. "This makes us even, Braston. I've no more debt to you."

"There is not now, nor has there ever been a debt, Sari. It's I who am indebted to you for the sins of my brother."

"The brother you refuse to overthrow?" She turned her green eyes, filled with anger, finally met his. "Where do your allegiances lie?"

"Actually, Samani and I discussed that, earlier, before you both arrived. He's convinced me to take Pirate's Cove from Stefan Nevra. After that I'll stage an attack on my brother. Would you like to join me in this endeavor?"

Eusari thought for several moments. "It's the only home I remember." She softened. "Yes. I'll help."

Looking at Wimbley, Braen inquired, "How many men do you have hiding in the forest, ready to attack when you give the signal?"

Shocked, the man went pale.

"This forest is the border between Loganshire and Fjorik, home of escaped slaves from the north and outlaws from the Empire. No one hunts in the Black Forest of Diaph, not with all of the outlaws who roam its' trails. Not unless you're one of them."

"I was scouting. I lead no one."

"No. I don't think that you're a mere scout. I think that you're the leader of a band of men, and I'm asking you to help us. What do we need to do for you, before you'll help us?"

Shon Wimbley picked up the axe from the table, turning it over and over in his hands while he thought. Finally, after a long, deep breath, he said, "I've approximately two hundred archer and crossbowmen surrounding this camp."

Braen did not outwardly flinch but watched as Eusari and Sippen turned ghostly pale. "And your demand?"

"We need to free about twenty-five of my men from the jail in Diaph and break into the Diaph Rookery. They have something of immense value to me." He looked at Braston and held out his hand to the Northman, "Get me into Diaph and I'll help you win your revenge."

Braen and Wimbley shook hands and Kernigan cleared his throat. Both men turned to look at him expectantly, since he had been largely quiet during the exchange. "Where can we get our hands on a lot of steel or iron for my genius friend, here." He gestured at Sippen.

All eyes turned to the little man whose face reddened at the sudden attention. Braen explained, "They need materials to develop a new type of weapon, Shon."

Samani reached down and removed the hand cannon from his belt. Placing it on the table, he explained, "This gadget is the sole reason that he and I escaped The Cove. He needs iron to make more. Lots more, and I have an idea to make them more effective at range. Sippen needs materials to crank out enough for a small army."

Wimbley frowned, "How is that little thing better than a bow?"

Samani picked it up off the table, cocked back the lever and pointed it at an empty wine bottle on the counter. He winked at Sippen, who had placed his fingers into his ears, smiling as he did. With a single motion of Kernigan's finger, fire exploded from the barrel and the wine glass exploded into bits of broken glass. The deafening sound rocked the little room and everyone else at the table fell from their chairs to the floor. All except Sippen, still smiling with his fingers in his ears. The wolf whined and ran from the room at the sudden blast

Dazed, Shon rose from the ground along with Braen and Eusari. Eyes wide, he looked at Sippen with amazement. "YOU made that?"

Taking his fingers out and lowering his hands, he nodded. "Yes."

"What do you need to make more?"

"Iron and charcoal.".

Wimbley smiled. "Well, this is your lucky day. As a matter of fact, I recently took a large amount of food, raw iron, and weapons from the Diaph army."

"Then we need a plan, gentlemen." Samani held up his mug and toasted the air before downing the contents.

Braen picked his chair up off the ground and dusted himself before sitting. "Tell me about Diaph. I haven't been there in over a decade."

Shon nodded and started marking on a piece of parchment that Sippen handed him. "The city is about five miles upriver from the mouth of the Logan. The fort is a half star with the longest side facing the water. A land assault is nearly impossible, given the angles of the walls."

"How so?" Eusari looked intently at the drawing.

Indicating with his pencil, he explained. "There are only two batteries facing the forest, but a small contingent of archers can pick off many foot soldiers from murder holes, essentially from any angle. That severely impacts my ability to get ground troops in. I've no artillery, so I can't soften the walls."

Braen pointed at the batteries that Shon had drawn atop the palisades. "How many guns are facing the harbor?"

"The harbor is huge. There are four batteries here, here, here and here. They're pointed at the river and each cover an overlapping radius. Not to mention, there're usually between five or eight imperial ships in the harbor." Shon sat back in his chair, as if to emphasize the difficulty of the raid.

Samani spoke, "Sippen, can you make some more carcass rounds? Something smaller that can be handheld and thrown by a man?"

The little man's eyes grew with understanding. "I... I have twenty rounds uh... aboard *Ice Prince.* I cuh... can repack those. Guh... give you about thuh... thirty, total." After some thought, he added, "Buh... but the fuse will be tricky."

Eusari nodded. Her men had been training hard and picked up quickly on the idea. "Shon, my team is smaller than it should be, and I need you to choose some of your most elite men to help us. If we go in with six teams of five, then we can clear the forest facing guns and most of the murder holes."

Shon nodded. "Ok. But what are carcass rounds?" He appeared confused.

Samani and Sippen smiled from ear to ear and Kernigan spoke, "You're going to love those fuckers."

Yurik took out another piece of parchment and handed it to Braen, who listed items and gear that they'd need for the assault. They planned throughout the evening and well into the night.

Chapter Thirty

Marcus nervously waited in The Room for the council to complete their vote. He had already downed an entire bottle of bad wine, completely ignoring the flavor. Tired of pacing, he settled down to play cards with Matteas. He had already lost several hands, but hardly noticed. He focused more on the door than on his hand.

"Relax, Your Highness. I assure you it's going as planned."

"How can you be sure? So calm?"

"Experience, My Liege."

Laying down his cards, he rose up and decided to try pacing, again. "What if they don't choose Campton? What will the Falconers do to me?"

"Trust in the process, Marcus." The Captain General leaned back in his chair with his feet on the table and fingers laced together behind his head. "This Empire is way older than you, and those cursed bird-men have been running things the entire time. Besides, what you did at the trial was genius. There's no way that anybody will dare to oppose your claim."

"We need to find my brother before I can relax completely." Pouring another glass of wine, Marcus looked at the soldier. "Are you sure about that report? Is it really accurate?"

"Yes. Weston opened the doors to the Pescari, and your idiot brother was humiliated. Now he's hiding out, afraid to leave but afraid to show his face."

"I want him found. Both him AND that General Reeves must be killed."

Matteas closed his eyes. "Trust in the process, Son."

"I've told you not to call me that." Marcus shot him eyes full of daggers. "I told you NEVER to say that out loud."

"Well, it's true. Your mother married a king who couldn't knock her up, and she visited me whenever the fancy took her. You'd do well to remember that, boy. You're half me and half your mother. Why do you think I am so damned loyal to you?"

"I'm sorry. I just don't want that information known."

"It won't be."

"What will happen in Weston, now. Should I send troops to force out the Pescari?"

"If you do, then you'll face a civil war. Those horse lovers out west will raise an army and blame you for starting it. No, I recommend that you send troops to Eskera, cutting off Robert's escape and trapping Reeve's troops out in the open."

"Make it happen, then."

"I already did, My Liege." A sarcastic smile lit up Brohn's face as he lay with eyes closed. "I sent a team of assassins to Weston to find and kill your brother. I also dispatched an additional five thousand troops to Eskera. That makes a total of seventy-five hundred against two thousand, in case your brother challenges."

"What if the northern king attacks?"

"He won't. He's a coward who likes to carve up women and kill babies. No, he isn't a general like his brother. Braen is the military genius in that family." He opened an eye and rested it on Marcus. "We should be more worried about that one if he ever defeats Skander."

"And in the meantime?"

Matteas closed his eyes, again. "Focus on your kingdom, find and kill Robert and let Nevra take care of Braston for you. He's one man and only has a couple of ships at his disposal. Honestly, it's not like he has an army or an entire fleet." Noises at the door caught the captain general's attention, and he snapped alert and jumped to his feet. One hand touched the hilt of his sword and he moved between Marcus and the door.

The heavy door opened slowly, and Lord Campton Shol strode in with a smile on his face. In a single bow, he was kneeling before the Esterling boy. "I, Campton Shol, High Chancellor of Eston, swear my undying fealty to you, My Liege. The council is ready to name you Marcus Esterling, King of the Eston Empire."

A smile broadened on the boy's face, "So it's done, then?"

Matteas nodded. "It's done."

Lord Shol regained his feet and gestured to the door. The council wants to see their new king." Marcus regained his composure and left the room with head held high and the captain general at his heels.

Campton Shol watched as the boy king left The Room and a voice from behind him echoed his own thoughts.

"He will be much easier to control than his mother was."

"No doubt about that." Shol turned to look directly at the large Falconer. "Kestrel, I need you to do something."

The specter bowed and answered. "Of course, anything for the Astian Council."

"I need you to travel to Diaph and root out the outlaws from the forest. I've sent several Falconers, but we've already lost two in the raids on our caravans to Fjorik. They captured a caravan carrying census documents. If those were to fall into the wrong hands, it would have damaging consequences."

"At once, My Lord." A look crossed Kestrel's face and he inquired. "What about the lost Falconer in Weston?"

"Yes. That's a problem and the Summer Oracle will already know about our failure. I expect that we will be hearing directly from the council, very soon."

Kestrel pressed, "I'd like to be part of the solution in Weston. The fire emote has considerable powers, far greater than any awakened since the experiments were abandoned."

Shol nodded his agreement and added, "Once we get the mess in the forest cleared up, then I'll send you to Weston. But right now, I need you in Diaph."

Kestrel bowed deeply and left through his secret entrance.

Shol straightened his robes, then left the room to rejoin the newly proclaimed king and his council.

CHAPTER THIRTY-ONE

Captain Alec Pogue descended the stairwell into the lower dungeons of The Cove. He had been informed that the prisoner had awakened and was eager to question him. Alec hated the dungeons, and had the subject not been so important he would not have come personally. It was a miracle that the man had survived at all, much less recovering from a punctured lung. The man was very lucky that Lord Nevra had dispatched a surgeon as quickly as he did.

The jailer met Alec on the lowest level and led him down two rows of cells, each occupied with Artema Horn's loyalists. Nevra had insisted on keeping these men alive, hoping that they would eventually be as useful to him as much as they were to Horn. Pogue doubted that possibility, based on how violently they had fought against Nevra's men. Even the stories that blamed Kernigan for the attack on Horn would not be enough to turn their allegiances.

The jailer finally reached the cell and addressed Pogue. "Captain, I'll be right outside the door in case you need me. The man's weak and recovering from injuries, but he's dangerous, I assure you."

"Thank you. I'll be fine." Shrugging, the jailer turned the key in the door and swung it open. As Alec entered, he saw the man lying on a straw bed in the corner. That was unusual, since most men didn't even get a blanket in the dungeons. He really was a special prisoner.

The man shifted his weight, raising up to a sitting position and holding his side as he did. *His stitches must still bother him*, Pogue thought. He hoped that they weren't infected, given the importance of the man. After he was fully sitting up, the prisoner addressed the captain. "To what do I owe this pleasure, to meet with the captain of the guard?"

"Hello, Amash. I hope that you've been treated well."

Amash winced from the pain as he answered. "I have been. I assume my identity has been discovered, then, Captain? I shouldn't be treated this well, given my lowly position in the guild."

"That's correct, my old friend. I'm sorry, but I had to tell Nevra who you really are. You were dying on that pier, and I needed his authorization to dispatch a surgeon. This was the only way."

"Why are you doing all of this for me? You know that I fought against Nevra's men. You know that I'm loyal to Horn."

"It isn't about Horn or Nevra, Amash. You're close friends with Braen Braston. Didn't you help Kernigan escape with his crew?"

"I am and I did, Alec." Amash narrowed his eyes. He liked Captain Pogue, but he disagreed with his allegiance. "I won't give them up. Even if I knew where they went, I wouldn't give them up."

"I know. I also know that you don't know their whereabouts." He sighed. "No one does." The captain shifted his weight, something weighting on his mind and bothering him. "What if I told you that Artema Horn was alive? That the coupe was arranged by him, so that he could go into retirement?"

Amash let out a laugh that hurt his ribcage. "Then I'd say that you're full of shit."

Pogue didn't flinch. He just stared into Amash's eyes. "It's true, my friend. He was onboard *She Wolf* when she left the harbor, and only a skeleton crew was onboard *Wench's Daughter*. Artema arranged the entire affair so that Stefan would appear the hero and take over the helm of The Cove."

"Holy hell. You're telling the truth, aren't you?"

"Yes I am."

Amash laughed again, ribs hurting on that one side. "What of Braen, then? Did the two of them sail off into the sunset of retirement, together?"

"No. I'm afraid, not." Pogue was taking a risk with the next piece of information. "Braston was to be sold to his brother in the north. Artema turned him over."

"You're shitting me?"

"No. I'm not. Look, I know that you two were friends, but things have changed in our world in just a very short time."

"What do you mean?"

"The Esterling Queen is dead. The word on the water is that Braen chopped off her head."

"Cheeky bastard. What else?"

"Your father's dead, and your sister opened the gates to the allow the Pescari into Weston. Mate, your city is overrun with a hundred thousand savages and your sister orchestrated it."

"I'm sure that Sarai had a good reason for doing what she did. What does all of that have to do with me?"

"Nevra is going to ransom you to the new king, Marcus Esterling. He thinks that the boy will want to use you to retake the city once he puts down his brother's resistance. Or, your presence might make your sister and her humanitarian allies come to their senses. Either way, you're valuable."

Amash laughed. "Valuable. That word hasn't been attributed to me since I left the university. My asshole father disowned me. I'm dead to everyone in that city, Alec."

"Maybe, but you're valuable to us."

The prisoner grew silent and stared at the floor, taking all of the information in and mulling it over. Finally, he lifted his head and looked into the eyes of his old friend. "Alec. You know that Nevra's a poor choice to lead The Cove."

"I'm loyal to him, Amash."

"Yes, but he's only loyal to himself. Don't forget that when I first arrived you had me attached to his personal guard."

"I remember."

"I saw a side of him that wish I hadn't. Even though I was living among a den of pirates, that bastard made my skin crawl."

Pogue ended the conversation. He rapped on the door and asked, "Are you sure that Braen didn't tell you where they're going?"

"Not a fucking word, Mate."

"That's too bad."

The door opened and Pogue turned to leave. Amash lifted his eyes toward the door and asked, "Alec?"

Without turning, the captain paused. "Yes?"

The prisoner squinted against the light pouring in from the open door. "How can you back him? Nevra, I mean."

"He is the rightful leader. It's what Artema wanted."

"You're sure of that?"

"I... I have to be, Amash."

"Follow the ledgers, Alec. They speak volumes and you should listen." The door shut behind the captain and the tiny cell went entirely black. Left alone in the dark, the son of Abraham Horslei wept silently for his dead father and his sister, alone in the world.

Chapter Thirty-Two

The moonless night sky loomed over the mouth of the Logan River. Although some stars peeked through the high clouds, a fierce winter storm closed from the north and threatened rage on the forest's southern edge. The wind still blew from the south but would shift as the storm neared. If high tide did not arrive soon, Eusari would scrap the mission.

She Wolf waited patiently at anchor in the mouth of the river. Her captain on deck, hoping that the impending storm would drive the city defenders inside, or at least divert their attention during the attack. Anxiety consumed Eusari. She and Shon had spent the past few days training their teams for the mission, but she wanted more time. So much could go wrong, and lack of precision threatened survival.

Her wolf companion stood at her side. She had tried to leave the animal in Estowen's landing, but it had raced up the brow and leaped aboard, much to the dismay of the crew. She absent-mindedly scratched its' head as she rehearsed the raid in her mind.

"You need a name, boy." The beast met her eyes as she spoke, letting out a low whine sounding more like a dog than a wolf. "Yeah. No time for that, now. We'll decide that, later."

A shout drew her attention when Devil Jacque announced the turn of the tide. This was the moment they awaited, when seawater backwashed into the brackish river. This change in current would last for the next hour, and a head start would help minimize rowing. The oar team rested below decks for now, but they expected to rely on them exclusively if the storm moved faster than expected.

Still anxious, Eusari signaled for Pete to raise anchor. The hull caught the stream and newly pitched boards creaked under the strain as it lurched.

"Here we go, Dearie." Shon had approached her on the rail, watching with a hint of excitement at the coming action.

"Are the teams, ready?"

"They're geared up and sitting below out of the cold."

"No. They need to be topside to acclimate. When this storm hits, I want them to barely feel it once the adrenaline kicks in." Eusari glanced at the two longboats they'd salvaged from Estowen's Landing. Sippen had refitted each and painted them black, ensuring low night visibility when they landed. "We have an hour to make it inland, more if the wind shifts and we're forced to row. Have the teams blindfolded when they come topside. I want their eyes adjusted to the dark when we deploy the boats."

"Aye, Dearie."

"Also, Sippen packed each man's bag with carcass bombs and some of those special primers. Make sure that they know to put one in every cannon, just in case."

"They'll be ready. Stop fussin' over them like they'll screw up the night." He went below to pass along her orders.

Once alone, Eusari's thoughts again turned to Braen. *He killed my father. He... killed... My father.* She let that thought wash over her from the inside out. He had answered without pause when Shon accused him, immediately owning the act. *Why am I helping the man who killed my father?* She felt that she should be angry and seeking his own death. *Instead I feel... I feel... What DO I feel?*

She considered her feelings about Braen Braston. He was a good man who had reacted to protect his own father, by going berserk on her father and his men. *That rage, though. He's dangerous when he frenzies.* She thought again at the way he had swung the axe on *She Wolf,* hacking and chopping while screaming and roaring like an animal above the cries of the mutineers.

Eusari had killed many men, even tortured some and destroyed their manhood. But she lacked emotion when she did, always cold and devoid of any feeling. *Am I any better than him? How many of my victims had families, daughters even, who mourn and seek their own revenge against me?* Killing was an act to Eusari. No different than pulling a weed in the garden. *I kill from the shadows. Is that why I find Braen's method so repulsive? He kills out in the open, raw and passionately covered in the blood of those in his way.* She killed with precision, intimately with eye contact like a lover's kiss. A kiss of death.

Eusari shook. She told herself that the reaction was a shiver against the wind as *She Wolf* raced upriver. Deep inside, she knew that she had shuddered against her own lack of humanity, *Lack of humanity, maybe, but not a lack of emotion.* There is plenty of hatred, anger, shame and humiliation within Eusari Thorinson. Of that, she was well aware.

Shon emerged with the teams. Each man donned an eyepatch under a blindfold before sitting down on the deck to wait out the remainder of the voyage. Eusari walked over to join them. She pulled out her own night vision gear, put it on, and settled down to wait. The remainder of the voyage would be one of apprehension and doubt, of that she was certain.

Braen watched his men tie off *Ice Prince.* Looking around, he counted six Imperial ships in the Diaph harbor. Six was better than eight but still worse than the five that Shon had predicted. He had chosen a center berth, so Imperials surrounded them with three on each side. He looked toward the sky. The lack of moon would bode well for Eusari's teams, but the wind was biting, turning slightly from the north. A complete shift would herald the arrival of the imminent storm.

The harbor master had been alerted immediately upon their arrival. As predicted, the sentries were uneasy with the sudden and unscheduled arrival of a Fjorik warship after nightfall. A full squad of crossbowmen lined the pier and a contingent of armored infantry formed up near the gangplank. They were on high alert and ready for any sign of open hostility from the vessel. The fact that they had arrived alone was in his crew's favor, but the harbor master openly displayed his irritation at being awakened and forced away from his warm hearth. Braen had his hood up to hide his face and pretended to be a deckhand, tying off lines and listening to Samani speak with the authority.

"You are seeking 'harbor from the storm,' you say, on your way to Eston?" The bookish man had lost nearly all of his hair, and what remained sprouted from his head in sprigs of grey. He pushed back his spectacles to look up from his logbook. He stole a glance northward at the horizon, then pulled his coat a little tighter around his small frame. His wrinkled face soured further when he looked back toward Samani.

"Yes." He pointed to the royal colors flying from the mainsail, the official flag of house Braston. "As you can see, we represent the royal family of Fjorik and are traveling under the diplomatic protection of the Esterling family."

"Where is your writ of passage?" Samani handed the man a piece of paper that Eusari had provided before their departure. She had lifted the seal off a document from an earlier mission and forged the words that would hopefully convince the sentries to stand down. The man looked it over, holding it up to a lamplight and nodding. "You won't mind if we look around your hold?"

"Actually, that would violate the terms of our diplomatic protection. So yes, good sir, I would mind, and no you may not." Samani was playing his part perfectly. Even his Fjorik accent was perfect, and with his disguise, he didn't even resemble himself. He handed the port authority a small bag, jingling the coins briefly in the air before placing it in the ready hand of the man. "What you CAN do is point me toward the tavern district. I would like to give a few of my officers a break from their duties, before finishing our journey at daybreak."

"Daybreak, eh?" The harbor master smiled at the thought of the northerners leaving at dawn and nodded. He pointed toward a row of buildings. "I can only allow you to take a few men into town. We have laws prohibiting your people from traveling in groups more than three at a time." He pushed his spectacles back on his nose and turned to walk away, hefting the purse as he did, trying to estimate its contents. With a motion of his hand, the troops fell into formation and followed him back to the port authority building at the end of the pier.

Samani casually walked back across the brow and stood before Braen. "That went easier than I'd hoped."

Braen nodded, "Perhaps too easy. Be on alert, out there. Remember, we most likely have bounties on our heads, so you need to get in and out of that tavern. Don't get recognized. If you do, tonight's lost."

Kernigan placed his hand on Braen's shoulder. "I won't screw this up. I believe in you, Braston. I want to see this thing through."

"Hurry, Sam. *She Wolf* should be floating by in about thirty minutes. That means that you have about one full hour before the teams are in place and the attack begins. When that happens, I need you onboard *Ice Prince* and ready to get the hell out of here."

"I'll be on time." Samani turned and indicated for a pair of crewmen to follow him. Geir was the largest of the men, highly intelligent and one of the best fighters on the ship. His accent was thick, though, and both Sam and Braen had worried that he may draw undue attention from the tavern folk. They had softened his look by dressing him in a more southern attire. Jan, the smaller of the two men, spoke almost entirely without a northern accent. He had spent part of his childhood in Eston and knew customs and courtesies better than Braen. He often accompanied his captain on more sensitive jobs, especially those that required getting past harbor security.

The three men left the ship without much conversation. Braen knew that they were wound tight with nerves and hoped that they would have luck on their side. Turning from the pier, he headed down the ladder toward the armory. Inside, Krill prepared the gunners for the impending attack. Braen signaled that they could begin moving the firepower to the deck, and the one-eyed man nodded acknowledgement. He then returned dutifully and quietly to his task of preparing the ordinance. They usually did this work topside, but tonight was clandestine, and they had to keep these special rounds out of the eyes of the authorities. Braen went back up the ladder to watch for *She Wolf*. He was anxious, and the deck provided much more room for pacing.

Chapter Thirty-Three

Sam, Jan and Geir made their way down the pier, trying their best to act like northern officers out to enjoy a night of drinking. As they passed the port authority, their eyes searched the shadows for lurking followers, no doubt tracking their movements and reporting back to the harbor master. Kernigan hoped silently that he was not recognized.

Geir lowered his voice, "I see six men on the starboard."

"Are they following?"

"They split up and three crossed the street, so I think that they'll just flank us for a while."

"Hopefully they're only supposed to observe and not apprehend." Sam felt butterflies in his stomach as he spoke. Normally, his contacts came to him. This was the first time that he had attempted to personally meet with his Diaph agent in fifteen years.

The men continued walking toward the tavern district, paying close attention to the shadows, but laughing and pretending to be unaware. As they approached a seedy looking inn called the Listing Barge, Jan grabbed the shoulders of the others and asked loudly, "Hey guys, why is Estonian Ale like sex in a canoe?"

Geir thought for a moment, but Kernigan responded immediately. "Because it's fucking close to water."

All three men erupted in laughter, and Jan leaned in close, whispering, "All six men are on the street behind us."

Kernigan, still smiling, answered, "Never mind them, we're here. This is the spot." He looked up at the old and weathered shop sign, which, as faded as it was, looked newer than the planks that made up the walls. The sounds inside indicated that there would be a large amount of witnesses. He hoped that would deter the guards from following.

The trio went inside and found a table next to the fireplace that was also near the kitchen door. They each turned their chairs so that they could watch the entrance. The room was crowded with travelers who wanted to get in before the storm, and a group of four men entered shortly after they did. Kernigan's eyes shot to Jan, but the small man shook his head with a low "no," as if to confirm that they were not from the group of six waiting outside. Nerves settling a little, he looked around. Samani could see that he and his companions were lucky to get a table at all, much less one in such a perfectly defensible position.

A busty waitress with black hair and piercing green eyes approached with a tray under her arm, wiping her free hands on a towel. "What'll it be, gents?" Jan ordered a Logan lager and Geir asked for an Estonian ale. This earned a questionable look from the girl as all three men erupted into laughter. She waited impatiently for them to finish, then pointed at Samani. "And for you?"

Sam finished his laugh, then watched the girl intently for a reaction when he said, "I want an Astian Pearl." Both pirates looked at him with serious wonderment, but the girl nodded and said that she would be right back with their drinks.

"What the hell is an Astian pearl, Sam?" Jan looked at Geir who merely shrugged.

"An imported amusement, I assure you." Kernigan smiled disarmingly and the men continued to talk and to watch the door. A few moments later, the girl returned with their drinks, placing them in front of first Jan, then Geir. In front of Sam she placed a glass of white wine with a perfectly round black rock at the bottom. Sam smiled and handed the girl a silver coin. She looked at it, nodded and then walked away to wait on another group of travelers. His two companions threw back their drinks, but he merely swished the contents of his own, frowning intently at the pebble.

After a few more minutes, an old woman with a black shawl wrapped around her silver hair entered the Listing Barge. On her arm hung a woven basket full of healing herbs and elixirs. Sam and Geir watched her as she moved from table to table speaking with each tavern goer, occasionally stopping to pull out a pouch and trade it for a coin before moving to the next patron.

Pointing at the woman, Geir prodded, "Maybe the witch has a something to make Jan less ugly." Upon hearing his name, the smaller man looked up.

"Or, she might have something to help Geir get up his willy." This made the bigger man's face change, the first time that Sam had seen him grow serious. Sam sat up in anticipation, hoping that the men did not start their own disruption.

Geir looked Jan in the eye and flatly asked, "Your mom told you about that problem, did she?" Both men threw their heads back in laughter and Sam relaxed.

When she finally approached their table, she sat her basket on the table and looked Kernigan directly in the eye. "You are taking a chance, coming here, Samani."

"Hello Pearl." A slight smile curved from the sides of his mouth when he greeted her.

Jan and Geir looked at each other, eyebrows raised incredulously, but did not speak.

"A messenger from The Cove arrived three days ago. He passed around descriptions of you and said that some "Lord Nevra" is offering a substantial reward for your return."

"Did he specify dead or alive?"

"No. He left that detail out. Who's Nevra? I thought Artema Horn led the guild, but rumor now has it that Horn was killed. Is that true?"

Samani shook his head. "Sadly, Artema is alive and a traitor. He sold out to Marcus Esterling and helped him kill the Queen."

Her face scrunched, wrinkles deepening all over her face. "I thought that was Braston."

"No. It was Matteas Brohn working with the brat and Horn."

"What about the northern prince, then? Why is he taking the fall for the crown?"

"Because he is a convenient target. Esterling had tried to sell him to his brother in Fjorik, but the trade broke down."

She nodded and then shrugged, "Well, he has a large bounty, also. Both the guild and his brother are hunting him, and there are a lot of thugs watching the waterfront for you both."

Sam shook his head and sighed. "Pearl, I need your help to get word out. All ships of The Cove that stand against Nevra must sail with haste to back Braen Braston."

"Word? Back? Are you interfering with Andalonian affairs?" Her face took on a look of shock and displeasure.

"Braston is planning to overthrow Nevra and will also retake Fjorik. He is the one, Pearl." He looked back at Jan and Geir and then again toward Pearl. He lowered his voice and quickly added, "He's awakened."

The old woman stood in silence as the words sunk in. After the long pause, she lifted her cloudy grey eyes to meet his, lips curling into a smile that deepened her lined face and she repeated the word in a whisper of excitement, "awakened!"

"Yes, Pearl." He leaned in close, mouth next to her ear so that his companions would not overhear, and said, "The prophesy is fulfilled."

The old woman nodded, eyes round in a mix of shock and glee, and placed her arm back through the handle of the basket. She turned in silence away from the three men and shuffled toward another table, again looking frail and very ancient. She paused at a table by the door, exchanged another tiny sack for an imperial coin from a sailor, and then waddled out of the door, leaving it open to let in the night. A blast of cold wind briefly blew large snowflakes into the room, and the sailor closest to it stood and slammed the heavy oak tight against its frame. Kernigan watched as the man pulled the collar of his jacket up around his neck before sitting to resume work on his drink.

Samani watched the door for a while. After the dusting of snow had turned to a puddle, he held up his glass in a silent toast to the old woman. Then, he threw back the contents, swallowing both the liquid and the stone. His eyes immediately grew wider, his pupils suddenly huge. Turning them to his companions he dropped his smile. Suddenly serious he said, "Gentlemen. We need to go NOW."

Abruptly the doors flew open and the cold wind, now fully blowing from the north, blasted the occupants and forcing everyone in the room to gasp. In the doorway was a man in a brown robe with feathered collar and a leather hood. Perched atop his right arm was a very large hawk. Snow swirled around the man, framing the hooded specter and adding to his hellish appearance. The bird of prey turned directly toward Samani and then spread its wings and squawked a high pitched and horrible cry. Six men dressed in city guard clothing rushed past the Falconer and pointed crossbows at all three men sitting by the fire.

Jan leaped to his feet and drew two short swords that were hidden beneath his cloak. But before they could be useful, a bolt sprouted from his chest, pinning him to the wooden mantle. Geir was slower with his own reaction and a bolt pinned his right arm to his side forcing him to leave his sword in its scabbard. Samani looked at his companions as blood poured from their wounds. He shook his head as Geir clawed at the bolt with his left hand, trying to pull the giant splinter from his bicep. Wisps of air wrapped tightly around his own hands, locking them in place as effectively as manacles. He shook his head as another bolt took Geir in the chest, putting him out of his misery. Frowning, he turned his wide eyes back up toward the Falconer. "Hello Kestral. I'd hoped that it would be you, who finally found me."

Eusari stood alongside her teams atop *She Wolf*. There were six in all, each comprised of five men. Everyone dressed in black from head to foot with an eyepatch over one eye. Even their faces were painted black to match the moonless night.

Her part of the plan was difficult. Two dark longboats were positioned on the port side of the vessel, each able to hold fifteen men. As they approached the third mile marker from the city, the first boat would disembark over the side, delivering three teams led by Shon, Marque and Devil Jacque to the first rendezvous point. The length of the protected harbor was another mile, and, after clearing the far side, they would deliver the second longboat and three more teams led by Eusari, Giovani and Porter.

As long as *She Wolf* was not delayed by other vessels on the river, the teams planned to reach their positions at approximately the same time. There were four batteries to the riverside and two on the forest side. After neutralizing each position, the teams would each move to their secondary mission targets. Each leader had their individual orders and would prioritize the secondary objectives.

Eusari held her breath as *She Wolf* approached the Eastern outpost. Inside, some bored junior sentry had the watch, and hopefully would be more intently watching the coming storm rather than looking for intruders. Torchlight burned from inside, but she did not see any activity that seemed alarmed. Finally, a head bobbed in front of the torch to look at the passing ship on the river, but then returned to the warm windbreak beneath the window. Once it was gone from sight, she gave the order and deckhands gently lowered the first longboat into the water without a splash. The first teams were away, and Shon gave Eusari a casual salute as they rowed gently to shore in the shadows of the tall pines.

After the boat had launched, she anxiously watched from the

stern, straining her eyes for any indication that the sentry had seen the longboat in the water. Holding her breath, she waited until she saw her men run aground, dragging the vessel into cover. Letting out a slow breath, she knew that as long as her men acted exactly as they were trained, that sentry would not be a factor on their return.

Peter Longshanks approached and joined her at the stern. "We have 'bout fifteen minutes before we cross the harbor and signal *Ice Prince*, Cap'n."

"Thank you, Peter. You and the crew are doing an excellent job, tonight."

Surprised by her expression of gratitude, the man stood dumbfounded. She turned her eyes away from the shore and looked up into his face, smiling a little at his shocked expression. "What? What is it?"

"Well. It's just that."

"Yes?"

He let out a breath and then locked his eyes on hers. "It's just that I've never heard you say, 'thank you,' Cap'n. I've also never seen you smile as much as you have, in recent weeks."

She raised an eyebrow at this, then thought about his words. He was right. She hadn't even realized it until that moment. "Well, I am doing a lot of things that I've never done." Indicating the remaining longboat, she added, "Including leading a coordinated raid with six teams on an amphibious assault."

"No. I don't reck'n many folk've done that, Mum." Peter looked down at the wolf beside Eusari. "He is stickin' around, is he? When you go ashore?"

"That is the plan. But he does seem to have a mind of his own and wants to be my side every moment."

"May I?" He pointed down, as if he intended to have a word with a child after asking for the parent's permission.

She chuckled. *Another new habit.* "Be my guest, Peter."

The peg legged man bent down until his nose was close to the wolf's. "My name is Peter. It is nice to be mak'n your acquaintance, mister..." He looked up at Eusari questioningly.

She shook her head, smiling at his foolery. "He hasn't told me his name, Peter."

"Well, he reminds me of a story about a nobleman long ago. When I was a wee one, mah mummy told me that the nobleman was out of his home and had left his family and favorite dog, behind. When he returned, the baby was miss'n from the cradle, and the dog had blood all over himself. Come to think of it, there was blood all over the house. The man lost his senses and killed the dog on the spot in a feverish rage. But the yelp woke the baby, who was sleepin' be'neath the cradle next to a dead wolf." He stopped the story and bent back down to the animal, "Sorry sir. Din't mean to be rude or alarm ya with talk of one of yer deceased ancestors." Surprisingly the wolf shook its' head and licked his face as if responding. Peter continued his story. "So. It turns out that the dog had protected the wee one, and the noble man wasn't so noble after all because he didn't get all his facts before killin' the pup. They say that the man never smiled after that day because of his mistake."

The story hit Eusari in the gut, thinking immediately about what she had done to Braen when she had confused him with his brother. She fought very hard to keep the tears out of her eyes and asked, "What was the dog's name?"

"Gelert, Mum. His name was Gelert."

The wolf sat up at the name and wagged its' tail like a dog. "He likes it."

"Yes, Cap'n. I think that he does." Peter looked over his shoulder and squinted his eyes. "Looks like the harbor is comin' up on starboard, Mum." The sailor ambled around with his wooden leg and began to stroll to the bow.

"Peter!" Eusari called after him, hesitantly. "Thank you." She gave him a small smile that felt warm on her face despite the bitter cold.

"For what, Mum?"

"Thank you for the story." She laughed a little, thinking that she had now thanked him three times in just a few minutes. "And for not giving up on me."

He swept out an exaggerated bow that looked hilarious with his wooden leg sticking out for balance. "Just don't lose that smile, Cap'n." With that he left her on the stern and went about his topside work, preparing the men for another longboat deployment.

She looked starboard and saw *Ice Prince* moored in the harbor. The wind had picked up from the north, and the crew below decks rowed hard against the current. Snow was falling, swirling around the night air and sticking to the wet surfaces that had iced in the cold. Focusing on a figure aboard the other ship, she smiled once more and whispered into the night, "Thank YOU, Braen. Thank you for forgiving me." She lingered for a moment, then joined her blindfolded team in the longboat. A few minutes later, the crew had lowered the craft into the dark water, and she was rowing toward shore. Thankfully her new pal Gelert the wolf had stayed aboard *She Wolf*.

PART III
EAGLE ROSE

All forces of nature have awakened,
Chaos sown without distinction.
No longer controlled by boundaries,
Siblings consume each other.

- The Oracle of Astian, 805th year of order

CHAPTER THIRTY-FOUR

Pain gripped Samani and his muscles spasmed as Kestrel dragged him into the cold. Snow blew everywhere, landing in his eyes that were locked open, unable to close from the drug. The specter half carried, and half dragged him from the tavern, finally tossing him down on the icy street. His tense muscles quivered and convulsed as he landed with a thud, unable to break his fall for the manacles of air around his wrists. Strong hands heaved him and tossed him into a wagon, surging pain wracking his entire body.

He willed the Da'ash'mael to hold off a bit longer and focused on the world around him. Unfortunately, the oracle bead had taken full effect and he slipped into the first stages. Idle thoughts about his childhood bubbled to the surface with tears from a different kind of pain falling for the family he would never see. The faces of two sisters lingered, then were gone after the drug fully took over his subconscious. With a surge he felt his mind leave his body, his stomach in the back of the cart. The omniscient sensation was one of flying and from this vantage he could see the top of the treetops and the storm on the mountains. It barreled toward a river winding through the trees.

He focused on the river with his mind's eye, clearly recognizing a black ship rowing against the current. Despite his pain he smiled as the figurehead came into view, a black wolf howling into the night with the bowsprit protruding from its' open mouth. Against all odds, *She Wolf* had gained a lead on the winds and made all three checkpoints on time.

Samani watched Eusari and the landing team row to shore,

silently cheering them on as they dragged their longboat into the cover of the forest. They wasted no time and split into three groups before heading for the walls. In the east, Shon and the other teams were already in position, ready to scale the walls. Splitting his consciousness, he followed all six teams simultaneously as they approached their first objectives.

Intense pain poured through every muscle of Samani's body. For a moment he returned to reality and left the dream state. His eyes focused on Kestrel standing above, stoically watching with incredulous attention.

"Why did you consume the bead, Samani? That was a foolish move and you drew the attention of every Falconer in the city.

"What will you... do with me?" It hurt to talk, but his voice worked fine. He discovered that he could anchor in reality while maintaining his view of the teams.

"First I will turn you over to the Astian council. They will likely make your death a public affair, as a lesson to the rest of the Society." Smiling, he added, "Not like your last death, where your body couldn't be found to properly put on display."

"Well..." Kernigan paused to breathe between convulsing muscles. "Since none of that will happen, will you at least tell my sisters that I'm alive and well?"

Kestrel let out a low, rumbling sound that resembled a laugh. "Oh, I assure you that it will happen, Samani. You wouldn't be able to escape me at full strength, much less in the state that you are in."

"Tell her. She needs to know that I took my mission to Andalon. That I will set these people free."

"They are not people. They are experiments that went wrong." Kestrel let out a sigh, then dragged Samani into the Rookery.

The stone inside of the Rookery was cold, and Kernigan was appreciative that the Falconers took the time to lift him up onto a table. His hands were still bound, and Kestrel had taken extra precautions of wrapping his arms and legs as well. Unless the lead Falconer released him, there was no way to escape, cell or no.

He let himself slip back into omniscience. All teams had tossed the "carcass grenades" into the murder holes and atop the gun positions. The smoke and chemical vapor worked very quickly, and the city guardsmen choked and gagged in the cloud of death. The luckiest of the men escaped to fresh air, but many hundreds were sleeping near their posts and died from asphyxiation.

Jacque crouched beneath the northeast battery, out of view of the murder holes. His team, like the others, wore eyepatches that kept one eye ready for night vision. On his cue they switched them over and tossed Sippen's inventions into the fortifications before climbing the wall to take out the first battery. Their knives flashed and throats of surprised men sliced open in a fog of smoke that billowed from the clay pots they had thrown.

Eusari's special teams wore masks that Sippen had given them, and walked into the clouds, unaffected. With haste each group raced to their assigned battery, placing primers in the barrels and inside casks of black powder resting nearby. They met little resistance since the guards were focused mostly on the gas, afraid to enter the clouds. He watched as Shon left the wall and led his team to the rookery. Marque turned south and led an assault on the harbor guns and Eusari headed for the northwest position by the gates. Remembering the mission briefing, he knew that Porter and Giovani would remove the southwest and harbor cannons overlooking Braen.

Samani shifted his view to watch *Ice Prince*. The bearded captain waited until he saw all four plumes atop the harbor wall and then signaled for Krill to fire both port and starboard guns. He aimed to cripple the enemy vessels before they could intervene. The first volley rocked his own ship in the harbor, causing waves to rip at the pier. The Imperial ships on both sides splintered from the attack, and Gunnery Sergeant Krill fired salvo after salvo into each of the six ships alongside.

The pounding from running feet on stone brought Kernigan's back to reality. He watched the Falconers sprint from the Rookery, racing to help fight off the attack. He tried his bonds and they still held, meaning that Kestrel had not gone far. He slipped back into the state but saw a different view.

The city of Diaph was gone and he gazed instead upon the city of Weston. The westernmost gate had been destroyed, and all that was left was a burned-out husk. The city had opened its' doors to tens of thousands of refugees, with more trickling across the Forbidden Waste. Shock turned to concerned, but eventually he felt proud that the people crossing the desert were Pescari.

As he focused on the palace, he found himself face to face with a teenage boy as shocked to see Samani as he was to see the boy. "I have to help her," the boy was saying, over and over again to him. "I have to save her before he burns her."

"How?" Samani was so shocked that he began to feel the dream slipping away and reality forcing its' way back into his mind.

With a violent rush his mind's eye clicked off and Kernigan lay on the table, effects of the bead completely used up. "How?" He thought. "How did the boy reach such a high level of Da'ash'mael without an Astian bead?" He stared down at his wrists, legs and ankles, swearing at the wisps of air that bound him. He finally lay back and waited, marveling at the implications in Weston.

Chapter Thirty-Five

Robert woke shivering but dry. It had snowed during the night, and a white blanket covered the city. Several weeks of growth showed on his face, and tiny icicles clung to his beard. Robert loved the snow but hated the cold wind. His breathing had been difficult every night since his humiliation, but the last had been the worst. His lungs felt like razor blades when he breathed in the icy air.

He had dreamed a scene so intense that he felt he had been there, watching the ship deposit the boats in the night. He remembered the adrenaline he felt as the soldiers, dressed in black leather, shimmied up the walls and deployed weapons the likes of which he had never seen. They tossed the little clay pots at the large harbor guns, causing gas to chase out the choking and gagged defenders. Most disturbing was the image of the man who shared his dream, and the Falconer who held him bound by shackles of air.

Of course, it was only a dream and he welcomed it over the others that plagued him every night since Eachann had taken charge of the city. Sarai dominated those visions, as she worked with the Pescari boy to settle his people. He had also seen her in reality, walking and holding the boy's arm though the city streets. Robert knew that boy was dangerous and prayed that she would realize for herself before it was too late.

He feared for her safety. His dreams of her were the reason that he had not rejoined Max and the rest of their army. It was always the same. Sarai would be sitting with Taros in the palace gardens, playfully tossing snow and smiling at their conversation.

Then Taros would be standing over her, face distorted in anger with flames again in his eyes. She would burn to a husk before he would turn off the fire, and Robert would be too weak and useless to stop him.

The prince rose from the bundled rags he used as a bed, stretching and moving blood back into his hands and feet. Pain rushed into his extremities as it did, but Robert ignored it, flexing his hands and toes as he planned out his day. First and foremost, he needed food. Then, he would return to the rooftops and find Sarai.

His little nest was built on the top floor of a burned-out apartment beside bakery that had somehow been spared from the fire. The loft provided the perfect vantage for spying on her window as well as the gardens below. He had watched over his love for several weeks. So long, in fact, that his crisp white uniform had turned unrecognizably black from the soot in which he slept.

He swung down to the street level, making an impression in the snow when he hit. He cursed at his mistake, realizing that if someone was looking for him, he had just given away the location of his nest. In the end, the uncomfortable rumbling of his stomach won out over his worry and he made his way down the street to an inn called, the Cozy Dog. He circled around to an alley in the back, knowing that the proprietor would leave the previous night's stew pot out on the step for vagrants. He smiled when he saw that there were also a few wooden bowls and spoons sitting nearby.

Robert sat on the step and filled a bowl. The stew warmed him from the inside out, and he felt his breathing improve with each bite. He closed his eyes and inhaled the steam through his nostrils, taking in the aroma of beef, mushrooms and leeks. When he opened them, the owner of the inn stood over him. The portly man was balding, white hair curving around the back of his head with only wisps of cotton on top. His fat cheeks were rosy, and his nose was overly large and scarred with tumors that made it as red as an apple.

"You need to come inside, Prince Robert. It isn't safe for you, today." The round bellied man was looking back and forth down the alleyway, as if he were expecting trouble.

"How? How did you know it was me?"

"Son, I knew it was you the first time you poked around my scrap bin. I didn't want you to starve, out here, so I started leaving the pot." The man looked anxious and even a little afraid. "Please, your highness. Please come inside."

Perhaps it was exhaustion from a restless night, but Robert rose and allowed the man to lead him into the kitchen.

"What's wrong? Something's obviously bothering you."

"There've been men about, asking everyone your whereabouts."

"Probably soldiers or officers acting on behalf of General Reeves." Robert dismissed the concerns of the man.

"No sir. These are harder men than soldiers. They stayed here, last night, and asked about you. They said that you conspired to have your mother killed so that you could take the throne. They offered to pay handsomely for information."

"My mother?" The young prince mulled over the words. Realization dawning. "Did something happen to my mother?"

"I'm sorry, My Lord. They say that you hired a pirate to behead her when she was trying to ransom back your brother." The burly innkeeper looked down at the ground, embarrassed. "I'm so sorry. I thought that you knew."

"That would mean that Marcus is claiming the throne."

"Yes, My Prince. He was crowned, last week after a huge trial in Eston. Apparently, the Chancellor was part of the conspiracy."

"Conspiracy." Robert shook his head in disbelief, dumbfounded by the news. "I had nothing to do with it. I've been dealing with issues, here."

"I know, My Lord. That is why I didn't trust them. We need to get you to your army, sir. The general has men looking for you, also. I can lead you to them."

"No. I'm not ready. I've important things to do, here." Robert was stunned. The news was slowly setting in, weighing his heavy melancholy further down.

"It ain't right, sir."

The prince looked up, focusing on the innkeeper. "What's not right."

"Moving the Pescari into the city. It ain't right." The man was fidgeting, rubbing his hands on a towel, drying them over and over, despite that they were already dry.

"Why do you say that?" Robert watched the man with increased interest. Something about the man's erratic behavior unnerved him. The prince stood to leave. "Thank you for the stew. I need to be going."

"No! I mean, please stay, Your Highness." The man's eyes darted toward the door to the common area then back to Esterling. "I need to keep you safe."

"Keep me safe? Or stall, you mean?" Robert grabbed one of the kitchen knives from the counter, holding it as he was trained by Max. The door to the common area swung open and two men rushed in. A split second later the door to the alley did the same and two more men entered the crowded kitchen.

One of the men handed a purse to the smiling innkeeper who ran from the room, door slamming shut behind him. The man who had produced the purse moved to block the door. "Hello, Princey," he gave Robert a short curtsey and then laughed, "you were a difficult man to find." The man signaled the others who rushed all at once.

Robert tried to control his breathing, feeling the passages constrict from his sudden leap to grab the knife. And then everything in the room came into sharp focus. A feeling of omniscience overwhelmed him, knowing where each man was going to step and the direction that their hands would attack. The first man reached him, but Robert ducked a blow from a cudgel and sidestepped, bringing his knife up into the man's armpit. With a turn of the wrist, he turned the man to face the other two attackers, using him as both a shield and a battering ram to push them off of their balance.

Having gained separation, he turned his body so that he could see all four men at once. Blurred shapes ran out from each man, each indicating a path of intended travel. The man at the door seemed to hesitate, showing no desire to get physical. Focusing on the other two, Robert saw that one intended to pull and throw a knife. He reached his hand up as it flew, watching it turn slowly end over end until he snatched it cleanly out of the air by the handle.

All three men hesitated at this, having never seen any feat like it. Smiling, Robert lunged at the solitary man, spinning with the blades through the air in an act of stunning acrobatics. He felt as if he were flying through the air as he lunged, and the look on the man's face was satisfying. He plunged the first knife into the man's neck, spinning him around so that he was between him and the other two. He rammed the second knife up between the ribs into the man's lung, feeling the escaping air around his hand.

He looked down and literally saw the air flow out from the man. Looking up he saw all kinds of swirling patterns like motes of dust around the room. The currents seemed to make sense to Robert in that moment, as if he could read them and predict their path. He reached out with his mind and caught ahold of one, drawing it toward the men. With a push he let it fly across the room, sending both men sprawling atop the man still bleeding on the floor.

He drew a deep breath into his lungs, filling them deeply and feeling no constriction. He marveled at the feeling whereas moments ago he had wheezed. Slowly letting out the breath he focused it into strands of air as fine and tight as tinsel. He reached out and wrapped the hands and legs of the two conscious men. He bound them in the same fashion as the Falconer had tied the hands of the man from the dream, with wisps of air.

The prince should have been terrified at what he just done, but he was strangely calm. He tucked the knives in his waistband and strode past the failed assassins, exiting the door beyond them and emerging in the alley. Looking down at the kettle of stew resting on the step, he thought about how he was lured into betrayal. He released another blast of air that sent the kettle careening down the steps, spilling its' contents into the alley.

He hustled back toward the burned bakery, glancing at his footsteps in the snow. No longer worrying about being found or followed, he pulled himself up, into the loft. As he did, he nearly collided with a hooded figure seated on a rafter. Robert jumped back, drawing his blades.

The man pulled his hood back, revealing his face. "Easy, now. Why would I want to hurt the rightful Emperor of Andalon?"

Robert relaxed, putting the knives away. "I missed you, Max."

"I missed you, too, My Liege." Wrinkling up his nose, he added, "Gawds. Your uniform smells like shit, boy."

Maximus Reeves sat across from Robert, sipping from a waterskin. Too dangerous to go about the city in daytime, he had decided to stay in the boy's loft. The prince had done well providing for his own survival, having collected non-perishable items in a basket in the corner. He had found a natural windbreak in the crook of the burned-out loft, and the hearth in the corner held warmth from the adjacent bakery.

He listened with interest at Robert's exploits over the past weeks, periodically nodding his approval at resourcefulness. He only interrupted on single time, when the boy discussed his most recent brush with death. "Tell that part again."

"About the men at the inn?"

"Particularly how you had bound their hands and feet."

Robert recanted the "Battle of the Kitchen," focusing on getting every detail accurate for the general.

"And you've never done any of that, before? Not even by accident?"

"No, Max. This was the first time."

"No, son. No, it wasn't." The boy looked shocked, so the general filled him in, describing the superstitious mumblings back in camp. "So, you see? You must have made a shield around us. That's why we didn't get hit with a single arrow."

Robert searched his mind back to that night. A single memory rose to his conscious, remembering the moment that Sarai had called his name and how he had dodged the arrow. There was no way that he could have moved so quickly, save for the fact that the projectile had been pathing much the same way that the men in the kitchen had. Only, it had been moving faster so Robert hadn't noticed reading the trajectory. He relayed this information to Max, who nodded.

"If I didn't know any better, I would say that you had the powers of a Falconer."

"Great. We saw what he did to two of them with his fire."

Maximus thought long and hard at this. "Don't be so quick to think that he's more powerful than you. They were bonded with their birds at the time, and we saw him fry those out of the sky. They were probably disoriented, and he caught them off guard."

Robert considered this for several moments, finally looking up at his friend and mentor. "Am I a freak like them?"

"You're not a freak, son. You are the rightful king of the Esterling Empire." Max walked over and put his hand on the boy's shoulder. "Now let's go back to the camp and march south to Eskera where I still have some officers loyal to me. If General Lourdes is sympathetic, we may be able to sway some troops into our camp."

"No, Max. I need to be here to protect her. I've seen what he'll do to her."

"You can't stay here, son. You just fought those assassins, and your brother's no doubt sent several teams at once." Shaking his head, he added, "No. I need to get you safely to camp."

"Give me a week, Max."

General Reeves looked closely at the young man sitting in front of him. Pride filled him as he thought about how much the boy had grown in recent months. "I'll give you three days, no more. After that I'll drag you kicking and screaming if I have to."

"Thank you, Max."

"You're welcome. I'm also sending you some supplies and rations." With that, the man put up his hood and started his climb down from the loft. Pausing, he added, "Oh, and be more careful about leaving tracks in the snow."

Chapter Thirty-Six

Eusari stood atop the city walls, surveying the first phase of her night's work. By now the murder holes and cannon outposts were neutralized and she scanned the night seeking confirmation. She smiled as she recognized six columns of gray gas and smoke billowing up, kept low and mixing into the storm clouds. She was pleased that the blinding snow had given extra cover as her teams entered the next stage of the operation.

On cue, she heard the retort of cannons from the harbor. Braen and *Ice Prince* had a difficult job of taking out the Imperial vessels, and she prayed that the primers had been properly placed by her team. Her friend and his crew would be sitting ducks for the large guns if they were recovered after the gas dissipated. None fired, so she felt satisfied that the water assault had worked. Silently praying that Shon's soldiers would be in position at the northern gate, she rushed to meet up with Jacque.

Everything had worked according to plan. Her team met very little resistance at the gate, as most of the city guard rushed to the waterfront. Braen would pin them down with grapeshot and more carcass rounds from the ship's guns, giving Shon's men easy access to the armory. She saw a small skirmish on the wall across from her, and worried that the other team couldn't get through. Finally seeing Jacque and his team break free, and she let out a breath. He ran up to her with a quick salute, proudly reporting that not a single man was lost in the first phase.

They quickly threw open the gates and signaled twice with a directional lantern. She marveled at the mind of Sippen who had invented the device. He had told her that he had "whipped it up just for tonight." So far, his gadgets were the main reason that the attack was going well.

She tired of waiting. She was starting to doubt that Shon's men had seen the signal through the storm and prepared to send a second set of flashes, but finally a response came. One. Two. Three lights. They were ready to begin the frontal assault.

Without a sound the men rushed the front gate, sprinting through and fanning out to the armory and several resource-filled warehouses. Any guardsmen caught out in the streets were cut down immediately by well-trained crossbowmen. More men drove wagons behind the first wave ready to load the night's spoils. Eusari and Jacque followed these, providing cover. When they reached the armory, Eusari noted that the men had already hauled out most of the armor and weapons onto the lawn. She ordered her team to load the piles into the wagons for extraction.

Looking up, she saw Porter rushing down the street with his team intact. A mass of people followed behind them and she strained her eyes to get a look at the freed prisoners. Expecting to count fighting men, she was shocked to count thirty children, running after Porter. Blinking in amazement, she noticed that some were little more than toddlers. They arrived at the armory panting and breathless.

"What the hell is this, Porter?" She pointed at the children. "Where are Shon's captured troops?"

"Ma'am, this is all we found. The jail was empty except for them, and I couldn't leave them."

"Holy hell." She couldn't believe the mess. "I guess we take them with us and sort it out, later. Get these children to Braen and load them aboard *Ice Prince*. There won't be time to get them on *She Wolf*." He saluted and took off running. Turning to Jacque, she added, "Take my team and rejoin the extraction. I need to go see what other surprises Shon has for us."

"Aye Mum." He ran off to round up both teams, who were busy loading wagons.

"And Jacque!" He skidded to a halt and spun around. "Be VERY leery of Falconers. I'm surprised we haven't seen any, yet."

Eusari sprinted toward the Rookery, cursing under her breath as she ran. Rounding the last corner, she stopped to let her lungs catch up. She observed that the building, although fairly large, was not elaborate. There were no windows on the first floor, and several large ones on the second. Two city guards lay dead in front of the building, crossbow bolts sprouting from their chests. She saw that the doors had been kicked open and Sippen's gas filled the foyer. She donned her mask and entered carefully.

Once inside she stepped over a dead bird sprawled on the floor. A few feet away she saw her first Falconer of the night. He had died with his hands clutching his throat, obviously having breathed in a full dose of the lethal smoke. *They can be killed. Good.* She picked her way carefully, irritated that her vision was poor in the mask. Reaching the other doorway, she braced herself for what lay on the other side and then pushed it open.

The next room served as either a dining hall or a meeting room. A long table ran the length of the floor, with a set of double doors on the other side. Two more guardsmen had bled out in front of the doors, swords drawn and laying on the ground. One of the doors was slightly ajar, and she gently slid through.

Eusari emerged into the strangest room she had ever laid eyes on. There were no candles or torches that she could see, but the entire room glowed with a strange light emanating from the ceiling. At first glance she assumed it was a room for the distillation of alcohol, as she traced hundreds of feet of glass and copper coils. These tubes connected vats of various sizes that sat atop small burners and drips. She silently wished that Sippen had been along to help her decipher the purpose of the room.

There were two additional doors that opened into the laboratory, one of which she was a supply closet and the other another room.

The door to the closet looked heavy and had once held a strong lock that now lay forced open on the floor. Sounds of movement from within reached her ears and she crept in that direction, careful not to give away her approach.

She slowly turned the handle and pulled open the door. As she peeked in, she immediately saw Shon and all four of his men filling their leather satchels with small objects, pouring them out of jars. She watched in silence as they dumped the contents into their bags and discarded the empty containers on the ground.

"What's all of this, then?" Her voice startled the men and caused one to miss his satchel, pouring hundreds of small black rocks onto the floor.

All five men froze at the presence of Eusari. Shon quietly cleared his throat, taking a step toward his niece. "You aren't supposed to be here, Dearie. You should be opening the gates and getting your teams out."

"I can be anywhere that I choose, Shon." She bent low to pick one of the black beads, rubbing the oddity between her fingers. It was perfectly smooth and round, about the size of a pearl. "I came to give you guys a hand, but it appears you don't need any help to steal rocks."

"Not rocks, Dearie." Wimbley carefully approached Eusari.

"Then what? Are these jewels? Some valuable commodity to help finance the coming war?" She slipped the black pearl into her pocket and placed her hand on one of her knives.

Shon's eyes shot to her hand as she did, halting his approach.

"Start talking, Shon Wimbley. You need to explain what's so important that we risked an entire operation."

"To do that, I need you to follow me."

Eusari stepped aside, allowing him to enter the laboratory. She glanced back into the storeroom, noticing that Shon's men immediately went back to work pouring the rocks into their satchels. Curious, she followed him through the other set of doors.

Lights turned on, illuminating the next room as soon as they stepped inside, and Eusari gasped in shock and disbelief. Rows of slab-like beds lined the room with hundreds of people lying atop them, nude and in a deep slumber. Tubes ran from every orifice of the sleeping subjects, and no effort was made to cover them. Eusari walked down the first row, immediately noticing that there was no regard to age. She saw infants, adolescents and elderly mixed in with adults. Tears welled in her eyes as she walked.

Pausing next to a male infant, she ran her fingers along the tubing. She had never seen anything so miraculous as the thin and flexible lines that ran from the base of the child's skull into a box nearby. Kneeling down, she saw that a clear fluid was circulating between the child and an apparatus beside the bed. Another line ran into the left hand while one more terminated as a mask that covered his mouth and nose. Looking around confirmed that every person in the room was similarly attached.

"The Rookery is a farm, Dearie. They harvest spinal fluid from the subject and extract what they need." Pointing at another tube that ran from the apparatus to the ceiling, he added, "They take that into the laboratory and make the beads."

Eusari was too shocked to comprehend. "What are they used for?"

"The best that I can figure is that the Falconers swallow the beads. I think that's how they get their powers, but it was mostly a theory, until tonight."

"But you convinced us to risk the attack, anyways? On a hunch?"

"Yes. Well, more than a hunch, really. I found some of the beads and several books during one of my raids. Look, we don't have much time and need to get what we have back to the extraction point. Can we discuss this back at the Landing?"

Before she could answer, Eusari heard a groan from one of the tables. Turning, she strained to see movement in the back of the room. One subject was fully dressed and without tubes in his body. Her hand came up to her mouth as she recognized Samani

Kernigan laying atop a slap, hands and feet bound by a swirling substance. She rushed over, reaching out to touch the shackles, recoiling when she realized that the man was bound by wisps of air. Unlike the others, he was awake and staring up at her with a blank expression. His eyes were wide open.

"Sam? Can you hear me?"

Without nodding, Sam answered in a voice that sounded trance-like. "Eusari? Thank heavens. Get me out of here before he returns." She shouted for Shon to help her. The other men had finished loading their bags and two of them picked the man up off the table, grunting under his weight.

Eusari looked with pity around the room, trying to form a plan that could get all of the people out of the Rookery.

Reading her expression, Shon looked around and shook his head in a sad, "no." Motioning to the tubes he said, "We don't know how to safely detach them, Dearie. Not without killing them all. Besides, how would we get them all out of the city?" With urgency in his voice he declared, "We have to, NOW."

Samani answered him, "He's right, Eusari. These people are little more than husks, now that the extraction process is so advanced. The thirty children that I saw Jacque rescue will have to suffice as tonight's humanitarianism."

"How did you...?"

"I'll explain, later. We have very little time. Kestrel is down at the docks with the two remaining Falconers, and they're facing off with Braen. You have to distract them and the Imperial troops so that we can get to *Ice Prince*."

Looking around remorsefully, Eusari nodded and swallowed back the tears. "You heard the man, let's carry him to the docks."

Chapter Thirty-Seven

The air filled with swirling snow and smoke as the cannon roared. All around him, Braen smelled gunpowder as cries rang out through the city, sounding the alarm. He stood atop *Ice Prince*, calling out shots to Krill. After he had seen the gas atop the wall, confirming that the guns were neutralized, he had begun firing upon the Imperial ships berthed in the harbor. Krill and his gunners made quick work of the other vessels, destroying them before they could even call away battle stations. Now, his crew focused all of their attention on the harbor gate.

Looking around, he saw a squad of twenty soldiers exiting the harbor master office, trudging through the piling snow. He pointed them out to his Gunnery Sergeant and waited. Just when they were within crossbow range, he gave Krill the second signal. Another set of guns erupted with a salvo of grapeshot that tore the advancing men into pieces. As soon as they were cut down, he saw several of Eusari's men rush into the street, making a dash for the harbor.

Among the men, he recognized Porter, carrying a little toddler in his arms. Braen could not believe his eyes, staring in disbelief as twenty or more children followed, ushered through the gate by the black-clad crewmembers of *She Wolf*. "Holy Hell. Cover those kids, Krill!"

Krill and his gunners worked fast to load the children, stowing them below decks and away from the fighting. Looking at Porter, he asked over the noise of the night, "What the hell? That wasn't part of the mission!"

"They're what we found in the jail, Braston. Eusari said to get them to you, and so we did."

"Where is she? Did she get out with the longboats?"

"Negative. She went alone to the Rookery to check on Wimbley. Haven't they extracted?"

"Shit. Krill hang on! We can't go, yet. We still have a team in the city!"

The Gunnery Sergeant turned his single eye toward his captain, pointing at the gate. "Well she best damned find another way out, Cap'n!"

Braen saw a platoon of Imperial troops forming up at directly where Krill had pointed. These men would be more cautious and would carry more firepower. He counted about fifty men in all, approached closely from behind by three Falconers. *Those are a problem*, he thought, and cursed under his breath as he wondered how he would fight three at once. Looking up, he saw three hawks struggling to stay aloft in the storm, getting tossed around like leaves. They quickly returned to their masters, perching atop their shoulders. *She still has a chance,* he realized.

"Krill," he yelled over the explosions, "keep your eye peeled for any more teams who have to egress via the harbor. Most of them have already started back to the boats, but I don't want to leave any stragglers."

"Aye Cap'n!"

Braen strained his eyes down river, waiting for the first signal from the shore. One flash. Two flashes. Three. There it was. The first teams were ready for their extraction, so he waited for the answer from *She Wolf*. "Hurry up," he thought impatiently. He finally saw two flashes as the ship began its' approach back upriver. Picking up the boats while riding the current would be trickier than when they deposited, and he prayed that they had timed it well. Peeling his eyes away, he again checked the gate.

"How many've formed up, Krill?"

"About one thousand men, Cap'n. I also saw a squad moving to the harbor guns."

Braen strained his neck to see atop the walls. Twenty men ran along the parapet to the first pair guns. Looking right he saw another twenty men running for the others. "Brace for shock, gentlemen! This is going to shake the harbor!" He watched as the teams fanned out, manning all four guns. Braen lashed his arms to the rail. "Hold on, men!" He bellowed into the night. His cry was met with four tremendous explosions as Braen prayed for the second time in two years.

Eusari and Shon emerged from the Rookery, scanning and taking in the scene. The snow had piled up fast, burying the city in a blanket of white. Bells rang a cacophony of alarm that mixed with shouts and the report of cannons from the waterfront. Straining her eyes, Eusari confirmed what Samani had predicted; three Falconers stood with a line of Imperial soldiers at the gate.

Shon spied a vegetable cart across the street and ran toward it, dumping out the contents and rushing back. After helping his men set down Kernigan in the wagon, he asked, "How the hell are we getting past them, Dearie?"

Eusari didn't know the answer. She desperately took in the scene, until she noticed two squads atop the wall, running toward the gun mounts. "Shit. Take cover, gentlemen." Just as they ducked behind the wall of a shop, four explosions rang out.

Shon's eyes grew large. "Sippen's primers?"

Eusari smiled back and nodded. "We placed one inside each cannon, in case they tried to use them against us. As soon as they loaded, the cannons and powder blew."

They both peeked around the corner, happy to see that the four-gun mounts were gone. Eusari peered forward. She could see large cracks and fissures all along the length of the wall, badly damaged from the blasts.

Shon pointed at the soldiers near the gate. The entire line had been blown backward, many of the men hit by debris. The Falconers were slowly getting up from the ground, trying to rally the troops back into formation. "This is our chance, Dearie. I think we can make a run for it!"

Eusari nodded and pulled her satchel close, peeking in to find four gas grenades. She passed these to the other men and said, "On the count of three we'll run for it. They all slipped masks and she showed the others how to pull the charge. "Throw on two. One. Two." Four grenades lobbed through the air toward the squad of soldiers.

The soldiers barely had time to turn as four tiny explosions released a grey cloud, causing them to choke and gag. Shon and the men pushing the cart sprinted by, making it onto the pier. Eusari was not so lucky. She felt tiny ropes lash around her as she tried to run past, pulling her to the ground. Through the eyes of the mask she saw a tall Falconer looming over her. She struggled against her invisible bonds, recognizing the same wisps of air that bound Samani.

Rolling over so that she could see the harbor, she watched as Shon and his men loaded Kernigan onto *Ice Prince*. At least they had made it, she thought. The Falconer was closer, now, peering down at the mask. With a quick swipe, he ripped it from her face, causing her to choke and gag as she breathed in. How was he not affected? She squinted her eyes and saw wisps of air around his head, as if he were wearing a helmet.

"What have we here?" When he spoke, his voice was distorted through the bubble of air. "So, you are the cause of my trouble, tonight." He reached into her pocket, pulling out the black bead. "And it appears that someone has been where they shouldn't. Seen things that they shouldn't see." The wisps of air constricted tighter against her skin causing her to scream out in pain, thereby breathing in more of the gas.

Eusari's vision was beginning to blur. The edges were dark, and she felt like she should close her eyes and give in to the darkness. It would be so easy to just sleep. Everything went dark.

Abruptly, Eusari was no longer laying on the ground in the city. She was onboard *She Wolf,* pacing back and forth, growling and whining as the boat drew nearer to the harbor. She could hear the voice of Peter as he tried to console her, "Easy now, boy. She's alright, she is. Steady now." And then he spoke to someone else, nearby, "Mate, pull in close as we sail by *Ice Prince.* I want to holler at Braen."

Braen had run to the stern of his ship and was flagging them down as they passed. "Eusari is still in the city!" He shouted.

"I'm right here, Braen!" She tried to yell to him, but only made a howl. Frustrated, she moved to the rail and stood up on her hind legs to peer at the harbor. She saw the soldiers, now advancing through the gate as Krill fired salvo after salvo of grapeshot to keep them back. She moved back from the rail, and with a running leap cleared the distance between the two ships, padded feet landing softly on the wooden deck of *Ice Prince* and then onto the pair. She raced toward the gate, ignoring both the grapeshot and the soldiers firing crossbows at Braen's crew.

Ahead she saw three Falconers standing over the frame of a small woman dressed in black. She looked dead, but Eusari sprinted toward the specters, somehow knowing that she could still help the girl. She leaped at the first Falconer and he spun around in shock, trying to move away. She adjusted in the air and her strong jaws grabbed his arm, dragging him down onto the cobblestones. Once she had him down, she grabbed ahold of his throat with her sharp teeth, ripping flesh and tasting the warm metallic blood on her tongue.

Satisfied that the first Falconer would not get up, she turned toward the others and squared off, growling and showing bloody fangs.

"No." The taller of the two said. "That's not possible. There's no way that Spring has awakened, too!" He tried to throw ropes of air around her, but he could not control three beings at once.

She fell to the ground as bonds formed around her muzzle and paws. Behind the feathered monster, the girl stood, freed and with eyes afire with hatred. She clapped her hands and the ground rumbled. She rubbed them slowly, and the earth shock beneath their feet, knocking the second Falconer to the ground. Faster she rubbed and faster and harder the ground shook until the weakened walls of the harbor gate fell atop hundreds of soldiers, crushing them beneath the weight.

All at once, Eusari was herself. She could see the crumbled walls and the remaining soldiers, scattered and trying to regain their footing. She faced two Falconers, one of which stood next to a tree by a market stall. She reached out became the tree. With a smile she wrapped her limbs around the man's throat, twisting and choking until he dangled from the tallest branches like a thief from the gallows.

Standing again as herself, she sensed thousands of tiny sentient lifeforms in the city. Smiling at the Falconer before her, she reached out and became them all. Spiders and insects of all shapes and sizes emerged from the shadows, converging on the tall, feathered man. Rats emerged in droves, biting and tearing at his flesh like fleas on a dog. When he had finally stopped struggling beneath their weight, the tiny army turned on the remaining soldiers and the ants cleaned his bones.

Braen and his men fell to the deck as the ground beneath the city rumbled, pulling against the ropes tied to *Ice Prince*. His ship shook violently, and terror gripped the crew. They desperately tried to cast off the lines, but the ropes were pulled taut and could not unwind from the chocks. Climbing to his feet, he strained his eyes to see beyond the fallen wall, desperately wishing he could see through the dust and snow. Moments later the shaking stopped.

Finally, after what appeared an eternity, he spotted Eusari and her wolf climbing over the rubble, carefully picking their way down the other side. He ran to them, catching her as she fell, exhausted, into his arms. He scooped up her tiny frame and carried her back to *Ice Prince*, tears flowing down his cheeks. Krill and the crew cast the lines and the sleek ship caught the river current. Together, the two ships raced to open sea and toward Estowen's Landing.

Braen had carried his friend below decks and laid her atop the bed in his stateroom. She was conscious and stared up with exhaustion. Smiling down at her, he whispered, "I thought I had lost you."

"I think you did, for a minute." Her smile was beautiful, green eyes taking on a bit of blue as his own reflected in hers.

"I don't think I could've handled that, if I had." He smiled shyly at how close they were, feeling her warmth and noticing her as a woman atop the bed. How had he missed her beauty? In that moment she was the most spectacular woman he had ever known. Trying to change the subject, he said, "You were wonderful, tonight. But how did you get away? I saw you laying on the ground, not moving."

She lifted a finger and gently shushed him. "Later. Let's talk later. Right now, I just want you to kiss me." And he did. Long and slow and with a lover's embrace.

Chapter Thirty-Eight

Taros sat next to Sarai in the Palace Garden. They came here, often, to sit and talk or to just enjoy each other's company. They talked about the snow that had fallen in the night, how it had blanketed the city and somehow quieted the world around them. She would point out a bird that had forgotten to fly south, or a squirrel not yet asleep for the season. Despite their actual conversation, every word that they exchanged fed his feelings and his love had grown.

He felt several emotions. First was joy from being near Sarai. He loved how his pulse quickened every time her skin brushed his own. Next was nervousness as he carefully tried not to upset her. In his mind Sarai was a beautiful bird that could fly away at any moment. But the feeling that overwhelmed him on this midday in the garden was fear that she would tire of his company and break his heart with rejection.

He wished so badly that his mother still lived. Lynette would have guided him through this, helping him find the words to express his feelings. His mother was always tender and understanding, unlike the other Pescari women who closed off their emotions. Like Sarai, his mother had lived with her feelings on the wind, finding joy in a breeze or a fallen acorn. Thinking of his mother brought more sadness to his heart, and he yearned so badly to touch Sarai's hand like he had in the market square.

He had tried speaking about these feelings with Teot, but his uncle had urged him to find a woman in his own tribe. He had even told him that Daska's granddaughter Flaya would be a good match.

"She is hearty and strong," he had said. "She knows our ways and will be your equal. Avoid the Westonese woman," he had warned, "she knows only servants and will make one of you, as well."

Sarai, as intuitive as ever, must have sensed his musings. She delicately reached out her hand and touched his arm. "Are you well, Taros? What troubles you?"

He blushed at her touch. "Nothing. I am just so happy to be near you. I enjoy our talks, very much."

Her smile filled her face at his words. "I do too, Taros. You're special, and I'm happy that you and your people are here."

"You have done so much for us, Sarai."

"Well of course!" Her smile was radiant and lit up her beautiful face. "You are good people who lost everything. I want you feel welcome as you get back on your feet."

"Thank you, for being so nice to me. Especially... Especially after what I caused to your father."

She grabbed his hand in her own and looked him directly in the eye, her face suddenly very serious. Taros drew a breath as she spoke, "I know that the others fear you for what you can do and for what you did. But I know that it was an accident."

"Sarai, I..."

She cut him off. "No. You listen to me. You are a good man with a sweet soul, Taros. I understand that you were grief-stricken. You don't need to apologize ever again. Do you understand me?"

He nodded silently, very much aware of his hands within her own. She was so close to him, now, that he could smell her scent. Pescari women smelled dull like the land, but Sarai always smelled like she had been rolling in a field of spring flowers. He felt drawn toward her. Leaning in, he closed his eyes and kissed her soft lips.

She recoiled in shock, pushing him back and laughing. "Woah! What was that?"

Taros leaped to his feet. "I... I'm sorry!"

Sarai was still laughing. "Taros, I don't feel that way about you. I'm sorry, I don't love you."

The words bit into the Pescari youth like a viper, and he stood. "So, all of this... All of your flirtations..." He narrowed his eyes as anger brimmed. "Was I a game to you?" Realization dawned. "Were you tasked with spending time with me?"

"No!" Sarai sputtered. "Well, yes I was asked to spend time with you, but you were not a game!" She looked afraid, as if she were hiding more truth behind her lies. "Taros." She moved in to touch his arm, but he pulled away from her touch.

"Who? Who told you to spend time with me?"

"Cassus did. He asked me to make you welcome and become your friend." She was too nervous and was definitely hiding more truth.

He felt the fire burn within, again building to dangerous levels. He wanted so badly to calm himself, to believe that she was truly his friend. "You have been lying to me. You made me fall in love with you so that you could use me and take advantage!"

"No Taros!" She pleaded, eyes round with fear.

Her eyes were enough for him and he spun around to leave before he lost his temper. She would not fear him if she was truly his friend.

She stood and ran toward him, grabbing his upper arm and turning him toward her. "Taros, I'm sorry. I like you, but I cannot love you. I..."

A blast of heat exploded from his body, sending her flying backward. She landed hard and sprawled in the snow, steam rising as it instantly melted around her. Her woolen dress melted into her skin as it burned and her once beautiful yellow hair singed atop her head. Large blisters filled half of her face, the other half red and swollen.

She said that she cannot love me. Not now. Not ever. She had not explained, but she did not need to. *She thinks I am a monster.* He looked at her, laying on the ground as pain racked her body. She convulsed as he watched, pitying her. He raised his hand to end her suffering.

Something hit Taros from behind and he was flung across the garden, his body hitting hard against the stone wall of the palace. Stunned, he tried to stand, head swimming from the impact.

Standing across the garden was Robert Esterling, the prince who had attended the council on the night of Lynette's death. "Leave her alone, Taros." The boy cautioned, his once white uniform turned completely black from dirt, soot and grime. He was walking toward the unconscious form of Sarai laying in the middle of the courtyard.

Taros felt his orientation returning and stood. In a way he respected the courage of the boy, but death was the prize for challenging Felicima's Shapan. He raised his hand and flung a firebolt toward Robert's head. It was deflected several feet in front of Robert, slicing off to strike the palace wall.

"You can't fight me, Taros, because I'm as powerful as you. Stop, now, and go back to your people."

The blasphemy from the prince's mouth infuriated the Shapan, even more. "I am a god, Andalonian. You are but a man." He focused his anger into a constant stream of fire that sped out across the courtyard, again failing to hit his mark. The prince was moving his hands in a circular motion, seemingly catching the fire in a whirlwind. The fire tornado grew in the boy's hands and he set it down in front of him, hurtling it back at Taros with tremendous strength.

Although the flames did not burn, he was too stunned to block the fiery cyclone as it struck him, exploding and sending him again flying through the garden. Dazed, Taros lay on the ground, head throbbing from a second blow to his head. He tried to stand. Barely able to keep his feet, he took two steps toward Robert and crashed into an invisible barrier. He tried to burn the shield of air that had formed around him, but only succeeded in filling the area around him with flames.

Within seconds, his flame had consumed all of the oxygen around him. He felt a surge of panic as he began to suffocate inside the sphere. His own fire extinguished, he finally lay down gasping for air. Helpless, Taros watched as Robert Esterling picked Sarai up into his arms and strode out of the garden. Tears formed in the Pescari boy's eyes as he closed them to die.

Maximus Reeves watched the city from his usual spot atop the hill. A glance at the sky revealed that it was midday, and the air was brisk from the fresh snow that had fallen the night before. He had promised Robert that he could stay for three more days, and today was the deadline. Tonight, he would sneak into the city and drag the prince back to the camp if the boy refused to come willingly.

Captain Titus approached him from the camp at a hurried pace. "General Reeves, we have an urgent dispatch from our allies in Eskera." He handed a slip of parchment to his senior officer and stood by for his orders.

Maximus took the paper and read it several times before addressing the captain. "Is this true?"

"It has to be, Sir."

"Then we need to get the boy out of the city, right now. If we cannot take and hold Eskera before these reinforcements arrive, then Robert's hopes to hold the throne are lost."

Titus nodded his agreement. "Shall I break camp, General?"

"Yes. Break camp immediately and prepare to move south. We'll have to keep a forced march pace if we're to beat the arrival of the boats."

"I estimate they'll arrive in four or five days, Sir."

"Then we will have to make it in three." With that the general rushed off without returning Titus' salute.

With a kick Max spurred his horse and the general raced toward the city wall. He did not stop at the gate as he blew past the city guard in his rush to find Robert. Ignoring the shouts from behind, he dismounted at the bakery. He pulled himself onto the upper level and found the nest empty, but an explosion from the direction of the palace turned his attention to the garden. The loft had a perfect view into the courtyard and he clearly saw the two boys squaring off in a fiery battle. Sarai lay on the ground between them, burned and unmoving.

The general froze. He watched as Robert caught Taros' fire, twisting it and mixing it with air. Then he sent the towering cyclone of fire racing toward the Pescari, sending him flying through the air and slamming against the wall. He jumped down from the loft into the snow and ran to the garden. Five city guardsmen followed in pursuit. He made it inside the gate just as Robert emerged with the limp body of Sarai Horslei draped in his arms. "You need to take her, Max. Get her to the camp and I'll follow."

Nodding, General Reeves took her into his arms and then turned to face the five men blocking his way. Before he could address them, Robert sent them flying across the street, clearing the path. Turning back, he hollered to his protégé, "You'd better do what you're doing quickly. Your brother is reinforcing Eskera and we need to get there before they arrive. You're in a civil war, now, Your Highness."

Robert nodded as the guardsmen tried to get to their feet. With another blast of air, he sent them sprawling backward.

Max set the injured girl across his saddle and rode out through the gate toward the camp. Ahead he saw the surgical tent and headed directly for it. Once inside he lay the girl down and a contingent of medics rushed to salve her burns. Tears filled his eyes as he looked at her hideously burned face. She would no longer be the visage of beauty that she had been, and his heart broke for her. He prayed that if she woke up, she would finally forgive his son.

Robert watched the general ride out through the gate, pleased that the guardsmen knew better than to follow him. Then he slowly walked back into the garden to finish with the boy. Taros lay where he had left him, unconscious from lack of oxygen. Kneeling down, he could see a slight bluish tint to the boy's lips. With a wave of his hand he removed the bubble and focused a stream of air into his mouth to restart his breathing. Taros awoke with a start, lurching up onto his knees and gasping in air on his own.

Robert leaned in closely, whispering low and clear into the ear of the Pescari boy, "I have wanted you dead since you burned her city, but I'm giving you a second chance to clean your mess. Not because I want to, mind you, but because that is what she would ask me if she still had a voice. I should kill you, now, and I still can." Taros stared up at him, hands clasped around his own throat and eyes large with both fright and awe. "You're not a god, Taros of the Pescari. You are a sniveling child who lives because I allow it. I own your life." With a final blast of air Robert pushed the boy to the ground, again knocking him breathless but only momentarily.

At that moment several people entered the garden, among them was Cassus Eachann. "Step away from the Shapan, Prince Robert."

"I can't do that, Councilman."

"You will."

"I won't." He shook his head. "He tried to kill Sarai."

"I sincerely doubt that. We just saw you kidnap and hand her off to General Reeves. Most likely Taros tried to stop you."

Robert looked around. Twenty city guardsmen stood beside the councilman and between him and freedom. "I'm going, now, Eachann."

"I'm afraid not. We're placing you under arrest. Your brother, the rightful heir to the empire, has issued a warrant for you. By that authority I arrest you for treason and kidnapping."

Robert could not help himself and let out a laugh. "You're a fool, Cassus." With a wave of his arm he sent the entire collection of men flying backward in a gust of wind. Casually he left the gardens, chose a horse from the stables, and rode out to rejoin his army.

CHAPTER THIRTY-NINE

Shon Wimbley sat across Braen and Eusari at the tiny kitchen table. Samani sat in a rocking chair next to the fire, feigning non-interest, but listening intently. The journey back to their temporary base was quick, and Shon barely had time to think of answers to their multitude of questions about the Rookery. In the end, he had decided to tell the truth and give the full story.

Eusari spoke first, breaking the uncomfortable silence. "How long have you known about what goes on in the Rookeries, Uncle Shon?"

"I've had my theories for about a year, but I only had proof a few months ago." He reached into his satchel and pulled out three books. "I found these during a raid on one of their convoys, along with a sack of those beads."

"Oracle beads." Samani interrupted.

"I beg your pardon?"

"Oracle beads. They're called oracle beads." Kernigan was staring intently at the fire, sullen and quiet without his usual flippancy or air of superiority."

"Okay, I found them along with a sack of those oracle beads." He shot the back of Sam's head an annoyed expression. "One of the books was a census report of children that had been culled from the area for the past ten years." He coughed a little, and continued, "When I was a constable, I had to escort these beasts around while they checked the newly born infants. If the baby was healthy, they were anointed with a jar with a red lid. If not, they were given a blessing from the blue lidded jar. After I did my own investigations, I figured out that they were culling out undesirable traits in every region of the empire."

Samani interrupted, again. "Latents."

"What's that?" Braen sat up, thinking about a conversation a month ago with Amash.

"Latents. They find children with latent abilities like yours and Eusari's and kill them before those powers awaken."

Braen and Shon shot Eusari a confused look. Braen spoke first, "You? You have abilities, too?"

Eusari nodded. Her pale cheeks blushing a deep red.

"You should have seen her, back there, Braen." Samani had picked up a stick and was poking at the burning logs. "She was magnificent. Took down three Falconers by herself."

Braen was flabbergasted. "What did you do? Did you drown them?"

"Not water, Braen." She shot Kernigan a deadly look, angry that he knew her secret. "I caused that earthquake and did some… some other things."

"She's a Spring Latent, Braen. Both warm and cool emotions by the looks of it. She bonded that wolf of hers and ripped out one of their throats. Then she strangled another by using a tree." He was poking the logs with more force, stirring up sparks as he spoke.

Eusari again nodded. "Let Shon finish. We can discuss me, later."

"Right." Shon continued, shooting his niece several uncomfortable looks as he did. "They haven't been killing all of the latents, though. The census records showed ten years of the lame children that they've been taking from the families. These were duly accounted for and listed at the Rookery for a period of time."

Everyone looked at Samani, who seemed to have all of the answers. With a grunt, he explained, "Autumn Latents. They've been stealing them because they have the genes they desire. Their spinal plasma and adrenal fluid can be extracted and made into a pill that passes on some of their latent abilities to someone who is sensitive to the same element."

"Oracle beads." Braen, Shon and Eusari spoke the phrase together.

"Exactly."

Shon spoke next, "I had a gut feeling that the beads were the source of Falconer abilities, but I didn't know exactly how. I was hoping to find more that I could study, and maybe free some of the kidnapped children."

"Only they weren't all children." Eusari looked down at the table, remembering the scene that she had stumbled upon. She cringed at the thought of the bodies lying atop the stark beds. "Some had aged several decades and there was no way to unhook them from the tubes."

"Not safely. No." Shon agreed.

At the mention of the children, Braen stood and walked to the window, looking out at the pier. Many of the children that they had brought back were running and playing in the snow, shouting and laughing as they did. "The children in the jail..."

"Were the most recent latents they had captured." Shon finished.

"Congratulations, Braston," Kernigan began, "you have an army of baby Falconers at your disposal."

Braen shook his head, pulling away from the window. "I must tell you that I feel less like a freak knowing that there are others like me." He moved back to his seat and sat down. "But what is waking up the abilities?"

Samani shoved the stick into the fire with great force, causing the fire to cough up sparks and a series of crackles and pops that made everyone at the table jump. "The Caldera of Cinder." He left the stick shoved into the fireplace and stood. Walking to the kitchen counter and picking up a bottle of wine, he added, "The atmosphere is more ionized, now, than it has been for nearly eight hundred years since the first explosion. The more it erupts the stronger and more frequent the awakenings will be."

Eusari paled. "There will be others?"

"Many more, I'm afraid." Samani tossed back the bottle of wine, taking a long drink. "The sole purposes of the Falconers are to stop the awakenings and farm the beads." He shook his head and resumed his seat by the fire. "But with this many already awakened the council may move to kill the inhabitants of Andalon."

Shon looked shocked. "Which counsel?"

"The Counsel of Astian, of course."

Braen added, "Which inhabitants?"

"All of them, Kraken. All of them."

Silence overcame the people in the room. After a few moments, Eusari asked the burning question. "Samani, how do you know all of this, and who are the Astians?"

He downed the rest of the bottle and then explained. "The Astians are the people who brought the latents to Andalon. You were an experiment, at first, to see if they could breed and develop humans with abilities like foretelling the future and moving things with their minds. Or even to read people's minds, really. They just wanted to develop what are called psychic abilities."

Braen looked mortified. "They succeeded."

"Well, yes and no. They succeeded in creating people who are predisposed to emotional latency connected with the elemental powers. Earth, Water, Air and Fire. Only, things got out of hand."

"Why would anyone want to breed people with powers like that? Especially fire?" Eusari thought of the Falconer swinging from the tree and she cringed.

He held his wine bottle toward her like a toast. "The experiment was considered a success, and the beads were created to fuel the oracles. Four in all, Winter, Spring, Summer and Autumn."

Shon nodded, "Or, Water, Earth, Fire and Air."

"Right. The oracles predict phenomenon for the Astians, and also act to keep the Andalonians in check. They help the Falconers by finding latents who slip through the cracks and help to suppress all other abilities while harnessing the air."

"Why didn't they just kill everyone, once they had the formula to breed air latents?" Shon seemed to be handling the details better than Braen and Eusari, since he did not have any abilities.

"That was the work of the Society. My work, actually." He shook the bottle, looking to find another drop but gave up and set it down. "I'm a member of the Humanitarian Freedom Society." Looking at their stares, he explained. "Yes, I am an Astian. I've dedicated my life to uncovering the atrocities that you've discovered, hoping to reveal how the beads are made to all of the Astian people."

Braen handed him another bottle and he continued. "Eight hundred years ago the Astians had a choice to kill all of the experimental rejects." Looking at Braen and Eusari he added, "No offense but you guys are the rejects because your emotional latency is not balanced." He took another long draw from a new bottle. "But we formed the society and fought to repopulate the continent that had been decimated when the Caldera first erupted. An entire civilization was either wiped out or forced to evacuate, and the Council had this land available to send the experiments."

Eusari rose and walked over to Samani, placing her hand on his shoulder. "What would happen if you're captured?"

"I would stand trial before the council and then put to death."

She nodded her understanding. "But you risked that by taking a bead and drawing the Falconers to you in Diaph. That's how you were captured?"

Kernigan nodded, "Yes. I wanted to give you all a chance to succeed in your raid, even if it meant that I was returned."

Braen lifted his head, spinning from all of the information, "Why did you do that, Sam? What's so important about what we're doing?"

"Like I told you, before, Kraken, you were prophesized one hundred years after the experiment began. You're the downfall of the Astian society, and they fear you. You're the reason that they cull your populations."

"I'm not special, Sam. I'm just a man like you."

"That's where you are very wrong, Braen. You're extremely special. I believe in what you're doing. I wasn't supposed to interfere with the prophesy, I am a part of it, now."

Shon looked at Braston. "What do we do, now, Lord Kraken? I promised that if you helped me, then I'd help you. What is next, Fjorik or Pirate's Cove?"

"I... I don't know and I need to think." Rising from the table and walking to the door, Braen added, "I need air."

Braen stood on the porch looking out over the harbor, watching the children play. *They have innocence,* he thought. One of the boys, a tall and skinny pre-teen of about eleven summers, picked up a ball of packed snow and hurled it, laughing. The bearded captain ducked, and the ball struck the door behind him with a splat. He couldn't help but laugh and it nearly made him forget about the strife in the world.

Beyond the children, Sippen fussed with Krill over weapon improvements aboard *Ice Prince.* They too were laughing, presumably at some off-color or inappropriate remark from the gunnery sergeant. They worked without a care in the world, acting as if the world wasn't going to end and that they weren't simply genetic experiments gone awry. Estowen's Landing had a beauty to it, and his private army acted more like a community than hardened fighters.

The door opened behind him and Eusari slid out, leaning on the rail and pressing her body close to his. He felt his pulse quicken a little at her touch, a feeling that he hadn't experienced since his boyhood in Fjorik.

"How do you do it, Braston?" He loved how her voice purred when she talked, now that she didn't say his name with dripping disdain.

"Do what?"

"Get kicked down as many times as you have and always get back up, again?"

"I don't understand, doesn't everybody?"

"No. They don't, Braen. Not like you do. Your father was murdered by your brother and you live as an outcast and outlaw without the comforts of your upbringing. But you hardly care and are happy with just a few friends and your favorite weapons." She leaned her head on his shoulder as she talked. "You've been repeatedly beaten, violated, lied to and betrayed by more people than any one man should ever have to endure." Pausing, she added, "I'm sorry about my part in that, by the way."

"I already forgave you."

Ignoring him, she went on, "But you wallow in your misery until you're completely awash, and then stand up, shake it off and forgive the very people who have done horrible things at your expense. How do you do it? How do you remain so calm, so loving, and most of all, so understanding and forgiving?"

"Think about what you're saying, Eusari. We've all lost a great deal. We're all broken a little inside, and we all experienced trauma beyond reasonable expectation of survival. But that makes us resilient. We're tempered steel made stronger by the flame."

"You're crazy."

"No. No, I'm not. Look over there at Sippen. What do you see?"

"Sippen."

"No. You see what he chooses you to see."

"How so?"

"Start with what you DON'T see. You don't see Sippen the scrawny stuttering weakling. See? He overcame his personal traumas and redefined himself as Sippen the Engineer. Sippen the weaponsmith and boatbuilder. Sippen the inventor. Most of all, Sippen the best friend that a man could ever ask for. Not because I wanted him to be, but because he chose to be."

"Ok, but he's special. He is an exception"

"No. He's the typical." Pointing at his gunner he added, "Look at Krill over there. You don't see Krill the pathetic man who's had half his body blown off. No. You see Krill the foul-mouthed, life loving, lucky son of a bitch. You see Krill the cheeky bastard who laughs at everything just to make others smile at the irony. The irony that we all stress over and call life."

"I see."

"No, you don't. Not yet, at least. Look at yourself, Eusari. What do you see?"

"No Braen. Don't."

"You don't see Eusari, the fragile survivor of repeated sexual trauma. You don't see Eusari, the girl who witnessed her mother's death and had her father ripped away from her."

"Stop, Braen." She lifted off of him, back ridged.

He gently grabbed her upper arms and turned her, looking in her beautiful eyes. "Eusari. You're not a broken and defeated girl who's afraid that everyone will take advantage of her or force her to hide in shadows. No, Eusari. You're a magnificent woman. A strong woman who has endured all that life has thrown and is still, somehow, standing. You are a capable military leader, the captain of the dreaded *She Wolf*. Most importantly you're a stunningly beautiful woman who has learned to command her body, claim it as her own, and do with it as she pleases."

Tears welled up in her eyes as he spoke, but she listened and stared into his.

"You're a fighter. A fighter who has compassion and love for those weaker than her. You're willing to fight for the weak, and that's what I love about you, Eusari."

"Wait. You what?"

"Yes. I love you for who you are and what you've shown yourself to be. You're my friend, Eusari. I love you for your scars, because without them you'd just be an ordinary girl. But with them, you're extraordinary."

She hugged him close for a few minutes, until a snowball hit them both in the side of the face. They looked up, shocked and a little out of breath as the children laughed and ran off down the pier. After a moment, they wiped off the wet remains of the snow and shared a smile. "What do we do, now, Braen?"

"We need to storm The Cove, and we need to do it before Nevra solidifies his power."

Looking doubtful, Eusari remarked, "We don't have enough ships for that."

"Don't we? What is The Cove built to defend against? Think about it."

She pondered for a moment. "Ships. The reefs prevent frontal attacks forcing a massive assault into a single file convoy. That makes it easier for the towers to pick off the ships like ducks in a line."

"Exactly. So how do you attack The Cove?"

"You don't."

"Exactly!" He was so excited that he kissed her on the mouth.

Pulling back, she kicked him in the shin. "Start speaking sense, Braston."

"Ouch!" He smiled, "There's that purr, again."

"I'm about to kick your ass, Braen. Stop kidding around and tell me what you mean."

"Come on. I'll tell you with the others!" With that, he swung open the door and dragged her inside.

Chapter Forty

Stefan Nevra looked out through the window in the great hall, marveling at the number of ships in the harbor. Six more had returned in the night and the sunrise reflected off the masts of thirty-two vessels of various sizes. He scooped up his ledger and furiously scribbled down the numbers and filled in the names of those he recognized. With a smile on his face he accounted, carefully documenting the new arrivals.

When he was finished, he looked toward the harbor entrance, pleased to see that the improvements were nearing completion. The batteries had been built up with masonry, forming a cap over the top to prevent the lobbing of gas rounds. Additional guns were added along the walls to facilitate mid and close-range coverage in the event that a rogue ship actually made it into the harbor. These were based on the designs found in Sippen Yurik's laboratory and were grooved on the inside of the barrel for accuracy and precision. Nevra smiled at the thought that an attack on The Cove would be impossible.

For a moment he wondered about Kernigan and Braston. The former had been spotted recently in Diaph, and word was spreading that he was helping Braen mount a rebellion. Unfortunately, no one was talking specifics about where the two men were. Oddly, the same night that Samani had been spotted, northerners had attacked the town and destroyed nearly all of its' defenders. The ship in the harbor had been flying the colors of the royal family of Fjorik, so either Braston was an idiot or Skander had resumed raids along coastal cities.

That wouldn't be so bad for business, he thought. The raids would open up the guild to attack northern ships and Fjorik, itself. Not to mention, merchants could be set up in a way to appear that the Northman had attacked those, as well, without violating the allotment agreement with the family. With the extra profits, Stefan Nevra would make out quite nicely.

Captain Pogue interrupted his thoughts with one of his annoying throat-clearing sounds. "Lord Nevra."

"What is it? Can't you see that I'm busy?"

A short and sweaty man pushed past Pogue and entered the hall. He was adorned in flashy colorful garments with a turban tied around his head of curly black hair. "I don't care how busy you are, Nevra, you'll explain yourself." The newcomer spoke from behind a sharply trimmed beard and when his mouth moved his mustache bounced with two long black braids. "What happened to Artema Horn?"

"Ah, Captain Creech. Samani Kernigan and Braen Braston conspired against him while you were gone. I was barely able to fight off the mutiny and restore order." He sat down in the throne with an exaggerated plop. With a sigh, he added, "I could have used your fleet's help, but we managed."

"You managed because you hold the city defenses in your palm, Nevra. I wouldn't doubt if you killed Artema, yourself."

Nevra stiffened in the high-backed chair. "I can assure you that I did no such thing. In fact, that accusation is complete nonsense."

"Regardless, I don't accept your legitimacy, Stefan."

"Are you challenging my rule, Adamas?" Nevra lifted his hand and six guards entered the grand doors.

Creech lifted his hands away from his sword hilt, showing the guards that their lord was not threatened. "I'll be calling a vote of the council."

"I dissolved both the council and the inner sanctum. Had you been here to vote, you could have dissented." The pox-covered man busied himself with dirt beneath his fingernails as he spoke. "Alas, you were not, and so your voice is silent."

"Then I'll be rejecting my letter of marque and leaving the guild, Lord Nevra." With a sweeping bow and a swirl of cloth, the flamboyant man left the chamber.

After Adamas Creech had left, Nevra signaled to Captain Pogue. "Captain, that man has no marque and is thus an outlaw to the Esterling Empire. Have him followed out of the keep, then arrest him before he gets to his ship. Before. Do you understand? I cannot stress that part, enough, Pogue. After you do, have his first mate brought to me so that we can begin negotiations. I'll grant a marque and percentages to him in his captain's stead."

"Aye, Sir." Pogue spoke quietly with his men and then led them out of the hall.

Stefan returned his attention to his ledger, opening it to a page and drawing a line through one of the names. "Forty percent," he said quietly to himself, "more like twenty-two percent." He scribbled some more and then closed the ledger, setting it on the throne beside him. Moments later, shouts erupted from the halls. His security detail rushed in and surrounded him as Creech ran into the room with blood dripping from his cutlass.

"Thought you could hide me away, Stefan?" He brandished the sword, taunting the soldiers who surrounded Stefan. "I'll cut you to ribbons and feed you to the tuna!"

Nevra froze. He stood motionless behind his guards, heart racing and adrenaline pumping. He wanted so badly to run from the room.

"You're a pox-faced coward! Come out from behind them!"

In a flash Pogue entered the room with dual cutlasses drawn. He was a flurry of metal as the two slashed and parried. The guards, seizing the moment to get their king to safety, ushered Nevra through the door to his chambers as quickly as they could. He did not look back as the ringing of steel on steel carried down the hallway.

Once safely in his rooms Stefan began to panic. In his haste he had left his ledger atop the throne. "I have to go back!"

His guards quickly moved into a position to block the door. One of them, a brute from Fjorik, spoke up with a deep northern accent. "Can't let you do that, Sire. The outlaw is still out there, and our job is to keep you in your quarters until the 'all clear' is sounded."

Alec had turned Captain Creech away from Nevra as quickly as he could while the security detail whisked him down the hall and into his chambers. Their swords clashed, ringing out and echoing in the vast and empty hall. Despite the little man's flamboyant appearance, Pogue's opponent was a master swordsman. The two dueled until the door shut behind the pirate king, sealing them out from the inside. He allowed Adamas to push him toward the throne, and then slipped his sword away, sheathing one cutlass and then scooping up the ledger with his free hand.

Creech held his attack long enough for Pogue to thrust out the book toward him. Through clenched teeth he whispered, "Get this to the resistance and meet me at a pub called The Leaking Sea Chest!" The little man nodded and took the book, turning to flee. "Wait!" Alec drew out his second cutlass and hissed in a whisper. "Make it believable!"

Creech drove his sword through the right side of the Captain of the Guard, intentionally missing any vital organs. Pogue blacked out and fell into a heap on the ground.

Chapter Forty-One

Forced marches were hard on men, beasts, and equipment, but the column made good progress in two days and was certain to reach Eskera by the next evening. Maximus rode in the middle of the procession alongside Titus. Together they mulled their options and conceived a plan that they hoped would prevent them all from getting killed. Their entire move was based on a hunch, and there was no certainty that they would succeed.

The general turned his destrier around and moved to the medical wagon, rapping against the doors in the rear. A nurse opened them from the inside, and Max looked in on Robert and Sarai within. The girl was still unconscious, which was a good thing for her while most of the nerve endings healed. No doubt she would awaken with the pain of her life, that is, if she awakened at all. Robert, as usual, knelt over the girl and used his powers to keep an aura of dense air around her body. He was keenly focused, paying close attention to any changes in her status.

"What are you doing, exactly, Robert?"

"I've increased the amount of air around her burns. Her tissues are badly damaged, and I am hoping that this will help the healing process." The boy looked exhausted. He had bags under his eyes, and he hadn't slept in either of the two days during the march.

"You need rest, boy. Otherwise you won't be worth a damn to anybody."

"How close are we?"

"One more day. We'll be able to camp, tonight, and I want you to get some sleep."

"I'll try, but it depends on her."

Max nodded and spurred his mount back to the front of the wagon. Titus was looking at him, expectedly. To the captain he asked, "What?"

"When are you going to tell him, Max?"

"Tell him what? That this fight is not a guarantee? That all of us may die, tomorrow night or the next morning?"

"No. That he's your son."

Max frowned. "Figured that out, did you?"

The captain nodded. "It wasn't hard." A moment later he added, "I've known for a while, actually. The resemblance is uncanny and getting more noticeable as he gets older." He looked up at the glare that Max shot him. "Don't worry, I've no intention of telling others. The Empire needs a Reeves in charge."

"Yeah? Well he's an Esterling, not a Reeves. And if word got out, we would all cease being fugitives, and would instead be heads on spikes."

"Every man in this camp is willing to risk that, General."

"I need them to risk it for him and not me, Titus. This empire is in trouble with Marcus in charge, and when the shit hits it will need Robert's compassion." With that, Max trotted off to the check the front of the formation.

The next evening, General Reeves brought the column to a halt about five miles from the city walls of Eskera. His men were exhausted, and he ordered them all to make camp and set picket lines. He doubted that the attack would come before the reinforcements, but he was careful, nonetheless.

"Titus, get the men well rested. I want them ready for anything at any time. Give them double rations, tonight, so that they can build back some strength. After that, I want you to dispatch a rider to General Lourdes in the city. Let him know that we're requesting a parlay with friendly intentions. As allies, Titus. Emphasize that part."

Titus saluted and rode off to make the arrangements. Max

moved to the medical wagon and peeked in, noting that Robert was fast asleep next to his lady, somehow maintaining his current of air around her wounds. Gawds but the boy did look a lot like him. If Titus had pieced it together then other people would, too. With a sigh he worried about the war that Robert was about to face. Even if he survived the military campaign, the young prince would have to battle accusations and criticism from political and personal attacks for the rest of his life.

After ensuring the boy was safe and finally sleeping, Max walked the camp. His men were tired and would need to see their general. All around him was fatigue. Men walked around with hunched shoulders, dragging their belongings as they worked with glazed expressions. He couldn't let them get sloppy. An orderly camp was part of military discipline, and men fought the way they camped.

He stopped to help two soldiers putting up their tent and returned their salutes with a quick nod. "As you were, men. Here, let me help you hold the pole."

"Thank you, General." One of the men said. Max watched them as they stretched the canvas out and staked the corners.

"Is it true, Sir?" The other man asked, earning a warning look from the other.

"Is what true, Private?"

"Is Prince Robert gifted like the Falconers?"

Reeves cringed at the question but decided to answer. "Would that matter to you or the others if he was?"

"No Sir. He's one of us. We've marched and trained alongside him for two years. Watched him grow up, really." The soldier paused, then stood to full height and looked the general in the eyes. "We'd die for him, Sir."

"Well, Soldier. Let's hope that you don't have to. Besides, I think he'd rather that you kill the other bastard." He looked at the first soldier and asked, "Do you feel the same?"

"Sir." The first soldier had decided that it was safe to speak to the senior officer, having witnessed the success of the second. "I do. Gifts or no, Robert's ours. We were there, that night, me and Gus." He had pointed a thumb at his buddy.

"What night was that?"

"The night that you two rode in on horseback. He had a shield around you both, shimmering and sparkly. It curved the air and the arrows followed its' shape, Sir."

Max nodded. "I reckon that what you saw was true, son. Just remember that he's your true king. When this battle comes, he'll be out front with you and doing what he can."

The men stepped back after pounding in the last spike and Max nodded his approval of their handiwork. Hopefully they would rest well inside of it. "Sleep well, soldiers." As he turned to leave, Gus asked a question that made him pause.

"Sir. Will we be fighting our own, then? Will the army split sides? Ol' Sarge said that's what happens in a civil war."

A quiet passed over the general in a way that he had only seldom felt, before. He finally found the words and responded with candor. "Yes son, I'm afraid that at some point we'll be forced to fight men that you have trained with or fought beside. Get some rest, now." The men nodded and gave a sharp salute that he returned before striding off. He walked the rest of the way to the command tent with a faster gait, returning salutes but not wanting to speak to any more of the men that night.

By the time that he arrived, Captain Titus was speaking with a courier. Seeing the general, the aide de 'camp rushed over to deliver news. "Sir, General Lourdes has agreed to meet."

"Good. What time, tomorrow?" He hadn't expected a response so quickly and had hoped that he could also get some sleep before the parlay.

"Not tomorrow, Sir. He wants to meet in an hour. He said that he's looking forward to meeting with you and Prince Robert as soon as possible."

Glancing at the medical wagon he frowned, not wanting to wake

the boy until he was completely rested. "Son of a Bitch." He shook
his head, "Well, I guess now is better than never."

The air above Eskera chilled Robert as he flew, and he somehow
knew that he couldn't stay airborne much longer. This dream was
different than those in recent nights, and he couldn't help but
notice a change in clarity as well. The city below rose up with
sharper details than the dreams of Taros burning Sarai, and he
felt that he was more corporeal. The cold air and sounds of the
night stimulated his senses much as they had when he watched the
pirates attack the town of Diaph. He somehow knew that he was
actually above the city.

Two armies camped within the walls of Eskera, the reinforcements
having arrived several days before Max had calculated. The
accounts provided by the general's spies were clearly accurate
as Robert quickly estimated five-thousand imperial troops by
counting the rows of tents in the city squares. Those, combined
with General Lourdes's forces, would ensure that his and Max's
small force would face nearly eight thousand if they could somehow
scale the walls.

To the north he recognized the orderly lines of his own army
camp as it lined the edges of a southward reaching swamp. Of
course, he thought, Max would have protected the flank of their
infantry against the imperial cavalry within Eskera. He focused in
on the camp and it rushed up with such speed that vertigo and
nausea washed over him for a brief moment. Once oriented he
could clearly see the medical wagon that held both Sarai and his
own sleeping form. About twenty yards away Max was mounted,
and Titus stood before him discussing an urgent matter. Hoping
to hear their conversation, he started his decent and came to a rest
atop the wagon.

"Don't wake the boy. He's been using a lot of energy to keep his girlfriend alive and I want him at full strength when the fighting starts."

Titus nodded and pointed toward the south. "Are you certain that it's safe to meet with Lourdes alone outside of the camp? At least let me send a security detail."

"No. The risk is huge, but it's one that I need to take, Titus." He gestured toward the wagon, "Keep the detail around the Prince. He's all that matters at this point."

Robert watched as Max rode south into the night and then spread his giant wings, preening his feathers and fanning them to help trap warm air close to his body. Ready for flight he pushed off, sending the cart shaking with the rhythm of his heavy and beating wings. He rose quickly into the cold air and kept his eyes on the horseman riding south. Maximus Reeves was no fool, but desperation gripped him on this night, and would need an extra set of eyes.

The general felt the cold wind on his face as he rode toward the meeting spot. He was not in a hurry, but he wished to arrive at the parlay before his old friend. So many thoughts raced through his mind, filling him with doubt and worry. In all practicality they didn't stand a chance against the larger force, and he prayed that the reinforcements hadn't arrived. The other concern was whether or not Merrimac Lourdes could be convinced of the legitimacy of Robert's claim.

Max had been aide de camp for the crusty old warrior ten years ago, serving in the same capacity that Titus does for him. Mac was fiercely loyal to the former emperor, having fought to put down rebellions and fended off raids from both Fjorik and the Pescari. The royal family rewarded his loyalty with a twilight command over the permanent army in place at Eskera, that assignment intended to take him into retirement and beyond. Max prayed that the man still had some fight left in him and was placing himself and Robert at the mercy of a man who could end the entire civil war with a single cavalry charge.

A torch burned on the road ahead, indicating that he had failed in his goal to arrive first. He pulled his horse back from a canter, walking the beast up to a cleanly shaven man in a crisp uniform and seated atop a fallen log. The hair upon the man's head had gone completely white, and what was left was cropped close to the scalp. Although he was weathered and old, he was still fit and in fighting form.

"You're late." The words came out as part of a low rumble.

Max shook his head as he dismounted. "I respectfully disagree, Major General, that you are early."

The older man grunted what could have been a laugh. "At my age I arrive when I damn well please."

"You always arrived when you damn well pleased. Remember the battle of Fort Falstaff? Sir John waited six hours for your cavalry to arrive."

"Sir John was a drunkard and deserved to bake in the sun a few hours. The fat bastard was always cracking jokes at my expense in the academy, and a bigger hangover was my gift that day."

"As I recall you ordered me to rest the men in their tents for the entire morning. I thought that you'd lost your mind." Max took a seat next to the old warrior.

"But you followed my orders, anyhow. Have you finally reasoned out my strategy for that day?"

"It was for the horses. The Pescari had a distinct advantage with their speed but had ridden three days across The Waste. John would have marched out to meet them, but you set up a faster charge down the hill instead of on the open plain."

"Exactly. Always strike when your opponent is exhausted."

Max blanched a little at the insinuation. "Is that your plan, tonight?"

Merrimac Lourdes laughed loud and gruff, "What the hell were you thinking, pushing your men from Weston to Eskera, like that?"

"I needed to beat your reinforcements." After a pause, he asked, "Did I at least pull that off?"

"Not a chance in hell, Max. You can't outrun an Esterling ship with a forced march, not when they have the wind." Putting a hand on the shoulder of his former protégé he added, "You're fucked, mate."

"Not necessarily."

"You have a miracle amongst your foot soldiers, Max? Something to turn the tide against ten thousand men?"

"Not ten thousand, but we can handle five or so with your help."

"I'm done fighting in wars, Max. If I charge on you then I save the crown one final time. If I don't, well, let's just say that I'm too damned old for an overland march to Eston."

"Not even for the true Esterling heir?"

Mac let out a snort. "We both know that Chuck was walking around with a limp sword that couldn't find the sheath. Not after that accident."

"That dancing horse of his did a number on him, didn't it?"

"Exactly why I don't trust trick ponies, and neither should you. No, we both know who the Esterling boys belong to, father wise. And that's exactly why I won't help you. Matteas is already spreading rumors about your tie to Robert and no one knows about his own relationship with Marcus." He shook his head, "Regardless of who wins, if word gets out that I helped you, then the rumors will be that nepotism favored your son over the true heir. No. I won't be on the wrong side of a rebellion, Max. A civil war, maybe, but not a rebellion." He stood up from the log with a slight groan and a pop from one of his knees. "My pages in the history books are already written, and I don't want to rip them out and throw them in the Caldera."

Reeves looked at the ground as he quietly spoke his next words. "He's as strong as five Falconers, Mac. Maybe stronger."

Lourdes froze in his tracks and stood, pondering what he had just heard. After a moment, he cleared his throat and said, "Well that's not good enough, Max. See you tomorrow morning."

As Maximus Reeves watched his former mentor mount up and ride south, an eagle screeched a mournful cry from a nearby treetop. It might as well have been a trumpet signaling defeat.

Chapter Forty-Two

The midday sun was high in the sky as Braen watched Samani. He lined the older children up in the town square and fifteen were chosen, their ages ranging between nine and fourteen summers. They were seven boys and eight girls standing before him as he coached the basics of air control. Despite that Kernigan had no power over the element, himself, Braston could tell that the man was doing his best to explain the art and was irritated with their progress. After a while, one of the boys succeeded in sending Kernigan flying backward and the northern captain laughed at the folly.

"Tell me this isn't what it looks like." A voice from behind broke his merriment and he looked up at Eusari's angry glare.

"We need their help." He looked back at the children, just in time to see a girl create a whirlwind in the snow. It was fascinating to witness, but it snuffed out as quickly as it had manifested. "If they can master their craft, that is."

"They're children, Braen."

"I learned to fight when I was their age." Shrugging dismissively, he added, "I've had an ax in my hand since I was ten." She still stood behind him and he could feel her eyes drilling holes in the back of his head. After a few moments of chilled silence, he turned to face her. "We can't get into The Cove without them, Eusari.

With a sigh she uncrossed her arms and moved beside him. "Just promise me that you won't use them in the battle."

Braen nodded, "Sure."

In a flash she had grabbed his tunic and spun him around

to face her, green eyes now showing a hint of grey. "I'm serious, Braston. They. Don't. Fight!"

He took in a deep breath and let it out slowly. "I can't make promises, but I'll try to keep them out of combat." She stared him down, so he added, "Ok. I'll only use them to get into The Cove. Then we'll leave them on the boats during the action."

"Swear it to me."

"Sari..."

She stepped closer, menacingly. "Swear it!"

"Fine. I swear that we'll leave them on the boats." Her sudden aggression caught him by surprise. Sometimes he forgot that she was a ruthless assassin, and times like this shook him into remembrance."

"Braen, they're children. They were stolen from their families and trust you and I to keep them safe." She stepped back with a crestfallen expression. "They'll probably do anything that we ask, and I can't live with it on my conscience if we lead them to their deaths."

"Sari." He stepped up and placed his hand on her shoulder. "I understand, but we need their talents if we're to pull off this attack. I'll do everything that I can to keep them off the front lines."

She silently stared up him and he assumed she was calculating whether or not she was ready to trust. After a time, she shook her head and said, "Fine. But if one of them dies then I'll never forgive you."

He nodded. "If something happens to one of them, I won't forgive myself." Changing the subject, he pointed toward the piers. "Sippen said that the boats are nearly ready. Come on. He wants us to see." They made their way to the harbor without further conversation. Braen worried a little, himself, about using the children, but their entire plan depended on their abilities and his combined.

They were met by an excited Sippen in the docks. He beamed

proudly and rushed to greet them. "Wuh... we have thuh... them fuh... finished!" Behind her were four specially designed longboats.

Braen raised an eyebrow at the design. Sleek and low to the water, they each had a large square sail that ran the length of the single mast. Each boat had rows of benches aligned so that weight was distributed evenly. "How many will they seat?"

Sippen smiled. "Fuh... fifty uh... each." He pointed at the waterline. "And Thuh... the draft is luh... low. They wuh... will glide over the reefs.

Braen clapped him on the back, causing the little man to lose his footing. "That will do it! Good work, Sippen!"

Eusari was not convinced on the design. "How are these supposed to survive on the open seas during winter? One storm could wipe out an entire army."

Braen had his turn to smile. "That's the beauty of it. I can calm the seas between here and The Cove, and with one or two of our air emotes in each boat..."

Eusari glared again. "Children. I believe you mean children."

Bowing a slight apology, he corrected himself. "With one or two of our children in each boat we can ensure a strong wind. We should be able to arrive within two days, beating any storm."

"And if one hits us, anyway?"

"Let's just hope that doesn't happen."

Eusari looked doubtful. "I don't like any of this, Braen. The entire mission sounds like a disaster waiting to happen." She turned to Sippen. "Show me the new weapons, at least."

Sippen nodded and led them up the pier back to the main road. Only part of the town had been remodeled, and those buildings were farther back from the waterfront. Intentionally, they had left the visible town abandoned in case a stray patrol ship passed by and used a glass. Other than *Ice Prince*, *She Wolf*, and the new longboats, there was no indication that Estowen's Landing housed over three hundred revolutionaries. Eventually they turned a corner and faced a large building that may have once been a brewery. Vines and overgrowth had collapsed a section of the roof, but overall the building appeared sound. Yurik pushed the door open and led his friends inside.

Braen had been in Sippen's laboratory several times since their arrival, but Eusari had not yet seen the marvel. Both men smiled at her reaction as the sight left her breathless. Two large kilns and four traditional blacksmith stations shared a large furnace in the back corner. The coals burned extremely hot and she watched as several men tended the heat source. Several other men were hard at work assembling longer versions of the little hand cannon that Samani had demonstrated. The entire line of men worked furiously and had already laid out fifty or so of the weapons on tables near the east wall. Sippen picked one from the table and grabbed a satchel from another nearby pile.

"Cuh... come on." With a smile he led them through door that opened into a clearing in the forest behind. There, several metal targets were laid out at fifty-yard intervals. A small table was set up in front of the targets and he laid the gear out as he talked. "I chuh... changed the buh... barrels, adding guh... grooves on the inside to spuh... spin the round as it flies." He turned the gadget to the sun so that they could look down the barrel. "I ah... also chuh... changed one uh... other thing." He picked up a small cloth pouch about the size of a walnut and in the shap of a rectangle. "Buh... bite the cuh... corner off and puh... pour the powder duh... down the barrel." He demonstrated as he talked. "Thuh... then drop the ball in like so." After dropping the ball, he raised the device up to his shoulder and aimed. With the slightest pull of his finger an explosion rang from the weapon, pushing him slightly backward as it fired. A metallic sound indicated that he had hit the first target with force.

Both Braen and Eusari were dumbfounded and Braen could not control his enthusiasm. "That's brilliant, Sippen!"

Eusari broke her own silence. "What do you call it?"

"Suh... Samani has been cuh... calling them rifles after the grooves in the barrels, which he called 'rifling.' He huh... has guh... great ideas."

"What about the smaller version?" Braen had picked up the rifle and mulled it over.

"Yuh... you muh... mean, this?" Sippen pushed back his coat to reveal a smaller and sleeker version in a holster on his belt. He drew it out, aimed at a target about twenty feet away and pulled the trigger. Again, the metallic retort of ball hitting metal rang true. "Suh... Samani calls thuh... this a puh... pistol."

Eusari shook her head in amazement, "This is going to change everything. Suddenly our small force is more powerful than a full-sized army."

Braen nodded, "I agree."

Abruptly a cry rang out from near the waterfront. Braen left the rifle on the table and the three raced back to where Samani had been training the children. When they arrived in the city square, they froze at the condition of Kernigan. He had been blown backward by one of the children with such force that was currently laying on the roof of one of the houses. He was too stunned to move and stared up at the sky.

The culprit was a young boy, probably between his ninth and tenth summers. He was sitting on the ground, visibly shaken by what he had done to his teacher with tears streaming down his red cheeks. Braen watched as Eusari crept up gently, crouching down to wipe his long blonde hair from his face. She revealed two ice blue eyes looking up at her. She smiled and spoke in a soothing and tender voice. "It's okay. He knows that you didn't mean to do it."

"I just... I got so MAD at him!"

"I get mad sometimes, too. Were you mad when you made the wind?" Through tears and sobs the boy nodded and she wrapped her arms around him. "My name is Eusari, what is your name?"

"I'm... Nikolas. My mother used to call me Niko, before..." He broke off as the sobs became inconsolable.

Braen cleared his throat, "That's enough training for the day. The rest of you go see Porter for your daily chores. Then you can all have the afternoon to yourselves." The other children ran off as soon as they were dismissed, leaving Niko behind with the adults. Braen moved over to the house and began setting up crates so that Samani could climb back down.

Eusari's voice drifted over to him and he strained to listen as she comforted the boy. "Did they take you from your mommy?"

He shrugged.

"Where does she live?"

He shrugged, again.

"You don't know the name of the town?"

"It's hard to say."

She smiled at him, understanding. "Try your best, Niko. Maybe I know it."

"Ata... Ata ratsy uh."

"Sounds like Ataraxia." A deep voice from behind signaled that Shon had arrived in the square after hearing the commotion. He looked up at Samani climbing down from the roof. He raised an eyebrow at Braen who inclined his head toward the boy, hoping that would explain.

Eusari gently asked, "Is it Ataraxia?" Niko nodded, tears welling up in his eyes at some distant and traumatic memory.

"That's just a few days sail north of here along the coast." Shon sat down on a bench to watch the exchange.

After shooting a look of thanks to her uncle, she focused again on the boy. "Do you want us to see if we can find her, there?"

"She isn't there." Niko whispered, body tensing.

Breaking his silence, Braen asked, "Where is she, Niko?"

"The bad men killed her."

Eusari pressed, "The Falconers?" He shook his head rapidly. It wasn't them. "What did the bad men look like?"

Niko lifted his head and met her eyes, anger filling them at being forced to remember. He raised a pointed finger directly at Braen. "Like him, only shorter."

Braen stood, shocked. "Did you see their ship?"

Another headshake. No.

"Did they have a crest or images on their armor?"

A nod.

Good. "What did the crest look like?"

"A cat eating a wolf."

Braen's heart might as well have stopped beating in that moment.

Eusari hugged the boy close. Finally, after a long while, the boy lifted his head and wiped his nose. She spoke to him very softly. "Niko, Shon is going to take you to your quarters so that you can get some rest. Does a nap sound nice?" He nodded. "Good. I'll find you, later, and we will talk some more."

Wimbley rose and led the boy away. Samani started to follow, but she stopped him. "Not you, Kernigan. We three need to have a chat about these children."

"Sari..." Braston started to speak but was cut off.

"No Braen. Don't try and argue. And don't you dare try and tell me how important they are to take The Cove. I know damned well how crucial their part is, but we're going to lay some ground rules."

Samani bowed his head and raised his palms upward in acquiescence. "What do you suggest, my dear?"

"First, you'll no longer be their teacher. You know a lot of theory, but you don't know shit about actually wielding the power." He started to speak but she put her hand up and he silenced. "I know. You have taken some beads and had visions. But that's not the same as using the elements."

He couldn't argue with her and so he again nodded. "You have a good point. So, what do you suggest?"

"Braen and I will teach them. You'll be the technical expert, but we'll practice the gift with them."

Braston thought about what she was suggesting and couldn't help but agree. "She's right. When I first used the gift, it was a surprise and not something that I planned. It seems that we could better describe what it feels like."

"Second, there will be strict rules regarding how they're used to aid us. Under no circumstance will they participate in a battle. Also, they're not soldiers, so you'll both stop speaking to them like they are. Don't even talk about them as if they're anything besides children." She was looking directly at Braen when she said the last part, eyes aglow with burning irritation.

"Finally, you'll both get to know each of them. A wise man once taught me that leadership is about making relationships. Well, that goes for the children, as well. You will both know each of their names, learn their stories and treat them like people instead of weaponry."

Braen smiled, "For the record I treat my weaponry better than I do people."

Her eyes burned a fierce green and she responded. "I know." With that she spun on her heels and left the square.

The two men watched her leave, then Braen broke the silence. "Why did you make the boy angry, Sam?"

"I had a theory. I noticed that every time you two have been strong with the power, it was because your emotions were surging."

"That makes sense. You were the one who said that the powers are tied to emotion."

"Specific powers are tied to specific emotions, yes. For example, if you're melancholy or lovesick you can make it snow or rain. You draw the water from the air, making it cooler. Then you manifest it somewhere else and don't always realize when you do."

"I've noticed that."

"But when you lose your temper you bend the water to your will. Remember the mutineers?"

"I'd actually like to forget that, Sam. Thanks."

"Braen, I wanted to piss him off to see if he could do more than make a puff of air, and it worked. A nine-year-old boy sent me flying onto the roof. Now that he's felt it, he should be able to tap into that memory and do it naturally."

"Eusari won't go for us doing that with each of them."

"No. She won't. But we're on a timeline."

Braen had always considered himself a morally upstanding man, and issues like ethics never worried his conscience. This dilemma was new territory for the northern captain, and he needed time to consider. Looking up, he saw the sun had moved well past midday and was making a descent in its' path. Time was indeed running out fast, and he feared that he would have to choose to ask her forgiveness at some point in the future.

Chapter Forty-Three

Amash Horslei felt stronger than he had over the past weeks. Despite that he lay in a dungeon, he fared well. The guards brought him food on a regular schedule, actual meals and not the slop or gruel that they fed the other prisoners. He also rested on a straw bed instead of the cold stone that surrounded him. His ribs mended well, and he had begun to exercise his muscles to prevent them from dwindling from lack of use.

Weeks had gone by since his first and only visitor had spoken to him, bringing news from the outside world. He was happy that his friend Braen was alive and elated that he was probably mounting a rebellion against Nevra. *But how can that fool think that he'll be successful?* The Cove was impervious to frontal assault, and everyone knew it. That was the allure of the island, knowing that not even the Esterling fleets could find a man hiding in the Pirate's Guild.

It was that allure that had brought Amash to The Cove after he had fled the University. His father had wanted him to take over the family fortune, to learn how to grow investments, and to someday take over as the Governor of Weston. But horses and riches meant nothing to the first and only son of Horslei, and so he left the school and ran to The Cove. Besides, there had been that incident that drove him away and into hiding.

That his father had died affected him more than he had thought that it would. He did not particularly care for his father, but he loved the man, nonetheless. Abraham Horslei was a brutal and hard tyrant, especially after the death of his wife. He would often explode in a tirade of verbal abuses aimed toward anyone around him, oftentimes turning them against his two children. Amash would shield his little sister, Sarai, but all too often his attempt was unsuccessful. When Abraham drank, he grew even more violent, sometimes even striking Amash but never Sarai. No, she reminded her father too much of their mother to strike her.

Sometimes he felt sentimental and thought about home, but he would never return. Even after learning of his father's death he would stay away. Sarai was safe and that was all that mattered. His father had no doubt told her that he had died, for that was easier than the truth. He was a disgrace to everything Horslei and did not deserve the name. No, Amash would stay far away from the green fields of Weston and be buried upon the sea.

A key in the door caught his attention and he slowly sat up in the bed with anticipation. It wasn't time for his midday meal, that was delivered hours ago. Fear and anxiety leaped through him when he remembered Nevra's plans to ransom him back to Weston. If they were here to take him back, then he would die at the tips of their swords before allowing them to profit at his expense.

He slowly reached his left hand to a slit that he had cut into the mattress. There, he had hidden a spoon that he had slowly and deliberately sharpened into a weapon. The handle was wrapped with straw and threads of burlap from the bed, making for a comfortable grip with which to plunge. His knuckles popped as he tightened his hand around the instrument, ready for whatever lay beyond his cell door.

Abruptly the door swung open and light flooded in, revealing the outline of a man in the doorway. As features came into focus Amash released his grip and pushed the weapon back into its' hiding place.

"Twice in one imprisonment? To what do I owe this visit, Alec?"

Pogue spoke not a word until the door was securely shut behind him. Then he listened to the retreating footsteps as the guard left them to privacy. Finally, he uttered, "You were right about the ledger."

"Of course, I was."

"How did you recognize what he is doing?"

"I am an accountant, Alec. That was all that my father taught me. How to cuss and scream and how to keep ledgers." Amash narrowed his eyes. "You realize the implications, then?"

"I'm good with numbers, but it took a thief and master bookkeeper to spot the discrepancies. And that wasn't until after the third read through."

Nodding, Amash agreed. "He's an accounting genius, I'll give him that. What did you find, Alec? I want to hear you say it."

Pogue sat down against the wall on the far side of the cell. "He's trafficking slaves from the mainland to the southern continent." Alec shook his head as if hoping to wake from a dream. "How can someone profit from such a horrible act?"

Amash nodded. "I wasn't positive, but I had my suspicions. That's why I asked for a transfer. I feared he would try and work me into it, somehow."

The captain stared at the ground, finally speaking quietly, "I'm ready."

"Ready for what?"

"I'm ready to help arm you and the rest of Artema's men. I've no idea how many of the city guard I can win over, but I think that I can get a few officers. The bulk of them follow the money, and we've none of it." Pogue's eyes were closed, strained against the words coming from his own mouth. "I know that I can get swords down here, I just don't know how soon."

"You realize that we'll get cut down rather quickly, don't you? One hundred and fifty men is barely a riot, much less a rebellion." Amash fought against the urge to smile at the lunacy of what Pogue was suggesting.

"If I can arrest and imprison him, then the core of resistance in the city will show itself."

"Who leads it? Who's their guy, Alec?"

"Adamas Creech."

"Creech?" Horslei was taken back. "That selfish prick isn't much better than Nevra."

"Maybe not. But he hasn't been trafficking humans back and forth to the mainland."

"No. I suppose he has that going for him." The both sat in silence for a moment, digesting what they were planning. "We could just wait for Braston."

Alec shook his head. "No. He's a poor choice because the Esterling's won't back him after he cut down their mother. I also doubt that he'd stand up to a vote of the council."

"If he takes this city by force then he won't need to put it to a vote."

"If he takes the city by force then he proves to the entire world that it's possible to do so. Ending our way of life forever."

Amash nodded, taking in the words. Finally, he offered, "Not if he takes it in a way that no one else can duplicate."

Pogue remained silent at that for a long time. After quite a few breaths he got down to business. "I'll get a set of keys and the first of the swords to you in a couple of days. There's an empty cell about five doors that direction," he indicated with his right hand, "I'll load up some chests and put them there. Wait for my signal and then release the others."

"They'll be too weak to swing swords, Alec."

"I'll double their rations during the night shift." The Captain of the guard, having said all that he had come to say, stood and pounded on the door for the jailer.

"Alec."

"What?"

"Thank you for trusting me."

"It wasn't just you, Amash. This man's just a total shit of a person and needs to be deposed." He paused as the door opened, as if he had more to say but couldn't with the untimely interruption. He finally stepped out into the hall with authority, the heavy door slamming shut behind him.

The room again plunged into darkness and Amash smiled for the first time in many days. "Braen," he said into the darkness, "wherever you are, whatever you're planning, you need to do it, soon." He let out a chuckle and added, "And you'd better have a bottle of 754."

Chapter Forty-Four

Eusari stared across the open waters at hers and Braen's pitiful armada. Four longboats packed full of men looked ready to capsize. It was a wonder that they had stayed seaworthy for so long. Miraculously, Braston had managed to keep his word and the seas remained calm within a mile radius around the fleet. Picking up her spyglass she peered into the distance. Anxiety welled up in her gut as forty-foot swells tossed the ocean around them. If he were to lose his grip for even a moment, their army would be destroyed in that instant.

Gelert whined at her feet. He disliked the unnatural calm of Braen's aura even more than his master. She reached down and stroked his ears to calm him, and he settled back down with a sigh.

"I know, Boy. I don't like it, either." Someone tugged at her sleeve and she looked down to see Niko grinning up. She swallowed her fears and feigned a smile before kneeling to look him eye to eye. "What is it, Nicolas?"

"I'm tired and I want to let Marita take over." He pointed at the girl who was standing by the helmsman.

"How does Marita feel about this? Is she ready?" She gave a thumbs up to the girl, a tiny thing despite her thirteen summers. The girl responded back with a smile and her own thumb sticking up into the air. "Okay. But let me signal the other ships, first." Moving to the signal deck, she ordered Jacque to send the message. He flashed his flags in the correct pattern and awaited a reply from each. *Ice Prince* was the last to respond but the answer came back, signaling that the other children and Braen were ready to coordinate a shift.

She smiled down at the boy who truly looked exhausted. He had been steering their sails for several hours and had pushed his little body very hard. "What did they say, Eusari?"

"They're ready." All at once the ships raised a blue flag and then dropped it on Braen's order. "You can stop, now."

The ship lurched a little as Nico let go of the winds. The sails on each vessel fell limp as the other children did the same, and Braen kept the aura of calm waters within the new slower speed. "Thank you, Eusari." He gave the captain a hug around her waist and then turned to leave.

"Go down to the galley and get something to eat, okay?" The boy nodded back that he would and then went below decks. The black preparatory flag raised up atop every ship and then dropped. "Now, Marita!" The ship lurched as the little girl took her turn on the sail. Eusari panicked as her vessel began to outpace the others. "Back down a little! Too fast!" She watched as the swells on the close horizon loomed toward her ship's doom.

"I'm sorry! I'm trying, Eusari!" After another moment the sails dipped just enough as the ship slowed to match the others. The girl flashed another smiling thumbs up.

"Good girl!" Eusari was convinced that she would die of heart stoppage before they actually arrived at The Cove.

Handing the spyglass to Jacque, she resumed her previous position pacing the deck and worrying over the attack plan. Her part of the raid would be easy. They would approach from the rear entrance, the pathway known only to Artema Horn, Kernigan, Nevra and herself. Even Braen had not been part of the inner sanctum long enough to know the secret. Using that approach, despite the narrowness of the passage, the shallow draft of the long boats would make it possible to skim over the tops of the reefs.

They sailed like this for many more hours, with Eusari fretting over every possible miscalculation. A few more shift changes had gone well enough, but one scared her badly when one of the longboats came too near the edge of Braen's aura. That boat had tipped against the swells, and several men fell into the sea. Thankfully, swift action on the part of Shon's soldiers resulted in the safe retrieval of every man. Eventually, they had reached their destination and Eusari signaled the all stop.

Eusari watched as Braen's crew shimmied down rope ladders to the longboats waiting below. He was a fool to attempt what he had planned, but he had wanted to make a grand entrance to The Cove. Not wanting to risk his men, he had encouraged them to accompany Eusari and her teams via the safer route. Only Sippen and Krill had remained behind. He had argued and tried to force them to leave him, but they unwaveringly refused their captain's order. Had she not spent so much time with the bearded man, she would not have appreciated the gesture by his friends. Looking across the deck toward Pete and Porter, she wondered if they would have made the same choice for her.

Gelert rose up onto his haunches and gave another whine. Through their connection Eusari shared his uneasiness and swallowed hard against their combined fear. She had made this approach dozens of times, but never failed to lose her breath when she did. A single misstep could toss a ship against the rocks in an instant, and those would be even harder to see in a fogbank. Regardless of her experience making the passage, she had never attempted in seas as rough and unpredictable as these. She had also never made an attempt in the dark.

Niko and Marita approached Eusari as she took the helm in her hands. The wood was dark, worn from the many years atop the seas and the salt had made the wood dry and pitted over the years. A moment of sadness and guilt passed over her as she thought about the last time that she had made this journey. Sa'Mond had been there, beside her on that day, calling out hazards as she navigated. On this day she looked to Pete and Porter to do that job, trusting these men to help her and the others safely through.

After she had swallowed down her grief, she signaled Jacque who waved a flag toward *Ice Prince* and the others.

Niko and Marita both smiled, eager to do this part of the plan. They had practiced for weeks how to invert the air, trapping a cooler layer beneath the warmer that they had lifted. From his own ship, Braen would do the rest. She waited until she could see vapor forming atop the water, rippling up like smoke until the entire fleet was encased in a dense fog bank. She let out a sigh of some relief that it had worked, and she was now invisible to The Cove.

Sails were bound tightly on all five vessels, and oars placed into the water. The entrance was not visible from the surface, and you had to know the order with which to sail from landmark to landmark. Slowly, she and the longboats entered the dangerous reef passage. Without Braen to calm the waters, they were at the mercy of the sea once they crossed the first barrier.

Artema had been with her the first time she had attempted the rear approach, and that was when he had revealed the secret. She had been so excited to learn the code, but excitement had dashed when he laughed at her disgust at his sophomoric joke. "Cliff, lighthouse, island and trees." he had said. She repeated the mantra once again in her head, just as offended by the acronym that Artema had taught her long ago. He had also relayed the navigational distances, "It's fifty-fifty that you avoid the rocks. The final stretch is thirty-six, twenty-four and thirty-six. Thirty-eight if the tide's out and her shoreline's exposed."

She sailed fifty yards with the bowsprit pointed toward the furthest edge of the cliff outcropping. Then, she turned sharply to the starboard and aimed for the lighthouse, sailing another fifty yards. Quickly making another compensation to port, she aimed the stern toward a distant island that had two hills shaped like a woman's breasts. She again shook her head in disgust and sailed onward another thirty-six yards. One more correction to starboard and she would head toward the grove of trees. Except there were no trees.

"Demon's Ass!" Eusari screamed. "Where are the fucking trees?" The distant shoreline had been changed, trees cut down and a large and armored gun mount had been set up in their place. Gelert stood on all fours and growled menacingly at the sudden change in his master. Pete and Porter looked up at her in shock and she screamed, "Get your eyes back on the water!" At that moment she needed their hypervigilance.

Her landmark gone, she could not be sure of the passage and only had a short time to guess where the center of the grove had stood. She quickly turned the helm to the right. "Brace for shock!" As *She Wolf* made the starboard turn it was late, dragging the hull against the rocks on the portside. She screamed as Nico fell over the rail.

Eusari called for Pete to take the helm. "Turn hard to port in twenty yards and take us in to the shore!" She rushed to the portside and looked over. Nico's small frame was floating above the rocks, with blood trailing out of a gash on the side of his tiny head. If she had killed him then she would never forgive herself. Her pulse throbbed in her ears as he pondered jumping after to retrieve him. Luckily, one of the longboats were able to navigate toward the boy, and crewmen dragged his lifeless form out of the water.

Pete followed his captain's orders exactly and the ship made a correction to port. All at once she realized her mistake. "Pete! Wait!" But it was too late. As he turned the ship to port the draft of the ship dipped, tearing a gash in the hull beneath the waterline. She cursed again as her ship took on water.

"Marita!" She called to the girl who had been crying uncontrollably since Nico had been tossed overboard. "MARITA!" She screamed to get the girl's attention, but she was inconsolable. "Gods damn it! Pete, maintain that heading toward the coast. We only have to make it thirty yards or so!" She also yelled up to the riggers who were staring down from the yardarms. Unfurl the sails! Quickly!"

When Nico had fallen the inverted air had lifted, and the fog was dissipating. Looking toward the gun mount she saw movement inside. Turning to the girl she tried again. "MARITA, pay attention!" With an open hand she slapped the girl so hard that her head turned to the side, a red welt forming in the shape of a hand. "Give us wind, NOW, Marita! Blow us to the goddamn shore!" The girl was stunned by the sudden aggression by Eusari. With tears in her eyes she heaved sobs as a gust of wind squared away the sails. The report from the gun mount was deafening as several large cannons fired at once.

Thankfully the sudden gust of wind blew *She Wolf* under the salvo. Wood creaked as the ship lurched forward in a full-on rush to the beach. As soon as it ran aground Eusari leapt with Gelert from the forecastle, landing hard in a sandy patch of ground. The men in the longboats rowed frantically to keep pace and within seconds had joined her on the beach.

Anger filled Eusari. She strode forward as her men lined up, rifles out behind the cover of the rocks. Glancing back, she saw Samani Kernigan following them with a rifle in his hands. "Not you! Get your ass to the boats and watch over Niko and the others."

"Yes, Ma'am." He turned back for the boats.

Deliberately she walked toward the gun mount as the men inside reloaded, ready to rain grapeshot down on her and her army. Behind her, she heard Shon calling out. "Dearie! Get down! Take shelter, Eusari!" But she ignored the shouts, hellbent on taking her anger out on the men inside of the fortification.

Finally, standing in full view of the men inside of the mount, she stopped. The island defenders had not fired, either not wanting to waste their shot on the crazy woman and her wolf standing before them, or out of shock at her boldness. They were no doubt watching for her next movement. Eventually they would have to fire upon her.

Kneeling, Eusari placed both hands on the rocks, head bowed as if in prayer. The rock was dry with a salty film and texture. She could smell the ocean all around her, but the smell of the sweet earth called up to her, drawing her senses and heightening her awareness. Behind her the shouts had stopped, and four hundred men stared in silence. She felt the world around her blur as she tried to become one with the ground itself. Only, something was in the way, preventing a true bond.

Slowly, she removed her gloves one at a time, revealing thousands of tiny scars running horizontal down her forearms and across the tops of her hands. Mixed among the cuts were hundreds of round burns that had dulled some forgotten pain. Eusari Thorinson examined the scars with a surreal disinterest. The girl who had made these cuts had been afraid and lost, wanting to leave the world but desperate to remain until she had punished all who had caused her the real agony.

Her eyes focused on a particular cut between her thumb and forefinger. It had been the first. After Skander Braston had finished with her, he had left her lying face down across the table, staring at the lifeless body of her mother. After she could finally pull her eyes away, she had drawn a knife from the block. Placing it against her wrist she had wanted to end it all, fully intending to do so. But she paused when she heard the voice of the prince laughing in the next room, looting her parents' home. In that moment she decided that she would live. She moved the tip of the blade and drew it across the sensitive skin beside her thumb. The pain was excruciating but it gave her control. It was her pain to give and so it was welcome.

Tears filled her eyes as she placed her scarred and disfigured hands flat against the ground. All of her tormented years had been bottled inside, represented by each scar and every burn. She breathed in and then out again. As she did, she felt agony flow out, causing her hands to tremble against the ground and causing it to shake.

At first only the ground beneath her vibrated. Focusing her attention on the gun mount the trembling intensified, moving out as a wave within the rocks below the fortification. After a few seconds the tremor had grown violent, tearing the rocks apart and shearing a cleft. That fissure also grew, as it radiated out from Eusari and became a fault that tore the small fort into pieces. The remnants crumbled, burying the men inside beneath the rubble.

Gelert licked the wet and salty cheeks of his friend, breaking her trance. She lifted her eyes toward the gaping chasm ahead and hugged the wolf, drying her face on his fur. Looking back at the men staring up from the beach, she pointed toward the city wall beyond the remains of the gun mount. A large crack had formed there, large enough for her army to make their way inside. She rose and quickly pulled her gloves onto her hands, ashamed that someone would see.

Shon approached her cautiously. She could tell that he was afraid, and his eyes reflected shock and amazement. "Dearie... That. That was incredible."

"That was reckless and stupid of me." She pointed up at the wall, indicating that archers ran to man the intact sections and city guardsmen hurried to form a shield wall in the crevasse. "We lost every element of surprise that we had planned for. Braen was supposed to be the distraction for us to get in under the cloak of surprise, and I ruined that."

"But we still have the advantage. And we have these!" Shon lifted his rifle up into the air to emphasize his words.

"Yes. We do, but that isn't the point." She shook her head, "We've deviated from the plan and lost our opportunity to minimize bloodshed." Pointing first at the open ocean behind them and then at the city wall, she added, "We can't go back the way we came in, and we can't charge that fortification without losing the army we came here to win over. We have to wait for Braen and hope for an opening.

Braen had waited until Eusari and the longboats passed beyond the reef wall and were on their way. His crew aided Eusari, and he sailed alone with his best friends, Sippen and Krill. He called to Krill to raise anchor and begin their circling approach to the front entrance of The Cove. After one more long look at the meager assault armada, he created a new current in the water, steering around the island and out of range of an eyeglass. *Ice Prince* lurched and began to pick up speed as they rounded the main island.

In no time at all massive outcroppings and stone walls marked the harbor entrance. He could immediately tell that several upgrades had been made to the massive batteries, including stone tops that would prevent their use of Carcass rounds. He smiled at the stories his friends had told him of their daring escape from the harbor. Of course, the account in his head was in Krill's voice and full of expletives.

"Prepare to come about! I want them to see us coming."

"Aye, Captain!" Krill ambled up to the main mast with his one eye and wooden leg. He had a bundle of cloth under his arm and attached it to the line that held the ensign. Lowering the Fjorik colors, he attached the new standard and quickly ran it up the mast. In a matter of minutes, a giant banner unfurled, much to the chagrin of the bearded captain.

"Krill! What the fuck is that?"

"Your colors, Cap'n!"

Braen flushed with embarrassment as the breeze found the piece of cloth, revealing the Kraken banner from his feast. It was so large that it would be visible from the harbor positions.

"Demon's nipples, Krill!"

The comical man smiled back at him from behind the eyepatch. "Twasn't me, Captain!" He pointed toward the first mate and smith who smiled a devilish expression from ear to ear, large head bobbing on his small frame.

"Gawds dammit, Sippen! Why would you do that to me?"

"Buh... because it suh... suits you, Braen!" The little man pointed around the ship. "Yuh... you need to listen to your crew. Thuh... they are proud to serve their 'Lord Kraken." "Wuh... whether you luh... like it or not. You... are the Kraken!" After a pause, he turned with an even wider grin than before. "Nuh... now let's kuh... kick some ass!"

Braen let out a long laugh at this. "Okay, my friend. Let's go kick some ass."

Movement from behind made him spin around, finding two small and timid children emerging from the hatch to the crew's quarters below. Their eyes were wide with admiration and stared up at the banner. The boy was Sebastian and the girl Suzette. They had been aboard *Ice Prince* during the crossing of open waters but were supposed to have left with the crew.

Braen narrowed his eyes and asked in a gruff voice, "Why are you still aboard? I ordered you both to disembark!"

The boy looked down at the deck and said nothing. Suzette, on the other hand, stared back at the captain with defiance in her eyes. *She's been spending too much time with Eusari,* he thought to himself. Finally, the boy broke his silence. "You need our help. Your powers are limited to water, and you'll need assistance once you get on dry land."

Braen nodded. The thought had crossed his mind several times in the planning. "Yes, Sebastian. But what I'm about to do is very dangerous and I promised Eusari that I would keep you safe from the fighting and not involve you two."

"That's bullshit!" Suzette broke her silence. "We're here because we want to be, not because we were made to be. This war is for all of us, and we're helping."

Braen almost smiled at her words. *Yes,* he thought, *she was definitely spending too much time with Eusari.* "Fine. Stay below decks and away from the forward compartments. Get as far aft as you can get and stay there until we reach dry land."

"Not a chance, Captain Braston." The girl again expressed defiance and this time Braen really did smile.

To the children he said, "Your funeral." Then he looked at Sippen and Krill who both shrugged. To them he said, "You two are no help."

Krill responded, "Sometimes that be true, Cap'n. Sometimes that be true."

Braen studied the fortifications. The larger main guns had a range of about four thousand feet, a little less than a mile. With that in mind he slowed the current to keep just at five thousand feet. His own guns had a range of about two thousand feet, limiting his attack capabilities if he ran into trouble and had to fight his way out. Suddenly, a thought entered his head.

"Sebastian, Suzette! Do you think you can blow a cannonball three thousand yards?"

The children thought long and hard before Sebastian answered. "I think we can."

"Sippen. Krill. Do the math and figure out the trajectory to pull this off. I want to do more than get their attention, I want to knock on one of their batteries." He knew that he couldn't destroy them with a single canon, but it would be fun to reach out with a long and accurate shot. "I want to say, 'hello,' to Nevra."

The calculations and adjustments were made, and Krill nodded back at Braen.

"Fire when ready, Master Gunnery Sergeant!" A single cannon fired from *Ice Prince* and the ball sailed long and true, pushed by the children through the air. When it hit the mark perfectly, the small crew cheered the explosion of rock and men flying over the side of the battery. They turned toward the harbor and lowered the sails to begin their approach.

From the walls, several large guns fired and Braen nodded knowingly that they would not be able to hit the ship so far out. "Hold this course, boys! Gunnery Sergeant count their reload time. Sebastian, get ready to blow wind like you've never done before." Turning to Suzette he added, "You'll help him, this time. I want to shoot that gap faster than they can load after their next volley!"

The tension aboard *Ice Prince* was thick as they made their approach, but every man and little girl on board were proud to serve their 'Lord Kraken,' as Sippen had called him. They were almost in range, when a second salvo fired from the heavily armored positions.

"That was sooner than I expected, Captain!" Krill's voice rang out. "They must have made improvements."

Shouting at Sebastian and Suzette, he gave the order. "Wind! Give me wind and let's shoot that gap!"

His plan was to speed under the salvo, expecting it to fly over their heads. But Nevra had indeed made improvements to his defenses, apparently stealing from some of Sippen's designs. The harbor guns rang true on that day, striking *Ice Prince* both below the waterline and atop the main deck. The repairs to the main mast failed to hold and it fell, crashing into the ship and sending splinters as it did. Little Suzette was sent flying backward and Braen watched a splinter pierce her chest. She lay on the deck, quickly forming a pool of blood around her. Her lifeless eyes stared up at the cloudless sky.

Braen froze. All was lost in a single blow and *Ice Prince* was taking on water very quickly. "Abandon ship!" He cried with agony, realizing that he had failed to retake The Cove.

Chapter Forty-Five

Robert awoke with pain pulsing through his temples. He groaned a little and reached up to press hands against his skull in hopes to dull the pain. He had rested but felt as if he had been awake the entire night. The images of the army and of Max were firmly embedded in his mind and he knew that it was all somehow real, just as he was right about Sarai.

Thinking of her, he turned and met her staring back, awake with the swirling currents of air still flowing. Even with the disfiguring scars she was so beautiful to Robert, and he knew that she always would be. He smiled at her awkwardly. "Good morning. How are you feeling?"

Her voice was weak and little more than a hoarse grown, signifying that her throat must have been damaged when she breathed in the heat. "Do you mean how bad am I hurting?"

"Well, no. How bad are you hurting, Sarai?"

Tears ran down her scarred face. "That depends. My entire body was burned and yet it still hurts less than what you did to my heart, Robert Esterling."

He reached up and touched a patch of skin by her left eye that was still intact. Tears filled his own eyes, as he whispered, "I was afraid. I was afraid that you would get injured or killed and I wanted to protect you."

"That was my choice, Robert. I knew my risks." She pulled her eyes away from his, staring up at the ceiling of the wagon with her mouth suddenly drawn tight. "Is he…" She swallowed painfully.

"Did you kill him, Robert? I passed out while you were fighting, and I want to know."

"No. I left alive. I had an opportunity to make a different choice and chose your path. If there's still an ounce of good in that boy, then he has another chance to find it."

"So, you finally understand that the entire people shouldn't be judged for the actions of one?"

"Yes. But I don't know how many more chances he should get."

She turned and again met his eyes. "That isn't for us to decide. That's up to him, Robert, but at least we've shown him the right way to live. He has choices to make that have nothing to do with his people."

The prince nodded. "Sarai, I am about to fight in a battle. My brother has claimed my throne, and I marched south to Eskera with Max. We're outnumbered three to one and our opponent has both cavalry and artillery."

"You brought me to a battlefield? You really aren't very good at romance. Do you know that?" She tried to smile but the pain in her face made her wince instead. "Don't surrender, if that's what you're thinking. Your brother will have you killed, no matter the outcome."

"I know. I just don't want these men to die when it only has to be me."

She looked deeply into his eyes, pondering something and saying nothing for a while. Finally, she responded, "You don't get it, yet, do you?"

"No. I guess not. What is it, Sarai?"

"Men will follow you, Robert. You wield so much potential that it isn't fair. You have wasted your entire life brooding over your insecurities and inadequacies, that you don't see how truly remarkable you are." She indicated the shimmering flow of air around her skin. "And this. I saw you fighting against Taros like a Falconer. I don't know how you did, nor how you are doing this, but you need to open your eyes to your potential. You're special,

Robert Esterling. You're special and men will follow you into the Caldera if that's where you take them. That's also why I love you."

"You... You love me? Even after... after that night?"

"Yes. I just want you to stop thinking that strength will solve all of your problems. You also need compassion."

"That's why I let Taros live, Sarai."

"And that's the only reason that I'm speaking to you, now." She closed her eyes, squeezing tears out from the sides. "I can't solve the problem of this battle for you, but I can tell you that there are other options to fighting."

When she finished speaking, he knew that the conversation was closed. He leaned over and placed a gently and cautious kiss on her lips, still perfect and unmarred if just a little chapped from the cold. Rising, he stepped out of the wagon and into the pre-dawn night. Cold air blasted him as soon as he emerged, forcing him to tighten his tunic. He quickly found Max and Titus leaning over a map in the command tent. They were in some kind of disagreement about strategy.

"Sir, with respect we need to cross the swamp and move north to here." Titus indicated a place on the map that appeared to be high ground.

"Foolish." Max shook his head. "We don't know how deep that mud is. We could lose half our force over what? High ground that will make it easier for their cannons to make us scatter over the top? No. We need another option."

"March them into the swamp, General Reeves." Robert spoke up from behind his mentor. "Find a sturdy footing and wait it out. Let them die trying to get at us with their infantry."

Max inclined his head toward the prince. "Nice thought, but same problem. Their artillery will scatter us and do the same to our own men. Besides, finding a footing is damned near impossible." After a short pause he added, "and that water is near freezing as it is. Our men would die from hypothermia if they happened to survive."

"I can get us across, Max. I think that I have a way." He pointed at the swamp on the map. "And out there we are protected from Lourdes' cavalry. Since he isn't going to help us, we need to keep him off our flanks."

"How did you know about that?"

"The same way that I know five thousand men reinforced them before we could arrive." And to himself he thought, *the same way that I know they have Falconers.*

This caught the old general's attention, and he turned to face him completely. "Even so, we'll be sitting ducks for their artillery."

"I have a plan for that."

The men listened intently as Robert explained his idea, pointing out flaws in their map as he did. After he had finished, Max and Titus stared dumbfounded. "How can you be so sure about the terrain?" Reeves asked. "Our best scouts were out all night putting this together."

The Esterling boy smiled, "They didn't have a birds eye view." With that an eagle screeched from the forest. Within seconds, the heavy flapping of wings could be heard outside and the men walked to the tent flap to look out. Robert pushed past them, and a large eagle landed on his shoulder, gently squeezing her huge talons into his tunic. Turning to face the men, Robert laughed at their expressions.

"You... You see through her eyes?" Max was astonished at the sight.

"I can. I can also hear if she is close enough."

"Last night? You could hear me talking to Lourdes?"

"Aye. I think we have a lot to discuss after the battle, Max. Or should I be calling you something else?"

The general looked down at the ground, embarrassed. "No. Max is fine."

Robert nodded. "Come on, gentlemen. Let's get ready for the battle."

Chapter Forty-Six

Water rushed into the belly of *Ice Prince* and Braen froze in place, helpless to save his friends. Krill had slid across the deck and would have blown over the side had it not been for dumb luck. He clung desperately to the rail while tangled in a rope and struggling to regain his footing. His wooden leg scraped uselessly against the slick hull of the ship, unable to give him the leverage he needed. His tenuous grip was failing.

Sippen was unconscious and laying near the helm. A spar had struck him hard across the face and blood ran down his bruised and swollen cheek. He should not even be onboard but had insisted on staying with his lifelong friend. Only Braen's overconfidence in the plan had allowed the little man to come along. Braen thought about how Sippen might never wake up, how he would slip silently beneath the cold waters and drown when the ship submerged.

Sebastian stood on his feet, staring down at Suzette and the giant piece of wood sticking out of her still chest. That sweet little boy should not have been exposed to so much carnage. He should be running around a village and tossing snowballs like the one he had thrown at Braen and Eusari back in Estowen's Landing. This image of his friend's death would add to the boy's own trauma, scarring him forever. Eusari was right and Braen should not have involved the children in his attack. His pride and ego had killed that sweet and defiant little girl.

The Crown Prince of Fjorik had never felt so defeated. Everything around him was hopeless as he prepared himself to die beneath the ocean. *Surely another salvo will be incoming,* he thought, *but we are sinking regardless.* Eusari and her teams were meant to take out the walls in the same manner as they had in Diaph but could only do so with the distraction of his arrival. If only he could find a way to help her disable the harbor defenses. *She should be on the beachhead by now,* he thought, *unable to move under the alert eyes of the sentries.* If they couldn't get to the guns, then the entire operation was lost.

His thoughts in that moment also turned to Skander, and how he had chosen such a dark path. He loved his brother and desperately wished that there was some way that he could restore his heart and soul. But the good was gone from that man, dead along with their father. Skander Braston's soul had bled out with Krist Braston's blood. He had to be stopped either by death or capture but Braen would die in these waters, unable to free Hester and Fjorik from their terrible tyrant.

Hester. Tears filled Braen's eyes when his thoughts turned to Hester. She had been his fuel for so many years. When he had fled Fjorik his thoughts of her had kept him warm and alive, always hoping that she still loved and thought about him as well. When he was hunted as a rogue and outlaw, the dream of reconnecting with her had driven him to dig harder. Thinking of her brought the scent of lilac to his nose. *How could I have forgotten that smell,* he mused, *how could I have forgotten her?* Hester was a sweet memory and nothing more than a ghost from his past that would never be held for real. He had to let go of her and move on.

He would have liked to have moved on with Eusari. When he held her close, he felt a different kind of woman than any he had known. Despite her emotional and physical sufferings, she had grown stronger than any person alive. Her resiliency was a product of her pain and she would not be Eusari without having lived through the worst of times. *She's probably dead by now.* Thoughts of her laying still on the rocks above the beach filled him and he began to sob. If he survived to ever love a woman, again, he hoped and prayed to the gods that it would be Eusari.

The gods. He truly did not know what to believe, especially after seeing and experiencing the events over the past months. If the gods existed as he had been taught as a boy, then one would think that they would have interfered to change his life's course over the years. If Kernigan was to be believed, the gods didn't exist at all, and had been replaced by people. People who manipulated and created this entire continent to supply their incessant desire to be as omniscience as the gods who they destroyed with their science.

Braen wept. The emotions of the past two years overwhelmed him as *Ice Prince* slipped deeper beneath the waves. He was no longer calming the seas, and those cold waves had grown dangerous as they tossed the vessel around. Cold. It had grown so cold that Braen could see his breath. Even the water on the deck had frozen and the wood around him frosted over as he cried over everything he had lost.

"Braen!" A voice snapped him back to reality. Sebastian stood pointing toward the harbor defenses. *Yes*, the bearded captain thought. *Those reinforced gun mounts had destroyed our chances and dashed our hopes. That boy will never live to see fifteen summers because of me.*

"KRAKEN!" Krill shouted as loudly as he had on the first morning the mythical creatures had saved them.

Braen looked the direction that the boy pointed. Two large squid had climbed out of the water and were wrapped around the harbor fortifications. Their huge eyes loomed over The Cove and men fled along the tops of the walls and leaped into the water to escape the tentacles. With unimaginable strength the creatures ripped the tops of the gun mounts and tossed them into the briny depths. The cannons were sent flying hundreds of feet as their huge tentacles swung back and forth, flinging men as well.

Very quickly, the entrance was free from threats and the harbor defenses had been neutralized. Braston marveled as the big squids slid back into the abyss, screams of dying men silenced by the water as the tentacles dragged them under. Only then did the prince understand what destiny demanded.

He truly was the Kraken. Like the beasts he had powers that were mythical and unmatched. Though not a god, he was a rarity among men. He must continue to serve and help less fortunate through his privileged birth. His father had raised him to rule over Fjorik as a servant to all and he would find a way to do so.

Rising to his feet Braen Braston stood atop the deck of *Ice Prince*. He screamed into the air with rage at the series of injustices that afflicted his friends. It wasn't too late. There was still time if he could reach The Cove and remove Nevra, and then no one would stand in his way as he made things right again. He had to continue the fight.

Emboldened and encouraged he connected with the water. Not just immediately around his ship, but the entire ocean around The Cove. His aura of power was huge and extended several miles. Slowly the water in the harbor began to flow outward until only dry land littered with rocks and shells remained. All along the piers wooden tall ships littered the seabed, laying on their sides and clinging to their moorings by crisscrossing lines. *These would have to be sacrificed*, he thought, *surely Sippen could rebuild the fleet.*

In his mind he felt something split. He could now control the moisture in the air around him and what had been a clear sky darkened and stormed. Lightning struck the tallest buildings of The Cove and picked off men who ran atop the walls. Rain washed over the city, flooding endlessly as he poured more and more moisture into the atmosphere.

Another split in his mind and he could sense the animals in the sea. Connecting with a gam of swimming whales, he brought them closer and under his fledgling ship. Slowly they rose up to the surface, lifting *Ice Prince* up toward safety. They held him and his friends there, floating atop the choppy waters like a raft in a storm.

And then he released the part of the ocean before him. A tidal wave raced toward the city, washing over it and rinsing the filth from the streets that had now become rivers of seawater. The ships in the harbor were crushed by the wave, splintered by the force of the impact. The height of the wave had even reached the highest balcony of the palace and Braen silently wondered if he had drowned the Pirate King he had come to depose. He surely would not be that lucky to end the revolution so quickly. Braen Braston, confident that the passage to The Cove was now safe guided the whales toward the city.

Behind him he could hear Sippen awaken. He turned and walked toward his friend, kneeling beside him.

"You okay, little buddy?"

"I thuh... think so."

"Can you stand?" The little man nodded back an affirmative and Braen helped him to his feet. Convinced that the concussion would be slight, Braen ran to Krill, heaving the man up and over the rail onto the deck. "How about you? Are you good?"

The man grabbed his own crotch and took inventory. "Aye. The important parts are intact. Nothing lost this time." Pointing up at the storm he added, "Can you turn off the storm, I gotta piss like you wouldn't believe."

Braen smiled. "You're fine." He then released his hold on the storm around them, ushering in an eerie silence broken only by the lapping of waves and the moans of the whales below the ship.

A few minutes later they had reached shallow water and the whales released *Ice Prince*. Braen made a current to push the ship the rest of the way, crashing what was left of the stern on the jagged rocks. The mismatched quartet scaled down a cargo net and surveyed the beach. The city was still standing but the entire harbor had been destroyed. Where there had once been a pier Braen found rocky shoals and splintered wood.

He looked around at the bodies littering the beach. These had all been friends and comrades at one time, the faceless people of

The Cove. Like him, they had sought safety and acceptance among outlaws, but he had destroyed that false security with a single crashing wave. *That's the way of life,* he pondered, *everything is fine until a single event washes the facade away, and you are left with nothing.* He wondered if the survivors would see him as a conqueror to be feared or a hero they could admire.

No one challenged the three men and a boy as they climbed up the shoreline. They strode through the city unopposed, with only the occasional frightened face peering out at them. Every set of eyes that Braen glimpsed held awe for the Kraken, having seen the powerful destruction that he had brought. Reaching back to touch the pommel of his father's sword he realized that men were more dangerous than the weapons that they carried.

Eventually they arrived at the palace and the bearded captain stopped his friends. A battle raged on the steps, but the fighting was not what he had expected.

Eusari stared at the archers formed up on the wall. She felt bad for what she was about to order, since many of those men could have some day fought alongside of her. She only had to kill a few to get the desired effect, but a few was too many when considering the coming wars. She worried about the range of the weapons, Sippen having told her that they would only be effective at close range if the enemy wore armor. Thankfully the archers were only clad in light chest plate.

Turning to Shon she gave the signal and then waited. A single shot rang out from behind. For such small weapons the report was deafening, and she jumped a little bit at the sound. Atop the wall one of the archers fell. The round had hit him in the forehead, and she prayed that the other shots would fly as true.

Another of Shon's men fired and a second archer fell. Men were running along the wall by then, investigating why their soldiers were suddenly dropping dead. And then Wimbley signaled the volley. Four hundred rifles fired simultaneously along the line, some hitting steel plate while others found skin and bone. The walls were cleared in seconds after that, as officers called their men back to safety.

Eusari then turned her attention to the shield wall formation that had filled the gap in the fallen structure. Rifles would not be able to penetrate both shield and heavy plate at any distance, so she had to disrupt them some other way. Behind the formation she could see a mounted officer peering over, trying to find the source of the small cannon fire. Eusari turned to Wimbley. "Shon, can you take out that officer on the white horse?"

"Aye Dearie!" Shouting to one of his men he asked, "Marque, do you see a pumped-up egotistical shit-for-brains on a white horse?"

"Aye. Didn't realize he was a Lieutenant. Want me to put him out of his troops' misery?"

"That I do, son! Take him when you have a shot." After a pause he fired his own rifle in the air to give the lieutenant something to look for.

Eusari smiled at their banter and waited. It was good that the men were loose, they would fight better. At the sound of the random shot the officer had moved closer to the shield wall, standing up in his stirrups to get a better view. As he looked out his head exploded, and Shon's men applauded Marque's marksmanship. As she had hoped the shielded men faltered, turning to see why their officer had fallen off his horse. "Fire another volley! Quickly!" The line of troops broke as men fell on the front lines.

All at once a storm raged above. Lightning struck at men in their metal suits and rain poured down from a cloudless sky. Beyond the thunder Eusari's ears perked as a deafening sound roared beyond the city fortifications. She watched as the foot soldiers froze in their retreat and then turned to run back toward the invading force. Puzzled, she called all men to the ready. "Reload fast! They're charging!"

And then she saw why they had changed their minds and

direction. Behind them a tidal wave as tall as the palace roared through Pirates Cove, cresting and breaking at the wall. The soldiers washed toward Eusari in a river of ocean, mud, people and debris. As the flow of water slowed, she could see that hundreds of people had been buried or trapped in the mud before her. The armor of the soldiers weighed them down and many looked as though they would drown as a result.

Demon's ass, Eusari thought, *we have to help them.* Turning toward Shon she shouted orders, sending her men into action. With their rifle stocks they dug, pulling citizens and soldiers from the mud and muck. She somehow knew that Braen had made the wave, but she worried that he would not have a city to rule over if she did not first help the people.

CHAPTER FORTY-SEVEN

Stefan Nevra sat the rear balcony of his private chambers. He was taking his morning breakfast when he saw a thick fogbank roll in across the reefs. *That's strange,* he thought, *fog doesn't normally form on the leeward side.* He stared for several minutes, watching as it rolled toward the island. *It's rolling in fast,* he thought, standing and walking to the railing.

He turned his gaze down to the rocks below the wall. That section had been largely ignored by Artema Horn when building the defenses, and Stefan had added a permanent gun mount. *Not like anyone would approach from that direction, only a few people know the secret to safe passage.* But Samani was one of those few people, and that caused him anxiety. He would sleep better at night knowing that Kernigan could not get at him undetected.

The fog continued to roll in, growing smaller as it did. A flash of something solid temporarily showed through the cloud and he strained his eyes. *What was that in the fog?* He quickly assumed he was mistaken but continued to stare. Abruptly the fog rapidly dissipated, and he could see a ship careen around a reef, dragging its keel along the rocks. Shock filled him as he recognized *She Wolf.* She appeared to be listing and taking on water.

Of course, Eusari knows the passage, he thought, remembering that she had used it frequently to enter and exit The Cove. He started to relax until he saw the other vessels and then spun around with fear pulsing through his body. Several Norse longboats skimmed over the reef following her approach to the beach. *This is a raiding party, but how?* Nevra was not a sea-going captain, he was a businessman, but even he knew that the longboats would not have survived the fierce winter seas north of The Cove.

A shot rang out from the battery and *She Wolf* sped forward with blinding speed sailing safely beneath the salvo. The burst of speed was unexpected from a sinking ship. *And from the leeward side? Where did she find wind?* He shook his head at the impossibility of what he had just witnessed. Even more impossible was the sight of Eusari leaping off the bow of her ship with a wolf landing in the sand beside her. He watched as she stood and casually walked toward the battery.

Hundreds of soldiers in light leather armor flooded out of the longboats as they beached one by one. A quick estimate revealed nearly four hundred men at her heels. Not a huge force, but a considerable one. The coming battle would be interesting to watch. Finally, as the last of the soldiers hit the beach, bells began to ring out in the city and somewhere horns blew, signaling the attack.

He had turned and was about to return to his chambers to change into a uniform when the ground began to shake. At first the rumble was low and nothing to fear. But after a while, the shaking became so violent that pieces of mortar fell from the ceiling. Stefan leaped in fright as a lamp fell off the bedside table, smashing into pieces and igniting the fuel as it hit the floor. Within seconds his bed was aflame, and he bolted from the shaking room.

As he entered the doorway the pirate king ran headlong into Captain Pogue, who was on his way to report the imminent attack to his liege.

"Get out of the way!" Nevra screamed, but Pogue stood, blocking the door. "Move, you idiot! We'll both die in here!" Pogue casually looked from Stefan to the flaming bed and for a brief moment the king thought that the captain actually wanted him dead. But then the man pointed out the window.

"Look! A portion of the wall has fallen!"

Stefan turned and saw that both the battery and the wall had fallen during the quake. No longer caring about the fire which had pretty much burned itself out, Nevra froze from panic at the damage. After a few moments he blinked and turned to the Captain of the Guard. "Why are you still standing here? Go muster up the soldiers and fight them off!"

"I've already given my orders, Your Highness. See?" Pogue pointed and Nevra saw lines of archers atop the wall while a shield wall formed in the gap.

Nevra nodded. All at once, another horn sounded. Something was spotted at the Windward entrance. *Another force, perhaps?* The two men looked at each other and sprinted to the main hall to look out upon the harbor. Out of breath, Nevra arrived after Pogue, who froze at the window. "Move aside! Let me see!" The Captain moved and Nevra saw that all was quiet in the bay. He could not see any attackers. Confused, he strained his eyes for any indication that something was amiss.

There, far out about a mile past the entrance was a single ship. The vessel fired a single shot that traveled several times farther than should be possible. The round hit its' mark and several men were blown from atop the battery. *Braston.* Nevra shook his head. "That damned fool." Pogue nodded his agreement but said nothing. Both men continued to watch as the city's improved cannons fired a full salvo with their extended range. The blast struck *Ice Prince* and she began to list as her mast crashed to the deck.

Stefan let out a cackle at the quick work that his guns had made of the invader and turned to address Pogue. The captain appeared crestfallen at the sight and this confused Nevra. "What? What is this? Didn't you want him to die?"

Alec Pogue shook his head and then opened his mouth to spew treason. In a calm voice he said, "I was actually hoping that he'd be the one to take The Cove from you. He wasn't a perfect choice, but he was a good one."

Nevra stared back in shock as Pogue drew his sword, holding the point at the king's neck. "What is the meaning of this? I am your rightful king! Artema left it all to me!"

"Even as pirates we have codes, Lord Nevra." Pogue took a half step closer, the tip piercing the pox-faced man's neck just barely, leaving a trickle of fresh blood on his sword.

"Whuh... What code did I violate? I ran everything correctly." *Wait,* he thought, *he knows about the extra coin?* "Is this about the extra taxes?" Nevra wracked his brain but could not think of anything that he had done to violate the code.

"No. Even Artema embezzled."

"It was the transport and delivery of slaves and human cargo, Stefan." The voice came from the doorway where Adamas Creech stood with several armed men.

Nevra stared back with eyes wide. "How did you?" And then a thought struck him. "You stole my ledger." He pointed at Creech. "You both worked together." Looking back at Pogue, he realized the truth. "You weren't protecting me! You choreographed the entire fight!" His pox-scarred face narrowed. "Then you know the truth about your wife and pretty little daughters?"

Alex's face dropped with confusion. "What about Mattie and the girls?"

A sinister smile curled the edges of Stefan's lips. "You don't know, then." He let out a high-pitched cackle and then roared with delight.

Pogue stepped closer, pressing the tip into the skin just enough to draw a more blood. Anger crossed his face and his next words came out a growl, "What do you know about my family?"

"Guards!" Nevra shouted. "Guards! To me! Save your king!" He was terrified. He knew that he was about to die.

"They aren't close enough to hear you. I sent the palace guard to man the wall against an attack." Pogue shook his head, "Your reign has ended, now tell me about my family."

"Alec! Stop!" A new voice had entered the room. Nevra tore free and ran to the corner of the room. The captain turned to see Amash Horslei standing with two swords in his hands.

"Stand down, Amash. He knows about Mattie."

"Our code demands a trial, Alec. You know that."

"Your precious Mattie was listed in the ledger, Captain Pogue." Believing that he had escaped death Nevra felt emboldened. "You are so stupid that you couldn't figure out that they didn't leave you. I sold them off and shipped them to be whores on the southern continent."

Tears formed in Pogue's eyes. He shook his head in stunned disbelief. "No."

"It's all true."

"Why? Why would you do such a thing?"

"She was just too pretty to be with a lowly guardsman. She fetched me a nice price, too. Did you see the entry in my ledger where I sold a thoroughbred? I called her that because she was tough to break in. I had to let Turat help, but he mostly enjoyed your little girls. So did Captain Dominique during his voyage, from what I understand."

Amash could see that his friend was quickly losing control. "Alec. Don't do this. He needs to stand trial."

"He dies."

"No. No matter what you just heard we have a code to follow."

"Ain't no one stopping him!" Adamas laughed at the thought. "There isn't a man alive that can best Captain Pogue with a blade. Even with his wound he's the greatest swordsman in The Cove."

"I wouldn't say that." Amash leaped at his former friend and captain, swinging the two swords just as Alec had taught him years ago.

Pogue parried with one blade while attacking with the other and the two men became a flurry of steel fighting with alarming speed. Stefan's eyes could barely keep up with the duel as the men spun around the room, razors flying and the sound of steel on steel ringing in his ears. Flashing a look toward the men at the door he could see that their attention was on the fight. He tried to inch his way around unseen, hoping to escape and get help.

Abruptly a wall of water crashed through the window, washing everyone against the far wall. Stefan sputtered and spit as he coughed and gagged on the ocean water. *How had ocean water reached the top windows of the palace?* Confused, he tried to reorient himself in the room. Thankfully the water had washed him closer to the door and he fled down the stairs, avoiding debris that had been left behind. Behind him shouts and heavy steps of soldiers announced pursuit.

He burst out of the main doors of the palace and saw that the streets had been deserted. He yelled, but no one was close enough to hear his cries for help. Running, he tripped over a log on the steps and fell a full flight, his arm cracking underneath his weight as he tried to catch himself. *No, not a log,* he thought as he held his arm, *that looks like it was part of the pier!* Opening his eyes and taking in the scene he realized that his entire city was awash under a tidal wave. The air was filled with the stench of dead sea life and seaweed and mud piled up everywhere. He stared confused, until he heard a shout.

Alec Pogue had recovered only one of his swords and charged at him as he lay on the stairs. Stefan cried and begged the man, "Please stop! Don't kill me!" between sobs he pleaded, "I'm the rightful leader! Artema told me it was mine! Please don't!" The captain's sword swung down.

Before the blade struck home, another person appeared in Stefan's vision. Amash Horslei tackled Pogue from behind, knocking him away. The pirate king lay on the ground sobbing as metal struck metal around him and the men resumed their combat. He trembled at the thought of death and begged the gods to deliver him safely.

Braen blinked in confusion at the battle raging before him. Two men, both expert swordsmen with talent beyond anything he had ever seen, fought with ferocity around a crumpled old man on the steps to the palace. *That man looks familiar,* he pondered before recognizing the hideously pox-scarred face of Stefan Nevra. Shock gripped him even tighter when he realized that one of the swordsmen was a dead man.

Sippen sputtered, "Buh... but I suh... saw him duh... die!"

Braen shook his head, "Obviously he lived, somehow. Did you know that he could fight like that?"

"Nuh... no."

More men staggered out of the palace. About twenty or so were dressed in tattered clothing that Braston recognized as former guardsmen to Artema Horn. Another ten were standing behind the Pirate Adamas Creech. All watched the display before them, not wanting to interfere.

Finally, Amash swung under a blow by his opponent and brought his hilt up into the man's face, crushing his nose. With his other arm he wrapped up Pogue's sword arm and shifted his bodyweight, breaking the bone and releasing the man's sword to the ground. Casting his own aside, he again struck, knocking him to the ground and stopping the show. Tears instantly flooded the big man's eyes as he bent over his former mentor.

"I don't want to kill you, Alec. But he needs to stand trial. That's how we do things in The Cove. If we have no honor, no code, then we're nothing more than pirates."

"We are nothing more than pirates, Amash." The man closed his eyes and gasped through the blood in his face.

"No, my friend. Here we're free to live our lives with justice and due process. I'll defend that until the day I die." Kneeling beside his friend he leaned in and spoke softer. "We'll find Mattie and the girls. I promise that we will."

"Amash! What's going on here?" Braen spoke, drawing the attention of Creech and his men.

"Braen? How did you get here? Wait, that was you in the harbor? That means that the tidal wave was..."

"More than I was going for, I assure you." He pointed at Nevra. "So, we're arresting him? Under what grounds is he to be tried?"

"His ships have been transporting slaves, mostly children for decades. Pogue found out that he'd sold his wife and daughters under his nose."

"I agree, Amash. He'll get a trial."

"And by what authority to you promise that, Braston? You lost your marque and are an outlaw." Creech had taken several steps and was dangerously close to Braen.

"So are you, I might add, Creech." Amash had placed his hand on his sword and positioned himself beside his friends.

Adamas bowed flamboyantly and drew his sword. The men behind him did as well. "It seems to me that the issue of leadership can be decided here, between you and I, Braston."

"No. There'll be a vote, Creech. Like Amash said, we have rules and a code that we follow.

"And plus, we have the numbers." A woman's voice purred from the corner of the building and all of the men looked up to see Eusari. She was flanked by fifty of her men, all covered in mud and holding rifles. "Marque?"

"Yes Mum?" The man stepped forward and leveled his rifle at Creech.

"Shoot that stupid fucking hat off his head."

Adamas held his hands up and threw down his sword, "No need for any of that, My Lady. We'll most certainly have elections."

Eusari nodded and Marque pointed his rifle at the ground. Then she walked up to Braen and threw her arms around him, holding him tightly.

Chapter Forty-Eight

The sun rose above two thousand men lined up with backs against the brown waters of the swamp. An island lay a few hundred yards across the water from the men, and dense forest provided cover from the only high spot on which the enemy could place artillery. The ground next to the waterline was too wet for the heavy guns, so they would have to shoot blind if they wanted to keep their firepower protected in the rear. General Merrimac Lourdes nodded his agreement on Reeve's choice of battlefields.

Turning to an aide, Mac gave orders for the troop placement. "Move the infantry line just outside of archer range. We are going to pound them with our guns to soften their position. The splinters off those trees alone should amplify the effective fire." Raising the spyglass, he scanned the meager force before him. He could clearly see Max and the boy standing at the water's edge behind their troops.

A rider made his way up to the hill. "Cavalry is in position in the forest north of the clearing, Sir. They're ready to charge on your signal." Nodding, the general again picked up the glass. "Where are their horses?"

"Perhaps they set them loose, Sir?"

"Perhaps. They may've abandoned them, knowing that they would spook when our artillery opens fire." The reinforcements had provided strong numbers. An additional five hundred cavalry brought his own totals up to three thousand, and an additional four thousand infantrymen brought his totals up to five. They also brought longer ranged cannons than he had available in Eskera, making the assault easier. This entire attack should be over in less than an hour.

Another aide approached from the south. "Cannons are ready, Sir. We should be able to zero in with only a couple of volleys."

He was about to answer when movement in the enemy ranks caught his attention. The entire column made an about face, turning their backs to his own infantry line. "Interesting. What are they going to do, march into the swamp? The fools are making this even easier." Abruptly the winds around them shifted from the west, blowing hard and with gale-force. Mac raised his glass and saw that the boy was standing on the water's edge with his hands outstretched. "What are you up to, Max?"

The winds around him intensified and blew down the hilltop toward an island in the swamp. Slowly, the water parted before the boy, forming a narrow bridge out to the island. "No." The old general shook his head. He remembered Max's words, the night before. *"The boy is as strong as five Falconers, maybe even stronger."* Staring at the marvel in disbelief, he came to his senses. "We can't let them get across and out of range." Give the order for the artillery. The first of the troops stepped out onto the mud, now frozen by the exposure to the cold air, and rushed to the island.

Cannon fire roared from the south and rounds rained down a few yards short of the fleeing infantry. Merrimac nodded his approval, estimating that the next volley would find their mark. He raised his hand to signal the next release when shouts of alarm turned his head. Archers on horseback had ridden within range of the artillery and were releasing volley after volley of flaming arrows into the exposed gun positions. Within seconds the powder barrels exploded, sending artillerymen scattering from the hill.

"Demon's Ass!" As he turned the last of the infantry safely make it across, forming new ranks and a shield wall atop the island and well out of range of the cannons. The boy was still standing on the water's edge, however. Slowly he turned to face the line of five thousand infantry before him, throwing his hands forward as he did. Abruptly the winds shifted from the east with more power than before, sending a microburst directly at the troops and blowing four rows backward with a crash of steel armor.

General Lourdes stared down at the boy with mouth agape. Coming to his senses, he signaled his aide. "Cavalry! Now!" The captain nodded reluctantly, pulling his own eyes away from the spectacle. He raised a signal flag and waved. All at once, the forest edge erupted with hoofbeats as three thousand cavalrymen charged one teenage boy standing alone on the coastline. Mac shook his head at the impending slaughter. "I almost feel sorry for you, Robert."

The boy raised his right hand as if to signal a halt, but the horses kept charging at top speed. One by one the lead riders smashed into an invisible wall of air next to the boy, breaking the necks of the horses as they made impact, throwing their riders against the shield. Unable to see the carnage in front of them, the rearguard continued headlong to meet the same fate as their comrades. Lourdes stared dumbfounded at how quickly his entire cavalry had exploded into a sea of blood and broken limbs, now piled ten feet high against some unseen wall.

Having seen the fate of the cavalry, many of the infantry broke ranks before the boy, throwing down their arms and running westward toward freedom. The officers tried desperately to hold the lines steady and to fill in the gaps. Mac stared, marveling at how one boy had singlehandedly embarrassed the might of the Eskeran force in less than five minutes.

Finally, ten figures stepped around the amassed infantry. They stood tall in their flowing robes and feathered hoods, walking confidently and converging upon the boy. A sudden westerly wind blew with such force that it sent him flying backward into the swamp. Mac raised his glass but could not find him after he splashed into the cold water, no doubt sunken into the wet mud by the weight of his armor.

Robert felt his breath leave his body when the massive blast struck him in the chest. With only a split second to react a bubble of air formed around his head, trapping enough that he could breathe while planning his next move. He had expected the Falconers and had been hoping for them. But not so many. He had also not expected such a powerful blast.

He lay on the bottom of the swamp both out of shock and a little fear. He knew that his next action should be swift, but he was still learning his abilities and the ten specters had been practicing theirs for decades. How many links could he make? As a boy he had always wondered about the powers of Falconers, marveling at their versatility and imagining what he would have done with their powers. But Max had told him that their powers, like everything in the world, had limits. With ten of them, they could make any combination of actions against him and his fledgling army standing on the island behind their shield wall.

He quickly did an inventory of how much he had extended his power. He could feel the force of air around Sarai, healing her wounds and forcing clean air into her lungs to assist her labored breathing. He could also feel the wall that held the southern flank secure. He closed his eyes and sensed the bond with his new friend the eagle, circling the sky and searching for any birds that were linked to the Falconers. He had made a fourth link when he had blasted the front lines of the infantry, but that strained him, weakening his foresight and preventing him from seeing the Falconers approach.

He reached out with his mind, solidifying his connection with the great bird. He watched from several thousand feet above as the ten Falconers stood on the shoreline of the swamp. Ten hawks flew beneath him, circling the water and searching for his body. One of them let out a call, and wisps of air shot out from five of the eerie men. Robert immediately felt manacles form around his hands and feet like ropes to draw him from the mud.

Focusing his strength into the bird he willed the giant eagle to dive at one of the Falconers. The specter looked up at the final second, but that mistake cost him his life as Robert gripped his throat with his sharp talons, ripping through the hood and gripping the soft flesh inside. He again released and rose up into the air out of the range of the other nine. One of the hawks, feeling the bond release from his master, flew southward to enjoy freedom.

Robert felt his body dragging across the swamp floor, mud seeping in through the cracks. If they failed to pull him out, then he would surely remain stuck, there, in the bog where he would surly run out of air. He concentrated on the bindings, focusing his mind on how they were constructed. When he had used them against Taros, he had not given this kind of thought, focused only on holding the boy. Looking closely, he detected a faint lashing like knots in a tangled string. Setting to work on the tangles, he slowly removed them with his fourth connection.

His hands freed first. He used these to remove the straps on his armor, quickly unlatching the buckles and letting it drop into the mud. Although the heavy weight greatly diminished, this exposed him to the pain and lacerations from the swamp floor. With renewed fervor he went to work on the bindings around his feet. All at once he stopped dragging across the bottom, realizing that his bubble of air was nearly spent. Had he delayed another minute he would have surely drowned.

Scrambling to his feet he leaped upward from the water, standing waist deep halfway between his army and the Falconers. Looking up, he saw that his great bird circled higher than the others who awaited his next plunging attack. He darted a quick look backward toward his troops, hoping to find a way out of his hopeless battle. Abruptly three shields moved, revealing the face of his father staring back at him, smiling proudly and nodding his encouragement.

Suddenly empowered, Robert sent out wisps of air of his own, trapping two of the Falconers and binding them to each other. Reaching out with as much power as he could muster, he managed to squeeze out another set of bonds, tying up two more in the same fashion. This fifth connection nearly broke him as intense pain shot through his temples and blood ran down his upper lip. Staggering in the mud and swamp he fought to right the spinning world around him.

Diving with his eagle he tried to attack the four men trapped on the ground and struggling to free themselves. But the hawks swarmed, and the eagle broke connection as it fought nine birds to save its' own life. Thinking fast, he used this newly freed connection to move the bonds around their hands. They slid up the bodies of the fallen Falconers like snakes until he moved them into place to bind their necks. These he squeezed, slowly and forcibly to choke his victims.

The other five Falconers stared in disbelief at what he had done. He watched as they quickly moved in unison and began waving their arms, weaving the air around them in an intricate pattern. Now able to see the individual threads as they worked, he recognized a very complex net forming before them. Obviously stronger than the individual ropes from before, his mind raced to find options. But he had maxed out his ability. He was split five ways and could not deflect or defend the net. Worse, he felt the muddy prison at his feet pulling him downward into the muck.

Robert panicked as defeat gripped his core. Closing his eyes, he reached out and allowed his mind to focus on the air around Sarai. Tears streamed down his face as he chose to die looking at her face instead of the Falconers before him. She was so beautiful, he thought. Despite her burns and scars she was the most beautiful woman in his world. Regret flooded him as he thought of the life that he would never spend with her and his gut wrenched his spirit.

"Robert, is that you?" She spoke her words into the air around her.

"It's over, Sarai. I failed. There were ten Falconers and they were too powerful. I couldn't split my power more than five ways."

"It's not over, Robert. You know what you need to do. Take this air off of me and use it to defend yourself." He could sense the love behind her words, and he hoped that she could sense the same through their connection.

"That could kill you. Your body will go into shock, and you may stop breathing. I can't do it. I won't put you through that pain. I don't want to lose you."

"Sweet Robert. If you die out there, then I'm lost, as well."

"No. I can't. I won't! I swore that I'd protect you until I die, Sarai."

"And you have. Even in Weston after I told you to leave, you stayed. You remained and you saved my life. You gave me more time to realize that I was selfish and put the needs of others above those of my love. You are my betrothed, and if we survive this then I vow to stand beside you and back you no matter what. Love is unconditional, Robert Esterling. Please forgive me for not loving you that way, before."

"I love you, too, Sarai."

With a snap he let her connection go, just as the net flew toward him. His shield raised in time to absorb the blow, somehow strengthened by the impact. With a final squeeze the four Falconers on the ground shook violently, succumbing to their deaths. He let go of their bonds, empowering himself with two free connections to the air around him. In a flash he threw up a shield around the five remaining Falconers, completely encircling them as he did against Taros.

The air around the Falconers strained as if it were ready to explode from the force within. From inside he felt the force of ten connections fighting against the shield around them. He reinforced it with his remaining four connections, but it would not be enough. He looked toward the west, observing that what was left of the cavalry had reorganized. Their horses had been crippled, but the men stood ready to charge on foot as soon as the shield dropped.

Looking beyond the Falconers he saw that the infantry was advancing with their shield wall. Behind the wall archers stood nocked and ready to fire upon the defenseless prince standing in the swamp. Robert fought to hold the bubble around the five specters as it strained against their power. Reluctantly, he let the barrier holding back the cavalry drop and used the last of his power to hold in the Falconers. The men immediately rushed toward the shoreline.

Merrimac Lourdes watched the display of courage by the young man standing in the swamp. Somehow, beyond all reason or comprehension, he had singularly stood against overwhelming odds and decimated half of the Imperial forces that he faced. In doing so, he had killed five Falconers and trapped five more. He could see the boy struggling to contain them in their invisible prison, and compassion mixed with awe as the general fought his own internal struggle.

He watched as the barrier holding back his cavalry dissipated and his men charged on foot toward the boy. Turning to his aides, he quickly signaled the halt and horns blared. Mac prayed that the men were not in too much of a fervor to hear the call, and desperately hoped that they would pull back. When they finally turned and reformed a position on the bank Lourdes let out a slow breath, watching as the boy still struggled with the hooded men inside of the bubble.

Spurring his horse, Mac approached the line of men. He rode past the infantry toward the Falconers, looking closely at their eyes within their hoods. Merrimac Lourdes had been a soldier his entire life, and if he knew one thing it was that fear always reflected from a man's eyes. He immediately recognized that terror gripped the five specters.

He reached out and touched the field around them. It was cold to the touch. He marveled that his hand could somehow pass slowly into the bubble and safely out, yet it had completely trapped the men inside. *You are afraid of him. There were ten of you bastards, yet you weren't enough to stop a teenage Prince.* Their eyes pled with him to help.

Looking out over the water he saw the Esterling boy struggling to contain them. He was determined and unafraid, despite that several thousand men stared him down from the bank. Blood ran down from both nostrils and from one ear, but the boy was unphased. Merrimac drew his sword and tapped it against the bubble which prevented a forceful blow from entering. A thought passed through him, and he slowly slid the sword into the field tip first. It entered as easily as a knife in butter. He pulled it back out and stared at the boy.

Beyond Robert, on the island, Maximus Reeves had moved out ahead of his own men and stood watching with wonderment at Lourdes's next move. The older man nodded at his former protégé and then saluted the boy with this sword, demonstrating the respect and full honors that he deserved. Turning back toward the force field he slowly plunged his sword, piercing the heart of the nearest Falconer. As he drew it back, he saw that the field had compressed even tighter around the hooded men. Twice more he plunged his blade until finally the remaining two imploded from the pressure and the field disappeared.

"Your Highness!" Lourdes addressed the boy standing in the swamp. "The blades of Eskera are yours to command." Dismounting, he strode into the muddy water, splashing as he approached Robert. When he finally reached him, Mac knelt with his sword held up and presented himself and his service to his new King. "With my honor I accept you as my rightful ruler and swear to protect and serve you as long as I live."

Robert reached out and took the sword, looking it over carefully.

He recognized the markings that were deeply etched in the blade and pommel. "This was my father's sword."

"No, Your Highness." The old general shook his head. "It was the sword of Charles Esterling, my friend and my sworn liege." He indicated Max who had waded carefully through the water to stand beside Robert. "Your father holds his own sword. Like him, I am sworn to protect the rightful Emperor of Andalon. You may have the name of Esterling, but you certainly have the courage of a Reeves."

"Rise up, General Lourdes. We have to get my infantry across this cursed swamp." At that, a mighty easterly wind parted the waters, once more.

Chapter Forty-Nine

Braen stood on the pier surveying the damage around him. The sun had risen high into the noonday sky, illuminating The Cove in a way that he had never seen nor believed possible. Even with all of the destruction, the sight was magnificent.

All around him were men who had trusted him with their lives, believing that he would pull them through to the winning side. They were already picking up the pieces, salvaging what was left so that they could rebuild their lives. He looked at each man fondly, silently thanking him for the part that he had played in the morning's battle. If it could even be called a battle.

Sippen and Krill picked through the wreckage of *Ice Prince.* The ship was beyond repair, the keel broken. Braen watched as the two men pulled several crates from the wreckage, each emblazoned with the numbers seven, five, and four. He smiled at their resourcefulness, pledging silently to open a bottle as soon as they could.

Eusari's crew moved from house to house looking for survivors and relocating them to an abandoned inn repurposed as a hospital. Shon Wimbley, the once constable and now freedom fighter, worked as a battlefield medic ensuring that all of the wounded from both sides of the battle were patched and given a chance to take part in the coming war against Fjorik.

Braen finally spotted Eusari, sitting away from the others, not in the shadows as when they first met, but seated on a rock facing the harbor. He marveled at her beauty as the breeze tossed her hair, revealing her pale face and rosebud lips. Her eyes were closed against the sun.

Samani Kernigan had noticed Braen and broke him from his thoughts. "Tough fight, but you did it."

Shaking his head, the bearded captain corrected, "No, Kernigan. We all did it. The cove belongs to everyone and all of us." With a motion he gestured around him. "Sam. This little town is the only free place on the continent."

Samani nodded. "Because of you."

"I only had a part in it."

"A part? Your humility is sickening, Braston. You're the inspiration to these men. They followed the Kraken because he gave them something to believe in."

"I never wanted to lead, Sam."

"I know. But you have to. You're their Pirate King, and now you're going to lead them against your brother and the Esterling family. They won't accept anyone else."

"No more kings. No more emperors. I heard Amash say that The Cove is a symbol of justice and freedom. The people will choose our leaders and the leaders will answer to the people."

"It doesn't work that way. The people can't lead themselves, and collectively they can't agree on anything."

"That's where you're wrong, Sam. I believe in a world where they'll at least learn to compromise."

"Compromise means giving something up. That won't be easy to get them to do."

"They'll have to see outside of themselves, eventually. Mankind is inherently good, Sam."

"Well, I beg to differ. I know of a group of peoples who tried the very system of government that you're describing. They consumed themselves, Braen. Their pride and arrogance tore them apart and drove them farther from their central ideology."

"Why? What happened?"

"They got too comfortable. Too complacent. There was no more adversity, so they created their own. They found turmoil in everything, forcing strife into every conversation. You can't do this, because it offends this person. You can't do that because it takes away that person's freedom."

"Isn't that contradictory? Preventing one person's belief in favor of what you believe to be your right? That isn't canceling out liberties?"

"Exactly. It is another form of oppression, and it's no different than what the Astians are doing to Andalon. Eventually, these people gave away their own liberty by building philosophical cages around themselves, forcing everyone to submit until too much power was given back to the government."

"Well, no more. We'll find a way to get free of the Astians, just like we toppled Nevra's grip on The Cove, today."

"But you'll have to lead these people until we learn how to do that. If you want elections, then we'll have to rig them. That is the only way that you can keep Creech from beating you. And I guarantee that he'll try to cheat."

Braen thought for a long time, taking in the words. He did not want to waste all of their efforts just to make Creech the new Pirate King. Finally, he sighed. "Alright, Sam. I will. But I won't do it, alone. I want a three-part leadership. You, me and one other until honest elections can be held."

"I won't do it, Braen, I'm not even from Andalon. I do promise to help, though. But not as front man. I'll guide and mentor you and whoever you choose, but I'll do it from behind the scenes. Who do you want? I'll ensure that all three of you win."

Braston paused, still afraid to fully trust this man, but realized that he had to start. "Have it your way. Who do you suggest?"

"Shon Wimbley."

"No. He isn't ready. He's too aggressive and full of hate."

"Then you tell me."

"Well, Amash Horslei, for one."

"Another noble-born? Your idea of democracy might be a little different than the people's if you keep stacking the deck with nobles."

"Amash has the right mindset. He's intelligent, well-schooled and will uphold the law at any cost."

"Understandable, but you may have to choose another. Who else?"

"The best woman for the job."

Samani looked thoughtful for a moment and then nodded, a smile curling up on his lips. "Good choice, Kraken."

Braen excused himself and left Samani, walking toward Eusari. He climbed on the rock beside her and said nothing, just stared at the harbor and thought about all of the rebuilding they had before them.

She broke the silence. "I can't do this with you, anymore. I won't."

"What part can't you do? The freedom fighting or the relationship?"

She looked up at him with a glare, "Relationship?"

"Well, what is it? You tell me." He braced himself for the letdown.

Releasing a breath Eusari let herself be vulnerable for the first time that Braen could remember. "I've never had a relationship, Braen. This concept is new to me, but I'm willing to try."

He felt the knot in his stomach let go. "Then what can't you do?"

"You're a good man. No, you're a great man. But you're so fucking selfish at times. Every time that I turn my back, you're doing something your way because you think it's better." Tears formed in her eyes. "And then you brought these kids along and look what happened! Niko died, Braen. They just told me. So did Suzette."

"I. I'm sorry."

"That makes two. I asked you not to involve them, but you did. You're responsible for their deaths because I won't have them on my conscience."

"Eusari, I…"

"I'm not finished." She glared at him, her green eyes burning with flecks of gold. "There are certain things that I'll never tolerate from anyone." She drew a deep breath and released it. "Breaking promises tops that list, Braen Braston. I can't let you lie to me ever again."

Braen sat for a while, taking everything that Eusari had said to heart. "I don't mean to break my promises. I get caught up in doing what I think is right. I guess that I just push my way through." He paused again, searching for the right words to say. "I'm going to change things. Samani and I were just discussing that we plan to have more than one leader of The Cove. We need that system if we're to have checks and balances and prevent tyranny. Eusari, I want you to be one of those leaders."

"I thought we were having elections."

"We are."

"Do you think that I would stand a chance in an election? Adamas Creech is more popular than me."

"Trust me. After what you did to help those people, today? You will be their first choice."

"I will do it if the people choose me. I won't take part in any system that forces our will on the people."

Braen felt a piece of him break. He had just promised not to deceive her, and he had already lied less than a minute later.

"Eusari?"

"Yes Braen?"

He felt her relax as she answered, resting her head on his shoulder as they sat. "I. I just. I don't know. I just want you to know that things are going to be different from now on. I promise."

Eusari smiled, fully trusting the words of a man for the first time in her life. "I believe you, Braen."

Epilogue

Fatwana Nakala felt exhausted. The Council was corrupt. Her brother had died trying to convince her of that, but she refused to believe him. That he had run off and joined The Society without a thought of how she and her sister would fare from his treason made her angry, even to this day. She was a reasonable woman, but she had refused to accept his words as truth until the latest transcriptions.

All four elemental latents had awakened. Water, Earth, Fire and Air. Most astonishingly, they had awakened with such power that each was five times stronger than anything science had been able to reproduce with their experiments. She stared at the parchment in front of her, wishing that she had acted sooner to help her brother. Perhaps she could have even prevented Ashima's death.

Tears flowed down her eyes as she saw inside of the Rookeries, rows and rows of people stolen and turned into farms. She had known that the beads came from human subjects, but she had not realized that her people farmed unwilling and enslaved subjects for their powers. That was a detail that the Chancellor and the Council had failed to share with the Oracles. *Surely a mistake had been made.* But she knew the answer immediately.

An initiate approached and handed Fatwana another piece of parchment. She accepted the latest transcription of the most recent Da'ash'mael, and then read the words with a trembling hand. *Since none of that will happen, will you at least tell my sisters that I am alive and well?* She felt her knees buckle at the realization. *Tell her. She needs to know that I took my mission to Andalon. That I will see these people free.*

Samani lived. He lived and she would do everything in her power to help him free these people. Her thoughts turned to the Chancellor and his fancy room with souvenirs from Andalon. His and the Council's exploitation of innocents must end. Knowledge is an uncontainable storm that would spread to all seven continents. The latents revealed by the oracles were just the beginning, and the people of Astian had a right to know that Andalon awakens.